A Holiday By Gaslight

"Matthews (*The Matrimonial Advertisement*) pays homage to Elizabeth Gaskell's *North and South* with her admirable portrayal of the Victorian era's historic advancements...Readers will easily fall for Sophie and Ned in their gaslit surroundings."

-Library Journal, starred review

"Matthews' novella is full of comfort and joy—a sweet treat for romance readers that's just in time for Christmas."

-Kirkus Reviews

"A graceful love story...and an authentic presentation of the 1860s that reads with the simplicity and visual gusto of a period movie."

-Readers' Favorite

The Viscount and the Vicar's Daughter

"Matthews' tale hits all the high notes of a great romance novel... Cue the satisfied sighs of romance readers everywhere."

-Kirkus Reviews

"Matthews pens a heartfelt romance that culminates into a sweet ending that will leave readers happy. A wonderfully romantic read."

-RT Book Reviews

The Lost Letter

"The perfect quick read for fans of Regency romances as well as Victorian happily-ever-afters, with shades of Austen and the Brontës that create an entertaining blend of drama and romance."

-RT Book Reviews

"A fast and emotionally satisfying read, with two characters finding the happily-ever-after they had understandably given up on. A promising debut."

-Library Journal

MIMI MATTHEWS

The
WORK *of* ART

THE WORK OF ART
A Regency Romance
Copyright © 2019 by Mimi Matthews

Edited by Deborah Nemeth
Cover Design by James T. Egan of Bookfly Design
Cover Photo by Richard Jenkins
Design and Formatting by Ampersand Book Interiors

E-Book: 978-1-7330569-0-8
Paperback: 978-1-7330569-1-5

www.PerfectlyProperPress.com

DEDICATION

For my mother, Vickie.

ONE

London, England
Spring, 1814

*C*aptain Arthur Heywood had never seen such an ill-mannered assortment of canines in his life. The three mongrels burst into the library, galloping past the maid as she exited the room after serving the gentlemen their tea. She moved to evade the largest dog—some manner of deranged wolfhound—only to lose her balance and drop the tea tray. It fell to the marble floor with a resounding crash.

The gentlemen in the library leapt to their feet. The Earl of Edgeworth bellowed in outrage. Viscount Darly grabbed the wolfhound by the scruff of its neck. And their host, the renowned financier Mr. Edgar Townsend, shouted for assistance from behind the safety of his enormous mahogany desk.

Only Arthur remained seated. He had little choice in the matter. One of the dogs had knocked his cane to the floor, where it had promptly skittered out of reach across the marble. As a result, he was obliged to observe the chaotic scene from his place on the library sofa.

And chaotic it was.

Indeed, unless Arthur was very much mistaken, the giant snarling beast Darly was trying to subdue was seconds away from ripping the viscount's head off.

"Basil, no!" a feminine voice called from the doorway.

Arthur looked up just in time to see a young lady rush into the room. She held a scraggly black terrier under one slender arm, much the way a great lady might carry a pampered pug. As she passed the sofa, she dropped the little dog straight into Arthur's lap. She didn't seem to notice he was there. Her attention was wholly fixed on Darly.

"Phyllida!" Townsend thundered. "What's the meaning of this?"

The young lady ignored him and went straight to Darly. "Please release him, sir." She placed a calming hand on the great dog's wiry back. "He's really quite gentle."

"Gentle! This brute?" Darly lifted his eyes to the young lady's face. And then he froze. "I beg your pardon, miss, I—"

"You must let him go," she said. "I promise he won't bite you."

Still staring at her, Darly withdrew his hand from the dog's neck and took a wary step back. Once released, the giant dog immediately ceased snarling and ran back toward the door and out of the library. The remaining two dogs—crossbreed collies by the look of them—quickly followed their rambunctious leader.

Arthur lifted the small terrier from his lap and lowered him to the floor to send him off with his fellows. The little dog squirmed violently.

"Oh no, sir!" The young lady hurried to the sofa and swept the terrier out of his arms. "He can't be let down. He's lame in one leg and finds it difficult to walk."

At her words, the room fell deathly quiet.

Arthur supposed he should feel something. A sense of embarrassment or personal mortification. In truth, he felt nothing. Nothing save the mildest twinge of annoyance that he was here at all. He didn't belong in Edgar Townsend's library any more than he belonged in London. That he was required to remain was a source of bitterness to him. The careless words of a stranger could make things no worse.

"Phyllida," Townsend said from between clenched teeth. "Haven't I told you—"

"Papa?" Townsend's eldest daughter appeared in the doorway. She was tying on a fashionable straw bonnet, giving every indication that she intended to go out. "What's all the commotion?"

"Your cousin's wretched dogs," Townsend snapped.

In response, the young lady—Townsend's niece, apparently—secured the little terrier more firmly under her arm and curtsied, rather gracefully, to the room at large. "My apologies, gentlemen," she said to no one in particular. And then, her head held high and her spine very straight, she walked out of the library with Townsend's daughter, shutting the door behind them.

Arthur leaned back against the cushions of the sofa, his injured leg stretched out before him. Darly crossed the floor to retrieve his cane. Arthur took it from him without a word. To the untrained eye it was no more than an expensively made walking stick, but everyone in the library knew full well that without it he couldn't even have managed to walk across the room.

Townsend cleared his throat. "Those dogs are a damned nuisance. No manners at all and every one of them a mongrel. My niece refused to come up to London without them. I should've put my foot down, but—"

"Your niece is uncommonly handsome, Townsend," Darly interrupted. "I knew you had a young female relation up from Devonshire to stay with you, but I never imagined..."

Townsend returned to his seat, his face settling into the same shrewd lines as when he discussed any other investment. "Yes. Miss Satterthwaite is a singular young lady. She's the granddaughter of Sir Charles of Satterthwaite Court in Devonshire. A distant relative of mine, recently passed away. He was knighted for services to the crown in '79."

Edgeworth frowned. "Satterthwaite Court. That's the estate you inherited six months back, is it not?"

"It is, my lord."

Darly laughed. "I suppose the girl came with it."

Townsend fixed the viscount with a repressive glare. "Miss Satterthwaite was left with no means of support. I had no obligation to her, of course, but I'm not a hard-hearted man. She's of an age with my two daughters, and I've plenty of room here in London. I invited her to stay until such time as she can be married. I have high hopes that now she's here in town, she'll make an excellent match."

"Her eyes are extraordinary," Darly murmured. "I've never seen anything like them."

Edgeworth snorted. The oldest man in the room, he had a great property in Hertfordshire and was, for all intents and purposes, little more than a titled farmer. "I had a sheepdog once just the same. One blue eye and one brown. Would hardly call it extraordinary."

Arthur hadn't seen her eyes. Even when she'd taken her dog from out of his arms, she'd most decidedly refused to look at him. He'd thought her behavior had something to do with his appearance. Now, however, as he listened to the other men discuss Miss Satterthwaite, it occurred to him that it likely had more to do with her own.

"Her eyes are hardly her only asset, Lord Edgeworth," Townsend said. "Even a man as particular as you are couldn't fail to see her other enticements."

Arthur hadn't paid much attention to Miss Satterthwaite's

enticements. She'd come into the room in a rush of radiant feminine energy and had left just as quickly, remaining only long enough for him to get an impression of a softly curved figure and a mass of dark auburn hair that was coming loose from the pins meant to hold it.

She might well be beautiful, but things of that nature made no difference to him anymore. He'd only come away from his estate in Somersetshire to transact some business for his father. Once it was concluded, he would return to the country, and as far as he was concerned, he'd be happy if he never saw another living person again.

During a few subdued chuckles, Darly addressed Townsend. "If you intend to see your niece married off, what are you hiding her away for?"

A ghost of a smile crossed Townsend's cadaverous face. "My sister, Mrs. Vale, has been overseeing the arrangements. Miss Satterthwaite will make her debut into society at Lord and Lady Worthing's ball on Saturday."

Darly burst into laughter. "So, that's your game, is it?"

"The Collector," Edgeworth said. "He never misses one of Worthing's soirees."

The Duke of Moreland was an avid collector of anything rare and valuable. He had a particular attraction to those priceless objects that were one of a kind—highly coveted treasures that, if possessed, would earn him the envy and admiration of other men. Indeed, many said his single-minded pursuit of such rarities pushed the limits of obsession and bordered on the edge of mania.

If he desired some unique item, Moreland would stop at nothing to acquire it. And if, by some chance, complete and total possession managed to evade him—an event which happened infrequently—there were apocryphal tales of the vengeance he'd exacted against those foolish enough to have deprived him of his goal.

Arthur knew of the man's reputation, but he'd had no idea that Moreland's passion for collecting extended to human beings.

"I heard Moreland's on the lookout for a new wife," Edgeworth said. "Last one died quite suddenly, I believe. Drowned in a fountain, or some such unlikely event."

"A tragic accident." Townsend gave a dismissive wave of his hand. "She was a foolish young chit just out of the schoolroom. He's made it known that his next wife will be of more mature years."

"How old is your niece?" Darly asked. "I expect she must fit the bill."

"She is three and twenty."

Edgeworth tilted back his teacup and downed the contents in one gulp. "If he's interested in your niece, Townsend, no doubt he'll make it worth your while."

Townsend bowed his head in silent acknowledgement.

"It's rotten luck that at his age he still gets first choice of all the young ladies," Darly said. "You should introduce her to us."

"And I shall," Townsend said. "When you all come to dinner next week."

Darly set his teacup and saucer down onto a side table with a clatter. "I see no need to delay."

Townsend frowned. "Regrettably, my lord, I believe Miss Satterthwaite and my daughters have already left for their afternoon walk. Perhaps some other time—"

"Then why don't we join the ladies?" Darly suggested. "It's damnably fine weather today. We could all do with some air."

Townsend was plainly not keen on the proposition, but he wasn't the type of man to offend his business partners. Especially not over something as inconsequential as an introduction. "Very well. A short turn about the park can do no harm."

Edgeworth glanced at Arthur. "What say you, Heywood? Are you able, man?" There was a trace of pity in his words. "No shame in begging off."

Arthur's hand tightened on the handle of his cane. "I'm confident I can manage."

"Splendid." Darly stood, straightening the cuffs of his expensively cut coat. "If we leave at once, I'm sure we'll catch up with them directly."

Phyllida Satterthwaite lifted her face to the sun, heedless of the danger its rays might wreak on her complexion. She loved nothing more than fresh air and exercise. Long rambles with her dogs had been a daily occurrence while living with her grandfather in Devonshire. She'd often walked miles to visit the tenants, or to call on friends in the village, with Basil, Jasper, and Dash trotting along at her heels and Fox held safe in her arms.

Those days were but a memory now.

It had been six months since her grandfather's death, and only a month since she'd first met Edgar Townsend. Uncle Edgar, as he'd encouraged her to call him, was the last living male heir to her grandfather's estate. At the end of her period of mourning, he'd arrived in Fox Cross and proceeded to make a thorough inventory of Satterthwaite Court—and of Philly herself.

He'd quickly come to the decision that Satterthwaite Court was to be let and those things of value within it sold at auction. Philly's own future was decided with no less efficiency. She was to return to London with her uncle. He'd finance a season for her so that she might find herself a suitable husband.

"It's the least I can do in memory of your grandfather," he'd said. "He wouldn't have wanted you to be forced into servitude upon his death."

Philly was decidedly unenthusiastic about this scheme, but she'd said very little in argument against it. Any influence she had remaining at Satterthwaite Court was exerted solely on behalf of the servants, with particular care for the nearly blind housekeeper and the butler who was so infirm he walked with two sticks.

Once all was settled, Philly and her four dogs had been whisked away to London.

There was nothing of the country ramble to her walks now— certainly not when accompanied by her two cousins. Elizabeth and Abigail Townsend were town creatures. They preferred a leisurely promenade. All the better to display the elegant fashions afforded them by their father's legendary business acumen.

"Lord Darly is a viscount," Elizabeth said as she walked at Philly's side. "An *unmarried* viscount." At four-and-twenty, Elizabeth was still unmarried herself.

Abigail trailed along behind the two older girls. She was a mere eighteen, her romantic future bright before her. "He's very handsome."

Elizabeth ignored her younger sister. "Then there's Captain Heywood. Heaven knows what he was doing there. He hasn't been out in society in ages. I suppose Papa has tempted him with some lucrative scheme bound to make them all heaps of money."

Philly's dogs tangled about the skirts of her plain muslin gown. With its faded blue pelisse, it was nowhere near as fashionable as the walking dresses worn by her cousins. Certainly not as fashionable as the dresses that had been purchased for her since arriving in London. Beautiful dresses of every variety. Far too beautiful to wear for a simple stroll in the park, or so Philly thought.

Uncle Edgar's widowed sister, Mrs. Vale, would be apoplectic to see her clothed as she was now.

Not that it mattered. Whenever Philly was left to her own devices, she always reverted back to the simple gowns she'd worn while living with her grandfather. It was one of her only acts of defiance.

She bent to let the dogs off their leads. They ran a short distance ahead, leaping and jumping in circles. Fox remained firmly in her arms. "Which one was Captain Heywood?"

"The dark-haired gentleman on the sofa. How could you not see him? He was holding your little brute just as surely as you're holding him now."

Philly hugged Fox closer to her chest. "I didn't pay him any particular attention."

Abigail caught up with them to walk at Philly's right. "Arthur Heywood is the second son of the Earl of Gordon. He was horribly hurt in the war."

"Was he?"

"Indeed," Elizabeth said. "I heard that, after he was injured, he lay on the battlefield for days, left for dead. And that when the other soldiers finally found him, he was half mad."

Philly reflected on this information a moment. "If he's half mad, why is he doing business with your father?"

"Well, he must not be mad *now*," Elizabeth replied with some irritation, "but everyone knows he's never been quite right since he returned from fighting in Spain."

"The story is rather romantic," Abigail said. "Before he left to fight, he was engaged to Lady Eliot. Her name was Caroline Battersby then, and—"

"It's not romantic at all," Elizabeth interrupted. "It's true that they were engaged, but by the time Captain Heywood came back to England, Caroline Battersby had already married Baron Eliot. She didn't even write to tell Captain Heywood she was ending their engagement."

"But he's never stopped loving her," Abigail said. "And he's vowed never to marry—"

"Who would have him? He's a thoroughly unpleasant man, and now he's come back from the war, he can hardly walk."

Philly remembered what she'd said when she'd retrieved Fox from Captain Heywood's grasp. She stifled a groan. Good heavens. What must he have thought of her? That she would make such a thoughtless remark about someone's infirmity!

"Lady Eliot has been widowed for over a twelvemonth," Abigail said. "I wonder, now Captain Heywood has come to town on business, he might not go and see her? Or perhaps he hasn't come to London on business at all? Perhaps he's heard that Lord Eliot died, and has come to reunite with Lady Eliot now she's out of her widow's weeds? Oh, he must love her desperately!"

"I saw him the year I came out," Elizabeth said. "He was a cold, unfeeling gentleman, even then. Too impressed with himself by half."

"He didn't ask her to dance," Abigail whispered. "He was frightfully rude."

Elizabeth's chin lifted a notch. "Rubbish. I never thought him handsome. And now he has altered so much I would hardly know him."

They hadn't gone much farther when Philly heard her uncle calling out to them. She stopped, along with her cousins, and turned to look.

Uncle Edgar and the gentlemen who had been with him in the library were walking toward them. To her dismay, Captain Heywood was with them.

As they approached, Philly discreetly took his measure. He was much taller than the other gentlemen, with broad shoulders and a lean, athletic build that seemed at odds with his use of a cane. Whatever had happened to him in the war, he still had the proud, upright carriage of a soldier.

His hair was jet black, with the barest hint of gray at his temples. His suit of clothes was black, as well; unnecessarily austere, as if he were in mourning. But it was his face that caught her notice most of all. It was solemn, almost to the point of harshness, and in it she had the distinct impression of pain.

It was hurting him to walk, as surely as it hurt when Fox attempted it. Why was he doing it, then? And why had her uncle and his friends been so insensitive as to impose such an activity upon him?

"Come, girls," Uncle Edgar said. "We're resolved to accompany you on your turn about the park. Lord Edgeworth, Lord Darly, Captain Heywood. My daughters, Elizabeth and Abigail. And my niece, Miss Phyllida Satterthwaite."

As the introductions were made, Philly felt herself under painful scrutiny, and though she made the necessary polite replies, she instinctively looked away from the gentlemen who spoke to her.

This was the part of life in London she enjoyed least. These strained encounters with sophisticated strangers. She never felt so shy—so completely out of her element—as when they were peppering her with questions, or gazing with open curiosity at her face.

Lord Darly wasn't any different. He made no attempt to conceal his avid stare. She supposed she should be honored. He was a gentleman of rank and fortune, eager to make her acquaintance. A handsome gentleman, too—if one liked golden-haired dandies of the fashionable variety.

As for Captain Heywood, it seemed he had no interest in her at all. He gave her the barest acknowledgement, his voice deep and a little rough, as if from lack of use, and then resumed looking fixedly off at some point beyond where she stood.

Why on earth had he come into the park? It was obviously not out of any desire to obtain a formal introduction to her. His mind was somewhere else entirely. Perhaps he was, even now, thinking of Lady Eliot?

"Shall we, ladies?" Lord Darly asked, giving Philly and her cousins a gleaming smile.

Philly wrapped both of her arms around Fox, holding him securely against her chest as she resumed walking. Basil, Jasper, and Dash meandered along beside her, their tongues lolling. They were too exhausted from racing around in the grass to pay the gentlemen any mind.

Lord Edgeworth and Uncle Edgar led their little procession. Philly, her cousins, and Lord Darly followed, with Captain Heywood walking a few steps behind.

Lord Darly talked easily to the ladies on a number of topics, ranging from the weather to Lord and Lady Worthing's upcoming ball. Elizabeth made frequent flirtatious responses, and Abigail joined in whenever her older sister would allow it.

Philly had little to say, and when asked a question, usually confined herself to one-word answers. It wasn't long until Lord Darly gave up his efforts to draw her out and directed his attentions to her much more obliging cousins.

Occasionally, Philly looked back and couldn't help but notice that Captain Heywood's gait was becoming more stilted, and the expression of pain on his face more pronounced.

Her heart swelled with compassion for him.

While Uncle Edgar and Lord Edgeworth talked together

rather loudly about the stock exchange, and Lord Darly and her cousins laughed about some comedy at Drury Lane they'd all happened to see, Philly began to walk a little slower, shortening her stride until she was, quite naturally, at Captain Heywood's side.

She took a deep breath. "I beg your pardon, sir. Might I avail myself of your arm?"

At the sound of Miss Satterthwaite's voice, Arthur's already uneven gait faltered. He'd been staring straight ahead, concentrating on putting one booted foot in front of the other, even as his leg screamed in protest. How long had she been beside him? Seconds? Longer? And now she desired a supportive arm? From *him*?

In another time and another place, he might have laughed. Her request was that ridiculous. That utterly absurd.

But a gentleman didn't laugh in the face of a lady.

Instead, he wordlessly offered her his arm. The gesture was stiff. Formal.

In answer, Miss Satterthwaite shifted her little terrier into her left arm and linked her right arm through his.

Arthur's entire body tensed. It had been years since he'd been in such close proximity with another human being. A feminine hand on his sleeve would have been challenge enough. But there was no ladylike formality in Miss Satterthwaite's touch. Her hold on his arm was firm and true. It took an effort to resume walking. A single-minded focus on the contractions of his muscles and the rhythm of his breath.

They'd gone no more than a few uneasy steps when understanding set in.

She'd positioned herself so close to his side that anyone watching them would have thought she was leaning on him. Indeed, he suspected she'd meant to convey just that impression. In reality, it was quite the opposite. Without a pitying look or a word of sympathy, Miss Satterthwaite had lent him her support. And she'd done it in just such a way as to spare his foolish pride.

Arthur was oddly moved, yet at the same time he recoiled from her kindness.

The rest of their party was much farther ahead now. None of them seemed to have noticed that he and Miss Satterthwaite were walking arm in arm. Edgeworth's booming voice carried on the afternoon breeze, as did the intermittent laughter of Darly and the Townsend chits. Arthur imagined they were all still talking about the same tedious subjects they'd been discussing twenty minutes before.

He considered saying something to Miss Satterthwaite. He could comment on the weather, perhaps, or ask her about her life in Devonshire. It was a foolish notion, and one he quickly dismissed. He'd seen her awkward interaction with Darly and Edgeworth, and unless he was very much mistaken, she was as little inclined to meaningless chatter as he was himself.

They walked on in silence, Miss Satterthwaite matching Arthur's stride with an effortless grace. She never hurried him, and seemed to know just when to slow down, and when to hold his arm more securely. He found it rather remarkable considering the fact that she appeared to be paying him no attention at all.

When he cast her a cautious glance, he saw that she was more focused on her dogs than on the humorless gentleman on her arm. He also saw the delicate line of her neck and jaw, the voluptuous curve of her lips, and the way the bright sunlight caused her dark hair to glow with warmth.

"Captain Heywood?"

He tensed, much as he had when she'd first taken his arm. "Ma'am?"

She looked up at him. "Would you mind very much escorting me back to the house? The dogs and I have walked enough for today."

Because she was speaking to him directly, Arthur felt at complete liberty to look at her face and immediately experienced for himself the rather startling effect of her mismatched eyes. One was a deep blue and the other the color of amber. They were large and fringed with thick lashes, set under a pair of dark, arching brows.

Such a striking feature might have overpowered the face of a woman less lovely, but for Miss Satterthwaite, her eyes only complemented and enhanced the whole. From her elegant cheekbones to her generous mouth and daintily rounded chin, the rest of her face bespoke the same soft femininity he'd observed in her profile and her figure. There was no hardness to her, no sharply hewn contours or harsh angles, only an inherent gentleness that manifested itself in every aspect of her person. Arthur had never seen the like of it.

He searched her sweet, rather serious expression for some sign of pity. He didn't find it. And yet he suspected that her desire to return home had more to do with his infirmity than with her own exhaustion. "If you wish. But perhaps you should first inform your uncle?"

She looked ahead at Townsend, who was deep in conversation with Edgeworth, and then to her two cousins who were still laughing with Darly. "I doubt it's necessary."

"Very well," he said.

Without another word, they turned and headed back to the townhouse. Arthur's gait was even stiffer, and they walked so slowly it felt as if they made no progress at all. The whole experience was an exercise in humiliation. He cursed himself for being so foolish and so proud as to accept the invitation to walk into the park in the first place. What had he been thinking? His leg was sure to cause him agony for days now.

When they finally reached the stone steps that led to the front door of the townhouse, Miss Satterthwaite tightened her grip on his arm. Arthur took each step with painful deliberation, as conscious of her presence at his side as he was of the pain in his injured leg.

She said nothing except to urge one of her dogs to hurry along into the house when the butler opened the door to admit them. Again, she seemed to take no particular notice of his infirmity, but Arthur leaned on her as they climbed the stairs, and whether she acknowledged him or not, Miss Satterthwaite gave him the full strength of her support.

She kept with him as they walked across the entry hall and into the library. Only then, within an easy distance of the sofa, did she relinquish his arm. "Thank you for escorting me home, Captain Heywood. If you'll have a seat, I'm sure my uncle will be back directly." She inclined her head. "Good afternoon."

"Ma'am." Arthur made a slight bow. By the time he raised his head, she was already heading toward the door—one small, bedraggled dog under her arm and three larger ones at her heels.

His face settled into a grim frown. He had no interest in society anymore. No interest, he sometimes felt, in life. But his gaze lingered on Phyllida Satterthwaite, his eyes following her graceful figure until she and her dogs were completely out of his sight.

TWO

Philly had come to Captain Heywood's aid just as she would to any creature in distress, and after leaving him in the library, she thought no more about it. The rest of her afternoon was taken up with her dancing lesson and writing letters to some of her friends in Fox Cross.

At dinner that evening, she was surprised when her uncle asked about Captain Heywood quite casually over his soup. Mrs. Vale had retired early with a headache, but both of her cousins immediately perked up, as if they expected Philly to receive the harshest reproof.

"Curious that he walked you home," Uncle Edgar said. "Rather unexpected."

"I was tired," Philly replied. "I told him I'd better return to the house, and he kindly agreed to escort me. Was that not all right, Uncle? I thought it must be preferable to my walking home alone."

"Hmm." He ate a few spoonfuls of soup, during which his daughters sat on the edge of their seats awaiting his response. "No harm in it," he pronounced at last. "Heywood's not likely to do any damage to your reputation." And with that enigmatic statement, Uncle Edgar returned to eating his dinner.

Elizabeth and Abigail caught each other's eyes and giggled. Neither said a word.

However, once they had retired to the drawing room so that Uncle Edgar could enjoy his after-dinner port in peace, her cousins lost no time in remarking on Philly's interest in the brooding cavalry captain.

"Do you think him handsome, Phyllida?" Abigail asked as she rifled through her playing cards. "He's nothing to Viscount Carlisle, of course, but he was once considered rather good-looking. He's tall and dark and all that sort of thing."

Philly glanced up briefly. "Viscount Carlisle?"

"He's Captain Heywood's older brother," Elizabeth said. "A notorious rake and a drunkard."

"Yes," Abigail agreed. "But ever so amiable."

Philly contemplated her cards with a frown. Unlike her cousins, she had no aptitude for games of chance. Her grandfather hadn't approved of them. While living at Satterthwaite Court, they'd never played after-dinner piquet, whist, or loo. Instead, she'd passed the time playing the pianoforte or reading aloud to him from one of his favorite books.

The memory of those quiet evenings filled her with an aching sadness.

She was determined to make the best of her new situation, but in her private hours she was terribly homesick and unhappy. Only the companionship of her dogs was able to give her any comfort in her grief.

"But perhaps you like a gentleman to be fair?" Abigail pressed. "Like Lord Darly?"

"Of course she doesn't think Captain Heywood is handsome."

Elizabeth lay down a card with a loud thump. "Who could, with that scowl of his?"

Abigail chanced a look at Philly. "I suppose it doesn't matter. After the Worthings' ball, you will be engaged."

Philly raised a brow at her young cousin. "You have a great deal of confidence in me."

"Why shouldn't I have?"

"Because," Philly said candidly, "I have a feeling that, despite Mrs. Vale's efforts, I shall make an abysmal show of myself at the ball and no gentleman will think of me twice."

Elizabeth and Abigail exchanged a look with each other from across the card table.

"Perhaps," Abigail said, "there may be someone at the Worthings' ball who will fancy you no matter how poor of a debut you make? Why, he may even be— *Ouch*!" She glared at her sister. "You kicked me, Lizzie."

"I did nothing of the sort. You must have bumped your leg against the table. If you'd pay attention to the game and not indulge in silly gossip, then maybe you wouldn't have these kinds of accidents."

The two sisters shared another weighted look.

Philly cast a curious glance between the pair of them. From the moment she'd arrived in London, Elizabeth and Abigail Townsend had been fighting with each other like two cats. Philly had made it a rule never to involve herself in their petty quarrels. Nevertheless...

"Is there anything you wish to tell me, Abigail?" she asked. "Elizabeth?"

"Nothing at all," Elizabeth said.

Abigail remained silent.

Philly sighed. "In that case..." She lay all her cards down before her. "I believe I shall retire."

"Phyllida," Elizabeth groaned. "You can't do that. Now you've ruined the whole game."

Philly rose from the table. "I'm so weary, I can be of no use to either of you. If you will excuse me."

"It's all right, Phyllida." Abigail gathered up the cards. "Now Lizzie and I can play piquet."

They both bid her goodnight, and Philly swiftly made her exit. She could hear them bickering softly as she stepped out into the hall.

"You know we aren't supposed to mention *him*," Elizabeth said.

"I didn't say his name," Abigail retorted.

A flicker of uneasiness traced its way down Philly's spine. Her cousins were keeping secrets from her. Secrets about something— and someone. A mysterious *him*. A gentleman Philly was to meet at the Worthings' ball.

She wondered who in the world he might be.

The next few days were spent in earnest preparations for the Worthings' ball. Philly remained alert for the slightest hint on who her mysterious suitor might be, but her cousins made no more mention of the man. They had little opportunity. Mrs. Vale was a constant presence. She sat in on Philly's dancing lessons, played cards with her every evening, and forced her to model various combinations of gowns, slippers, and wraps so she could determine which ensemble would be the most impressive for Philly to wear when she was introduced into society.

Philly found it all stifling and anxiously awaited the brief moments she could escape with her dogs to the park.

It wasn't complete freedom. Indeed, since she'd come to live in London, she'd never once been allowed to go out alone. Even when walking her dogs, Uncle Edgar insisted that she be accompanied by a vigilant maid.

Still, it was liberty of a kind. And Philly relished every second of it.

The Friday before the ball, she was just rushing down the front steps of the townhouse with Fox in her arms, her three larger dogs at her side, and Sara, the maid, hurrying behind her, when she saw Captain Heywood alighting from a carriage.

She resolved immediately not to acknowledge him. He seemed a proud sort of man, and she didn't like to remind him of how she'd lent him her arm. She started to walk past him, her eyes averted.

"Good morning, Miss Satterthwaite," he said.

Philly came to an abrupt and rather awkward halt. She hadn't expected he'd address her, and now felt rather foolish that she'd attempted to avoid him. "Captain Heywood. Good morning."

He was leaning on his cane, his solemn face as hard as granite. "I see you're off on another walk."

"Yes, sir."

"It's a fine day for it."

"Yes. The weather is very pleasant."

He was silent a moment. "Do you often walk in the park? I suppose you must with so many dogs to care for."

"I go to the park at least twice a day."

"Morning and afternoon, I presume."

"Yes, sir. I would take them out more often if I could, but I'm afraid my time is not my own."

Captain Heywood nodded. "Well, Miss Satterthwaite, I won't keep you."

Philly thanked him, and then—heart thumping—headed off down the street with her dogs.

When she returned to the townhouse an hour later, Mrs. Vale was waiting for her in the entry hall, her arms folded across the bosom of her gray bombazine dress, and her jaw clenched so tightly that a muscle worked rhythmically in her cheek.

Prudence Vale was as tall and thin as her brother, with the same sharp eyes and shrewd expression. Her lips were perpetually pressed into a thin line, and she wore her hair scraped back from her forehead in a tight knot at her nape.

Her personality was no less severe than her coiffure.

She hadn't invited Philly to call her *Aunt*. Indeed, since Philly's arrival, Mrs. Vale had offered Philly precious little kindness at all, save for the benefit of her instruction.

"How many times must I tell you?" she scolded. "If you insist upon going into the park with your dogs, put on one of your *new* walking dresses. This isn't Fox Cross. You can't scamper about unremarked. The finest ladies and gentlemen in society are bound to see you, and what will they think of you dressed like this? I'll tell you what they'll think. They'll think you're some ramshackle hoyden up from the country without anything to recommend her. Once that impression is made, it will be fixed. Fixed, I tell you."

Philly started up the stairs to her room without a word.

Mrs. Vale followed. "Is something wrong with your new gowns, pray? Or is it merely your own obstinacy that drives you to defy me?"

"I'm sorry, Mrs. Vale. I promise I'll remember next time."

"You had better. When you go walking this afternoon, you'll wear a proper walking dress. And if I discover that you've ventured out of the house again in one of these gowns that aren't even fit for the rag bag, why, the rag bag is just where they'll go!"

Later that afternoon, when Philly went to the park with her dogs, she wore an ensemble chosen for her by Mrs. Vale. The elegant cambric dress came down to her ankles, and the sarsnet spencer jacket she wore over it was Sardinian blue with decorative cuffs, braiding, and epaulettes. The maid had arranged her hair so that the bulk of it was elaborately pinned in three low, intertwining rolled sections behind her head, and over it all she wore a village hat made of chip with deep blue ribbons to match her spencer.

She shifted Fox under her arm, inwardly fuming at having to dress up just to take her dogs out for a run. In the country she'd been allowed to dress practically, but here in London, she was expected to display herself in the park like some manner of peacock.

Having been born with dark auburn hair and mismatched eyes was quite conspicuous enough. The last thing she wanted to do was to draw further attention to herself with her clothing. She'd attempted to explain this to Mrs. Vale during their first shopping excursion, but Mrs. Vale wouldn't hear of it. For a woman so unerringly conservative in her own dress, she seemed to have no compunction about outfitting Philly in daring styles, bright colors, and some of the lowest necklines in England.

As Philly walked farther into the park, she let the dogs off their leads. They ran out onto the grass to race each other.

Sara attempted to corral them, but the more she chased after them, the more the dogs attempted to evade her, believing it to be some sort of game.

Philly wasn't worried. Her dogs wouldn't stray far, and she didn't begrudge them their exercise. It was bad enough that she must be constrained and stifled. She wouldn't allow it to happen to her pets.

She continued down the path, and Sara and the dogs made some progress along behind her. From his place in her arms, Fox took in the sights around him, intermittently looking up at her for reassurance. In response, she pressed a kiss to his scraggly forehead, so lost in her own thoughts that she didn't even notice the gentleman sitting on a bench they passed until he said her name.

"Miss Satterthwaite."

She started, turning back to see who had addressed her, even as a shiver of awareness informed her about whom the deep, low-pitched voice belonged. "Captain Heywood!"

Arthur moved to rise and greet her properly.

Miss Satterthwaite anticipated him. "Please don't get up. I was just about to sit down awhile myself. If you don't mind my joining you?"

"By all means." He gestured to the spot on the bench next to him. He had no doubt her actions were motivated solely by consideration for his infirmity. For a moment, he had to steel himself against the resentment that consistently rose within him at any perceived sign of pity.

"Miss?" Miss Satterthwaite's maid eyed Arthur with suspicion. "Shall I stay with the dogs on the grass?"

"Yes, do," Miss Satterthwaite said. "I'll be right here. Oh, and Sara! Don't chase them. They'll only run faster. If you're very still and quiet, they'll come to you of their own accord."

The maid didn't look convinced. "Yes, miss."

Miss Satterthwaite took a seat beside him, carefully situating her bedraggled dog next to her. Once she'd assured herself of the little beast's comfort, she turned to face him. "I'm sorry I passed you. I wasn't paying any attention."

"It's quite all right." His gaze drifted over her clothes. "I hardly recognized you myself. You've changed a great deal since this morning."

She cast a frowning glance downward. "Now I'm in London, I'm required to dress well even for a short walk with my dogs. It's all rather a nuisance."

"Is this your uncle's directive?"

"In a manner of speaking. He's put me under the care of his sister, Mrs. Vale. She's chosen all my clothes while I'm here in town. If I don't wear them, she falls into a state."

"I see."

She tugged at the braiding on her spencer. "I feel rather foolish."

"You look very well, Miss Satterthwaite."

"I wasn't fishing for a compliment, sir."

"Of course not." Arthur's gloved hand tightened reflexively on his cane. He'd never been adept at casual conversation, but since he'd come back from the war, he found even the simplest of exchanges to be agonizingly difficult. He didn't know why he was subjecting himself to it except that, for the past several days, he'd thought of little else but Phyllida Satterthwaite and her quiet act of kindness toward him.

"I know I shouldn't complain," she said. "They're lovely clothes. Any other lady would be happy to have them. I'm really...very grateful...for my uncle's generosity."

"It is not the best position to be in," Arthur said after a long pause. "Being grateful, that is."

"No. It most definitely isn't." And with a heartfelt sigh, she looked out across the park.

Her three dogs were playing on the grass under the careful supervision of the much put-upon maid. Arthur wondered what Miss Satterthwaite was thinking about as she looked at them. It occurred to him, quite suddenly, that she might be homesick. "Is this your first visit to London?"

"I confess it is. Up until two weeks ago, I'd never left Devonshire except for twice accompanying my grandfather to Bath so he might take the cure."

"My estate in Somersetshire is very near Bath."

"Is it?" She looked at him with renewed interest. "I didn't know you were from that part of the world, sir. Have you ever had occasion to go into Devonshire?"

"Many times. Whereabouts are you from?"

"A small village called Fox Cross. It's near Dartmoor."

"Ah, yes. I've been there."

Her eyes brightened, and then she smiled. "Have you?"

Arthur was momentarily transfixed. Never in his life had he encountered a woman with so much genuine warmth in her expression. "In my younger days. My brother and I stopped off there once on the way to visit family friends in Cornwall."

"I wonder if... Is it possible you might remember my grandfather? Sir Charles of Satterthwaite Court?"

"I fear I don't. I was only a boy then. My father may well have known him. I'll ask him in my next letter, if you like."

She beamed. "I'd be so very much obliged to you."

It wasn't a very bright day—indeed there was scarcely a patch of blue in the cloudy sky—but somehow what little light there was seemed to shimmer in the red highlights of her hair and illuminate her skin in a soft, golden glow. It wasn't only her expression that exuded warmth but the entirety of her person.

Arthur tried not to stare.

He failed miserably.

"Were you always in your grandparents' care?" he asked.

"My whole life."

"And your parents...?"

"My father was my grandparents' only child, and my mother was the daughter of a widowed vicar in Fox Cross. My grandparents arranged the match between them. They hoped my mother would settle my father. He was rather wild, you see." A slight frown marred her brow. It was quickly dispelled. "My mother was said to have been one of the loveliest ladies in Devonshire, and the closest thing in the West Country to a living saint. She was steady and kind. A paragon, really."

"You didn't know her?"

"No. I didn't know either of my parents. My mother died bringing me into the world, and my father died in a carriage accident one week later."

"So, your grandparents brought you up as their own."

"Yes. Well...not quite as their own, for they vowed they would never raise another child as they had my father. They'd spoiled and indulged him, which must have been quite natural since he was their only child, but in time they grew to believe it was the root of all his wildness. So, though they loved me, they dealt with me very strictly. There were no balls or assemblies. No visits to town. We lived an exceedingly isolated life."

"It sounds a grim existence."

"Oh no. I had my pets about me for company. And there were villagers and tenants to visit. Decent, hardworking people. Friends I've had my entire life. I wasn't ever lonely."

"Did you never yearn to venture farther? To see something of the world?"

"I never thought of it. It seemed such an impossibility—and not suited to my temperament at all. And yet....when my uncle came to Satterthwaite Court and told me I must return to London with him, I climbed into his coach and left Fox Cross without a word of protest." She tugged absently at her glove. "Do you think I did right, Captain Heywood?"

He had an overwhelming impulse to cover her anxious hands

with his own. He didn't act on it. "I beg your pardon, did you not want to come to London, Miss Satterthwaite?"

"No, but I very much wanted to do what was right. What was expected of me."

"Have you no other family that you could go to?"

"I have no one." She looked out at her dogs for several seconds. "What a maudlin thing to say. Pray forgive me. I don't mean to sound as if I'm blue-deviled. I really have a great deal to be...to be..."

"Grateful for?" he suggested.

A hint of a smile edged her soft mouth. "Yes. Exactly."

Philly wondered how so much of the conversation had gotten away from her. Captain Heywood didn't look like a man one could confide in. In fact, he appeared as if he were the sort of man who would rebuff even the slightest attempt at personal conversation. Yet here she was telling him the story of her life—and asking for his advice, no less. He must think her some sort of hoydenish madcap, or at the very least, a country oddity.

"Do you remember much about your visit to Fox Cross, Captain Heywood?" she asked. "Did you have a chance to see a bit of the countryside?"

"Unfortunately, no. We stayed only one night at an inn near the main road. I think it may have been called the Hart and Hare."

Philly brightened. "I know it well. It's run by a woman named Mrs. Carter. You may have met her. She's rather thin and quite tall for a woman. She may even be as tall as you are. It's through her that I came by Fox. She named him after the village." She lifted the little terrier onto her lap. "Can you believe he was thrown from a carriage on the main road? Mrs. Carter said he likely bit someone and was tossed out in a fit of anger, but I don't think that's any justification."

Captain Heywood stroked Fox's head. "Is that how he hurt his leg?"

"Yes, I believe so. When first Mrs. Carter brought him to me, he was in a dreadful state. He's much better now."

Captain Heywood's large hand moved gently over Fox.

"You know," she said, "it's rather remarkable. He doesn't seem to be afraid of you at all."

"Is he usually frightened of people?"

"He will bite, I'm ashamed to say, but his ill temper is solely reserved for men. My grandfather said it was almost certain his injury was inflicted by a man."

"Yes. Men can be very cruel."

Something in his tone caught Philly's notice. She looked up, only to see that his gaze had grown distant, and he appeared to have withdrawn from her.

He was not an unhandsome man. With a noble brow, a strong, chiseled jaw, and penetrating gray eyes, he might even have been called dashing. But there was a permanent air of melancholy about Arthur Heywood, and an ever-present cast of pain that clouded his features. Philly began to comprehend that his pain was not merely physical.

What horrors he must have been through in the war. And to then come home from it all only to find that his one true love had married another man?

"Do you have more business with my uncle this afternoon?" she asked, for want of anything better to say.

"No. I won't meet with him again until Monday morning."

"Then perhaps I'll see you when I go out for my walk?"

He looked at her then, the expression in his eyes hard to read.

"Perhaps you will."

Philly was just about to say something more when Sara approached with the dogs in tow.

"Miss, we must get back. Mrs. Vale said I was to be sure you weren't late for your dancing lesson again." Sara cast a narrow glance at Captain Heywood. "She said to remind you there's much to be done before the ball."

"Yes, thank you, Sara." Philly was conscious of the maid's attention. She wondered what tales the girl might carry back with her to the servants' hall. Trying not to give any of it too much notice, she gathered Fox close to her and stood.

Captain Heywood rose, as well. "Miss Satterthwaite, it's been a pleasure."

Philly gazed up into his stern face. How many smiles had she given him today? Far more than she'd managed in the past two weeks in London. And yet, somehow, without the slightest effort, she was smiling again. It was the kind of smile one would give to a very dear friend. "For me, as well, Captain Heywood. Good afternoon."

THREE

The Earl of Gordon kept a fully staffed townhouse in Mayfair, and everything had been made available for Arthur's stay. The servants all treated him with near-embarrassing deference, and the coachman would have no doubt been willing to wait the day away while Arthur sat in the park. None of them had ever even dared look at him askance. Arthur suspected that their behavior owed a great deal to some high-handed command of his father's.

His older brother, George, might be his father's heir, but the bulk of the earl's affections had always been reserved for his younger son. When Arthur had gone away to fight on the Peninsula, no father could have been prouder. And when he'd come home, a mere shell of the man he'd been before, no father could have grieved so much.

He'd been tolerant of Arthur's desire to seclude himself down in Somersetshire, and—for the most part—had respected his wish for privacy. But as Arthur's thirty-second birthday approached, marking nearly three years spent alone in the country, his father's letters had started to become stern. The words *hermit* and *recluse* were used with increasing frequency.

"At least have some visitors down to stay," the earl would exhort him. "Nothing good can come of so much time spent alone."

When all his suggestions failed, the earl had issued what amounted to a royal decree. His son must immediately go to London to transact some business on his behalf. It was of the utmost importance. It must be seen to personally.

Arthur hadn't been fooled for a moment, but he'd obeyed out of respect for his father.

The pressing business had turned out to be nothing more than a consortium of investors being formed by Edgar Townsend, a man Arthur considered barely deserving of the title of gentleman. He'd never met anyone so lacking in finer feeling. Townsend's only code seemed to be that of making money.

Arthur's poor opinion of the man had been further cemented when he heard of Townsend's plans for his niece. In fact, he found it all so distasteful, that had *he* been the one in control of the matter, he'd have terminated his business with Townsend then and there. As it was, he expected that all would be completed to his father's satisfaction within three weeks. At which point, Arthur intended to return to Somersetshire without delay.

If his father had anticipated him enjoying himself in London— going out into society, or availing himself of the varied entertainments available to a wealthy gentleman—the earl would be sorely disappointed. Since arriving one week before, Arthur had rarely left the house except to attend the agonizingly dull meetings with the other potential investors in Townsend's library.

It was therefore quite a shock to the coachman, when after his brief visit with Miss Satterthwaite in the park, Arthur asked to be driven to his club in St. James's Street. The coachman's wiry brows shot up, but he said only "Yes, Captain Heywood," and gave the horses the office to start.

Arthur's club was much as he remembered. He crossed through the main room, making his way to a great leather chair located in a secluded corner. Ignoring the sound of murmuring voices and the curious stares of the few gentlemen who deigned to look his way, he ordered a bottle of brandy and opened up a newspaper. He had no intention of reading it. He didn't expect he would be sitting alone for very long.

Sure enough, within ten minutes he was approached by a man he hadn't seen in almost seven years.

"Heywood, what the devil are you doing in London?"

Reggie Forsythe was an impeccably coiffed dandy, with the same lean face, flaxen hair, and slender build of his father, Sir Clement Forsythe. The Earl of Gordon and Sir Clement were acquaintances from their youth. In his own younger days, Arthur had met all of Sir Clement's six sons at some point or another.

Unlike Arthur, who had purchased a commission not long after coming down from Oxford, Reggie Forsythe had eschewed military service in favor of living on credit in London; his life one of dissipation and debauchery. Arthur remembered hearing a story, widely bandied about some years ago, that Forsythe had lost the money for his own commission at some gaming hell. Like much of society gossip, Arthur didn't know if it was true, but it bore a close enough resemblance to Forsythe's character that he tended to believe it.

"Business for my father," Arthur replied. "And you?"

"Here for the season, of course." Forsythe took the chair across from Arthur, and after crossing his legs, spent a long while attending to an imaginary speck of dust on his biscuit-colored pantaloons. "It must be six or seven years since you and I last met.

Where was it? Let me think..."

Arthur had no desire to reminisce. He was here for information, nothing more.

"Business for the earl, you say?" Forsythe asked, giving up on his recollections. He withdrew a small bejeweled snuffbox and opened it with a practiced flick of one hand. "Must be something important to draw you out of Somersetshire." He took a pinch of snuff. "Understand you never leave your estate anymore."

"I'm overseeing various investments. With a fellow named Townsend."

Forsythe snapped shut his snuffbox. "Edgar Townsend? A veritable Midas. Can make money out of water, I hear."

"Are you acquainted with him?"

"He has two whey-faced daughters. Don't expect you've met them. Had too much to drink once and asked the elder one to dance." Forsythe gave a dramatic shudder. "He has a niece recently up from the country. Not a proper niece, mind you. Their grandfathers were distant cousins or some such thing. A rare beauty, people are saying. Haven't seen her yet myself, but I've heard all the talk."

"Have you?"

Forsythe needed little prompting. "Grandfather was a Sir something or other from somewhere or other not very important. Grandmother's related somehow to the Earl of Merrivale. Good bloodlines, but no great fortune, apparently. Townsend hasn't brought her out yet. Plans to introduce her at the Worthings' ball tomorrow. Rumor has it he intends to dangle her in front of the Collector. Don't envy her that!"

Arthur took a swallow of his brandy.

"I knew his last wife. Little Molly Cartwright, as was." Forsythe helped himself to a drink. "Damned shame how she died."

"Drowned, did she?"

"So they say."

"You have reason to suspect otherwise?"

"The thing is, Heywood..." Forsythe leaned toward Arthur, suddenly serious. "I know for a fact Molly only pretended to be a featherbrained little fluff. It was all an act she put on, you understand. She was an intelligent girl. Knew exactly how she must behave to get herself a rich husband. To think she fell into a fountain and drowned..." He shook his head. "It couldn't have happened the way they say."

Arthur frowned. "I've been away from town too long. I don't know the whole story, I'm afraid."

"Have you ever been down to Moreland Park?" Forsythe asked. "There's a great big fountain on the grounds. Deep enough you could dive into it if you like. When the Collector married Molly, he took her to Moreland Park straightaway. Molly was furious. Little point in contriving to become a duchess if you can't lord it over everyone in town, she said. Any rate, they say she used to walk along the edge of that fountain. Made a game of it; balancing on it for a while and then jumping off. They say she was doing it one night after coming home from a ball. She was wearing a heavy cloak. She slipped. Fell in. The water soaked through her clothes and pulled her straight under."

"Is that so improbable?"

Forsythe moved even closer to Arthur, his voice dropping to a half whisper. "Molly would never have walked on the edge of a fountain that deep. She was terrified of the water." He fell quiet for a moment as another gentleman passed them. "Besides, if that's what truly happened, then why did one of the grooms who pulled her out of the water claim she had bruises round her throat?"

Arthur lowered his glass. "Another rumor, surely. No different from the others that have plagued Moreland these many years."

Forsythe's eyes glinted. "You think so?"

"Do you have evidence to the contrary?"

"That very groom left Moreland Park shortly after and came to work for me. He told me everything, and a nasty picture he painted, too. Always knew the Collector was a brute, but had no idea the extent of it. Of course, Molly could have been spared all that. I would've married her myself if she'd have had me. But what's the second son of a baronet compared to a duke?" He threw back the entire contents of his glass of brandy. Once he'd swallowed it, his cheerful demeanor was restored. "As I say, I don't envy Townsend's niece. The Work of Art. That's what they're calling her. And we all know how the Collector feels about works of art."

"The Work of Art?" Arthur was incredulous. "Where the devil did you hear that?"

"The betting books, old chap." Forsythe filled his glass again. "You in town long?"

"A few weeks."

"Expect you're anxious to get back to Somersetshire."

"Quite anxious." Arthur rose from his chair. "If you'll excuse me, Forsythe. I've business I must attend to. I can delay it no longer."

"Of course, of course." Forsythe stood, as well. "Will you be out at all while you're here? The Worthings' ball is tomorrow. No need to dance in order to enjoy it. Quite interesting to see what type of young lady Townsend's been hiding away from everyone. Might be amusing to watch the old duke's reaction when he sees her for the first time."

"I won't be attending." Arthur headed toward the door.

Forsythe followed, making no effort to hide his interest in Arthur's uneven gait. "Naturally. Lady Eliot will be there. Wouldn't precisely be the thing to run into her after all these years. Especially in your, uh, current condition."

Arthur said nothing. What could he say? Caroline was the last thing on his mind at present.

"An unfortunate incident all around," Forsythe continued. "Personally, I thought she'd have waited for you. You did cut a dash back then. Four-Horse Club, Corinthian, and all that. And then a captain in the Dragoons. A war hero. But women *will* prefer a title. I know that as well as anyone. Can hardly blame them, when it comes down to it. Granted, old Eliot was only a baron, as well as a bit of a boor, but you must know she was happy. He treated her well enough while he was alive, the old sod. Clothes, jewels, all the things a lady desire. She wanted for nothing. That must put your mind at ease, at least."

Before exiting the main room, Arthur stopped in front of the high table where the club's leather-bound betting book was kept. Only half listening to Forsythe, he began to peruse the pages.

"She hasn't aged a day." Forsythe leaned against the wall next to where Arthur stood. "Still a right beauty. No woman could ever compare."

"Indeed," Arthur said absently.

There were several entries in the betting book mentioning the Collector. The wagers ranged from ten guineas to one thousand pounds.

Mr. Fullbright wagers Mr. Mills one hundred pounds that The Collector will marry The Work of Art in one month.

Sir Windham wagers Lord Bryce Pembroke twenty pounds that The Collector will take The Work of Art for a drive in the park on Monday.

Lord Darly wagers Lieutenant-General Culpepper one thousand pounds that The Work of Art and The Collector will be engaged in a fortnight.

Arthur wasn't surprised Darly's wager was so extravagant. He'd met Miss Satterthwaite, after all. He must have no doubt that Moreland would act quickly to secure her.

"Thinking of laying a wager, Heywood?" Forsythe asked. "I put down ten guineas myself. Things are a little thin right now, or I might've bet more. Seems a sure thing to me."

"I won't be wagering anything today." Arthur turned to leave, but at the last instant something in the betting book caught his eye. It was an entry written in barely legible script near the bottom of the page:

Lord X wagers Mr. X five hundred pounds that The Collector will be widowed again by Christmas.

FOUR

Philly and her cousins arrived at the Worthings' ball late Saturday evening accompanied by Uncle Edgar and Mrs. Vale. The street was lined with carriages. Everywhere Philly looked were dandified men and sumptuously clothed women. There were sparkling jewels, bobbing feathered head-dresses, and a sea of pastel gowns. She'd never seen so many people all entering the same townhouse at once. It was so crowded, that by the time they'd made it through the initial crush and into the ballroom, Philly could scarcely catch her breath.

She was first introduced to Lord and Lady Worthing, and then to what seemed an endless succession of strangers. Philly was well aware she was a novelty, but never had she experienced curiosity on such a grand scale. The constant chatter and unending stares had the effect of making her even shyer than usual.

It didn't help that her dress left her feeling practically naked. It was a flowing gown of Sardinian blue crepe over a delicate satin slip, with tiny puffed sleeves, and a neckline low enough to expose the swell of her bosom. The modiste had assured her that it was the very height of fashion.

The gentlemen at the ball certainly seemed to approve of it.

Within minutes of arriving, Philly's dance card was filled—except for the single waltz of the evening. Her uncle commanded that she leave it free.

Philly's mind instantly flashed to the mysterious *him* mentioned by her cousins. "Do you have a particular gentleman in mind for my partner?"

Uncle Edgar gave her a smile that didn't quite reach his eyes. "That I do, Phyllida. That I do."

Her heartbeat quickened in nervous anticipation. "Who is he, Uncle?"

"You shall know him when he comes," Uncle Edgar said. "*If* he comes. I'll not raise your hopes."

Philly suppressed a flare of irritation at her uncle's lack of candor. She wondered again who the gentleman might be. Was he someone of importance? Someone who had seen her—in the park perhaps—and expressed a specific interest?

There was no opportunity to reflect upon the matter. It took all of her faculties to attend to the people already surrounding her. There were names to remember, and steps, as well, when the music started.

She danced the first set with an older gentleman, and the second with an energetic younger fellow. The third set—a country dance—had been spoken for by an immaculately groomed flaxen-haired gentleman garbed in elegant black-and-white evening attire.

"Forsythe," he reminded her as she fumbled with her dance card. "An easy enough name to forget."

"If I have forgotten," she said apologetically, "it's only because I've met so many people this evening."

He took her gloved hand in his and led her out onto the floor, his thin mouth curling into a smile. "Everyone wishes to meet *you*, Miss Satterthwaite."

The couples lined up to face each other as the orchestra began to play. And then the dance began. She and Mr. Forsythe were separated several times as they performed the steps.

It didn't prevent him from conversing with her. Indeed, he seemed rather determined to engage her. "Are you enjoying London?" he asked when they joined hands to promenade.

"I've seen very little of it, sir." It wasn't for lack of interest. Much as she preferred life in rural Devonshire, she would have liked to visit the British Museum at least once, and she longed to see the performing horses at Astley's Amphitheatre. But entertainment hadn't been the focus of her visit thus far. Uncle Edgar and Mrs. Vale had been far more interested in seeing she was properly outfitted for her debut than in squiring her about town.

"No ices at Gunter's?" Mr. Forsythe pressed.

"Not yet," she said. "But I hope I shall taste one soon." Had she come to London with her grandfather, they would have visited Gunter's Tea Shop on the very first day. Grandfather had loved sweets in every form, and never missed a chance to try some new confection. An ice, eaten in an open carriage on a warm summer afternoon, would have been a temptation he couldn't resist.

"And what about Vauxhall Gardens?" Mr. Forsythe asked.

"I haven't had the pleasure."

They separated once more, only to reunite a moment later. "Let me guess," he said. "Books are your passion. You prefer the circulating library."

Philly thought of the small stack of books she'd brought with her to London. Two leather-bound novels and a volume of poetry. Books taken from the sprawling library at Satterthwaite Court. By rights, she should have left them there. They didn't belong to her anymore. Nothing at Satterthwaite Court belonged to her. Not as far as the law was concerned. It all belonged to Uncle Edgar now.

"I do enjoy reading," she admitted, "but I—"

"Don't say you haven't visited the circulating library? A travesty!"

They were parted again before Philly could answer. When next they reunited, he grinned at her.

"You must see something of the city, ma'am. If ever you have the inclination, it would be my pleasure to show it to you. All you need do is say the word."

Philly only smiled and shook her head. She'd love to see something more of the city, but she wasn't certain she wanted to do so in Mr. Forsythe's company. He was amiable, to be sure—and just as handsome as Lord Darly, who partnered her for the next set. But neither gentleman made her heart beat faster. And they certainly didn't inspire the sort of confidences she'd shared with Captain Heywood.

As the night stretched on, Philly's feet began to ache in her thin dancing slippers. She looked for her mysterious suitor in the faces of every gentleman she met, but he'd yet to make an appearance. Soon, exhaustion outweighed curiosity. She was ready to return home, and thus to bed. Uncle Edgar, however, was insistent they stay through supper. As the hour approached, Mrs. Vale took a seat at the edge of the ballroom and sent Philly and her cousins off for refreshments.

Out of the presence of her father and aunt, Elizabeth was quick to convey every small detail about the gentlemen with whom Philly had been dancing.

"The short, plump one is heir to a great fortune. He's set on finding a wife this season, and I've heard that any woman will do."

Elizabeth took a glass of lemonade from an obliging footman. "His skinny friend has a title, but no money. He'll marry an heiress, or no one at all."

"The fine-looking blond gentleman is Mr. Forsythe," Abigail chimed in. "Do you think him handsome?"

"Reggie Forsythe may be handsome, but he hasn't a feather to fly with," Elizabeth said. "He's seeking an heiress, too. I can't think why he paid you any attention. The novelty of it, I daresay."

"I expect you're right," Philly replied.

Elizabeth hadn't danced much herself. Whenever Philly had glanced in her direction, she'd seen her sitting in a high-backed chair along the wall, wafting her fan with vigor. "You were lucky to have danced with Lord Darly. I've heard he's an excellent partner. What did you think, Phyllida?"

"I'm sure he's very accomplished," Philly said, "but I couldn't tell. I'm not a good enough dancer to appreciate it, I suppose."

"Fiddle. I think it's only that you must hate dancing as much as you hate cards, shopping, and every other thing. It seems you're determined to be miserable."

Philly gave her cousin a thoughtful look. Elizabeth was only a year older than she was, but in London, a lady's years weighed heavily. Especially when that lady had had no success on the marriage mart. Whether Elizabeth's waspishness was the cause of her failure or the unhappy result of it, Philly didn't know. She rather suspected the latter. "You're very harsh, cousin."

Elizabeth's lips compressed in a fair imitation of her aunt. "I speak as I find."

"Oh look!" Abigail exclaimed. "There's Lady Eliot."

Distracted from her exchange with Elizabeth, Philly looked out across the ballroom. "Which one is she, Abigail?"

"She's wearing a white-and-silver gown. Like a Grecian

Goddess."

Philly couldn't see her at first, but in seconds the crowd shifted, and there across the floor, on the arm of a fashionable gentleman, she first beheld Caroline Eliot—the lady who had broken Captain Heywood's heart.

She was classically beautiful, with a tall, stately figure, and a magnificent bosom showcased quite daringly in a very low-cut gown. Her cropped blond curls were secured with a silver bandeau and accented with a single white ostrich feather, and her dark eyes roved over the ballroom as if she found the entire party exceedingly dull.

"Is she not the most elegant woman you've ever seen?" Abigail said in tones of awe.

Philly hated to agree. "Who's the gentleman with her?"

"Him?" Elizabeth smirked. "Why that's Mr. Ludlow, Lady Eliot's very *particular* friend."

As Philly and her cousins watched, Mr. Ludlow repeatedly leaned in to Lady Eliot and whispered into her ear. Each time he did so, Lady Eliot threw back her head and laughed, baring her long white throat.

"They've been lovers for over a month," Elizabeth said under her breath. "Before that, Lady Eliot was seeing the man over there. The portly gentleman with the red face. I heard that he bought her a necklace with a diamond as big as a quail's egg."

Philly's gaze flicked from one gentleman to the other in dismay. "How do you know all this?"

Elizabeth shrugged. "Lady Eustace and Lady Eliot are bosom friends. Whenever I visit Lady Eustace, she always shares the latest on-dit."

"She's coming over," Abigail whispered. "Perhaps she wants to be introduced to you, Phyllida?"

Lady Eliot and her paramour advanced upon them from across the floor. Up close, she was even more beautiful. Her skin was pale as alabaster, and the elaborate silver embroidery along the edge of her gown sparkled in the flickering light of the chandeliers.

"Miss Townsend," she drawled. "You must introduce me to your cousin."

While Elizabeth hastily dispensed with the introductions, Lady Eliot's dark eyes settled on Philly.

"What an original you are," she said before Elizabeth had finished speaking. "I vow I've never seen eyes like yours in my whole life. Did your mother have eyes just the same? Or your father?"

Philly met Lady Eliot's gaze. She found no friendliness there, only a glint of something cold and faintly amused. "They did not, ma'am."

"What a mystery." Lady Eliot laughed. "I wonder if your children will have eyes like yours. And maybe red hair, as well? Can you imagine that, Ludlow?"

Mr. Ludlow chuckled. "Rather singular."

"You're fortunate, Miss Satterthwaite, that you're not cursed with freckles. But then, your hair isn't truly red now, is it?" Lady Eliot reached out one white-gloved hand and twined a lock of Philly's hair between two of her fingers. "Dark brown, I think. With just a touch of red. What would you call it, Ludlow?"

"Auburn?" Ludlow suggested. "Or something approaching auburn?"

Heat flooded Philly's cheeks. She had little experience with this type of banter, and didn't know in what spirit to take it.

"I think it's chestnut." Lady Eliot withdrew her hand. "And that's how I'll refer to it when I describe you to everyone at my salon next week." With a languorous smile, she linked her arm through Mr. Ludlow's. "I must tell you, I'm rather envious of you, Miss Satterthwaite. My poor brown eyes are quite plain next to yours."

"Your eyes have no equal, my lady," Ludlow declared. "I challenge anyone to say otherwise."

Lady Eliot smiled at her admirer. "I won't believe it. Miss Satterthwaite has outshone me in every respect tonight." She gave Philly a small, mocking nod. "I congratulate you on your victory."

And with another tinkling laugh, she turned away in a sweep of white-and-silver fabric, and along with her gentleman, disappeared back into the crowd.

"I don't understand," Philly said. "Did I do something to offend her?"

Elizabeth heaved an exasperated sigh. "Heaven's sake, Phyllida. It's perfectly clear."

"Is it?"

"Why, Lady Eliot is wildly jealous of you, of course."

Philly stared at Elizabeth, dumbstruck. The idea that a creature as lovely as Lady Eliot could find anything in her to be jealous of was frankly astonishing. It wasn't that Philly valued her own looks so meanly, but that she'd spent her whole life thinking herself more odd than beautiful. If she'd been gawped at or made a fuss over, it had never been on account of being pretty. It had been on account of being different.

In Fox Cross, those differences hadn't seemed to matter so much. Her grandparents had taught her that there was no great value in outward appearances. It was the inside of a person that mattered. The heart and soul of them. As a result, except for a shyness about her mismatched eyes, Philly had never given her own appearance much thought at all.

Without another word, she followed her cousins as they made their way back across the ballroom toward Mrs. Vale.

"I'm famished," Abigail said. "Thank goodness it isn't long

until supper—"

"I don't know how you can be hungry," Elizabeth interrupted. "You've hardly danced at all. If anyone should be famished, it should be—"

"*There you are!*"

A gloved hand shot out of the crowd and closed on Philly's forearm so tightly that she jumped. It took her several pulse-pounding seconds to realize that the hand was attached to Mrs. Vale.

She pulled Philly close to her. "Let me look at you. Stand still. Now turn. Wait. Some of your hair has come loose from your comb. Elizabeth! Give me one of your pins. Hurry, girl."

Elizabeth drew a pin out of her own hair and handed it to Mrs. Vale, who promptly used it to secure one of Philly's stray locks.

"Is he here, Aunt?" Abigail stood on her tiptoes, peering over the crowd.

Mrs. Vale didn't answer her. "How do you feel? Not faint, I hope. Not too tired. I won't have you lightheaded. I don't want anyone to think you're prone to illness."

"I'm perfectly well, ma'am," Philly said. It wasn't entirely true. Her legs were trembling beneath her and her heart threatened to pound straight out of her chest.

Her mysterious suitor had come.

She felt, all at once, the full import of the moment.

"Very good, Miss Satterthwaite." Mrs. Vale smoothed the skirt of her own severe gown and then patted her hair into place with her hands. "Come along then. Quickly, ladies, but mind you, not *too* quickly."

They followed Mrs. Vale to the opposite side of the ballroom. As they made their way, the crowd fell quiet. Up ahead, a circle had formed around a small group of people. Mrs. Vale put a hand under Philly's elbow and urged her forward.

Lord and Lady Worthing were standing within the circle,

along with Uncle Edgar. Beside him stood an impeccably dressed gentleman who had to be at least a decade older than her uncle.

He was taller than she was, with a sturdy build and silver hair swept back from a deep widow's peak. His eyes shone like two luminous black stones, and coupled with his aquiline nose, gave him the appearance of a dangerous predatory bird. As soon as Philly entered the circle, she felt those eyes sharply upon her.

"Your Grace, may I present Miss Phyllida Satterthwaite?" There was more reverence in Uncle Edgar's voice than Philly had ever heard before. "Miss Satterthwaite? His Grace, the Duke of Moreland."

Philly dropped into a curtsy, even as her stomach clenched with anxiety. She had never in her life met a person of such exalted rank. "Your Grace."

Moreland bowed. "Miss Satterthwaite. Your uncle informs me I've been saved the waltz."

Philly glanced at her uncle for confirmation. He gave her a curt, rather impatient nod. "Yes, Your Grace," she said.

The orchestra began to play the first notes of the dance.

"Excellent timing." Moreland offered his arm. "If you will do me the honor?"

Uncle Edgar and Mrs. Vale watched as Philly put her hand lightly on the duke's arm and allowed him to lead her away.

They weren't the only ones to show interest in Philly and her new partner. As she and the duke walked through the crowd, many people stopped to watch them. There were countless knowing glances, and a rush of hushed whispering as ladies murmured to each other behind their fans. It was something of a relief to Philly when the orchestra began to play in earnest and everyone's attention returned to their dancing.

Moreland led her to a far corner of the ballroom, and then,

abruptly, stopped and turned to face her. Before Philly could get her bearings, he stepped forward and encircled her waist in a powerful embrace. It was vastly different from the light holds she'd been practicing with her dancing master. Something inside her gave a primitive shudder of fear.

He caught her hand in his, and without pause, rapidly began to turn her across the floor.

Philly was so disconcerted she temporarily forgot the steps of the dance.

The duke didn't slow to accommodate her awkwardness. He continued his energetic pace, dragging her right along with him.

It took her several seconds to regain her composure. Long, agonizing seconds during which she must have looked utterly graceless. Thank goodness Mrs. Vale couldn't see it! All those dancing lessons, only to make such a mull of it when she was actually called upon to dance the waltz at a real ball.

"Do you find the waltz distasteful, Miss Satterthwaite?" Moreland stared down at her. "Or is it merely that you don't care for dancing?"

"No, Your Grace," Philly said.

"It seems to me you're not enjoying yourself." Moreland turned her so violently that, though she opened her mouth, she could make no reply.

Was he taking some perverse delight in keeping her off balance? Or was he simply the kind of dancer who naturally dominated his partner?

"Perhaps a drive in the park would give you more pleasure?"

The knot of anxiety in Philly's stomach tightened. A drive in the park? With the Duke of Moreland? She'd never been for a drive with a gentleman before. It seemed something only done by courting couples.

She knew she should be flattered by such an offer. There were only a handful of dukes in England. To be courted by one of them was surely the stuff of dreams.

But there was nothing dreamlike about Philly's present situation. Rather the opposite. She was filled with a sense of impending dread.

What in the world had Uncle Edgar got her into?

"Your uncle has informed me I may call for you on Monday afternoon." Moreland's eyes didn't leave hers. "What say you to that, Miss Satterthwaite?"

"I would be honored, Your Grace." Philly didn't know what else she could say. Between her discomfort at dancing the waltz, and the notion that the Duke of Moreland might consider her a prospect for marriage, she was feeling quite overwhelmed.

Moreland continued to wordlessly move her around the floor, all the while staring at her face with his unblinking black eyes. It was as if she were some rare creature he'd discovered in the natural history museum.

To ease her discomfort, Philly began to ponder things she might converse with him about. But Moreland didn't seem like the sort of man who would appreciate any of the things she had to say. No doubt he'd find her wretchedly uncultured.

Unbidden, an image of Captain Heywood sprang to her mind. With it came a distinct pang of sadness. Those brief moments with him had been the closest thing to companionship she'd had since coming to London. The way he'd looked at her. The way he'd listened. But it was more than that. She'd felt something when she was with him. A kinship. A shared sense of...something.

Moreland swept her into another turn, startling Philly so much that she lost track of her footing again, as well as any fleeting thoughts she might have had about Captain Heywood.

Thankfully, it wasn't much longer before the music swelled to a finale. She attempted to step away from Moreland then, but he held her fast for just one second more than was decent before, finally, letting her go.

"I shall escort you to supper, Miss Satterthwaite." He offered her his arm.

She could do nothing but take it, letting him lead her back through the very interested crowd of onlookers.

Up ahead, Uncle Edgar, Mrs. Vale, and her cousins waited to join them. They all made their way into the supper room together.

"Your niece is not much for talking, Townsend," Moreland said to her uncle. "I find her silence suits me rather well."

Uncle Edgar gave a watery chuckle and made some polite reply.

Philly did her best to pretend that she hadn't heard the remark.

As they walked, the two men continued to talk to each other as if she wasn't there. She was relieved rather than offended, grateful for anything that would draw the duke's gaze from her face.

FIVE

Monday dawned overcast and cold. Philly hoped it might rain in the afternoon, thereby postponing her drive in the park with the duke. She wasn't looking forward to the outing. Quite the reverse. She was dreading it. At the same time, she was all too sensible of her obligation to Uncle Edgar. He'd brought her to London to make a good match. And a match with a nobleman—a duke, no less—would be better than good. It would be illustrious. A match for the ages.

Philly was beginning to feel rather depressed about the whole thing. It was a relief to get out of the house for a walk with her dogs.

Since the ball on Saturday, Mrs. Vale had become even more dictatorial about what Philly wore on her outings. "Everyone's eyes will be upon you now. You must take the utmost care with your appearance."

Not wanting to upset the woman any further than was necessary, Philly had dressed for her morning walk with particular care, pairing a pale-yellow cambric walking dress with a close-fitting pelisse of rich, dark amber sarsnet.

"I hope we won't see that man again," Sara muttered as they entered the park.

Philly settled Fox more firmly in her arms. She didn't mind the young maid's impertinence. She'd always encouraged candor in the servants at Satterthwaite Court. "Why do you say so?"

"He's not right. And he's got no business talking to you in the park."

"Captain Heywood is a war hero." Philly spoke with unerring confidence. Though she didn't know anything about Arthur Heywood's service in the war, her instincts told her that such a man could be nothing but noble and heroic.

"That's not what I heard, miss."

Philly shot the maid a questioning look. "What did you hear, Sara?"

"Only that he's dangerous. That he's not to be trifled with."

"Who says so?"

"All of them belowstairs." Sara's expression turned mulish. "He's no hero, miss."

"Well, I know for a fact that he is. He was hurt fighting in Spain. In future I hope you'll correct any of the servants you hear saying otherwise."

Sara pursed her lips for several strides before offering another comment. "When I serve tea to the master and them in the library, I never heard that man say so much as a single word, but he sat here last week talking to you easy as anything. What's he up to, I wonder?"

"I could be accused of the same," Philly pointed out. "I don't talk much in company, and yet I'm able to converse freely enough when alone with someone. I daresay you wouldn't accuse me of being up to something."

"Humph. 'Tis not the same."

Philly gave the disagreeable little maid an indulgent glance before continuing on ahead as she often did. It was early enough in the day that they weren't likely to see many people. The path she liked to walk wasn't often travelled by other visitors to the park. She preferred the solitude. It gave her dogs more freedom to run and play, and allowed plenty of time for quiet contemplation.

As she strolled along, Sara not far behind her with the dogs, Philly fretted over her drive in the park with the duke.

There was no getting around it; she hadn't liked the man. She didn't know exactly why. Except for staring at her and holding her a little too tightly in the waltz, he'd done nothing very wrong. Nevertheless, he'd made her exceedingly uncomfortable, and she'd been glad when he'd left them shortly after escorting her to the supper room.

She'd assumed he had gone off to dine with his other acquaintances, or perhaps to play cards, but during the carriage ride home, Uncle Edgar had informed her that after taking his leave of them, the duke had left the ball.

Mrs. Vale had been triumphant. "A declaration of his interest for certain. To stay only long enough to dance the waltz with you and escort you in to dinner? No one can doubt his intentions now. And when you're seen driving in the park with him next week, everyone will know you may well be the next Duchess of Moreland."

Philly could see no fault in Mrs. Vale's logic. What she couldn't understand was the why of it. A duke could have his pick of any of the young ladies on the marriage mart. Why would he have any interest in her at all? She was three-and-twenty with no fortune and no connections. An oddity. A country nobody. And she certainly hadn't dazzled him with her brilliant conversation or vivacious personality. It was all most perplexing.

She'd attempted to discuss the matter with her cousins, but the most they would offer was that the duke was a man of large fortune with a great estate called Moreland Park. This worried Philly more than anything, for Elizabeth could find a wealth of information to gossip about on persons of only the slightest acquaintance. That she had so little to say about the duke was exceedingly strange.

Philly had no friends to consult. She hadn't been allowed to go visiting with her cousins, and hadn't had any opportunity to meet other ladies her age that she might turn to with her questions. The only person she'd had anything close to a personal conversation with since she'd come to London was Arthur Heywood, and as luck would have it, he hadn't turned up to meet with her uncle today.

She hadn't seen any of the gentlemen arrive to meet her uncle this morning, and as she'd gone through the entry hall on her way out of the townhouse, she hadn't heard the customary sound of deep murmuring voices coming from the library.

It was therefore quite surprising to Philly that when she turned along the bend in the path, taking the exact same direction as she had the Friday before, she came upon Captain Heywood sitting on the very same bench.

Arthur was looking intently down the path and saw her immediately.

"Captain Heywood!" she exclaimed as she approached him.

He rose to greet her, momentarily unnerved by the warmth of her smile. "Good morning, Miss Satterthwaite."

Her maid was close behind, disapproval written on her face.

"Beg your pardon, miss, but the dogs are restless. We shouldn't be stopping."

"No, of course not." Miss Satterthwaite extended a gloved hand to one of her dogs as he leapt to get her attention. "Would you take them just up ahead onto the grass, Sara?"

"And you, miss?"

"Well, I..." She looked at Arthur. "Do you mind if I share your bench for a while, Captain Heywood?"

"Not at all."

"I think I might sit down for a moment, Sara. You go on ahead."

"Yes, miss," the maid said with grudging obedience. "But I'll keep you in my sights at all times!" she added tartly, before turning to go off with the dogs.

Arthur stood, supporting himself shakily with his cane, while Miss Satterthwaite sat down on the bench. He waited for her to situate her little dog next to her, and only then did he lower himself down beside her. He'd walked into the park too many times in the past several days. As a result, his right leg was throbbing. He could barely bend it, so was forced to keep it stretched out in front of him.

"I'd thought I might see you when you arrived to call on my uncle," she said. "Was there no investor's meeting today?"

"Your uncle has decided that the dinner party tomorrow evening will stand in place of it. He sent a note round on Sunday to that effect."

Arthur tried not to give in to the urge to stare at her. In her shimmering amber pelisse, she was more striking than on any other occasion he'd seen her. More than ever, she gave the impression of sunlight and glowing warmth, a person around whom it was impossible for cold or darkness to dwell. A man like himself, so often consumed by the shadows, could become addicted to being around such a lady. It wouldn't do to keep indulging himself this way.

"Oh, yes," she said. "The dinner tomorrow evening. I'd almost forgotten."

"Will you be in attendance?"

Her smile faded. "I think I must."

"The prospect doesn't appeal to you."

"It's not that. It's only..." She hesitated. "Since I've come to London, I sometimes find social gatherings rather difficult."

"The society in London must be very different than what you've been used to in Fox Cross."

"I'm afraid there wasn't much society to be *had* in Fox Cross. My grandfather preferred a quiet life. We had guests to stay once or twice a year, and Sunday dinners with the vicar and his wife." She broke off, looking up at him. "It must sound awfully dull."

"I assure you it doesn't. In fact, it sounds much like my own life in Somersetshire. Quiet, with little society."

"What do you do to pass the time?"

Arthur reflected on the years he'd spent down in the country since coming back from Spain. He had isolated himself there, not even employing enough servants to properly run Heywood House. "Sometimes it seems as if the time doesn't pass at all. Or if it does, it moves so slowly that one can hardly feel it. I'm sure your life in Fox Cross was quite exciting by comparison."

"Will you be going back soon?"

"In another week or two. As soon as this business with your uncle is completed." He watched her awhile. She was looking out across the expanse of grass at her dogs in the same pensive way she'd done the last time he'd sat with her. "Perhaps one day you'll return home to Fox Cross?"

She didn't respond right away. Instead, she continued to look out over the park, as if contemplating some dilemma of her own. "I dearly wish I could, Captain Heywood. But in truth, there's no home to go back to. My grandfather is gone now, and Satterthwaite Court is to be let. I have no one else except Uncle Edgar. I must make the best of things."

"That's often easier said than done, I've found."

"What other choice is there? One mustn't give up."

Arthur fell silent. The sentiment she expressed, so undoubtedly earnest and determined, only served to remind him of his own loss of hope and optimism. "I don't think I was half so pragmatic when I was your age," he managed to say at last. "Indeed, I cannot claim to be so now."

"I'm three and twenty, Captain Heywood. Surely not that much younger than you are yourself."

"You're nine years younger than me, Miss Satterthwaite."

"Am I?" Her brow creased.

He watched the play of emotions on her face, unable to fathom what he'd said to disconcert her so. "I think I've offended you."

"No, indeed, you've only reminded me of two people I met at a ball on Saturday evening."

Was she speaking of the Collector? If so, who was the other person to whom she referred? A young gentleman who had caught her eye, no doubt. "Would this be the Worthings' ball?"

"Yes, it was. Do you know Lord and Lady Worthing?"

"Once. A lifetime ago. They throw quite fashionable parties, if I remember."

"It was certainly well attended. I've never seen so many people in one place. Between the crowds and the dancing, I could scarcely draw breath."

The throbbing in Arthur's injured leg was more acute than ever. As he looked down at it, a familiar coldness seeped into his veins. "I expect you must enjoy dancing."

"Regrettably, no. I'm afraid I don't seem to enjoy much of anything here in London. I've been trying to make myself more agreeable, but the people are so different. At the ball, everyone stared at me so, and they sounded as though they were mocking me, even when they were being kind." She turned her focus back to her dog. "I suppose I'm not yet sophisticated enough to appreciate such subtleties—or to respond to them in kind. I'm determined to try harder."

The hint of sadness in her eyes made Arthur inexplicably angry. "Miss Satterthwaite, these subtleties you speak of are nothing more than cruelties disguised as amusements. They're not worth your notice. And as for these two people you met, if they've upset you—"

"They didn't upset me. They puzzled me exceedingly." She assisted Fox into her lap, wrapping her arms around him. "Captain Heywood...do you happen to know the Duke of Moreland?"

The cold drifting through him was positively icy now. "I know of him."

"I met him at the ball." Her expression was troubled. "He partnered me in the waltz."

"*The waltz?*" The very idea that the Collector had partnered her in a dance so intimate unsettled Arthur deeply. He couldn't think why. His own feelings for Miss Satterthwaite—if they could even be called that—were far from romantic. He was drawn to her, it was true, but only because of the way he felt in her presence. It was a selfish attraction and nothing more.

"The Worthings allowed one waltz for the evening, and my uncle said I must save it. I didn't know who I was saving it for until the moment I was introduced to the duke. And now he's arranged with my uncle to call on me this afternoon and take me driving. I think he means to court me, but I..." She trailed off, a blush rising in her cheeks. "I beg your pardon. I should not have presumed to—"

"You needn't apologize. You've done nothing wrong."

"Indeed, I have. I seem to find myself confiding in you about all sorts of things each time we meet. It's an inexcusable behavior. All I can say in my defense is that since I've come to London, you're the only person I've met that I feel at ease with. I suppose it sounds rather silly, since I hardly know you."

Arthur's fingers clenched the handle of his cane. He wasn't an eloquent man. He never had been. He'd been a man of brutal action. Of rare physical skill. Words didn't come easily to him. "Miss Satterthwaite, I beg you, don't distress yourself. What you've just described..." He hesitated. "It's no different than how I feel myself when I'm in your company."

She turned to look at him. "Do you, sir?"

Something deep within Arthur's chest tightened almost painfully as Phyllida Satterthwaite rested her blue and amber gaze softly on his face. "Yes. I do. And I'm honored to listen to anything you'd like to tell me. Anything at all."

She exhaled. "Thank you, Captain Heywood. You're very kind."

"Not kind. Rather selfish, in fact."

She looked as if she might question his remark, but had no chance to do so. At that precise moment, her dogs came bounding up to them. Sara, the little maid, was close behind. Any chance at conversation was at an end. Whatever Miss Satterthwaite had meant to tell him about Moreland would have to wait until another day.

"What do you call them?" he asked as one of the dogs came toward him.

"This one is Basil." She reached to scratch the wolfhound's wiry ears. "The red one is Jasper, and the spotted one is Dash.

They're not usually so friendly toward strangers."

Arthur stroked Basil's head, his gloved fingers brushing against Miss Satterthwaite's. She didn't pull away.

"Miss!" Sara cried as she approached them. "We've no more time to spare. Mrs. Vale says you mustn't forget—"

"Thank you, Sara." Miss Satterthwaite gathered up Fox and rose from the bench.

Despite the pain in his leg, Arthur stood. He failed to suppress a grimace.

"Captain Heywood..." She began, sounding very formal toward him in the presence of her maid.

"Yes, ma'am?"

"This is the second time I've seen you on this bench. Perhaps you have a preference for it? If not, might I recommend the bench just there? Not far from that cluster of trees? I pass it as soon as I enter the park each day, and have always thought it seemed a rather pretty location."

The cluster of trees she indicated was near the edge of the park, so close to the entrance that he'd be able to reach it in less than half the distance it took him to walk to the bench where they were now.

He looked at her face, expecting to find some hint of pity in her expression, but there was no such emotion. "It's certainly not as remote a location as this," he said carefully.

The maid's eyes narrowed, suspicion and disapproval etched into her sharp little features.

"No. It isn't," Miss Satterthwaite agreed. "But if you intend to come to the park often... That is, if you expect to come in the mornings..."

"The mornings," Arthur repeated, not certain he fully comprehended her meaning.

"The park is always much less crowded then." Miss Satterthwaite glanced at her maid before taking her leave of him with a subtle inclination of her head. "Good day, Captain Heywood."

Arthur touched the brim of his hat. "Good day, Miss Satterthwaite."

He watched as she walked off with her maid and her dogs, her amber sarsnet pelisse catching the light with every step she took.

The Work of Art.

The Duke of Moreland had waltzed with her on Saturday and was taking her for a drive in the park this very afternoon. Darly had wagered they'd be engaged in a fortnight, and at the rate Moreland was progressing, it wasn't too far from the mark.

Was Phyllida Satterthwaite the kind of young woman who aspired to be a duchess? Arthur didn't think she had such mercenary ambitions. And yet, he knew of no female who would ever consider refusing so illustrious a match. Indeed, he doubted very much that such a lady even existed.

SIX

In the afternoon, Philly's dogs were sent out to the back garden. There was a small shed there where they were often banished when they couldn't be with their mistress. Philly hated to be parted from them, but felt herself lucky to have made friends with one of the footmen—a lad named William—who promised he'd look after her dogs himself.

"You are fortunate those mongrels are allowed into the house at all," Mrs. Vale had said during Philly's very first days in London. It was a fact of which Philly was well aware, and she always made sure not to complain too much about the temporary separations lest the threat of permanent separation be carried out.

While her dogs languished outdoors, Mrs. Vale sat in a chair in Philly's attic bedroom, supervising as she dressed for her drive with the duke. Philly had once been mortified by the lack of privacy, but Mrs. Vale had observed her like this so often since she'd first arrived in London that she was now resigned to it.

"Your hair, miss," whispered Clarice, her cousin Elizabeth's lady's maid, as she assisted Philly into a pale-blue muslin gown.

Philly lifted her heavy tresses out of the way so the maid could attend to her buttons.

"You shouldn't have worn the amber pelisse this morning," Mrs. Vale remonstrated. "It's by far the most striking color, and would've done much better for your drive in the park."

"I thought you'd decided the deep blue pelisse would be more suitable," Philly said. "Had I known you preferred the amber, I wouldn't have worn it."

"Humph. The blue items in your wardrobe do very well with your blue eye, and the amber items do very well with your brown one. Madame Aubert said they both suit your complexion, but I can't say which is preferable. I've never had to choose a wardrobe for a girl with two different colored eyes." Mrs. Vale sniffed. "Naturally, I won't complain, for it's the thing His Grace fancies most about you. Still, I—"

"Does he?" Philly looked up with a start. "How do you know that? Has he said so?"

"The duke admires anything that's out of the ordinary. One moment, Clarice. Hold up the celestial blue pelisse. Ah, yes. And here, the blue feathered bonnet. What do you think of that, Miss Satterthwaite? It should make a fetching picture."

Philly frowned at her. "If you like."

"Or perhaps the darker blue carriage gown? Clarice, bring back that one. No, you stupid girl. The darker blue. Just there. That will do. With the blue feathered bonnet? Or should we pair it with the darker hat?"

"What do you mean by 'out of the ordinary'?" Philly asked.

"What's this?" Mrs. Vale looked up, her eyes narrowing. "Out of the ordinary?"

"Yes, you said the duke—"

"Never mind that." Mrs. Vale gave a dismissive wave of her

hand. "You must turn your attention to the task before you. It won't be long before His Grace arrives."

"But I know so little of him," Philly persisted. "Would it not be useful to learn a few things—"

"What is there to learn? He's here for the season in search of a new wife, just as are countless other gentlemen."

"A *new* wife? Do you mean to say the duke has been married before?"

"What a question. He's a man in his prime, not some young buck. Here, Clarice, I think this one will do. Paired with that hat. No. The other one. My word, must I handle everything?"

There was no more time for talking. The Duke of Moreland called for Philly at exactly half past five, and after politely greeting Uncle Edgar and Mrs. Vale, extended his arm to Philly and escorted her out the front doors of the townhouse.

He'd arrived in the most luxurious-looking landau she'd ever seen. It was gleaming black with shining red wheels, and pulled by two perfectly matched black horses, identical even to the height of the snowy white socks on their hind legs.

The impeccably liveried coachman remained in his seat, his eyes straight forward and his posture ramrod straight. A similarly attired footman stood outside the vehicle, and to Philly's delight, held two leads on which were attached a pair of elegant black dogs.

They had narrow noses and flowing hair. Their legs were long and slender, and their backs sloped in a graceful curve to their thin tails.

"Your uncle informed me you had a fondness for dogs," said Moreland. "Perhaps you will find these two amusing."

"They're beautiful." She was enchanted. The two dogs were almost as tall as Basil, but far more finely built. "I've never seen anything like them."

His mouth twisted into a complacent smile. "They're the only two of their kind in England."

She extended her gloved hand out to the dog nearest her, intending to pet him. The large dog raised his lip in a threatening snarl. She immediately withdrew, but the dog lunged toward her, snapping its jaws even as the footman pulled it back on its lead.

Before she could discern his intention, Moreland stepped forward and cuffed the offending dog across the muzzle two times in sharp succession. The dog yelped in pain, cowering away as Moreland raised his hand to deliver a third blow.

"*Stop!*" Philly cried out. "Oh, please stop!"

Moreland took a moment to compose himself, tugging his waistcoat back into place, and brushing off his sleeves. When he turned back to her, his black eyes were as cold and inscrutable as they'd been at the Worthings' ball. "Come now, there's no need to make yourself ridiculous over it." He held his hand out to her to assist her into the landau.

Philly couldn't bear to touch him. She was in shock, astonished by his brutality.

Her hesitation wasn't borne well by Moreland. When she didn't willingly put her hand into his, he forcibly took it. "Miss Satterthwaite, you try my patience. I begin to think you as stupid as my dogs. Come now. Look at them. They've benefitted from my correction."

Her eyes went to the two dogs even as she climbed numbly into the landau. They were sitting in the same elegant way they'd been when first she'd walked out of the townhouse. Rather than set her mind at ease, it distressed her even more. *He strikes them often,* she thought with a deepening sense of dread. They've become used to it. No wonder they snarled and snapped at her.

Moreland climbed into the landau. He took the seat across

from her, fixing his gaze on her face just as he had during the waltz. The dogs leapt into the seat beside him, and the footman vaulted easily up beside the coachman.

As the carriage began to move, it occurred to Philly that such a vehicle was ideal for the duke's purpose. He could keep his eyes upon her for the entire drive.

Unable to face him, she stared unseeing at a point just beyond Moreland's right shoulder. Her heart pounded against her rib cage, and her hands trembled in her lap. She wanted to go home, but all she could do was sit very still and look out into the distance, realizing that what she'd sensed in Moreland at the Worthings' ball had been cruelty.

She wasn't so naïve as to believe such behavior toward animals didn't exist. Living in the country all her life, she'd seen many cruel acts perpetrated by humans against animals. Indeed, each of her own dogs had come from situations of the most severe mistreatment. However, something in the way the duke had struck his beautiful dog had shaken her to her very core. His face had become a stark, impenetrable mask, and his eyes had appeared void of all emotion.

He hadn't struck the dog in a fit of anger, she was certain. There was something extraordinarily coldblooded about the act. And suddenly she knew, with a sickening sense of clarity, that the Duke of Moreland would strike his wife as easily and as remorselessly as he would strike his dogs.

If Moreland had any idea of the direction her thoughts were tending, he gave no indication. He said not a word, merely sat back in his seat and looked at her as the landau entered the park and joined the rest of fashionable society, out in force on their daily promenade.

The dull gray of the morning had given way to a bright, sunny afternoon, and the park was filled with all manner of carriages and riders. Philly saw ladies in beautiful gowns with stylish bonnets of every variety, and gentlemen in gaudily striped waistcoats driving sporting curricles. What appeared to be an entire family travelled in a barouche, and smaller rigs carried courting couples or gentlemen driving alone, intent on flirting with any passing female.

"Afternoon, Your Grace," a young dandy called as he drove by in a brightly colored phaeton, a young lady on the seat beside him.

"Your Grace." An older gentleman in a carriage bowed his head.

It seemed each person who passed bid good afternoon to the duke, and to every salutation the duke gave a cool nod in response and nothing more. A few who had met Philly at the Worthings' gave her a greeting, as well. She even saw Mr. Forsythe. He was standing near some trees along the edge of the park, staring at the duke's carriage as it passed, and looking far more serious than he had when last Philly had seen him.

She expected some form of acknowledgment from him, but Mr. Forsythe didn't seem to see her at all. He was looking, rather intently, at Moreland.

Not that it mattered. Philly was in no mood for polite conversation. Indeed, whenever she was addressed, her reply was no less coldly civil than the duke's.

She'd never taken part in this sort of display. If she hadn't been in such a state of shock, she might have felt self-conscious. From the moment the landau entered the throng, all eyes were upon them. No one made even the slightest effort to be discreet in their stares and whispers.

"All of this attention is for you, Miss Satterthwaite," Moreland remarked after they'd driven some distance in silence.

It was the first time he'd spoken to her since assisting her into the carriage. Philly forced herself to look at him. The two dogs were sitting up in the seat beside him, their noses in the fresh air, giving every appearance of enjoying themselves. The duke himself looked quite comfortable, showing no sign of being affected by the earlier incident.

"No one has seen your equal," he said with smug satisfaction. "And they're not ever likely to."

Philly wondered how much longer the drive could possibly last.

"You don't seek attention, do you Miss Satterthwaite? You merely sit there, as still and silent as a statue. As if you were a sculpture carved from stone." His mouth curved. "Do you have any idea what they're calling you?"

"No, Your Grace."

"Of course you don't. I suspect you don't even care."

She held her hands tight in her lap, having no desire at all to engage with him in conversation.

"The Work of Art," Moreland pronounced. "As if you were a Botticelli or a Titian. I expect it was thought up by some young fool while in his cups, but it's an apt title for you, I must say. When you marry, perhaps your husband will have your portrait painted?"

Philly suppressed a shudder. The Work of Art? She supposed it was meant as a compliment, though it seemed a rather strange one. She was no great beauty. Certainly nothing on par with a famous painting. Perhaps it was merely another society cruelty? An unkindness disguised as a witticism?

Moreland was watching her carefully. However, when she betrayed no interest, he said nothing more, and shortly after, seemed to lose interest himself.

The rest of the drive took place in silence. Philly continued to look off into the distance and Moreland continued to look at Philly, but neither said another word. She was relieved when the landau finally exited the park.

When they arrived at the townhouse, the footman leapt down from his seat beside the coachman and came to assist the duke. Once Moreland had alighted, he handed Philly down himself.

Uncle Edgar and Mrs. Vale were waiting in the entry hall as the duke escorted Philly into the house. He exchanged a few brief words with them, and then, after giving Philly a curt bow, took his leave.

A flurry of questions from Mrs. Vale followed, but Uncle Edgar only looked on for a moment with the same appraising expression he always wore before disappearing back into the library.

"I have a dreadful headache," Philly said when she could take no more. "I beg you would excuse me."

Once out of Mrs. Vale's presence, Philly headed to the back garden to retrieve her dogs. William, the young footman, caught sight of her and followed after to assist her.

"I looked in on them three times while you were gone, miss." William opened the shed and attached leads to the larger dogs. "They've been no trouble at all."

"Thank you, William." Philly ignored the tremor in her voice. She gathered Fox up in her arms, and took the leads of her other dogs from William. "You're such a help to me."

"Happy to do it, miss."

She thanked him again for his assistance and made her way back into the house. As soon as she was in the relative safety of her attic room, she took off her carriage gown and curled up on her bed wearing only her shift. Fox came to lie in her arms and Basil stretched himself out by her feet. Jasper and Dash couldn't fit on the narrow bed. They took up positions on either side of it as if standing guard.

Surrounded by her pets, Philly indulged in a rare bout of tears. Her sobs were muffled by her pillow, but once started, seemed to have no end. She wept over the loss of her grandfather and the loss of her beloved home in Fox Cross. She wept over how unhappy and alone she was in London with these strangers who now stood in place of her family. And she wept over her future; a future which she now understood was to be very bleak indeed.

SEVEN

*A*fter seeing Phyllida Satterthwaite in the park on Monday morning, Arthur went back to his father's townhouse in Mayfair. He had no desire to visit his club again, no wish to hear any gossip or be reminded of people from his past. Nor was he inclined to receive any callers, though a few stopped by and left their cards.

Instead he spent his time alone, ensconced in the library, attempting to write a letter to his father and making some effort to read a book. He could focus on neither task. His thoughts kept drifting, meditating on the loveliness of Miss Satterthwaite's countenance, and worrying about the Duke of Moreland.

Reggie Forsythe's melodramatic tale about the untimely demise of Moreland's last wife had made Arthur uneasy, but he couldn't entirely believe it. Forsythe had always been inclined to adopt a sneering attitude toward his betters, and Arthur was willing to wager he'd despised the Duke of Moreland well before the man had married Molly Cartwright.

If Miss Cartwright had rejected Forsythe in favor of marrying the much wealthier, more prestigious duke, it had likely only added fuel to the fire of Forsythe's resentment. No doubt the betting book entry referencing the late Duchess of Moreland's death was fueled by similar ill feeling.

It wouldn't be the first such rumor to plague Moreland.

Arthur remembered years before, when he was just a boy, hearing a story about the duke's pursuit of a rare painting. It was a priceless item, done by a Flemish master, and had been in the possession of a rather temperamental member of the country gentry down in Hampshire, who desired to keep the painting in his family. The duke had attempted to acquire the masterpiece to no avail.

A fortnight after refusing the duke's offer, the capricious country squire had given the painting to his only daughter's betrothed, an impoverished baronet who accepted the work of art in lieu of a dowry. The baronet had been conveying his prize back to his smallish estate in the neighboring county when he encountered a highwayman on the road.

The robbery had been a strange event. The baronet was unharmed, and no money or jewelry had been taken from him or the companions with whom he travelled. But in the course of the altercation, the Flemish painting had been completely destroyed.

There were similar tales: a rare piece of porcelain ground into dust, a famous racehorse dead in a stable fire, and a sapphire brooch—said to have been commissioned by Peter the Great— which had simply vanished into thin air.

The duke had never been implicated in anything, but it was enough to give him his rather sinister reputation. If the Collector wanted something, people had said, he must have it. And if he could not have it, then no one could.

Arthur had spent all of Monday afternoon and evening brooding on these fairytales, which he'd once considered to be ridiculous. When he found himself tempted to go to the park in the afternoon in order to assure himself that Miss Satterthwaite wasn't in any danger while on her outing with the duke, he realized that his preoccupation with the matter had finally exceeded the limits of casual interest and passed over into idiocy.

What was she to him, anyway? Absolutely nothing. He didn't know her and she certainly didn't know him. She was kind and gentle, to be sure, and he felt safe and easy in her presence, but though she was a woman of warmth, she was no beacon. And while she might be calm and steady, she was no ballast. He wouldn't allow himself to succumb to the temptation of mistaking her for either.

In a week, he'd return home, and very soon she'd marry the duke. There was no point in seeking her out anymore. All it served to do was make him feel like some desperate, pathetic fool. And Arthur Heywood wasn't willing to sacrifice any more of his dignity.

Not even for a few moments of peace in the presence of Phyllida Satterthwaite.

On Tuesday morning, Philly had breakfast in her room. She had no interest in being subjected to more of Mrs. Vale's questions, and was anxious to change and go out for her walk. She was looking forward to seeing Captain Heywood, and hoped he'd taken her advice and only walked as far as the bench near the entrance to the park. She'd seen that his leg was causing him more pain of late and didn't want him to push himself beyond his endurance.

After putting on a white jaconet muslin dress and a blue

sarsnet spencer ornamented *à la militaire*, she ran down the stairs with Fox under one arm, her bonnet in her hand, and her three large dogs at her heels, only to find both her cousins dressed and waiting in the entry hall. It was enough to bring her to an abrupt and very dispirited halt.

"Thank goodness you're ready, Phyllida," Elizabeth said. "We've been waiting ten minutes at least."

"You're coming with me?" Philly asked in disbelief.

Abigail, who was wearing a jonquil robe and holding a quilted silk parasol, smiled broadly. "Aunt Vale has said we must from now on."

Elizabeth straightened her stylish bonnet so the trimmings showed to best advantage. "Where are your gloves, Phyllida? And what of your hat? Aren't you going to put it on?"

Philly tugged on her gloves and her bonnet without a word.

They all walked out together with the dogs surrounding Philly, and Sara trailing behind. Philly glanced only once at the maid. Sara swiftly looked away, her cheeks splotched with red.

Her expression told Philly all she needed to know.

Sara must have mentioned Captain Heywood to Mrs. Vale. It had been clear the maid hadn't approved of Philly's visits with him, no matter how short or well chaperoned.

Disappointed that she wouldn't be able to talk to Captain Heywood by herself today, Philly directed her attention to her dogs as they walked the familiar path into the park. She fully expected to see him on the bench waiting to greet her.

He wasn't there.

She tried not to look too crestfallen lest Sara notice and realize the reason.

Perhaps he'd forgotten her suggestion, and was, even now, waiting on the same bench he'd been on yesterday? With renewed hope, she walked on with her cousins. "Shall we go that way?"

"You always walk that way, Phyllida," Elizabeth complained. "You're so dull in your habits. We shall go by the lake. I see two gentlemen there."

"I can't set the dogs loose by the lake," Philly said. "There are far too many people. But just down that path there's a perfect spot."

"I like the path you walk on Phyllida," Abigail said. "It's so private. We're not likely to run into another soul."

"I'd think it would be rather nice to run into another soul," Elizabeth retorted. "Why, I heard that Mr. Goodrich often walks in the park."

Mr. Goodrich was another of her uncle's business associates. A young gentleman of fortune, or so Philly understood.

"Aunt Vale says I'll sit next to him at dinner this evening." Abigail twirled her parasol. "She says I'll have Lord Darly on one side and Mr. Goodrich on the other."

Elizabeth scowled. "Fustian. She told me the very same thing. It's not possible for us both to sit between them."

Philly looked up ahead, certain she'd see Captain Heywood. The bench stood empty. Her heart sank like a stone in her chest.

He hadn't come.

She felt a fool to have expected he would. He was a gentleman with many responsibilities. It would be a waste of his time to come into the park every day.

And even if he *had* come, it wasn't as if she could have sat and talked with him. She had her cousins with her. There would have been no privacy. No opportunity to speak to him as a friend.

"I expect you'll be between Lord Edgeworth and Captain Heywood, Phyllida," Elizabeth said with a laugh. "That should be to your liking. You find Captain Heywood amiable enough."

"Yes, I do," Philly said. "He seems a very nice gentleman."

"Rubbish. You haven't yet met him at a ball or a party. Just wait until he comes tonight. You'll see how unpleasant he is. Why, he'll not speak to you throughout the entire meal."

"Lord Edgeworth won't, either," Abigail informed her. "He thinks it beneath him to address young ladies. He rarely even speaks to his own wife."

"I suppose then that I will eat my dinner in utter silence." Philly smiled slightly. "Or perhaps I shall occupy myself listening to the scintillating conversations that the two of you will be having with your seatmates?"

Elizabeth's eyes narrowed. "You may well laugh, Phyllida, but 'tis a fact that Lord Darly and I have much in common. He adores the musicals at Drury Lane and declares he loves nothing better than a game of loo."

"I asked Papa if the duke might not come," Abigail said, "but he says the dinner is only for his investors."

"Has the duke dined at your house before?" Philly asked.

"No. But he may yet, now he's courting you."

Courting me, Philly thought bleakly. She walked along in silence for a few moments. "Mrs. Vale has told me the duke was married before," she said at length. "Did either of you know his last wife?"

Abigail exchanged a fleeting glance with her sister.

"My aunt has told you that?" Elizabeth looked skeptical.

"Of course she has," Philly continued blithely. "I've already heard so much from the duke himself that these things are hardly secrets anymore."

Elizabeth's brow furrowed. "Oh, yes. Quite."

Philly met her cousin's eyes. "They're calling me The Work of Art, you know. Rather strange, is it not?"

"I think it's ever so flattering, Phyllida," Abigail said in a rush. "I suppose they mean to say you're like a beautiful painting or a sculpture."

"Nonsense." Elizabeth could be mute no longer. "They've simply named her that because the duke is called the Collector and everyone assumes he'll want to have her. It's meant to be clever, but I think it utterly stupid."

"The Collector?" A current of cold fear trickled through Philly's veins. She remembered what Mrs. Vale had told her the previous day. "Because of his appreciation for things that are out of the ordinary?"

"Out of the ordinary?" Elizabeth scoffed. "Is that what you call the things he collects? Why, Lady Eustace told me that the duke's art collection rivals that at Carlton House. Everyone knows that if there's anything rare or valuable, he must have it. Why else would he be interested in you?"

Philly held Fox tightly in her arms as she recalled how the duke had stared so fixedly at her face from the first moment he'd met her. "My eyes."

"Don't be offended, Phyllida. If you were ugly it wouldn't matter how rare your eyes were. But because you're so beautiful—"

"Obviously," Elizabeth said. "But if her eyes weren't so rare it wouldn't matter how beautiful she was, either."

Philly looked between the two of them. "I'm not beautiful."

"No," Elizabeth agreed. "Not in the common way. Which suits His Grace very well."

Abigail nodded. "He only wants things that are one of a kind."

Philly had difficulty finding her voice. "Was his last wife very unique?"

"Not like you are," Abigail said. "But she *was* a renowned beauty. Delicate as a little bird, with raven hair and skin like cream—"

"She was a ninny." Elizabeth interrupted her sister again. "Just out of the schoolroom. I don't know how she tricked the duke into marrying her, but as far as I saw, Molly Cartwright was nothing but a—"

"You mustn't speak ill of the dead. Besides, I think she was quite amiable. She was always laughing, and said the most brilliant things."

"She can't have been so brilliant," Elizabeth retorted, "to have drowned in a fountain."

Philly's pulse quickened. "Drowned in a fountain?"

Elizabeth cast her a suspicious look.

"I didn't realize," Philly said quickly. "I thought she drowned in a...in a pond."

"Indeed not; it was the great fountain at Moreland Park. She fell in, and her clothes pulled her under the water." Abigail bowed her head. "May she rest in peace."

Elizabeth gave her sister's arm a hard pinch. "You hardly knew her. There's no need to pretend that you did."

"You wretch!" Abigail rubbed her arm. "You knew I was going to wear my gown with the short sleeves. Now I'll have a horrid bruise." Her eyes welled with tears. "I *hate* you, Lizzie!"

As the argument escalated, Philly continued walking, contemplating what she'd learned. If the duke did have a penchant for collecting rare things, it would explain a great deal about why he'd shown any interest in her.

But she was no painting. She was a human being.

Did the duke collect people, as well as artwork? If so, whom had he collected before? And what of his last wife's death? A tragic accident, surely. Had he been married another time before that? At his age, he must have been. And what had happened to that wife? Was she dead, as well?

Philly thought of his beautiful dogs. He'd said they were the only two of their kind in England. But though they were rare and possibly very valuable, it hadn't stopped him from treating them with cruelty.

It was all too disturbing, and Philly trembled to think of it, but she counseled herself to be reasonable. Nothing about the duke made any matter now. She'd made it clear that she disliked him. Indeed, Moreland had barely looked at her when he bid her goodbye yesterday afternoon.

Whatever initial attraction he'd felt for her was surely at an end.

EIGHT

*Arthur arrived at Edgar Townsend's house at half past seven. He was wearing evening black, with a white waistcoat and a simply tied cravat. His suit of clothes didn't become him as well as it once had. Alone in the country, more often than not submerged in a deep melancholy, there were times he failed to eat properly. He was nowhere near as sickly as he'd been upon returning to England two and a half years ago, but he was far from the athletic figure he'd been before leaving to fight on the Peninsula.

"Our dashing Captain Heywood!" a lady had called out to him at one of the last balls he'd attended in London before departing with his regiment.

It seemed a lifetime ago.

As he climbed the stone steps to the front door of the townhouse, Lord Darly arrived, alighting from his carriage and bounding up the steps to join him.

"What say you, Heywood? A rather grim evening ahead of us with the two Townsend chits. The younger is jolly enough, I grant you, but if Townsend is angling for one of us to take the older one off of his hands—"

Darly broke off as Townsend's elderly butler opened the front door to receive them. He greeted them both in somber tones, informed them that the rest of the party was already in the drawing room, and proceeded to escort them up to the first floor.

The steep interior stairs were challenging for Arthur, but not impossible. After a day and a half of rest, the excruciating pain in his leg had calmed to its normal level of discomfort, and though slow and unsteady, he managed to ascend to the drawing room without too much difficulty.

Darly took full advantage of Arthur's slow pace, talking to him as if the butler weren't a mere few steps away. "Townsend's latest scheme is dashed risky, but I like a gamble. The earl does too, if I recall, so I can't understand your hesitance. Do you intend to join with the rest of us on his behalf? Or have you decided to bow out?"

Arthur's reluctance had more to do with his dislike of Edgar Townsend than anything else—a fact he had no intention of sharing with Darly. "I believe that Goodrich is uncertain, as well."

"Goodrich is uncertain about everything. He'll go along with what everyone else does in the end, mark my words." Darly dropped his voice. "I expect Townsend to press us all for our final word during port. Why else go to the trouble and expense of a dinner? If you have no intention of joining, he'll expect a devil of a lot more from the rest of us in lieu of the earl's share. Dashed inconvenient, Heywood. Some of us were hard pressed to scrape up the funds to begin with. The whole blasted scheme is likely to fall apart if you withdraw. I hope you'll keep that in mind."

When they reached the first-floor landing, the butler directed them down the hall to the drawing room. They'd gone no more than a few steps when a soft noise on the second-floor staircase caught Darly's attention. He looked up, a smile spreading over his face.

Arthur followed his gaze to see Miss Satterthwaite coming down the stairs, one hand resting lightly on the banister as she descended. He froze where he stood, feeling the now-familiar tightening in his chest.

She was wearing a gown of deep amber silk, delicately embroidered with glass beads that twinkled and flashed in the candlelight. Elbow-length sleeves hugged her daintily rounded arms, and the neckline was low enough to display the gentle curve of her bosom. She wasn't looking in their direction, her thoughts clearly somewhere else as she brushed a stray lock of hair from her face, tucking it back into the elegant arrangement in which she wore it. It was an innocent feminine gesture and nothing more, but the sight of it provoked a deep, stirring ache within Arthur's heart.

She stepped down onto the landing and turned toward the drawing room. When she saw them, she stopped, hesitating a fraction of a second before coming forward to greet them.

"Miss Satterthwaite," Darly said, making his bow. "Forgive our impertinent stares. You look as fine as fivepence this evening. Why, I believe you look even more beautiful than you did at the Worthings' ball. You were wearing blue that night, were you not? I distinctly remember admiring how well it became you whilst we danced together."

Arthur shot an annoyed glance at Darly. He briefly envisioned how satisfying it would feel to slam his fist into the golden-haired dandy's face. Not much imagination was required. They'd boxed together at Jackson's before the war, and more than once, a punishing left had sent Lord Darly to the ground. Arthur savored the memory even as he intervened to save Miss Satterthwaite the trouble of supplying an answer to such inanities. "I trust you're well?"

"Very well, sir." Meeting his eyes softly with hers, she gave him the barest trace of a smile.

Arthur was rendered temporarily speechless.

Darly laughed. "Heywood has no idea how to talk to a handsome woman. Allow me to escort you into the drawing room, Miss Satterthwaite. I promise I won't bore you."

"Thank you, my lord, but I should not. My cousins have been looking forward to your company all day. If I were to enter the room on your arm, it would only bring them displeasure."

Darly's smile dimmed. "Ah, yes. Your charming cousins. How could I forget?"

Arthur didn't know what compelled him to action. He'd counseled himself to let Phyllida Satterthwaite go. She wasn't for him. And no good could come of forming an attachment to her. Nevertheless, upon her refusal of Darly's escort, he quite naturally stepped forward. "If you please, ma'am. Your cousins can have no objection to my escorting you."

"No, I don't suppose they can," she replied, and to Arthur's profound satisfaction, she tucked her hand gently in his arm.

The rest of the party was already assembled in the drawing room. Goodrich was by the pianoforte, engaged in meaningless banter with Townsend's two giggling daughters. Darly went to join them. Townsend himself occupied a chair near the fireplace, where he was absorbed in low conversation with Edgeworth. Townsend's sister, Mrs. Vale, and Edgeworth's redoubtable wife, a portly woman with a great deal of her bosom exposed, sat close beside each other on the sofa. Lady Edgeworth, whose booming voice echoed throughout drawing room, was complaining to Mrs. Vale about how inconvenient the war had been.

"Terribly inconvenient," Mrs. Vale agreed.

The room might as well have been empty. Arthur's attention was fully engaged by the young lady on his arm. Up close to her now, he could see the jeweled pins that decorated her hair. Garnets, or possibly even rubies. They glittered like fire, as warm and vibrant as every other part of her.

"I believe you're escorting me into dinner, as well, Captain Heywood." She took a seat on a small, silk-upholstered settee.

"Am I?" Arthur sat down beside her, much as he did when they were conversing together on one of the benches in the park.

"Yes, you see, my uncle will escort Lady Edgeworth, Lord Edgeworth will escort Mrs. Vale, Lord Darly will take Miss Townsend, and Mr. Goodrich will take Abigail. I'm not sure that precedence is being entirely respected, but..." She trailed off with a rueful grimace. "I beg your pardon. I've no talent for small talk."

"You're doing very well."

"No, indeed, I'm utterly hopeless. You'll find me a rather dull dinner companion, I fear."

"I shall find you a perfect dinner companion. I've only to wonder what sort of dinner companion you'll find me."

"The best kind. Truly, Captain Heywood, if you hadn't come tonight, I'd planned to plead a headache and excuse myself to bed."

Arthur opened his mouth to reply, but across the room, Lady Edgeworth's loud voice arrested his attention. The conversation about the war had escalated from a single stupid sentiment to a full dialogue of offensive nonsense.

"...our soldiers do love to fight," she was saying with blustering condescension. "One cannot begrudge it them. But in my view, Mrs. Vale, it would be far better to die on the battlefield with full honors and glory than to come home fit for no occupation at all. In our village alone, Edgeworth and I have seen men who..."

Arthur's hand tightened on his cane. "Would that we could both excuse ourselves this very moment."

Miss Satterthwaite cast a fleeting glance in Lady Edgeworth's direction. "And go where, sir?"

"Wherever you'd like, ma'am. The further the better. I'm completely at your service."

"Shall we take my dogs along with us?"

Arthur turned his gaze back to Miss Satterthwaite's face. His anger over Lady Edgeworth's remarks faded. "Naturally. Though it will limit our options somewhat."

"Not at all. We shall simply go to the park."

"I don't advise it at this hour. It will be black as pitch, and no doubt filled with all manner of villains."

Her brows lifted. "Will it really?"

"I should think so."

"Well then, I'm afraid there's nothing for it. We shall simply have to remain here and make the best of things."

"There are worse fates, I'm sure."

She smiled. "In all seriousness, Captain Heywood, the park can't be so dangerous, can it?"

"London is a dangerous city, Miss Satterthwaite. I'm glad you don't venture out of doors without your dogs and your maid."

"And my cousins."

"Your dogs and your maid and your cousins? That's quite a large party."

"Rather *too* large. Unfortunately, I've been informed that my cousins must accompany me on all of my outings from now on."

A flicker of apprehension put Arthur on his guard. "How did they come by this decision?"

"It's rather ridiculous, but I think Sara has been expressing concern to Mrs. Vale about who I talk to when I go into the park."

His jaw tightened as apprehension quickly gave way to anger. "You've done nothing improper. And I shall be glad to address the matter with anyone who dares say otherwise."

"Oh no, Captain Heywood." She set a hand on his sleeve. "You mustn't say anything. I'm not certain that Sara has mentioned your name, you see, and I've no wish to put you into any difficulty with my uncle."

The warmth and weight of her touch set his heart to thumping. Foolish, really. He was no green lad. "There will be no difficulty. I'll speak with your uncle directly."

"You're very obliging, sir, but please, I must insist you not say a word. It will do nothing but alarm everyone further, and who knows what they might do then? Why, they may get it into their heads to forbid my going for walks altogether."

"Don't distress yourself. I'll remain silent if that's what you wish. But I must say...it seems to me that this maid of yours has done you a very shabby turn."

Miss Satterthwaite removed her hand. "Yes, I suppose it does appear that way, though I don't believe she meant any ill."

"No?"

"She's overprotective of me, that's all."

Arthur was sure that she was. No doubt the sharp-eyed little maid had dreams of one day serving the Duchess of Moreland—dreams that would hardly come to fruition if the future duchess were seen trysting in the park with unmarried gentlemen.

After his last visit with Miss Satterthwaite, the maid had likely gone straight to Mrs. Vale. He'd seen the suspicious expression on her face when Miss Satterthwaite had suggested a certain bench and remarked that mornings in the park were far less crowded.

The uneducated young servant had recognized instantly what her far more innocent mistress could not.

Their chance encounters in the park were well on their way to becoming assignations.

NINE

Contrary to her cousin's predictions, Lord Edgeworth talked a great deal to Philly during dinner. He was seated between Philly and Mrs. Vale, and when forced to choose between them, settled on Philly as the beneficiary of his long-winded pontificating.

He spoke of the workings of his estate, the exile of Napoleon to Elba, and the strain of coach travel on a man afflicted with gout. He was a gentleman of considerable girth, and helped himself to each of the dishes on the table with enthusiasm. In so doing, he forgot his obligation to the ladies seated on either side of him. He never passed a dish or helped to carve off a slice of meat for either Philly or Mrs. Vale.

Fortunately, Captain Heywood sat on Philly's right, and though he didn't say much, he was unfailingly courteous, serving her from all the best dishes within his reach. As Lord Edgeworth expounded loudly on the questionable value of a horse too fine-boned to carry a man of his size, Captain Heywood carved a small piece of mutton and silently put it onto Philly's plate. His manners at table only emphasized what Philly already knew about him. Arthur Heywood, whatever else his faults may be, was a kind and thoughtful gentleman.

"You've spent your life in the country, Miss Satterthwaite." Lord Edgeworth swallowed a large draught of wine. "I daresay you're a competent enough rider."

"Yes, my lord." Philly half listened to him as Captain Heywood served her a small portion of curried rabbit. The dining table was ablaze with flickering candlelight, and as he wielded the serving spoon over her plate, she noticed that the back of his left hand was covered with scars.

On every other occasion they met, he'd properly been wearing gloves, but having taken them off for dinner, she could now see quite clearly the remnants of what appeared to have been a particularly brutal injury. The scars were raised and ran in sharp intersecting lines all the way up to the back of his fingers.

It was an old injury, she could tell. Had it happened to him in Spain? She couldn't imagine how. Would someone have cut the back of his hand during battle? Perhaps once, but not so many times, surely.

"Everything is too fine-boned," Lord Edgeworth continued. "Can't find a mount anymore that's worth having. Strong legs, Miss Satterthwaite, and a strong back. No need for beauty, in my opinion."

Philly raised her eyes from Captain Heywood's hand and saw, to her chagrin, that his brooding gaze was upon her. There was no doubt he'd seen where her attention had been directed. A knot of anxiety formed in her stomach. She'd always been so careful never to draw any notice to his injuries, and was horrified to think she might have inadvertently done something to hurt or humiliate him.

"Wouldn't you agree, Miss Satterthwaite?" Lord Edgeworth asked. "Not particularly elegant, but by God, it's practical."

Philly had no idea what he was asking her. "Yes, my lord," she said, still looking at Captain Heywood. She wanted to apologize to him but was sure it would only make the situation worse. Instead, she affected as normal a demeanor as she could. "Captain Heywood, would you mind very much passing the stewed mushrooms?"

Her request broke the uncomfortable tension between them. Indeed, it seemed that the captain was relieved to be given another task to occupy himself.

"Lady Edgeworth is of the opinion that gentlemen of a certain age and size should no longer ride," Lord Edgeworth went on. "But I say when a man can no longer ride, he might as well give up on life altogether."

Philly winced at the implication. "I can't agree with that, my lord."

Lord Edgeworth was impervious to subtlety. "Heywood, you had a fine piece of horseflesh if I remember." He leaned across Philly to address Captain Heywood. "A Greek name, I think it had. A blood bay from the earl's stable. You didn't lose him out on the Peninsula, did you?"

"No."

Lord Edgeworth waited in vain for Captain Heywood to elaborate. "Humph! Know quite a few lads who lost their horses down there. Shot right out from under them. A waste, I tell you. Some very fine horseflesh left to rot on the field—"

"I had a lovely mare in Devonshire," Philly declared.

Lord Edgeworth stared at her. "What's this?"

"Her name was Persephone."

"Another Greek name? A dashed coincidence. What did you

call your horse, Heywood? Can't quite recall—"

"She wasn't as fine-boned as some of the horses you've been describing, my lord," Philly continued determinedly. "In fact, I believe she was the unfortunate offspring of a carthorse and a hunter. The combination produces a particularly sturdy mount."

"Carthorse, you say? Now there's an idea. What manner of carthorse? A Shire? A Suffolk? Why, I knew of a fellow..."

Having successfully diverted Lord Edgeworth from topics that might offend Captain Heywood, Philly was able to eat a little something while the older man droned on about various equine crosses which might produce a horse suitable to his purpose.

"What became of your horse, Miss Satterthwaite?"

The sound of Captain Heywood's low-pitched voice broke through Philly's thoughts. She turned to him, offering a slight smile. "My uncle wouldn't allow me to bring her to London," she said, her voice just as quiet as his had been. "She remained behind at Satterthwaite Court."

"Is she to be sold?"

Philly's fork trembled in her hand. She set it down beside her plate.

"Forgive me for asking," he said. "It's none of my affair."

"It's perfectly all right. I'm sorry to be so silly over it, but I raised her from a foal, you see. The fact is, she may be sold; however, there's a chance the new tenants at Satterthwaite Court might allow her to remain there. She'd make a perfect riding horse for a young lady or a little girl. I have every hope it will all come right."

"I hope it shall, Miss Satterthwaite," Captain Heywood said. "I very much hope it shall."

It was an hour before Arthur and the other gentlemen joined the ladies. When they finally entered the drawing room, there wasn't a man amongst them who didn't have a dark, stormy expression on his face. Even Darly, normally as cheerful as anyone, looked as if he'd been forced to swallow a bitter tonic.

Townsend's daughters descended on Darly and Goodrich, who had promised during dinner that they'd play a game of loo with them. The gentlemen looked little inclined to keep their word until Edgeworth said he'd join them, for Edgeworth was known as a man who wagered extravagantly and played poorly.

Arthur found Miss Satterthwaite seated in the window embrasure. She had a bit of embroidery on her lap and was plying her needle with elegant dexterity. He admired her for a moment before making his way to her side. "May I join you?"

"Oh, please do." She put aside her needlework as he sat down beside her.

"Do you play, Miss Satterthwaite?" Darly asked as the table was arranged for their game.

"She does not," Miss Townsend said. "And she has no money to wager, either."

"We've been trying to teach her," the younger Townsend girl chimed in. "She isn't very good."

Miss Satterthwaite made no attempt to answer the questions that were asked her, and she didn't seem to mind that her cousins answered in her stead. Arthur wondered how she could show such forbearance. "Don't you care for cards?"

"Not very much."

"Nor do I," he admitted. "Besides which, they all appear to be settling in to make a night of it, and I won't be able to remain much longer."

"Yes, of course. With so little diversion, the evening will drag on for you, I fear."

"No, Miss Satterthwaite, not at all. I..." He struggled for the right words. "It's not out of boredom, for I would be happy—I would be honored—to sit here with you all evening. But my business with your uncle has come to an end, and my presence here isn't very welcome at the moment. In truth, I think your uncle would rather I'd left directly after port."

Her eyes flew to his. "You've concluded your business with my uncle?"

"I find that I must."

"Then...will you go back to Somersetshire early?"

"I hope to leave Friday morning."

"As soon as that?" She stared at him. "Can you not stay awhile longer? Perhaps, if you were to meet again with my uncle...?"

"I'm afraid there's nothing that can be done on that score. I've made up my mind on the matter, and I believe your uncle has done the same."

"I see." Her mouth was tugged down at the corner, and her mass of dark hair, so artfully arranged at the beginning of the evening, was beginning to come loose from the jeweled pins that held it.

Arthur had never seen her look so vulnerable, nor so very beautiful. "I would have left next week in any case. It's only a few days difference—" He broke off as, right before his eyes, one of the little ruby-encrusted pins began to fall from her hair. Without considering the intimacy of the action, he reached out and gently removed it.

Her cheeks flushed pink. "What a nuisance. I expect I've lost several of them already."

He turned the hairpin in his fingers so that it caught the light. In Miss Satterthwaite's hair, it had looked like a precious gemstone, but in his hand it looked like nothing more than what it was: a gold-painted pin on which was fixed a cluster of the same glass beads that trimmed her gown. It struck him then, quite forcibly, that Phyllida Satterthwaite had the rare gift of transforming everything that came near her into something better than it actually was. If he were a more eloquent gentleman, in the manner of Lord Darly or Reggie Forsythe, he might have told her so.

"Phyllida!" Miss Townsend called out. "Play something on the pianoforte, won't you? I must have some music."

"Yes, Phyllida," Abigail Townsend agreed. "Play 'Robin Adair.'"

"Capital!" Edgeworth bellowed from his place at the card table. "Always fancy a good Scots melody."

Miss Satterthwaite hesitated but a moment before politely begging Arthur's pardon and rising from the window so she might go and do as her cousins had bid her. "I'll likely be relegated to the pianoforte for the next hour at least."

Arthur rose, as well. "Then I shall take my leave of you."

"Now?" She looked up at him, at first with some little surprise, and then with a sad resignation that tore at his heart. "Oh, yes. Of course. I see that you must."

He extended her hair decoration to her.

"Keep it," she said.

"Miss Satterthwaite, I couldn't possibly—"

"Please. It's only a small thing, I know, and has no value at all, but I hope that...that if you have it...you won't soon forget me."

Arthur's fingers closed around the hairpin. His voice, when he found it, sounded very unlike his own. "I have no intention of forgetting you."

"Nor I you, sir." She gave him a small smile. "Goodbye, Captain Heywood."

Arthur stared at her. He knew then, as sure as anything, that he was never going to see her again. "Goodbye, Miss Satterthwaite."

The words had a stark finality to them, and as he watched her walk away, all of the cold and darkness of his life once again enveloped him. Whatever small degree of light and warmth that had been his by virtue of proximity to Phyllida Satterthwaite was snuffed out as easily as a candle.

TEN

The next day Philly kept to her room for most of the morning. She didn't expect that anyone downstairs would notice her absence. The entire household was suffering from the aftereffects of the dinner party. All the servants were exhausted from their labors. Mrs. Vale—who had indulged in far too much sherry with Lady Edgeworth—was bedridden with a blinding headache. And Elizabeth and Abigail were both sleeping late.

Only Uncle Edgar seemed unaffected by the previous evening's festivities. He woke at the same early hour he always did, and after breakfasting, went straight to his library and shut the door behind him.

At half past eleven, Philly called in the maid to help her dress, and by quarter past twelve, she was walking out the front door of the townhouse wearing one of her favorite old gowns. She carried Fox under her arm, and Basil, Jasper, and Dash ran along at her heels. Her cousins and Sara trudged behind. They were quieter than usual, tired from their late night and resentful that they'd been forced to act as chaperones on Philly's outings.

"If you'd only go in a different direction occasionally, perhaps it wouldn't be so tedious to walk with you," Elizabeth grumbled before falling silent.

Philly didn't respond. She had no intention of exploring a new path. Even though she wasn't likely to see Arthur Heywood ever again, there was still some small hope within her that she'd find him sitting on the bench where she'd come across him twice before. As they turned down the familiar path, her heart beat rapidly in anticipation. But when the bench came into view it was empty. There was no sign of him anywhere.

He'd left the party last night only moments after she sat down at the pianoforte. Her heart had been so heavy as she watched him go that she could scarcely finish playing the Scottish love song her cousins had requested of her.

She hadn't known until then just how much he'd come to mean to her.

Her grandmother would have called it a tendresse. Her grandfather would have called it calf love. Philly wasn't sure what to call it. All she knew was that she felt more fondness and affection for Arthur Heywood than for any other gentleman of her acquaintance. He'd been her first and only friend in London. She despaired of finding another as thoughtful and sympathetic as he'd been.

Of course, she understood his desire to return to his home in the country. He had nothing to keep him in London, and he preferred a quiet life, much as she did herself. And yet, when he'd spoken to her of his home in Somersetshire, he hadn't sounded as if he were looking forward to returning there. Instead he'd been grave and melancholy, referencing the slow passage of time in the country as if he were a man who had been banished to some sort of half existence.

He was going to be dreadfully lonely there. Far lonelier than she was on her own here in London. It wasn't what she wished for him. She cared for him deeply and wanted him to be happy. She wondered what would make him so, and unbidden, an image of Lady Eliot garbed in a diaphanous white-and-silver gown came into her mind. Once conjured, it was hard to dispel.

With a disheartened sigh, she attempted to focus on something else. It wasn't a day for feeling sad. The sun was shining brightly, and there was hardly a cloud in the brilliant blue sky. She turned her face to the sun, feeling the warmth of it on her face, and—as she walked along with her dogs—her mood began to lift a little.

The sun had a similar reviving effect on her cousins. Soon, Elizabeth and Abigail's sullen silence was replaced with lively chatter. By the time an hour had passed, they were in as fine a form as always, snapping and arguing with each other so aggressively that neither could finish a complete sentence.

Basil, Jasper, and Dash ran in circles around their little procession, and Fox, held tight in Philly's arms, strained his head so he could watch them. Sara trotted along behind, as harried and nervous as ever, regularly reminding the three young ladies that they shouldn't tarry too long in the park lest Mrs. Vale become cross with them.

"She's not likely to care today." Elizabeth kicked a stone with the toe of her half boot. "When I went into her room this morning, she could hardly open her eyes."

"Constance Penniman says drink is the devil," Abigail pronounced with some authority. "A real lady should never forget herself with the sherry as Aunt Vale did last night."

"If she did overindulge a little," Philly said, "I'm sure it was only because Lady Edgeworth was doing so."

Elizabeth snorted. "Lady Edgeworth has a great capacity for

drink. As much as her husband has for food, I daresay."

Abigail was in rare agreement with her sister. "He ate ever so much Savoy cake."

"As if he were a starving man!"

"While Lord Darly and Mr. Goodrich were as gentlemanlike and elegant in their manners as—"

"I suppose you think yourself an expert on Lord Darly and Mr. Goodrich? Merely because you sat between them at one silly dinner?"

A blazing row commenced directly. Philly did her best to stay out of it. Elizabeth had been jealous that her younger sister had been placed between the two eligible gentlemen, but Philly didn't think it was so wrong for Mrs. Vale to have arranged it so. Elizabeth had been on the marriage mart for years, after all, and had shown no promise whatsoever. It wasn't unreasonable to think that her younger sister might fare better if given an opportunity.

"And you had to make a show of yourself at cards, as well!" Elizabeth accused Abigail as the argument continued. "Pretending you didn't know when to pass or when to miss just so Mr. Goodrich would help you."

"I never did!"

Philly noticed her dogs were panting. She shielded her eyes with her hand and squinted up at the sky. "It must be nearly two o'clock. We'd better start back before it gets any later."

Sara exhaled with relief.

"Two o'clock! Why didn't you say so, Phyllida?" Elizabeth hurried back up the path with Abigail close behind her. "I'm to call on Lady Eustace at three."

At a far brisker pace, they made their way home. Their arrival was anticipated by Evans, the butler, who opened the door for them before they'd finished ascending the front steps of the townhouse. His face—usually a mask of bland subservience—betrayed a high color, and perspiration dotted his brow.

"Miss Townsend, Miss Abigail, Miss Satterthwaite," he intoned as they filed in. "Mrs. Vale insists you join her in the drawing room at once."

"Whatever is the matter, Evans?" Elizabeth untied her bonnet strings. "You look as if you've seen the specter of doom."

Evans winced. "I beg you, Miss Townsend, please moderate your tone. Your father has a distinguished visitor in the library. You must all go to Mrs. Vale. She was most insistent that you not linger in the hall." He turned to Philly. "Your dogs, Miss Satterthwaite. They're to go directly to the garden."

"Of course." Philly didn't like to cause the old retainer any more anxiety. "I shall take them—"

"No, miss, you must go to the drawing room. I can't begin to convey to you the urgency of the situation." His eyes darted to the closed doors of Uncle Edgar's library. "Sara can tend to your dogs."

"Fetch William, Sara," Philly said as the maid came to assist her. "He knows how to look after them."

"Yes, miss."

She eased Fox into Sara's arms, feeling the little terrier's entire body stiffen with outrage. He tolerated the young maid but didn't like her.

Evans looked thoroughly pained. "Miss Satterthwaite, time is of the essence."

Philly waited until Sara had control of all the larger dogs, then started up the stairs after her two cousins.

They found Mrs. Vale partially reclined on a gilded settee in the drawing room. Her eyes were red and her skin was tinged the same gray color as her severe bombazine gown. When she saw them enter, she rose to her feet. The simple action caused her sallow face to momentarily turn green. For several seconds, it looked as if she might cast up her accounts on the drawing room carpet. She fumbled about her person, at last producing an engraved silver vinaigrette, which she waved at some distance below her nose. The results were instantaneous.

"Where in heaven's name have you been?" she demanded in an urgent undertone. "This is unpardonable."

"We've only been to the park, Aunt." Elizabeth sank into a chair. "Phyllida insisted upon going for her walk, and you said Abigail and I must attend her."

Mrs. Vale's bloodshot gaze fell on what Philly was wearing. Her cheeks flushed with anger. "Miss Satterthwaite, this is not to be borne! Is this how you dress the moment I'm not available to advise you? Have you learned nothing at all from my instruction? Oh, you'll be the death of me." She rang the bell. A footman appeared almost instantaneously. "Send for Clarice. I need her upstairs quickly. Quickly, I say!"

Abigail's eyes widened. "Whatever is the matter, Aunt?"

"The matter, you ask? Why, the Duke of Moreland has come, girl. He's even now in the library with your father."

The blood drained from Philly's face.

"He may well send for you, Miss Satterthwaite, and you were nowhere to be found. And now you've returned hardly fit to be seen. Oh, that I should have such a task before me. My head is splitting." She took Philly firmly by the elbow and propelled her out of the room. "We haven't a moment to spare. Elizabeth. Abigail. Don't dawdle. Go to your bedrooms and change. I'll send Clarice when she's finished with Miss Satterthwaite."

Philly could scarcely formulate a thought as she was hurried up the stairs to her attic bedroom and stripped down to her chemise. Mrs. Vale rifled through her wardrobe before choosing a gown of fine white muslin with a low neckline that Philly thought more suitable to a ball or an assembly.

"Virginal. Just what's required. Here, Clarice!" Mrs. Vale snapped her fingers, pointing to a pile of wraps and shawls. "The celestial blue shawl, I think."

Clarice gave the shawl to Philly, who draped it gratefully around her partially exposed bosom.

"No, Miss Satterthwaite." Mrs. Vale rose from her chair and snatched it away. "Gracefully, twined through your arms. Thus. And now draped behind your back. Yes, yes. Very elegant. Very Grecian. Clarice, the hairpins with the cut glass posies." She snapped and pointed several times in quick succession as the lady's maid ran to and fro like a confused chicken. "Stupid girl. Where's your sense? They're right in front of your eyes."

Philly was made to sit down in front of her small wooden dressing table while Clarice arranged her hair, decorating it with a few floral hairpins as directed by Mrs. Vale.

No sooner had Clarice secured the final pin than Mrs. Vale urged Philly back up. "Here. Turn round. Let me look at you. Yes, this will do nicely."

"Why is the duke here?" Philly asked at the first opportunity. "Does he mean to take me for another drive? For I must tell you Mrs. Vale, I don't think I care to—"

"Clarice, go straight to Miss Townsend, and then to Abigail. I require them back in the drawing room as soon as possible." Mrs. Vale nudged Philly forward. "Miss Satterthwaite, we must hurry. Don't let your shawl drag on the ground."

There was a brisk knock at the door. Everyone froze where they stood.

"Come!" Mrs. Vale called out.

A housemaid ducked into the bedroom. Her eyes were round

with excitement. "Mr. Townsend requests the presence of Miss Satterthwaite in the library, ma'am."

Mrs. Vale covered her mouth with her hands, stifling a gasp. "I knew it. It's just as we planned."

Philly's heart pounded. It had been only two days since the duke had taken her driving. Did a second visit so soon afterward mean that he was officially courting her? Was that why everyone was in such a state?

What an awful tangle. And to see her relations so excited at the prospect! It simply wouldn't do. The sooner she set them straight on the subject, the better. "Mrs. Vale, there seems to be a misunderstanding—"

"There's no misunderstanding, Miss Satterthwaite. Hurry now. As quickly as you can." Mrs. Vale pushed her out the door. "But carefully. You mustn't trip on your shawl. If you broke your neck at this stage, all would be lost."

"Are you sure the duke is still here?" Philly descended the stairs, looking back over her shoulder at Mrs. Vale. "Perhaps he's gone and it's only Uncle Edgar who wants to see me? Indeed, I think that must be the case. His Grace and I did not get on at all. He can have no interest in me anymore."

Mrs. Vale was deaf to Philly questions. "Slowly now. Take each step with care. You mustn't appear out of breath when you enter the room."

Evans was waiting in the entry hall. He'd managed to compose himself, his face once again set into lines of distinguished indifference. "Miss Satterthwaite. His Grace and Mr. Townsend are expecting you."

"Thank you, Evans. Did they happen to say why—"

"Miss Satterthwaite, there's no time for this!" Mrs. Vale cried. "Now, listen to me. What is this? Are you trembling? Never mind.

His Grace will appreciate it. It shows you have the proper fear of him, and that you know the inferiority of your own position. But you mustn't cower. Your posture, Miss Satterthwaite. Be ever mindful. And don't speak unless you're spoken to."

Before Philly could utter another word in protest, one of the footmen opened the door to the library and Mrs. Vale pushed her into the room.

ELEVEN

As soon as Philly entered the library, her uncle, the duke, and a short, rather fussy-looking man in spectacles all rose from their seats. The duke's eyes were as black and glossy as she remembered. They settled on her immediately. She was reminded of a hawk fixing its predatory gaze on a field mouse.

The Collector.

The name alone was enough to send a cold trickle of fear through her. She knew now why he stared so intently at her face, but the knowledge did nothing to make it more bearable.

"Miss Satterthwaite." Moreland gave her a rigid bow.

Philly curtsied. "Your Grace."

Uncle Edgar nodded in the direction of the short man in spectacles. "His Grace's solicitor, Mr. Pritchard."

His solicitor?

Philly's mouth went dry at the implication. "Mr. Pritchard."

The little man came forward to greet her. She could smell at once that he was of the school of gentlemen who eschewed regular bathing in favor of copious amounts of cologne. His hair was powdered, and he was sweating profusely, causing his wire-rimmed spectacles to slide partway down his nose.

"Miss Satterthwaite." He cleared his throat. "It is indeed an honor and a privilege to make your acquaintance."

"Sit down, Phyllida," Uncle Edgar commanded, his hands clasped behind his back.

The library was Uncle Edgar's private lair. The furnishings in it were larger, darker, and far more masculine than those in the rest of the townhouse. Across from the three heavy chairs in which her uncle, Moreland, and Pritchard had been sitting was a velvet-upholstered sofa. Philly perched as delicately as she could on the edge of it lest the outsized piece of furniture swallow her up.

Moreland resumed his seat. Uncle Edgar and Mr. Pritchard remained standing.

"Phyllida," Uncle Edgar said. "His Grace wishes to speak with you alone. Your Grace." He bowed low to Moreland. "I shall remain nearby. Mr. Pritchard? If you'd care to repair to the drawing room for some refreshment?"

"Oh, yes, sir." Mr. Pritchard blotted his forehead with a large white handkerchief as Uncle Edgar led him out of the room. "So many details to agree upon. It's all quite taxing."

A footman closed the doors behind them with all of the ominous significance of the sealing of a tomb.

"Miss Satterthwaite." Moreland's sharp voice cut through the silence.

Philly jerked her head to look at him.

He was watching her closely. "My intentions will be of no surprise to you."

Her pulse skittered. "No, indeed." His intent couldn't be plainer. He'd brought his solicitor with him, for heaven's sake. A gentleman with a solicitor in tow wasn't thinking of courtship.

He was contemplating marriage. "But I do own to being a little confused, Your Grace."

"In what respect?"

"After the ball and our drive in the park, I thought you realized, as I did, that we have precious little in common to justify a courtship, let alone a—"

"I haven't come to court you, Miss Satterthwaite. I've come to make an offer for you. My solicitor has spent the last two hours settling all of the details with your uncle."

Her breath stopped in her chest. "The details? What details?"

"The settlements and so forth. It has all been arranged."

"How can it be? I've only a small stipend left me by my grandfather. It barely suffices as a dress allowance. And, as for a dowry, I haven't anything at all."

"Indeed, you do not."

Philly clasped her hands together in her lap. She'd forgotten how uncomfortable the duke was capable of making her, and just how much it seemed he enjoyed doing so. "I'm sorry. I don't understand."

Moreland continued to watch her with the same unblinking, emotionless expression. "Miss Satterthwaite, have you any idea what I might be willing to pay for a work of art?"

"No, Your Grace."

"Rest assured that your uncle does."

She stared at him, stunned. "Do you mean to say that you've settled money on my uncle? So that you might marry me?"

"I've shocked you, I see." Moreland's mouth twisted at the corner in a faint mockery of a smile. "You think it distasteful, perhaps. Or is it that you fear you've been undervalued?"

"Your Grace, I..."

"Have no doubt, Miss Satterthwaite, you didn't come cheaply.

Your uncle has got full value. In truth, I would have paid far more had he demanded it."

A rare spark of anger flared within Philly's breast. "I'm no work of art, Your Grace, no matter what people have been calling me. You can't simply acquire me from my uncle like you would a painting or a porcelain figure."

He raised a brow. "You think not? What do you suppose I've spent the last two hours doing?"

"I think you've very likely been wasting your time."

"No, indeed, Miss Satterthwaite. I believe I've made a wise investment of both my time and my money." He leaned forward in his chair. "I have a consuming passion, you see. If something exceptional catches my eye, I must have it. I cannot rest until I possess it utterly; until it's mine alone."

Philly drew back into the cushions of the sofa. "It sounds an unfortunate condition," she said with more bravery than she felt. "For you must know that there are some things that cannot be bought."

"That has rarely been my experience. Everything has its price."

"An object, perhaps, but—"

"You get right to the point, Miss Satterthwaite, and therein lies the dissatisfaction I have with my present collection. Objects can be bought. Paintings or porcelain figures, as you say. You can own them, display them, touch them, but you cannot truly possess them. They have no body. No soul." He leaned incrementally closer, just enough to see her cringe. "A woman, on the other hand, is something a man can wholly possess in every sense of the word—"

Heat flooded Philly's face. "Your Grace, I must protest—"

"Your uncle is a clever man to have struck on this. I'd never considered it myself. But then, how many women, however beau-

tiful, would qualify as a work of art? I've seen none but you."
Slowly, and with obvious reluctance, Moreland reclined back in
his chair. "A long engagement won't be possible. I have business in
the West Country I must attend to in August, and then I return
to Moreland Park. We shall marry in the second week of June."

"Really, Your Grace, you go too far." Philly marshaled her
courage. "You've given me no opportunity to make my answer."

"Your *answer*?"

"You've asked for my hand in marriage." She ignored his apparent incredulity, forcing herself to continue lest she lose her nerve.
"I'm aware of the great honor you have bestowed upon me, but
I cannot marry you. Not in June or any other month of the year.
I regret you have wasted your afternoon—"

Moreland rose abruptly from his chair. "You mistake me, Miss
Satterthwaite. I require no answer from you."

She looked up at him in astonishment.

"I didn't come here this afternoon to ask for your hand in marriage, as you so charmingly put it. I came here to make an offer
for you. An offer no different than I would make on any other
piece of art I desired for my collection." He smiled, his black eyes
glittering. "That offer was accepted two hours ago."

TWELVE

Philly watched in stunned silence as the Duke of Moreland gave one rapid jerk to the tasseled bell pull that hung by the fireplace. Within seconds, a footman opened the library doors and Uncle Edgar strode into the room.

"Your Grace—" he began.

"Townsend, your niece has a mind to refuse me." Moreland betrayed no emotion except that of mild irritation. "I'll spend no more time on the matter. Expect me Saturday afternoon. I trust that will give you sufficient time to make her amenable."

Uncle Edgar's face hardened. "I will see to it."

Moreland bowed curtly to Philly, and without another word, walked out of the library.

Philly's gaze found her uncle's. She hadn't expected he would be sympathetic to her refusal. Indeed she'd anticipated a harsh reproof. But she wasn't prepared at all for what she saw. He appeared to have transformed into a complete stranger. A man she'd never met before in her life.

"Am I to understand that you have objections to this match?"

Uncle Edgar lowered his cadaverous frame into the chair where the duke had been sitting only moments before.

A shiver of foreboding went through her. She had a sense that something was terribly wrong. It was true that she didn't know her uncle very well. She'd met him for the first time only two months before. But he'd always seemed an impassive, rather indifferent man, consumed with his investments and schemes, and sparing little emotion for the ladies in his household. As he looked at her now, she had the distinct impression that another man was staring out from behind her uncle's eyes.

"Well, Miss Satterthwaite?"

Miss Satterthwaite?

She couldn't remember when her uncle had ever addressed her so formally. He'd made free with her given name since the moment of their first meeting. That he was no longer doing so only intensified her feeling of his being a stranger. "We scarcely know each other," she managed to say.

"Many marriages are made after a single meeting in a crowded ballroom. You've met the duke on three occasions already. You're acquainted with him well enough. There will be plenty of time to know him better after you're wed."

"I suppose, but he's so very..." She wanted to tell her uncle that the duke had scared her. That he might, perhaps, even be mad. But she was so disconcerted by the change in Uncle Edgar's demeanor that she had difficulty finding the words. "He's so very..."

His eyes narrowed. "So very old?"

"No! Well, rather, he is old, but that isn't what I was going to say—"

"Were you expecting a love match? Some handsome young man of large fortune, perhaps? Come now, I'd thought you a practical-minded lady."

"I hope I am practical, sir, but I—"

"When I brought you back with us from that miserable little village in Devonshire, it was on the understanding that once here in London, you would make a successful marriage. Now you're here and I've spent a small fortune on seeing you made presentable for society, do you intend to go back on your word?"

"No, of course not, but—"

"For I must warn you, Miss Satterthwaite, I've kept a record of every farthing I've spent on you, and if you don't fulfill your end of the bargain, I'll expect every single farthing repaid."

Philly recoiled at his words. Her uncle had never been warm to her, that was true, but she hadn't thought him cruel or unreasonable. He'd taken her in, after all, and even allowed her to bring her dogs. "I have every intention of making a suitable marriage, if I can."

He gave a humorless laugh. "And yet you think to refuse the Duke of Moreland? Do you expect to do any better? A prince, perhaps? Or do you have designs on a king?"

"I didn't refuse him because I think I can do better, sir. I refused him because I know we're not suited. I don't expect a great romance or a young, handsome man, but I cannot marry someone who gains pleasure from tormenting me."

"From tormenting you!"

"Yes. He seems to enjoy it." She hesitated before continuing, uncertain of her uncle's reaction. "And that isn't all. He seems to be laboring under the delusion that he has bought me."

Uncle Edgar fell into an ominous silence.

"He claims to have settled a large sum of money on you in exchange for my hand in marriage. If he's promised you something, sir—compensation for all you've laid out on my behalf, perhaps—I'm sorry you must be disappointed in your expectations, but I—"

"I shall not be disappointed, Miss Satterthwaite. You may depend upon it."

"I'm glad to hear that, sir, for I cannot marry him. I won't. Not on any terms."

Uncle Edgar observed her for a few moments. "Do you know how I earn my daily crust, Miss Satterthwaite?" he asked at last. "I discover investment opportunities. Some would say I have a preternatural skill for it. But investments are not without risk. With each failure, I lose the confidence of the gentlemen who invest with me. And I lose money. The very coin that keeps my daughters in pretty frocks. That serves to provide their dowries."

Her conscience panged. "I hadn't realized you were in financial difficulty, sir."

"We're not paupers yet, though last night's debacle has certainly not improved our circumstances. Had Heywood stayed the course—" Uncle Edgar stopped short. "But none of that matters. Not in light of your impending marriage to the Duke of Moreland. Such an alliance will undo every failure of the last six months. It will also secure my position in society—and that of my daughters."

Philly didn't know quite what to say. She didn't wish her cousins to suffer because of her choice. Truly she didn't. But to marry the Duke of Moreland? A man who was cold and cruel? Her spirit rose up in objection at the very thought of it.

She'd spent her whole life being obedient and obliging. Always doing what was expected of her, no matter the sacrifice to her own happiness. But this was too much. "I want to help you. But I can't do what you ask of me."

Uncle Edgar's eyes turned cold. "Is it possible you can be so insensible to your position? I must say, I find that astounding. You have no fortune of your own and no connections. In short, nothing at all to recommend you except for a rather unique beauty."

She suppressed a rush of indignation. "My grandfather was a gentleman, sir. And my grandmother, as you well know, was the daughter of an earl. I may have no great fortune, but I'm a gentlewoman of good family."

"You have no family, Miss Satterthwaite."

He might as well have struck her. Indeed, Philly felt as if he had.

"I would have you think carefully about what would become of you if I were to turn you and your four mongrels out of my house. To whom would you go? There is no one who will take you in, and London is not a very hospitable place for a young woman alone."

She tightened her hands in her lap to stop their trembling. "You needn't consider turning us out, sir," she said, unwilling to show how much his words affected her. "I have every intention of making a good marriage. However, I've only attended one ball. If you would but have patience, I'm sure that, in time, I shall meet a gentleman who is much more suitable. At the next ball—"

"Oh, there will be no more balls, Miss Satterthwaite. No more parties. In fact, I believe it would be best if you kept to your room until the duke returns on Saturday."

Philly sat very still on the sofa as the full import of her uncle's words sank in. Her thoughts raced over all that had happened to her since the day Edgar Townsend had first come to Satterthwaite Court. With a sickening clarity, everything suddenly fell into focus. She had only to wonder how she could have been so blind—so very naïve—as to have not seen it before.

"I thought I was brought here for the season to make a suitable marriage with someone," she said. "With anyone. That's not so, is it? All of this preparation hasn't been for the season. It's been for one man alone."

"I won't deny it."

"That's why I've attended no ball but the Worthings', and why you haven't allowed me to go out visiting with Elizabeth and Abigail. That's why my walks must be so heavily chaperoned. Why I'm not allowed to meet anyone or speak to anyone." Philly's brows drew together in distress. "You haven't wanted me to meet any other eligible gentlemen, have you? I'm to be for the duke and no one else."

"Moreland is one of the wealthiest men in England," Uncle Edgar snapped with a touch of impatience. "Is it such a surprise that I've brought the two of you together? That I've taken the trouble to arrange a match?"

"No," she said softly. "No surprise at all. I've known for some time that you and Mrs. Vale cherished hopes in that direction. But I never imagined..." She shook her head in disbelief. "When you came to Satterthwaite Court, you said you'd finance a season for me so that I might make a suitable match. You didn't tell me I'd have no choice in the man I married, and you most certainly didn't tell me you'd already chosen for me. If I'd known the whole of your scheme, I'd never have agreed to come here."

"Nevertheless, you're here now. In my home. Upon a few days' reflection, I believe you'll do what you must." He rose. "We've discussed this enough for today, Miss Satterthwaite. You're becoming overset."

Philly stood, as well. Her eyes were tearing, but she was in no danger of having the vapors. "I'm not overset. Nor am I a child. I'm three and twenty. It's my right to marry where I will."

"Your right?" He looked down his nose at her. "Would you care to know of my rights? It's my right to evict you from my home this very moment. To turn you out without a ha'penny. It's my right to have those four mongrels in my garden destroyed. We both of us have rights. I trust you won't forget that."

She stared up at him, aghast. "You would threaten my dogs, sir?"

"I don't make threats, Miss Satterthwaite. I'm a man of business. I deal only in facts and figures. And the fact is I could tolerate much while you were a grateful and obliging guest, but if you prove yourself otherwise, I must tell you that my patience has grown thin with those beasts. I allowed you to bring them here as a gesture of my goodwill, but I see none of them very fit to live. Why, one of them can't even walk."

With each icy word he spoke, Philly grew colder. All that she'd intended to say in argument froze upon her lips, and for the first time, she saw Edgar Townsend for exactly who and what he was.

A devil.

THIRTEEN

The Earl of Gordon's library was as different from
Edgar Townsend's library as night was to day. It
wasn't a room designed for business or high finance, and the
décor hadn't been chosen to intimidate and overwhelm. It was a
room meant for reading and quiet study, filled with dark wood
bookcases lined with well-read books, a large globe in a mahogany
stand, and a collection of maps spilling over the sides of an
inlaid drum table. The walls were richly paneled, and the sofas,
armchairs, and carpets were done in shades of red. The entire
room had the feel of distinguished age and comfortable wealth.

After a light supper, Arthur had retired there as he often did
while here in town. He sat in a leather chair in front of the fireplace,
a book spread open on his lap. He'd been attempting to read,
but more often than not found himself gazing into the flickering
flames of the fire. His thoughts had been much distracted since
leaving Edgar Townsend's dinner party the previous evening. He
couldn't seem to focus on anything.

More and more, he found himself wondering what he'd do in

this particular situation if he were the same man he'd been before the war. Would he return to Somersetshire? Would he resign himself to never seeing Miss Satterthwaite again?

No.

The old Arthur Heywood would stay in London and use all his strength and resources to pursue her. He'd go to every ball she attended and claim every waltz. He'd take her out riding and for long walks in the park. He'd offer to escort her and her two cousins to the opera, to Astley's Amphitheatre, and to see the fireworks at Vauxhall Gardens. He'd subject himself to all the London diversions he'd spent most of his life avoiding. He'd do whatever it took to remain in her presence, whatever it took to win her heart.

It was a pointless fantasy and served no purpose except to sink him further into melancholy. He'd never pursued a woman in such a determined fashion, and it was ridiculous to imagine doing so now. Besides which, even if he'd never been injured in the war, Miss Satterthwaite was still not likely to ever look at him as more than her friend. She was on the verge of becoming a duchess, after all. And, as Reggie Forsythe had said, what was a second son when compared to a duke?

Arthur was in his shirtsleeves, his cravat removed and his hair disheveled. Every aspect of his person attested to his restless state of mind. There was nothing for it except to get himself good and drunk. It wasn't his usual course of action, and in general he disdained it, but after saying goodbye to Miss Satterthwaite in Townsend's drawing room, there was little else to do.

A cut-crystal decanter of brandy stood on a marble-topped table beside his chair. He was just unstopping it to refill his glass when his father's butler soundlessly entered the room. "Yes, Underhill? What is it?"

"There's a young man here to see you, Captain Heywood. I've told him you're not receiving visitors, but he's most insistent. He claims to have an urgent note he must deliver."

Arthur hadn't received a single caller since coming to London. He had no intention of starting now. "He's welcome to leave it with you."

"The young man informs me he must put the note into your hands himself, sir."

For the first time, Arthur glanced up at Underhill. "Where is this young man come from?"

"His name is William, sir. He works for Mr. Edgar Townsend."

Arthur frowned. What the devil could Townsend want from him? He'd told the man in no uncertain terms that he wouldn't be doing business with him. There was nothing more to be said on the matter.

"Shall I have one of the footmen run him off, sir?" Underhill asked with bland indifference. "He's not willing to leave of his own accord."

Arthur muttered an oath under his breath. The bloody nerve of Townsend! "Send him in. I'll deal with him myself."

Underhill glided out of the room. He returned a brief moment later with Townsend's servant in tow.

Arthur leaned back in his chair and surveyed the young man. He was clad in the livery of one of Townsend's household servants. "You have a note for me?"

"Yes, sir." William looked pointedly at Underhill who was standing close behind him. "I'm to give it to you in private."

Arthur sighed. He was beginning to feel rather exasperated by the whole affair. "Leave us, Underhill."

The butler bowed and left without a word.

"Well?" Arthur prompted.

William withdrew a letter from inside his waistcoat and extended it to Arthur.

"You may go now," Arthur said as he took it. "You've fulfilled your duty."

"I can't, sir. My mistress bade me stay until I have your answer."

Arthur went still. Very slowly, he raised his eyes to the young man's face. "Your mistress."

"Yes, sir. Miss Satterthwaite, sir. She said I'm to stay with you while you read the letter and..." William hesitated. "Please, sir. I must return with an answer. She expects one."

Arthur tore open the letter. It was short, written in an even and elegant hand. He read the contents quickly, and then, after he'd finished it, he read it again.

> *Dear Sir,*
>
> *Please forgive me for writing to you. I would never presume to do so if it were not a matter of the utmost urgency. You are my only friend in London, and I hope with all my heart you will see fit to do me the service I must request of you. Will you meet me tomorrow at sunrise on the bench where we first talked together?*
>
> *I await your answer.*
> *Yours in friendship, P.*

Arthur stared at the sheet of foolscap, awash in conflicting emotions. Phyllida Satterthwaite didn't strike him as the type of woman who would ever write a letter to an unmarried gentleman, let alone arrange a clandestine meeting with one. That she'd just done both disturbed him greatly.

"There was something else, sir. She said to tell you..." William's brow furrowed. "She said to tell you that no matter what you decide, her good opinion of you won't be altered. She said to make sure you understood that, sir."

"Do you know what all this is about?" Arthur asked. "Has something happened at Townsend's?"

The young footman dropped his eyes down to the floor. "I shouldn't say, sir. Mr. Townsend is... He can sometimes be... Well, no matter what he is, he's my master, sir."

"But something has gone wrong there."

"Yes, sir."

"William. Look at me."

The young footman immediately lifted his gaze. "Yes, sir?"

"Is Miss Satterthwaite all right?"

"No, sir." William shook his head. "She was very upset. Indeed, I've never seen her so poorly. I hope your answer might cheer her. If you'd but give it to me, I'll return to Mr. Townsend's directly. If I stay any longer, Mr. Evans will notice I'm gone, and I could be in ever so much trouble, sir. I might even lose my place."

Arthur looked again at the letter, his stomach twisting with frustration. More than ever he felt his own limitations. He was utterly powerless. Whatever had happened at Townsend's, he could very likely do nothing to help her. Why had she turned to him? What could she possibly expect? Could she not see that he was in no condition at all to be of service to anyone anymore?

"William," he said abruptly.

"Yes, Captain Heywood?"

"Tell Miss Satterthwaite that my answer is yes."

FOURTEEN

Arthur had his coachman drive him to the entrance of the park, and with no little difficulty, walked down the secluded path that led to the bench where he was to meet Phyllida Satterthwaite. The landscape was shrouded in a thick blanket of fog. It rolled over the ground and clung to the blossoming trees. A sliver of sunlight rested on the edge of the horizon, too faint yet to give any warmth.

He hadn't been waiting long when a single dog barked in the distance. It wasn't an uncommon thing to hear in the early morning hours, and at first, he paid it no mind. But when the dog barked again—the sound even closer—he rose from his seat on the bench in anticipation.

Seconds later, the giant, wiry-haired figure of Basil padded out of the fog. Miss Satterthwaite was right behind him, the mist swirling around the folds of her amber velvet cloak. As she approached, she raised her gloved hand to push back the hood of her cloak. At that very moment, the sun came up from behind the trees, illuminating her hair and face in a dazzling array of golden light.

"Captain Heywood," she said with a sigh of relief.

Arthur stared at her, resplendent in the sunrise. "Miss Satterthwaite."

She sank down on the bench, her cloak pooling around her. "Thank you for agreeing to meet me, sir."

He came to sit beside her. With the sun no longer glittering on her face, he saw for the first time that her hair was down. It fell in a mass of dark, lustrous waves over the front of one shoulder, secured rather haphazardly with a satin ribbon. It took an effort for him not to look at it more than he ought. "The footman who delivered your note said something had happened at Townsend's to upset you."

"Did he?" She bent her head. "Yes, well, things haven't been going particularly well since last we met."

"I'm sorry to hear it."

"I wouldn't like you to think I wrote to you lightly, sir. If it hadn't been absolutely necessary, I'd never have been so bold. The fact is, as I said in my letter, you're my only friend here in London, and I've no one else to turn to. I hope you won't think too ill of me for my presumption."

"Not at all," Arthur assured her. "I'm at your service."

Miss Satterthwaite appeared to be heartened by his words. She looked up at him, eyes peculiarly bright. "Might I enquire, sir, whether you still intend to depart for Somersetshire tomorrow?"

"Yes, I leave first thing in the morning."

"Then, I would like to ask you—to beg you—to please take my dogs with you back to the country."

Arthur blinked. "You want me to take your dogs?"

"Yes, I do. Very much. I noticed from the first time we met that they all took to you. Even Fox didn't mind you touching him. Do you remember? They'd be very little trouble. Indeed, they would thrive in the countryside. And I know you wouldn't be cruel to them, Captain Heywood, for I've seen how very kind you are." Her eyes filled with tears. "Fox would have to remain in the house at night, for his injury requires warmth. The rest of the dogs would do quite well in the stable. Jasper and Dash are excellent ratters and Basil is the most fearsome guard dog you could ever want. If you would—"

"Miss Satterthwaite," Arthur interrupted gently, "what has happened?"

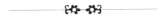

Philly dashed the tears from her eyes with her hands, only to notice afterward that Captain Heywood was holding out his linen handkerchief to her. She took it gratefully. "My uncle says he will have them destroyed." The admission brought on a small sob, which she tried her best to stifle. "It's no idle threat. If I don't do what he wants, he'll have no compunction in carrying it out. He's made that quite clear."

Captain Heywood leaned closer to her, his posture oddly protective. "What's brought this on? What is it that he expects you to do?"

She blotted her tears with his handkerchief and tried to collect herself. She'd only intended to talk to him about her dogs, but as she looked up at Arthur Heywood, his eyes were fixed on her with the same thoughtful expression they'd held so many times before. He was her only friend. If she couldn't share her misfortune with him, with whom could she share it? She had no one else.

"Oh, Captain Heywood," she said in a tearful whisper. "The Duke of Moreland made an offer of marriage for me yesterday. And when I would not have him—"

"You *refused* the Duke of Moreland?"

"I did, sir. I could never marry such a man. But he won't countenance my refusal. He says... He says he's bought me from my uncle. That he's purchased me like any other work of art he would buy for his collection."

"The devil he has!"

"I'm afraid he has, sir. His solicitor came and drew up the papers with my uncle. They spent two hours negotiating my price." She raised his handkerchief once again to her face as she choked back a fresh sob. "I've discovered that my uncle has been behind the whole scheme. From the day he first met me in Fox Cross. He lied to me. Tricked me. All of the clothes and dancing lessons and everything else...it was never for the season. He meant to keep me isolated from everyone but the duke."

As he listened to her, Captain Heywood fell silent.

That very silence, which appeared to be a sympathetic one, encouraged Philly to share more than she'd ever intended. Before she knew it, the entire story was pouring out. She held nothing back.

She told him about the duke's behavior during the waltz at the Worthings' ball, how he'd viciously struck his dog before taking her for a drive in the park, and how he'd loomed over her in the library just for the enjoyment of seeing her cringe. She told all the things he'd said to her, even those statements that caused her the deepest feminine mortification. Most painful of all, she revealed her uncle's part in the whole affair, and how she'd been so deceived as to his true character.

While she spoke, Captain Heywood stared fixedly off into the distance, his expression unreadable. With every single sentence she uttered, he became more and more withdrawn.

"I suspect the only reason he allowed me to bring my dogs with me to London was so he might use them to force me into compliance," Philly said. "If he knew me any better, he'd have realized that such threats would have quite the opposite effect. No sooner had he made them than I resolved to leave his house forever. I have every confidence I can find a position as a paid companion or perhaps even a governess. I intend to go to an agency this very day, but first I must see to the safety of my dogs. That's why I wrote to you, Captain Heywood."

Philly hadn't initially noticed the captain's inattention. However, as she came to the close of her tale and he still hadn't said a single word, she began to realize that she'd been boring him, or even worse, offending him.

Whatever he'd wanted to know in the beginning, it was apparent she'd told him far too much. Perhaps she'd revealed more than she ought about Moreland's behavior? It was surely not very ladylike to list out the flaws of one's suitor, no matter how justified one's complaints. She was just about to say as much, when he anticipated her.

"Miss Satterthwaite, your situation is an unfortunate one indeed, but as you can see, I'm in no position to do anything about it." His voice had a sharp edge of bitterness to it.

She'd never heard him speak in such a tone. It immediately put her on her guard. "You misunderstand me, sir. I didn't intend for you to do anything except for...well, I very much hope that you'll take my dogs back with you to Somersetshire."

"Moreland has grievously insulted you."

"I shall be all right. As long as—"

"Townsend has, as well."

She didn't know what was wrong with him. He was behaving

so strangely. "It doesn't matter. I don't care about any of that."

"It *does* matter, Miss Satterthwaite. It matters to me, *as a gentleman*. And yet I can do absolutely nothing about it. I can barely walk, let alone challenge either of those men—"

"I would never want you to!" she objected, horrified at the thought. "I only wrote to you because of—"

"Because of your dogs. You've been insulted and threatened, but my task as a *gentleman* is to tend to your dogs."

"You won't do it?"

"Of course I'll do it. Your dogs will at least be safe." Captain Heywood's hand tightened on his cane. "What about you, Miss Satterthwaite? Who will keep you safe?"

"You needn't worry about me, sir. I know everything will come right. I'm not too proud to work for a living and haven't the least qualm about seeking employment. Perhaps I may even find a place somewhere in the country?"

"Moreland will never leave you alone, do you realize that? It makes no difference whether you run away from Townsend's. If he wants you, he'll find a way to have you. As a governess or a companion, you'll be even more vulnerable to him than you are now."

A chill ran through her. What he said was true. Moreland had told her as much himself yesterday in the library. "You sound as if you think my situation is hopeless, sir, and it may well be, but what else do you propose I do? Simply give up my plan and consent to marry the duke?"

"Three years ago, I would have proposed that I put a bullet in him," Captain Heywood said brutally. "Now I can offer you no such assistance in that regard. In truth, Miss Satterthwaite, the only thing I have left to offer you, as worthless as it is and as undesirable as it may be to you, is my name."

Philly stared at him. His face betrayed no emotion and he was still looking off into the distance. She didn't understand him at all. "I beg your pardon?"

"There's only one way you'll ever be out of Moreland's reach and that's if you marry another. If you're truly desperate, perhaps you will consider marrying me."

"Marry *you*?" Philly was stunned.

"It would be a marriage in name only, of course." He ground out the words. "A way to protect you; to keep you safe from Moreland."

Everything about his demeanor confused her. There was no sympathy in his eyes, or in his tone. Instead, he managed to sound almost angry. And why would he not look at her? Had she done something wrong?

He said nothing else, and Philly was speechless for what seemed an interminable amount of time.

Had it been a real proposal—had he fallen in love with her and wanted her as his wife, she'd have known how to answer. But a marriage in name only? What would such a thing even be like? Would she live with him in Somersetshire as if she were a distant relation he'd taken in? Would she run his household just as she'd once run Satterthwaite Court for her grandfather?

It was a dispassionate offer, and one that spoke more of the role of housekeeper than wife. She supposed she should be insulted. And yet...

The more she thought about it, the more the idea appealed to her. To live with Captain Heywood and no longer be constrained every time she wished to talk to him or be near him? To have the run of a home of her very own? To be once again in the countryside with all her walks and rambles? Philly had never dared hope for such a happy solution. Indeed, she'd never even imagined such a one existed.

But even as her excitement over the prospect grew, a leaden feeling in her stomach told her that it could not be. There was one thing that would be intolerable about the situation, for him, as well as for her. "Captain Heywood," she began.

He flinched slightly, but still didn't look at her. His hand was gripping the handle of his cane so tightly it seemed as if he would break it into splinters.

"I thank you for your kind offer, sir," she said. "But I cannot accept it."

He closed his eyes briefly against her words.

"I couldn't allow you to make such a sacrifice. It would be cruel to you and dreadfully unfair. No matter what else I may feel or how desperate my own circumstances, I could never come between a gentleman and the lady he is most devotedly in love with."

"What the devil are you talking about?" Captain Heywood turned to face her at last.

Philly was so taken aback by the intensity of his expression, it was all she could do to stop herself from instinctively drawing back from him. "Why, about Lady Eliot, sir. It's well known that you're in love with her."

His eyes fairly blazed. "Is it?"

"Yes," she said, more hesitant now. "My cousins told me the day we all met in the park. They said that...when you came back from the war, she'd broken your engagement and married another, but that you've remained steadfast to her, and now she is widowed—"

"Miss Satterthwaite, when I came back from the war, the last thing on my mind was Caroline Battersby. My engagement to her was the thoughtless act of a young man with poor judgment and no sense. When she broke it and married another, I considered it a blessed release. I didn't love her before the war, and I don't even think about her now."

He spoke with unwavering conviction. Philly had no doubt but that he was telling the truth. She had now only to wonder how she could have ever believed her cousins in the first place.

He was watching her reaction carefully. "I'd hoped that you, of all people, would realize that my desire for solitude has little to do with pining away for the love of some society lady. The truth is, Miss Satterthwaite, you're the only person in quite a long while whose company I can tolerate."

Her heart thumped. "Captain Heywood, I..."

"I wouldn't like to see you married to the duke any more than you would like it. You're right, he's a cruel man and bound to make your life a misery. I dearly wish I'd some greater assistance I could offer you in the matter, but at present I can barely walk across a room unaided. And, though I can do a creditable job of carving your mutton, my left hand isn't capable of holding a pistol steady any longer."

Philly could hear the wry humor he attempted to infuse into his speech. It made her feel inexplicably sad. Without a thought for propriety, she placed her gloved hand on his arm. He immediately stilled. "Your name is quite sufficient. I would be honored to have it."

Captain Heywood had plainly not expected her answer. When she gave it, he searched her face with something akin to desperation. "Miss Satterthwaite...I can't have heard you correctly. Are you saying that you'll marry me?"

"Yes, Captain. I will marry you. But I feel obliged to tell you... Well, perhaps you haven't considered that...the benefits of such an arrangement would all be on my side?"

He didn't answer her right away. Indeed, it seemed that he was still very much affected by her response. But when at last he made his reply, the bitterness and frustration that had characterized his voice only moments before were gone. "I'm sure you're wrong, ma'am."

Her hand fell from his arm. "I wish I were, but the fact is, I've little in the way of a fortune and even less in the way of connections. There's no doubt that, if you were to marry me, I'd be forever hanging on your sleeve."

"Those sorts of things mean nothing to me."

"Don't they?"

"Less than nothing."

"Oh, I'm glad of it. But there's more, I'm afraid." She dropped her eyes, sincerely wishing that her conscience didn't compel her to be so honest with him. "I wonder if you've given proper thought to what might happen if you were to one day meet a woman for whom you have a true affection?"

"On that score, Miss Satterthwaite, you need have no apprehension. I can promise you quite faithfully that there will never be another woman I wish to marry."

Philly lifted her gaze back to his. "I daresay you think I'm worrying over trifles, but I'd be a selfish creature indeed if I said nothing at all."

"You're the most unselfish person I've ever met. Now, tell me, are there any other warnings you feel compelled to issue me?"

"No. That is, I'm certain there must be, but I can think of nothing else at present."

He regarded her with solemn attention. "And is your answer to my proposal still yes?"

"Yes. Yes, of course it is. But how can such a thing even be done? The duke will return on Saturday, and any moment my uncle may make good his threat against my dogs. There's so little time."

"There's time enough. I should have no trouble procuring a special license. We can marry tomorrow morning and leave at once for my estate in the West Country without delay. Unless..." His expression turned grave. "Do you think it safe for you to spend another night under Townsend's roof?"

Philly's head was spinning. Married tomorrow morning! "Yes, I think so, but do you really mean for us to marry *tomorrow*?"

"It will enable us to leave immediately for Somersetshire. The plans for my departure are already in place, and the sooner you're out of London, the better."

"But if you were to call on my uncle and tell him of your intentions, then perhaps—"

"Your uncle would never countenance an offer from me. He and Moreland may even take steps to try and prevent our marrying. No. It's better if he knows nothing until after it's done."

"Oh, yes. Quite." She was feeling a trifle overwhelmed, but took comfort in the fact that Captain Heywood now appeared completely in control. He looked, for all the world, like an officer planning a military campaign.

"I'll make the arrangements. You needn't worry about anything except meeting me one final time tomorrow morning." He met her gaze. "If you will but trust me, Miss Satterthwaite—"

"I do trust you, Captain Heywood," she said. "I trust you enough to put my fate and the fate of my dogs in your hands. I know you won't let us down."

He regarded her steadily. "I shall endeavor not to."

FIFTEEN

*U*pon leaving the park, Arthur told his coachman to drive him to Doctors' Commons. The coachman flashed him a look of surprise, but complied without a word. Once there, Arthur took care of the necessary paperwork at the archbishop's office, and then waited for the clerk to write out a special license.

While waiting, he planned out exactly what he'd do next, trying to focus on the tasks that needed to be done as dispassionately as he could. It was harder than it otherwise might have been, for every few minutes the reality of the situation struck him afresh, and he experienced a vague sort of euphoria as he realized that he was, in fact, going to marry Phyllida Satterthwaite.

He hadn't planned on proposing to her. His offer had started as a response to all she'd confided in him, born of frustration that he could do nothing else to help her. But no sooner had he said the words than he knew beyond all doubt that he must have her.

It was this certainty, this very determination to keep her in his life by any means, that had compelled him to utter those fateful words *a marriage in name only*. Even then he'd never truly believed she would consent, and now, as he awaited the license which would enable them to marry, it seemed to him somehow impossible.

No doubt he'd arrive for her in the morning as planned and find she wasn't there. Or, perhaps, a note might come later this evening telling him that she'd changed her mind.

She'd accepted him under the influence of a great emotion. She was scared and upset, overwhelmed by all that had happened with Moreland and Townsend. After calm reflection, she'd likely realize that a marriage to him—even a marriage in name only—wasn't anything worth having at all. And then all of the plans he was making would come to naught.

He'd end up looking like a fool.

It was a distinct possibility, but he didn't let it deter him from his course.

Once he had the license in hand, Arthur had the coachman drive him to the office of his family's solicitor, Mr. Ombersley.

Ombersley was knowledgeable on most every matter and was more than happy to conduct a few items of business on Arthur's behalf, as well as to furnish him with the direction of a clergyman who might be willing to officiate on such short notice, and at so early an hour.

With this information in hand, Arthur proceeded to his next errand.

At each consecutive stop they made, the pattern of their business became clearer, and the coachman was less and less able to hide his astonishment. When Arthur directed him to a jeweler in Bond Street, the normally stoic servant could barely suppress his grin.

Arthur hadn't been out for such a prolonged period of time in the entirety of his stay in London. He was physically exhausted, but his leg—though painful after the day's exertions—was causing him nowhere near as much agony as he'd expected. He had a vague idea that all those walks into the park to see Miss Satterthwaite might have effected some minimal improvement.

Nevertheless, he was still in far from ideal condition. If the inducement hadn't been so great, he'd never have hazarded a visit to Bond Street. The shops were busy at this time of day, and the streets were teeming with carriages, street sellers, and pedestrians. He was almost guaranteed to run into some former acquaintance, or even worse, one of the myriad gossiping tabbies of the *ton*.

Thankfully, the jeweler wasn't prohibitively crowded, and as it was an establishment that had been patronized by the Heywood family for many generations, Arthur was at once recognized and promptly attended.

"A wedding band, you say, Captain Heywood?" The proprietor beamed. "Very good, sir."

Arthur had intended to purchase a plain band of gold. Something dignified and distinctly unromantic. But as he stood at the jeweler's counter, a flash of fiery brilliance caught his eye, much in the same way that Miss Satterthwaite often did herself.

The canny proprietor followed his gaze, and without a word, brought the item out onto the counter for Arthur to examine. It was a gold ring with five inlaid oval rubies. The band was slender and elegant, etched with an intricate floral pattern. "The stones are flawless, as you can see. And the workmanship is exquisite."

As Arthur looked at the delicate little ring, he recalled how he'd mistaken Miss Satterthwaite's glass hairpins for rubies. Quite suddenly, he wanted nothing more than to give her the real thing, and after a short discussion with the jeweler, the purchase was made.

While he waited for it to be wrapped, he scanned the jeweler's other offerings. There were filigree butterflies with sapphire eyes, ropes of gleaming pearls, and several jewel-encrusted snuffboxes. Amongst the glittery baubles, his eyes lit on a pair of ruby earrings. They weren't too dissimilar from the ring he'd just bought, and when the proprietor returned with his neatly wrapped purchase, Arthur asked to see them.

While he was standing at the counter being shown the ruby drop earrings, two new customers entered the shop.

"Heywood! This is a dashed coincidence." Reggie Forsythe's voice sounded from the doorway.

Arthur turned to acknowledge him. Only then did he see that Forsythe was not alone.

Clinging to his arm was Caroline Eliot.

She was dressed all in white with a fur-trimmed Cossack mantle thrown round her shoulders, and her cropped blonde hair artfully curled under a fashionably garish hat. When she saw him, she fluttered one gloved hand to her mouth in surprise.

"Captain Heywood! Why, it's been absolutely ages."

Arthur greeted them both with excruciating civility. Caroline had changed little in the years since he'd last seen her. She was as cold and brittle-looking as he remembered, and her personality seemed no less artificial.

"It's been six years at least since last we met." Her dark eyes roved over him. "You must tell me how you've been keeping."

"He's keeping bloody well, by the look of it." Forsythe approached the counter. "Buying rubies for some ladylove. Expensive little trinkets these, eh, Heywood? Who is she? Anyone I know?"

Caroline joined them at the counter. She picked up one of the earrings to examine it more closely. "When Forsythe told me he'd seen you at the club, I didn't believe him. I'd no notion you were even in town. I wish you'd seen fit to call on me."

"Heywood isn't in London for the society, m'dear. He's here on business with Edgar Townsend." Forsythe leaned against the counter in a manner that would give his stylish suit of clothing the best effect. "By the by, Heywood, why in blazes didn't you tell me you'd already met Townsend's Devonshire niece? I had to hear it from Darly. Would've been a good bit of information to have before I made my wager."

"You know, Captain, my conscience has never been easy since last I wrote to you," Caroline continued, as if Forsythe hadn't interrupted her. "Why, I'd even considered calling on you myself when I go down to the West Country next month for the Markhams' house party. That's how heavily it's been weighing on my mind." She affected a grief-stricken expression that was somewhat spoiled when she held one of the earrings experimentally up to her earlobe. "After my husband died... Well, one has regrets, you know."

"You need have none where I'm concerned." Arthur shook his head at the proprietor who promptly collected the ruby earrings and put them away.

"Met her myself at the Worthings' ball," Forsythe went on. "Danced with her, as well. A work of art indeed. Had I put down a little more, I might be in line to make a pretty packet."

"Would you like to see anything else, Captain Heywood?" the proprietor asked.

"That will be all."

"I thought her nothing very special," Caroline said languidly.

"Oh, she's no rival to you, of course," Forsythe said at once. "Can't even compare."

Arthur collected his package and prepared to take his leave.

"You've seen us both, Captain." Caroline's mouth curved into a feline smile. "How do you judge? Is Mr. Forsythe, right? Or do you think Miss Satterthwaite my rival?"

Arthur briefly met her gaze. "Phyllida Satterthwaite has no rival." And before either could recover from his assertion, he bid them a curt good day and walked out of the shop.

SIXTEEN

Philly's escape from her uncle's house on Friday morning didn't go as smoothly as it had done the morning before. After dressing in a sprigged muslin gown and blue spencer robe, she'd wasted quite a bit of time trying to arrange her hair. It was so thick that no sooner had she put in a hairpin than it popped right back out again. Following several attempts, she finally had it in some semblance of order. Only then did she pack as many clothes as she could carry into a valise and make her way downstairs with her dogs.

Just as she was preparing to descend the last flight of stairs and creep quietly out the front door of the townhouse, she heard the unmistakable sound of voices in the entry hall.

Upon further inspection, she discovered it was Evans reprimanding William.

"As that may be, sonny boy," Evans was saying in an accent far less genteel than the one she usually heard him use. "But you don't work for Mr. Townsend's niece, do you? You work for Mr. Townsend. There won't be no more ducking out to the garden.

If she wants her dogs to be looked after, she can bloody well—"

"Good morning!" Philly called cheerfully. She came down the stairs and into the hall. "I'm just going to walk my dogs out onto the green."

Evans turned to look at her. His gaze flashed to the traveling bag in her hand. "Miss Satterthwaite, it's half five in the morning."

"It's not so terribly early. I often woke at such an hour in the country. Besides, I can't sleep and I've a mind for some fresh air. If no one is available to accompany me, I'll be quite content to go out alone with my dogs—"

"Mr. Townsend and Mrs. Vale wouldn't allow it," Evans said. "*I* won't allow it."

She swallowed her growing anxiety, and with a purposeful stride, moved toward the front doors. "Enough of this nonsense, Evans. I'm resolved to go, and I shan't wait a second longer."

"Hold a moment!" Evans rushed toward her, as if he meant to bar her way or perhaps even grab hold of her.

Basil growled low in his throat. Fox joined in with a threatening snarl from his place in Philly's arms.

Evans took a few cautious steps back.

Philly seized the opportunity. Tugging her dogs behind her, she hurried the rest of the way to the door and opened it.

"William!" Evans exclaimed. "Go with Miss Satterthwaite. Just to the green, mind you. She must come back directly." His eyes darted from Philly to her dogs. "I'll have to send a maid to wake Mrs. Vale. She and Mr. Townsend said you weren't to leave the house—"

"Do whatever you think you must," Philly said, and without waiting a moment longer, she went out the front doors of the townhouse.

Her pulse raced as she and her dogs skipped down the front

steps and to the street. She didn't say a word, only walked briskly toward the park.

"Wait, miss!" William caught up to her. "I thought we were walking to the green?"

"No, William, I'm going somewhere else. I don't wish you to get in any more trouble, so you may turn back if you like. In truth, it's probably better if you do."

"And leave you here?"

"I'm quite all right with my dogs, as you can see— *Oh*!" Philly held tight to Jasper's lead as he attempted to bolt off, nearly toppling her over in the process.

"Let me, miss." William took charge of the three larger dogs, showing no inclination to leave Philly's side. "Where are we going?"

"Just to the entrance of the park."

"You mean to walk your dogs in the *park*? But I promised Mr. Evans we were only going to the green. If we aren't back right away, he'll have my head."

Philly chewed her bottom lip. She contemplated how much she could confide in William. He'd always been good to her. Surely he wouldn't betray her now. "I'm not going into the park precisely, only to the entrance of it. I'm...I'm meeting Captain Heywood's carriage."

"Captain Heywood!"

Her cheeks burned with sudden warmth. "You needn't be concerned. Captain Heywood is a gentleman. Nothing untoward is going to happen."

"This is going to be the end of me," William lamented as he followed her. "First, I delivered that letter to him, and now, if you don't come back, they're all like to think I helped you run away. Mr. Townsend will let me go without a reference. I know he will. I'll be left to starve in the streets."

"I won't leave you to starve in the streets," Philly promised. "I shall mention it to Captain Heywood, and if he can't help, then I..." She thought rapidly of what remedies would be within her power. "I shall pay your wages myself out of the stipend left me by my grandfather."

William protested this generosity, but the prospect of it appeared to soothe his fears. For the remainder of their journey, he was silent.

When they turned the corner that led to the entrance of the park, Philly saw Captain Heywood's town carriage. It was glossy black, with the Earl of Gordon's coat of arms emblazoned on the door, and a team of fine bays in the harness. A liveried coachman sat on the box seat with a similarly attired footman standing on the footboard.

As Philly, William, and the dogs approached, the footman leapt down and opened the door of the carriage. Within seconds, Arthur Heywood had alighted.

He was dressed for the country in buckskin breeches, top boots, and a coat of dark blue superfine that set off his shoulders to magnificent effect.

Philly's heartbeat quickened. She scolded herself. It was only Captain Heywood. Her friend and confidante. But he looked extraordinarily tall and handsome—and much more intimidating than he had in the park yesterday.

She supposed it was nothing more than wedding day nerves. A rational explanation, to be sure. And yet, as he approached her, she still found it very hard to look at him.

"Miss Satterthwaite, I hope nothing is amiss." There was a note of uncertainty in his gruff voice.

Good gracious, had he thought she wasn't coming? That she wouldn't keep her word? The very idea made her feel a little braver.

"Good morning, Captain Heywood. Forgive me for being so late." She paused as he lifted her valise from her hand and passed it off to the waiting footman. "There have been a few difficulties, but all is well now. Except—"

"What is it?" he asked at once. "I'll remedy it if I can."

"It's William, sir. He kindly came along as my chaperone, and now, as a result of my leaving with you, he may well lose his place."

An odd expression passed over Captain Heywood's face. Was it relief? "Yes, of course." He turned to address William. "As it happens, I'm in need of someone who is capable of helping with Miss Satterthwaite's dogs on occasion. If you're prepared to leave service with Townsend and come down to the West Country, I can offer you a place with us."

William looked between Philly and Captain Heywood in confusion. "With *us*?" he echoed. "Do you mean...with the *both* of you, sir?"

"Miss Satterthwaite and I are to be married this morning."

William was dumbfounded. "Well, I never would've... Why, this is..." He smiled broadly. "It would be an honor, sir. I'll just have to fetch my things from Mr. Townsend's and—"

"I'd rather you come along with us now," Captain Heywood said. "I'll send someone to collect your belongings after the wedding."

"Yes, sir. Whatever you say." William thanked them profusely, and then, in his exuberance, proceeded to assist Philly and Fox into the carriage.

Captain Heywood waited for Basil, Jasper, and Dash to jump in before climbing into the carriage himself and sitting down in the seat across from Philly.

"I began to think you wouldn't come," he said once they were underway. "When half an hour had passed, I was almost sure of it."

Securely inside the carriage, Philly began to experience the full effects of her ordeal. All the courage she'd mustered to get past Evans drained away. "I began to think so, as well." Her voice trembled. "Evans was in the hall when I came downstairs. He attempted to take hold of me and prevent me from leaving, but Basil and Fox scared him away. I was so frightened."

Captain Heywood moved from his seat and came to sit beside her.

"He said he was going to wake Mrs. Vale, and by now he must have done so. She and my uncle will know I've run away. Do you think they'll have any idea where to find me? Do you think they'll try...?" Her voice trailed off as Captain Heywood picked up her gloved hand and held it gently in his. She looked at him, her heart pounding hard in her chest.

"Is this all right?" he asked.

She moistened her lips. "Yes."

"You needn't be afraid anymore, Miss Satterthwaite. You're safe now. No one save William knows you've come to meet me, and I've made sure he won't be free to speak of it until after we're wed."

"I hadn't thought of that. In truth, I've overlooked so many things."

"Have you?"

Philly's hand was small and slender in his larger one. It was his left hand. The one that was so badly scarred. She couldn't see the scars now, for he was wearing gloves, but the memory of them compelled her to squeeze his hand.

Captain Heywood's fingers immediately closed protectively around hers. "What sorts of things?"

She swallowed. "As you see, I've come to you with practically nothing except for myself and my dogs. The little I managed to pack won't get me through more than a day or two. I'd hoped to send for the rest of my belongings once we arrive in Somerset-shire, but now I think of it, I'm not sure Mrs. Vale will be in any mood to oblige me."

"I've arranged for all of your things to come with us when we leave London. You needn't waste a moment of worry over it."

"Have you? But how?" A jolt of alarm went through her. "Surely you don't mean us to go to my uncle's house on our way out of London? I don't think it advisable. They'll all be furious, and there's certain to be an awful scene."

"Don't make yourself uneasy. You'll never have to see your uncle again, I assure you. My solicitor will deal with him. The servants will tend to the packing of your things and your trunks won't be long behind us on the baggage coach. At the very most, you'll be without them for one night."

Philly exhaled an unsteady breath. "Thank you, Arthur. I believe you've thought of everything."

Captain Heywood went very still. There was an oddly arrested expression on his face. "That's the first time you've ever called me Arthur."

"I suppose it is. But if we're to be married today, I think it must be permissible."

"It's more than permissible. In fact, I like it very well." He paused. "Shall I call you Phyllida from now on?"

"If you prefer it, but I'd much rather you call me Philly."

"Philly?"

"No one ever called me Phyllida until I came to London." She raised her eyes to his in guarded expectation. "To my real family I've only ever been Philly."

He met her gaze, seeming to immediately comprehend the significance of what she was telling him. "Then you shall be Philly to me, as well." His thumb moved across her hand. "Unless we're being very formal, in which case I'll be obliged to call you Mrs. Heywood."

"Mrs. Heywood," Philly repeated. "She sounds like another person, and yet in less than an hour, I shall be her."

"Yes," he vowed. "You most definitely shall be."

SEVENTEEN

*U*pon arrival at the Earl of Gordon's townhouse, Philly asked for a few minutes to repair her hair and dress. With the assistance of a very competent housemaid, she removed her spencer robe, revealing the same sprigged muslin gown she'd often worn to church on Sundays in Fox Cross. It wasn't as dazzling as some of her newer London-made clothes, but it was her own best gown and she was really quite pleased with the elegant simplicity of it. The maid helped to arrange her hair, and after re-pinning it, tucked a small spray of white flowers into her tresses. Philly didn't think she could have looked any better.

When she came back downstairs, Arthur and the vicar were waiting for her in the lavishly appointed drawing room. Several vases of flowers had been placed throughout for the occasion, and William, the earl's butler, Underhill, and two of the house-maids were in attendance. It all felt very much like a real wedding ought, and as Philly took her place at Arthur's side and the vicar began to read out the ceremony from the Book of Common Prayer, she found it harder and harder to accept that theirs was to be a marriage in name only.

When Arthur took her bare hand in his for the first time, Philly's heart beat so heavily that she was sure he must have heard it. And when he put the sparkling ruby wedding ring on her finger, her breath caught in her throat.

If Arthur was similarly affected, he didn't show it. He evinced a quiet satisfaction at Philly's response to her wedding band, but otherwise seemed intent on getting the business of the marriage over and done with. On one occasion, Philly thought his hand might have trembled as it held hers. She was sure she must be mistaken. Arthur had fought in the Peninsula. A wedding ceremony was hardly going to shake his nerves.

For Philly, however, every single word that was read by the vicar excited a new depth of feeling. By the time the ceremony was complete, she was so overcome with emotion that she could say precious little to anyone. They were congratulated by all of the servants, enthusiastically by William (who was the first to call her Mrs. Heywood), and more sedately by Underhill and the rest of the staff. They partook of a small wedding breakfast, which neither had much of an appetite for. And then, before Philly knew it, the same maid who had helped her to dress for the wedding was assisting her back into her spencer robe—which was to serve in lieu of a carriage gown—and she and Arthur were ensconced in his luxurious travelling coach and on their way out of London.

It was a cold morning, and Philly kept her gloves on against the chill but discarded her hat as soon as they climbed into the coach. It now lay on the seat beside her, along with Fox and Dash. Jasper was resting next to Arthur, his wet nose nestled between his two front paws, and Basil had managed to curl his large body comfortably on the floor.

Philly had a copy of *The Odyssey* she'd borrowed from the

earl's library spread out over her lap. The leather-bound volume was filled with beautiful etchings. She spent the first hour of their journey poring over them as the coach traveled at a rapid clip down the Bath Road. Whenever she glanced up from her reading, Arthur was still gazing out the window, deeply immersed in some melancholy thought of his own.

"Do you dislike talking during a long journey?" she asked.

Arthur turned to look at her. "I beg your pardon?"

"I'll be quite happy to continue with my book if you like it to be quiet, but if not, then I thought that perhaps we might talk."

"If it pleases you. What would you like to talk about?"

Philly stroked Fox's head with her gloved hand. "I have some questions about my role in your household."

"Your role?" His brow creased. "You're my wife, of course."

"Yes, quite, but you said it was to be a marriage in name only. That you were offering me your name and nothing more. I wouldn't like to presume anything."

"What would you be presuming?"

"Well, if our marriage were to progress like any other marriage—" She broke off with a flush of embarrassment. "That is to say, a new bride upon arriving at her husband's home would begin to oversee things related to the household. She'd meet with the housekeeper and—"

"I didn't marry you to gain a servant to run my household."

"No, of course not, but I don't wish to run your household as a servant might do. I..." She hesitated for a fraction of a second. "I'd like to be mistress of your house, Arthur, as any wife would be. But if you'd rather I not interfere with things—"

"You have all the authority of the Heywood name, Philly. You may do with it what you will. Don't forget that no one else even knows of our particular arrangement. To the rest of the world, you're simply my wife, with all of the rights that come with it. I won't gainsay you in household affairs."

He acceded to her so easily that Philly was given to suspect that he had very little interest in the running of his household. She brightened nonetheless. "You won't be disappointed. I have a particular talent for managing a great house, you see. Why, I was running Satterthwaite Court while I was still sewing samplers."

"I've no doubt." He looked once more out the carriage window, his expression grim. "Heywood House may not be as great as you imagine."

"No?"

"Don't mistake me, it's a grand old place, but most of it's shut up now, and I've kept on very few servants."

She nodded. "You've preferred to live quietly."

"I don't know if it's a preference, but it's how I've lived since coming back from the Peninsula."

Philly hesitated. Arthur had never mentioned anything related to the war before. She was wary of saying the wrong thing. "Did no one come to stay with you when you first returned? Your father or your brother, perhaps?"

"In the beginning, yes, there was an excessive amount of company. I found myself quite unequal to it. I couldn't bear the noise and all of the activity. Nor could I bring myself to be amiable to my guests for any length of time. Within two months, everyone had happily gone and left me alone again. Since then, I've had no one to stay, and there have been few callers. It's...easier."

She sighed. "Oh Arthur, will I disrupt your life very much?"

He turned his attention from the window, his gaze coming to rest on her face. "No, Philly. Not you."

"I shall try not to. But even in a large house, we won't be able to avoid each other completely."

"Did you think I intended that we would?"

"I hoped you wouldn't, but I wasn't certain. Everything has happened so quickly, and there's been no time to discuss any of the particulars. I don't know anything about Heywood House or the servants. Why, I don't even know the name of your village."

"Heycombe."

"Heycombe? Your family must have been there a very long time."

"Several generations. Heywood House was the estate of Richard Heywood, a second son of the Earl of Gordon over one hundred years ago. When his elder brother was killed, Richard inherited the earldom. He gave Heywood House to his own second son. It's been the residence of the second sons of the Earls of Gordon ever since."

"So, you have charge of the estate quite independently of your father?"

"For the term of my life."

"It must be a great deal of responsibility."

"It's not a heavy burden. The lands are prosperous and the tenants keep to themselves. My steward handles much of the day-to-day business of running the estate. In truth, he could do it quite well without me, and has done so during the years of my absence."

"What is his name?"

"Bernard Pebmarsh."

Philly committed the name to memory. "And your housekeeper?"

"Mrs. Lamb."

"Mrs. Lamb," she repeated to herself. "Oh, I do wish I'd thought to bring a bit of paper and a pencil. I might have taken notes on these things."

"You needn't worry about any of this, Philly. If you took it in your head to dismiss the entire staff and start afresh, I'd have no objection. They're none of them the sort of lifelong retainers you had at Satterthwaite Court. Save for Pebmarsh and a few others, most were newly employed when I returned from Spain."

"I shouldn't like to start out my tenure as your wife by dismissing all of your staff. I'd much rather get along with everyone. Naturally, the servants won't be disposed to like me at first—"

"Why the devil not?"

"Servants like to be prepared for things so they can show themselves at their best. They take a great deal of pride in their work. It will put them in a taking to have a new mistress appear so unexpectedly—"

"They *are* expecting us."

She looked at him in surprise. "Are they?"

"Yesterday morning, I sent my butler, Crofton, an express. I informed him we'd be arriving late this evening, and that we'd have your four dogs with us. The servants will have had ample time to see that all is in readiness."

"Oh, Arthur, you *have* thought of everything." Philly sank back into her seat. "I do so want to start out well. With the servants—and with the villagers in Heycombe."

He raised his brows. "The villagers, too?"

"Naturally. In Fox Cross, I often accompanied our vicar's wife, Mrs. Webb, on her visits to the sick and the poor. I'd bring them special hampers from Satterthwaite Court, and sometimes, if they wished it, I would read aloud to them or help with their sewing."

"An angel of mercy, in fact."

"Hardly that. Most of the villagers wished us at Jericho. Mrs. Webb had the disagreeable habit of sermonizing to every poor soul we called upon. They would endure it, of course, but I used to think it a high price to pay for nothing but a hamper full of supporting broths and restorative jellies."

"Good God, not *Dr. Ratcliffe's Restorative Jelly*?"

"You have some familiarity?"

Arthur grimaced. "More than I care to remember."

"It *is* vile," Philly agreed. "But you needn't fear. When you're next ill, I shall feed you nothing but cream cakes and jam tarts."

No sooner had she uttered the words than she wished them back again. The very idea that *she'd* be the one to care for him when he was ill, as if she were a real wife, and theirs a real marriage.

But Arthur didn't seem to mind the intimacy of her jest. He leaned back against his seat, stretched his legs out in front of him as far as he could in the close confines of the carriage, and said, quite gallantly, "I see I shall have to contrive to become ill more often."

Philly laughed, even as her stomach turned over. Was he flirting with her? Surely not. It was merely harmless banter. The flattering sort that gentlemen indulged in with ladies. And yet...

"I've never heard you laugh before," he said.

She blinked. "Haven't you?"

"I've often wondered what it would sound like."

Had he not looked so dreadfully serious, Philly might have thought he was teasing her. He'd been thinking about her? He'd been wondering about her laugh? For a moment she didn't know where to look. "You were no doubt disappointed," she said, thankful her voice didn't betray her quaking heart.

"On the contrary. It was everything I'd hoped it would be."

She waited for him to elaborate, but he said nothing more on the subject, instead resuming their previous conversation as if no interruption had taken place.

"Are you in earnest about continuing your charitable endeavors in Heycombe?" he asked.

"Completely. Why? Would it not be welcome?"

He folded his arms, his broad shoulders straining against the fabric of his coat. "You may be disappointed. The village is an exceedingly small one, with precious few people worth visiting. And there's no vicar's wife. Frankly, I can't envision a woman who would willingly fill the position. Mr. Fordham is a dour, miserable man with more about him of fire and brimstone than Christian charity."

She frowned. "These older vicars can sometimes be difficult. They're set in their ways, and often their advanced age makes them cantankerous and short-tempered. Perhaps Mr. Fordham might be persuaded to retire soon?"

"Mr. Fordham is not yet thirty years old," Arthur said. And, for the first time in their acquaintance, a smile flickered across his face.

Philly didn't fail to recognize it. "You think me very silly, don't you?" she said with a faint smile of her own.

"I think you very sweet."

She blushed with self-conscious pleasure. To her amazement, Arthur reddened a little himself. Had he not, she might never have had the nerve, but the sight of his discomfiture so emboldened her, that without stopping to consider, she declared, "If I were sitting next to you, I would take your hand just as you took mine this morning."

Arthur looked steadily back at her, an expression in his eyes that was hard to read. "Would you indeed?"

She sensed a hint of a challenge in his words. "Yes. I do believe I would."

He cast a glance at the small space on the seat that existed between him and Jasper. "Regrettably, your dog has not left any room for you."

"Oh, hasn't he?" Driven more by impulse than sense, Philly rose from her seat. At that very moment, the coach shuddered heavily, and without warning, careened sharply to one side. Philly was hurled across the cabin.

Arthur reacted instantly, lunging forward to catch her around the waist before she fell. "Careful!"

Philly had instinctively clung to his neck as he caught her, and now, draped across his chest with her face only inches from his, she found herself in the rather singular position of being held, for the very first time, in Captain Arthur Heywood's arms. "My goodness," she breathed. "Did we break a wheel?"

"No. It was likely nothing but an uneven patch of road." His voice was rough with concern. "Are you all right?"

"Perfectly all right." She moved her hands to his shoulders, making an effort to right herself.

He helped to ease her off of his lap and down into the seat beside him. "Perhaps you shouldn't get up again while the coach is moving?"

"I suppose not."

Basil raised his head to see what had happened, and Fox's ears twitched in annoyance, but as soon as the carriage was rolling along again on even ground they all resumed their former positions of drowsy indifference.

"The dogs don't appear to have minded the upset at all." Philly stole a sidelong glance at Arthur and saw that his eyes were still upon her. A wave of shyness assailed her. Her impulse to hold his hand seemed clumsy and childish now. The action of a young girl rather than a newly married woman.

She wondered what Lady Eliot would have done in the same situation. She was far too sophisticated to have lost her balance and fallen. But if she had, she wouldn't have blushed and lowered her eyes when Arthur caught her in his embrace, nor would she have pulled away from him. No. Lady Eliot would have stayed in his arms and waited for him to kiss her.

Or she would have kissed him.

Had they kissed before? The thought struck Philly almost painfully. Arthur said he'd never loved Lady Eliot, but he must have felt something for her once in order to have proposed. And, as Philly had observed at the Worthings' ball, Lady Eliot was an accomplished flirt with a string of lovers to her credit. She wasn't the sort of lady to have shied away from kissing her own betrothed.

"Philly."

Arthur's quiet voice wrenched Philly from her rather disheartening reflections. She looked up at him. "Yes?"

He held out his hand to her.

Her heart leapt in her breast. She met his gaze for a moment, and then, before she could question the wisdom of such an action, she removed the glove on her left hand. Once she'd done so, she watched with a quickening pulse as Arthur stripped off his right glove.

When his hand was bare, he held it out to her again. In response to the invitation, she slid her hand slowly into his.

His fingers closed over hers.

Neither said a word, but in that moment, all thoughts of Lady Eliot were banished from Philly's mind.

EIGHTEEN

*W*ith the temperate weather and their well-sprung coach, they made remarkably good time on their journey out of London. Their stops thus far had all been brief ones, made only out of necessity. They never spoke of Philly being in danger from her uncle, or from the Duke of Moreland. Even so, Arthur couldn't help but feel that, on some deep level, she understood the urgency in getting quickly and safely to Heywood House.

He didn't believe Moreland or Townsend would send someone to recover her. What could possibly be achieved by such an act? She wasn't some young girl who had been spirited away to Gretna Green. She was a woman grown who had been wed to him quite respectably by a vicar in the Earl of Gordon's drawing room.

Their marriage couldn't be undone. Townsend would have known that within two hours of her having run away, and the duke would likely have heard of it soon after.

No, if Moreland decided to send someone after them it wouldn't be for the purpose of retrieving Philly. It would be for the purpose of vengeance.

But what sort of vengeance could the duke possibly hope to exact?

Philly may have been referred to as The Work of Art for a time, but she was no painting that could be slashed to ribbons by a highwayman. Besides which, though stories abounded of Moreland's swift and brutal retaliation against those who denied him possession of an object he desired, none of those stories had ever been proven true. They were probably nothing more than sinister fictions perpetuated by gentlemen in their cups.

Arthur had been reminding himself of that ever since they left London. And yet, as he looked at his new bride sitting so contentedly next to him in the coach, her slender fingers idly turning the pages of the book she was reading, the stories about Moreland's vengeance—stories of robbery, arson, and murder—no longer seemed so unbelievable. Arthur was possessed with an almost primitive urge to protect her and to keep her safe from harm.

Philly glanced up at him, appearing to notice for the first time how intently he was watching her. When she met his eyes, her expression softened and her mouth lifted into a smile.

Warmth crept up Arthur's neck. He felt a resurgence of the same painful ache of longing that had been his near constant companion since the beginning of their journey.

If I were sitting next to you, I would take your hand just as you took mine this morning.

Did she have any idea how much those words had affected him? How much they'd encouraged him to hope? And then, when she'd removed her glove! How the devil had he managed to keep his countenance? He had wanted to embrace her. To kiss her full, soft mouth and tangle his fingers into her hair.

Instead, they'd held hands for over an hour. Periods of companionable silence broken only by the occasional exchange about

Heycombe or Heywood House. Had Fox not woken and proceeded to scrabble about on the opposite seat, they might be holding hands still.

"He must be frightened," she'd said, gathering the little terrier up into her arms. "No doubt he's remembering those terrible people who threw him from that carriage in Fox Cross."

But as she'd hugged Fox close, even going so far as to place a much-coveted kiss on his scraggly head, Arthur could have sworn that the smug little beast met his eyes rather shrewdly. As if to convey to him the superior position he held in the hierarchy of his mistress's affections.

Arthur couldn't recall when he'd ever been more irritated with an animal.

"Would you like to see the etching?" Philly angled the book for him. "It's Odysseus imprisoned in Calypso's cave."

The flickering flames from the carriage lamps cast the pages in shadow. "How can you manage to read anything in this dim light?"

"It helps that I'm so familiar with the story. I used to read it aloud to my grandfather—though his copy of *The Odyssey* wasn't so grand as this. Did your father have the etchings commissioned?"

"He may have done. You can ask him yourself when you meet him."

She turned another page. "Do you expect I shall meet him anytime soon?"

"Within a month, if I'm not mistaken."

"A month!" She looked up at him with a start.

"Yesterday, when I was at my solicitor's, I sent an express to my father informing him of our intention to marry." Arthur paused, adding, "It wouldn't have done for him to hear it first from someone else."

"Who do you imagine might have told him? So few people know of it."

"Within a week, all of England will know of it. I instructed my solicitor to put a notice of our marriage in the papers." Arthur winced at the look of alarm that came over her face. For a half second, he wondered if he'd been too high-handed in his arrangements. "The gossip would have spread like wildfire in any case. I hoped we could forestall some of it by seeing that everything was done properly. Unfortunately, there was no time to take you to meet my father, but he'll have received my express by now, and if I know anything about him, he'll already be arranging his affairs so he might leave Hampshire in as early as a fortnight."

"Yes, I see. You did quite right to tell your father, of course, but...whyever would he want to come so hastily? Do you think... Will he be very angry that you've married?"

"Angry?" Arthur was surprised by her conclusion. "Not in the least. He'll be elated." The countryside was glowing softly in the moonlight. He could just make out the high steeple of the village church in the distance. "Look out your window, Philly."

She did as he bid her. Her face instantly brightened. "Is that Heycombe?"

"It is. Heywood House is just beyond those hills. We should arrive in less than half an hour. And when we do, I suggest you go straight to bed. William can take charge of the dogs."

"I'm not at all tired."

Arthur gave her an appraising look. For all he admired her beauty, he couldn't deceive himself that Philly was anything less than thoroughly worn down. Her gown was creased and rumpled, most of the pins had worked free from her hair, and despite having briefly availed herself of his shoulder, she hadn't closed her eyes even once during the more than fifteen-hour journey.

"You're plainly exhausted," he said.

She glanced at him over her shoulder, her eyes sparkling with sudden humor. "I daresay I am," she admitted. "I'm just far too excited to notice it yet."

Heywood House appeared in a swathe of moonlight as they crested the final hill in their path. The classical Palladian structure was built of granite, which had weathered over the years, and under the full moon, made the house look as if it were composed of silvery shadows rather than gray stone. It was a building of perfect proportions, set back amid untamed parkland, and completely unmarred by any of the hotchpotch of sprawling architectural additions that had characterized Satterthwaite Court.

"Do you like it?" Arthur asked.

"Very much," Philly said. "Very much indeed."

As the coach advanced smoothly up the expansive drive, she could see even more how the countryside had grown up around the massive house. It was as wild and rustic as a wilderness garden, lending Heywood House an air of enchantment, as if it had been untouched by human hands for several generations, frozen in time under some magic spell.

Torches lit the way to the front entrance of the house, and as the coach slowed to a halt, a flurry of servants hurried out to meet them. In no time at all, a footman was opening the door and lowering the step. Behind him, William stood waiting to assist with the dogs.

During the course of the long journey, William had proven himself invaluable. He'd taken charge of the dogs at every stop;

calming a snarling Basil, preventing Jasper and Dash from chasing after a postilion they'd taken a dislike to, and narrowly stopping Fox from biting the hand of a small child who had attempted to stroke his head. Now, he moved swiftly to apprehend the three larger dogs as they leapt from the carriage.

Arthur alighted after them, and then handed Philly down himself. "There will be a fire in the kitchen," he said to William. "You might take them there."

"Yes, do, William." Philly settled Fox in the young footman's arms. "Fox's leg will be aching from the cold. It's no wonder he's been so cross."

"I'll look after them, ma'am," William said. "You needn't worry."

Having seen to her dogs, Philly tucked her hand into Arthur's proffered arm. He led her to the stone steps that flanked the arched entryway of Heywood House. Glancing up at him, she was startled to see an expression of pride on his face. Pride in her as his wife, she realized with amazement. She immediately resolved that she wouldn't disappoint him.

They were met by Crofton, the elderly white-haired butler, and Mrs. Lamb, the severe-looking housekeeper, as well as a handful of other servants who had lined up to see their new mistress. The sight of Philly's mismatched eyes invariably caused them to start, and many looked from her to their implacable master with unconcealed bewilderment. Despite their dismay, and her own shyness, Philly offered a kind word and a warm smile to each person who greeted her.

She received few smiles in return.

Her spirits sank a little at the lukewarm welcome.

"There's a light meal if you're hungry," Mrs. Lamb said as she accompanied them into the house. "Cold meat and a little wine. The fire in your room has been lit, and I've seen to a thorough cleaning and fresh linens. Violet! Tend to the unpacking of Mrs. Heywood's bags. Violet will be at your service until you engage a lady's maid, Mrs. Heywood."

A dark-haired girl with a pale, pinched face gave Philly a neat curtsey.

"I'll not keep you from your duties long," Philly told her. "I hope to engage a girl from the village by the end of the month."

"Yes, ma'am." Violet curtsied again before taking Philly's valise from one of the footmen and disappearing back into the throng of servants.

"From the village, Mrs. Heywood?" Mrs. Lamb's voice was as cold and unwelcoming as her expression. "You'll never find a proper lady's maid amongst the girls in Heycombe. They wouldn't know the first thing about caring for fine clothes or arranging your hair."

"I don't mind inexperience, Mrs. Lamb. At Satterthwaite Court, I always trained my own lady's maids from girls in the village."

Mrs. Lamb looked skeptical, but held her tongue.

After the initial furor of their arrival, things calmed enough that Philly was able to speak once more with William about the care of her dogs. When she'd satisfied herself that all would go well with them for the night, she joined Arthur at the immense mahogany table in the dining room to have something to eat.

As she passed through the house, she saw that the interior was very much in the same classical style as the exterior. There were molded ceilings with gracefully ornamented plasterwork, and white-paneled walls spaced with Ionic pilasters. The carved marble fireplaces were enormous, rivaled in size only by some of the great landscape paintings that covered large expanses of the walls. And the furnishings, though obviously old and out of fashion, still retained a comfortable elegance with their faded silk damasks and well-worn velvets.

After they'd eaten, Arthur advised that she retire for the night. He'd seemed to be increasingly preoccupied since they sat down together. Philly assumed he must have some estate business to attend to before he could retire himself.

"Sleep well," he said to her as Mrs. Lamb came to take her to her room.

"Goodnight." Philly wanted to say more. To thank him, and tell him that she would be forever grateful—forever in his debt—for the service he had done her.

But such words would be inappropriate in front of the servants.

She followed Mrs. Lamb back into the main hall, and up the grand, sweeping staircase that curved to the floors above.

The housekeeper led the way down a dimly lit corridor. She stopped in front of a large paneled door and opened it for Philly to enter. "I'll send up Violet. If you need anything more than she can provide, have her fetch me."

Philly thanked the housekeeper and bid her goodnight. After shutting the door firmly behind her, she turned to look at her new bedroom. It was not as well lived in as the other parts of the house she'd seen. Indeed, she had a sense that this particular room had been shut up for a very long time. It was large and rather lonely, though the thick Aubusson carpets that covered the floor and the crackling fire in the hearth made everything seem cozier than it otherwise would have been.

She paced the length of the room, running her hand along the carved mahogany furniture and the faded blue damask hangings that surrounded the four-poster bed. There was a truly monstrous wardrobe, a cheval mirror with a tarnished plate, and a writing desk stocked with foolscap, quills, and ink. A paneled door led into a well-appointed dressing room and a second paneled door appeared to connect her bedroom with another.

Curious, Philly went to the connecting door and tested the doorknob. It turned easily in her hand. She was just opening it to take a peek inside when she realized exactly whose bedroom the connecting door must lead to.

She jerked her hand from the doorknob, a jolt of anxiety running through her as quick and sharp as a lightning strike.

Did Arthur know that the servants had placed her in the room adjoining his own? And why was the door unlocked?

She gave herself a little shake. Gracious heaven. There was no reason to act like a silly pea-goose. She was Arthur's wife now. Naturally the servants would have put her in the room adjoining his. They didn't know that she was his wife in name only.

Turning her attention back to her own bedroom, she spent a few more minutes in exploration, before sitting down at the draped dressing table and unpinning her hair. She brushed it through, a full hundred strokes, as she waited for Violet to come and help her undress.

The maid had obviously already been there once. The few belongings Philly had brought with her had been unpacked. Her rose soap and toothpowder were on the washstand, and her lawn nightgown was laid out on the end of the bed next to her ruffled white dressing gown. When she was done brushing her hair, she came and sat on the bed beside them for a while.

After a time, when Violet had still not arrived, Philly began to undress on her own.

She was able to strip down to her chemise and stays without too much trouble. However, when she attempted to unlace her stays, she found they were tied in an immoveable knot. She struggled with it, straining to see behind herself as she felt the laces with her fingers.

It was no use.

In her hurry to dress that morning, she'd tugged her laces so tight and tied them so securely that they could never be undone without a maid's help.

With a heavy sigh, Philly sank down in the large velvet arm-chair in the corner of her room and waited for Violet to arrive. She debated summoning someone, but didn't like to ring the bell pull so late at night. She was certain Violet had been waylaid with some task or other and would come eventually.

An hour passed.

Too tired to wait any longer, Philly resigned herself to going to bed in her stays. She rose from the chair.

And immediately stilled.

Voices sounded from the adjoining room, followed by the closing of a door. It was Arthur, finally retiring for the night. It sounded as though he'd just dismissed his valet.

Philly bit her lip. She didn't want to sleep in her stays if she could avoid it. And Arthur was not only her husband, he was her friend. Surely, he wouldn't mind unlacing her before he went to bed? She fretted over asking him for help, changing her mind several times before at last slipping on her dressing gown and going to the connecting door. She took a deep, steadying breath.

And then she knocked.

NINETEEN

rthur had already discarded his coat and cravat when he heard the tentative knock. A jolt of alarm shot through him. Philly had retired hours ago. He hadn't expected to hear from her until the morning. Was something amiss?

He crossed the floor of his room and opened the connecting door, not giving a thought to his state of undress. His mouth opened, and—

Whatever he'd meant to say evaporated into the ether. He was confronted by a sight that robbed him of speech, as well as breath.

Philly was in her dressing gown, her dark auburn hair falling in a magnificent cascade around her shoulders.

It took him several seconds to compose himself. "What is it?" he asked gruffly. "Is something wrong?"

"No, I..." Philly's gaze drifted from his chest, to his shoulders, and then to his bare neck. She moistened her lips. "It's rather silly. The maid never came to help me undress—"

"Have you been waiting this whole time?"

"Yes, but—"

"I'll ring for someone."

"No." She caught his arm as he began to move away. He stilled at her touch. "Please don't, Arthur. It's far too late, and now I've waited too long. It will be terribly embarrassing. I've managed very well myself, and there's only a slight problem, which I hope you might help me with, and then I shall go to bed. I can start fresh with the servants tomorrow."

Arthur frowned. He couldn't for the life of him understand Philly's concern over what the servants thought of her, but he had no intention of going against her wishes. "What would you like me to do?"

"I can't get my stays untied."

"*Your stays?*"

"I had to dress myself this morning, and I've somehow got the laces into a terrible tangle. I've been trying to unknot them myself for the last hour, but I fear I've only made things worse."

His heart thumped hard. He didn't know what to say. She was standing in front of him looking so beautiful and so vulnerable, and all at once he no longer felt merely protective of her, he felt possessive. She was his wife. No matter what arrangement had brought them to this point, she belonged to him now. Would it be so ungentlemanly, so dishonorable, to take her in his arms?

"Arthur, do you mind trying to untie them?" she asked.

"No, I don't mind." He glanced at his cane. His mood instantly sobered. "But unless you think I can do it one-handed, we'll have to sit down."

"Oh, yes, of course." She looked about his room, her eyes finally alighting on his bed. It was a giant carved mahogany four-poster, not unlike the one in her own chamber.

Arthur followed her gaze, and after a few weighted seconds, he motioned toward it. "If you like."

She went ahead of him and sat on the edge of the mattress. He sat down next to her and waited. After a brief moment of hesitation, she turned her back to him, untied her dressing gown, and let it slide off her shoulders and down to her waist. She then gathered up the bulk of her hair, holding it out of the way so that he could see what he was doing.

If she'd intended a more seductive scene, she couldn't have designed one. Arthur could only stare at her: the graceful curve of her neck, her daintily rounded bare arms, and her slender fingers threaded through the mass of her thick hair. His blood warmed and his mouth went dry. Only by focusing with a single-minded intensity on unknotting the laces of her stays was he prevented from reaching out to her in some more intimate manner.

"I expect you had business to attend to this evening," she said.

"Business? What business?"

"You've been preoccupied since we arrived, and you're late coming to your room. I thought..."

His hands stilled on her laces.

"Forgive me," she said. "I didn't mean to pry."

"You needn't ask my forgiveness. You're right, I've been preoccupied since we arrived, but it has nothing to do with matters of business."

She asked him no more about it, and after several fraught seconds, he resumed his efforts to untie her stays. She was as quiet and immobile as a statue, only moving once to gather a few stray locks of hair that had escaped from her grasp.

"Are you making any progress?" she asked after another long while.

"By God, no," Arthur muttered. The knot was so fast and secure that he couldn't see where it ended and where it began.

He continued to work on it for some time in a state of abject frustration. As he struggled, he was struck more and more by the utter absurdity of his situation. It was almost humorous. "Do you realize what this is, Philly? It's a blasted Gordian knot."

She smiled at him over her shoulder.

"I believe I'll have to apply the Alexandrian solution." He rose and went to his desk to retrieve a pair of scissors. "Do you mind if I cut through the laces?" he asked as he sat back down behind her.

"If you think you must."

"I'll be exceedingly careful." He placed the scissors against the back of her stays and, with one sharp snip, cut through the knot. "There," he pronounced. "I've freed you."

Philly let her hair fall from her hands and slid her arms back into her dressing gown. She fumbled with the tie for a moment, cinching it tightly around her waist, before turning on the bed and lifting her eyes to his face.

Arthur met her enquiring gaze and held it, a deep well of longing pooling inside him as he looked at her. All the control he'd exercised while leaning over her knotted stays melted away. He could no longer stop himself from reaching out and touching a lock of her hair. It was glossy and thick between his fingers, shimmering with warmth in the flickering candlelight. "I've wanted to do this since the first day I met you."

She swallowed. "Have you? I didn't know you thought of such things."

"With increasing frequency. Indeed, it's been the source of much of my preoccupation since our wedding."

"Your desire to touch my hair?"

"Amongst other things."

"I had no idea." Seeming to be encouraged by his boldness,

Philly slowly reached up to lay a hand alongside his face. He went still as stone beneath her fingertips, ceasing to move or to breathe. "Is this all right?" she asked in a whisper.

"Yes." He spoke gruffly, but his eyes were fixed on her with extraordinary tenderness.

She stroked his cheek. "Your face isn't as smooth as it was this morning. I should like to have felt it then."

"I wish you would have."

Amusement flickered in her eyes. "That would have been rather forward of me."

"You're my wife now. You can touch me whenever you like."

"Even though ours isn't a usual marriage?"

Arthur didn't answer her. Instead, he removed his fingers from her hair and very gently stroked her cheek in an identical manner to how she was stroking his. "Your skin is softer than silk." He drew his hand down the delicate line of her jaw to cup the edge of her face, his thumb grazing gently across the side of her mouth. "I've never felt anything like it."

"I've never felt anything like you."

He gave her a fleeting smile. "I should hope not."

She smiled briefly in return as she mirrored his gentle touches with those of her own. She caressed the hard planes of his cheek, his stubble-roughened jaw, and even that sensitive part of his throat usually concealed behind an elegantly folded cravat.

He watched her face as she explored him, feeling a tremor of anticipation as she lightly touched the nape of his neck, unintentionally drawing him closer. "My God, but you're lovely, Philly."

Her eyes met his. "I think you very handsome, as well."

His heart lurched in his chest. "Do you?" He made an effort to keep his tone light. "I had no idea. But then, I didn't even suspect you were fond of me until you threatened to hold my hand."

Her hand fell from his neck. "Please don't laugh about that, Arthur."

"I wouldn't laugh. If I find any humor in the situation at all, it's only in my own reaction."

"You had no marked reaction."

"Not outwardly, perhaps, but on the inside, I assure you, I was as anxious to hold your hand as an untried youth courting his first young lady."

"I wish you were an untried youth."

At Philly's words, Arthur's hand froze on her face. He stared down at her.

"I'm sorry," she said in a rush. "I shouldn't have said that. It's just that..." A blush rose in her cheeks. "I think all of your previous ladies must have been terribly sophisticated. Every time I say or do something, I imagine you're comparing me with them."

Arthur didn't know how to respond to such an admission. "Has this truly been worrying you?"

"I know I shouldn't have said anything. It's silly and foolish and—"

"I don't compare you with anyone, Philly."

She looked up at him, startled by his vehemence.

"Since the day I met you, I haven't even thought of another woman. Indeed, I've been hard pressed to think of anything else at all." He brushed a lock of hair from her face. "As for these 'previous ladies' you speak of, there haven't been so many as you suppose. Besides which, it was all a very long time ago, and none of it worth remembering. I'm far more interested in the present. Here with you."

He continued to stroke her face and her hair. Under such gentle ministration, the shyness and anxiety she'd exhibited only moments before faded away. It wasn't long before she was once again touching him with as much tenderness as he touched her.

"What am I to do with you, Mrs. Heywood?" he asked quietly.

"Do with me?"

"I've vowed to you that ours will be a marriage in name only, but I find such a vow difficult to keep at present."

"I don't mind it."

"You're not thinking clearly, my sweet. You haven't been thinking clearly since you came to me yesterday morning in the park. I've already taken advantage of you by marrying you so quickly. I won't compound the damage by breaking my promise to you."

"You haven't taken advantage of me."

"I proposed to you when you were desperate and upset. Had the circumstances been different—"

"My answer would have been the same. Truly, Arthur, I would have accepted you had you proposed to me the night of my uncle's dinner party."

He drew back from her. "What?"

"When we parted in the drawing room, could you not see how grieved I was to lose you? My heart was breaking."

"Philly..." He shook his head. "You don't know me. You don't know what kind of man I am. If you did—"

"But I do. You're a man of honor. The only one I could turn to for help in my time of trouble."

"You're grateful to me."

"It's more than gratitude. Can you not see that? Why, I even gave you my hairpin as a token of my affection. Surely you must have recognized my feelings for you then? It was a rather childish gesture, I know, but..." Her words died on her lips as, before her eyes, he reached into a small pocket in his waistcoat and produced the hairpin of painted gold and glass. She stared at it in disbelief before raising her eyes back to his. "You've kept it with you?"

"I wanted to believe that you cared for me. That I was more to you than just your friend. But it seemed somehow impossible. I dared not hope—"

"I do care for you, Arthur. I care for you most dreadfully."

Arthur looked down at her, his chest tightening on a flood of emotion. Caught up in its swell, he took her in his arms, and with a fierce tenderness, lowered his mouth to hers and kissed her.

Philly's lips parted in surprise, resulting in his initial kiss being far more intimate than he'd intended. Arthur knew he'd alarmed her. Perhaps even frightened her. She'd clearly never been kissed before. But she made no protest and she didn't pull away from him. He didn't know what he would have done if she had.

"Arthur," she breathed, one hand clutching weakly at the fabric of his waistcoat.

"I know, love. It's all right."

She looked up at him, eyes luminous, as he kissed her again. He drew her closer, pressing her firmly against his chest as his mouth moved on hers. She was so trusting. So vulnerable. It would be easy to become carried away. It didn't seem to matter that he was closer to her now than he'd ever been before. It was still not sufficient. He wanted more of her. *Needed* more of her.

But he didn't take more.

Instead he softened his kiss, gentling her and coaxing her until her eyes closed and her lips yielded endlessly to his. Philly had lips made for kissing. They were voluptuous and soft, her top lip slightly fuller than the bottom. They gave in to the slightest pressure, molding to his mouth with an unconscious sensuality that sent his pulse racing.

She didn't return his kiss. Not yet. But she was warm and sweet and trembling with passion. He framed her face in his hands, meeting her gaze for a moment before softly capturing her mouth again.

Another kiss followed.

And then another.

Each was deeper and more thorough than the last.

Philly's arms twined around his neck. She leaned into him. And the next time his mouth closed over hers, she kissed him back.

Arthur's whole body tightened in response. "Is this to be my reward, then?" he asked thickly, when they finally broke apart.

"What reward?"

"For untying the Gordian knot." He trailed kisses down the delicate flesh of her throat. Her fingers tightened in his hair and her body melted into his. He could feel every luscious contour of her small, feminine frame through the thin fabric of her night-clothes. His breath became heavy, his kisses more urgent.

"The Gordian knot?" she murmured. "Oh, yes. Of course." She caught his lower lip in hers as he kissed her.

Arthur stifled a groan deep in his throat. It had been a very long time since he'd been with a woman, but never had he experienced anything to compare with this. Philly's unschooled passion stirred his senses. She was sweet and soft, generous and welcoming. And when she looked at him, her cheeks flushed and her lips swollen from his kisses, he realized that he wanted her more than he'd ever wanted anything else in his whole life.

"What reward did Alexander the Great claim?" she asked as he began to ease her slowly back onto his bed. "I can't seem to remember."

"He became king of Asia." Arthur lowered himself down alongside her and gathered her up in his arms. "But somehow, at the moment, this reward seems entirely more satisfying."

TWENTY

Philly woke many hours later, still in Arthur's arms. For a moment she couldn't remember where she was or how she'd ended up there. When she did, a warm blush flooded throughout her entire body.

Her marriage to Captain Arthur Heywood was no longer a marriage in name only. It had been well and truly consummated. Thoroughly consummated, in fact, for after a brief period of rest, and several whispered assurances that she was, indeed, perfectly agreeable to the idea, Arthur had taken her a second time.

Philly had never experienced anything more wonderful. Or more terrifying. She'd been woefully ignorant of the intimacies of the marriage bed and hadn't known what to expect at all. She needn't have worried. Arthur had been a patient and unfailingly gentle teacher; coaxing her, caressing her, and soothing her maidenly fears with dozens of sweet words. He'd told her she was beautiful, and called her his darling and his sweetheart—endearments that still resonated in the deepest part of her being.

He hadn't said that he loved her, not in so many words, but

every kiss and every touch seemed to proclaim the depth of his feelings, and by the time Philly had drifted to sleep in his arms, she felt wholly secure in his affections.

Arthur's arm was still around her, his hand resting on her hip with a strangely possessive heaviness. Philly sighed. She felt safe where she was, but soon the sun would rise, and no matter how intimate she'd been with Arthur in the dark, she was far too shy to wake up next to him in the bright light of day without any clothes on.

With that in mind, she carefully extricated herself from his embrace and quietly rose from his bed to look for her chemise. She found it lying on the floor, not far from her mangled stays and Arthur's discarded shirt and waistcoat. She slipped the thin linen garment back on over her head, and after raking her fingers through her tangled hair to put it in some semblance of order, climbed back into bed.

As she knelt on the mattress, preparing to lie back down in the crook of Arthur's arm, she heard a deep, unintelligible murmur emanate from his side of the bed.

She went still, listening. Had he said something? If he had, she couldn't make out the words. She leaned a little closer in the darkness just as he turned his head fitfully against the pillows.

A surge of compassion rose in her breast. He was having a nightmare, poor dear. She placed her hand on his chest so that she might gently wake him up.

It was the last movement she was capable of making.

There was no warning at all. No chance to cry out or to pull away. Arthur came awake in a rush of savage power, and in one incredibly violent movement, seized her by the throat.

Philly gasped, her eyes widening in shock and confusion. Her heart slammed painfully against her ribs, and her pulse roared to life in her ears. Instinctively, she began to struggle, but in response his fingers only tightened around her. Panic threatened.

And then it was over.

Whatever dark nightmare had engulfed Arthur was lifted, and just as suddenly as he'd taken hold of her, he let her go.

Philly fell back from her knees onto her hip, fighting for breath. An uncontrollable shudder ran through her body, and the sting of tears blurred her vision. Even so, she could make out the look of dawning horror on Arthur's face.

"*Philly. My God, what have I done to you?*"

His ragged, anguished voice was unrecognizable in the darkness. He moved toward her, reaching out as if to help or offer comfort, only to stop short of touching her. He was afraid to touch her, Philly realized. Perhaps she should have been afraid, too. Afraid of him and what he might do to her. But she wasn't afraid. She went into his arms without hesitation.

"You were dreaming," she said through her tears. "You didn't know me."

At her words, every last vestige of color drained from Arthur's face. "Are you all right?" he asked roughly. "Please, Philly, tell me that you're all right."

She took a deep breath. "I'm all right." She drew back from him to wipe her face. "I don't know why I'm crying."

"I've hurt you." He groped for the tinderbox on the bedside table, his shaking hands somehow managing to strike a spark to light a taper. "Here, love. Let me look at it."

From the flickering light of the candle Philly could see for the first time how pale and stricken Arthur was. Whatever brief distress he'd caused her bore not even the slightest comparison to the torments he was putting himself through now.

"I'm truly all right," she protested as he lifted her hair away from her neck. "You let go of me right away. You couldn't possibly have harmed me."

Arthur was deaf to reason. He seemed determined to view his actions in the worst possible light. He looked at her throat, seeing the impressions of his fingers on her skin, and his expression became a mask of self-loathing. "I've hurt you," he repeated. There was a raw and helpless despair in his words.

"No. You merely startled me. That's why I was crying. I was a little scared. But I'm all right now. Perfectly all right."

"How can you ever forgive me for this?"

Not wanting him to look at the evidence of what he'd done any longer, Philly put her arms back around him and buried her face against his shoulder. There were no assurances she could give him that would make the situation any less terrible than it was. She gave them anyway. "There's nothing to forgive. It was only a dream. A terrible dream."

Arthur wrapped her close to him. His embrace wasn't as strong as it had been before. He held her as if she were made of fine porcelain. As if, at any moment, she might shatter into a million little pieces.

Philly said nothing else. Her frightened tears had run their course, and now she imagined she was comforting him more than he was comforting her. She stroked the nape of his neck, soothing him. She didn't know if he was even aware of her touch. He was still and quiet, sunk into some brooding thought of his own. She had a sense he was coming to a decision, and wasn't surprised when, after a while longer, he pulled away from her.

She expected he'd say something more about what had happened, apologize again or even confide in her about his nightmare, but Arthur only touched a lock of her hair, just as he'd done after cutting her out of her stays.

"It's nearly morning," he said, his voice strangely flat. "It would be better if you went back to your own bed."

Philly stared at him. "What?"

"But if you prefer to remain here, then I must go."

She blinked away the threat of more tears. "You don't want to stay with me anymore?"

Arthur looked pained by her question. He dropped his hand from her hair. "It doesn't matter what I want. I can't trust myself with you like this. Had I not come to my senses when I did—"

"Don't dwell on what might have happened. Pray don't. You woke up and all is well now."

"It's far from well."

"But I'm in no danger."

He shook his head. "Philly, please don't."

"Can we not stay together awhile longer? At least until sunrise? If you told me what your nightmare was about, then perhaps—"

"Talking about it won't change anything."

"Then we won't talk, but you mustn't send me away, Arthur. Not now. Not when you're so upset. It would be worse than anything."

"No. It wouldn't be worse than anything," he bit out in a sudden flash of anger. "What would be worse than anything is if I'd killed you."

A shiver of fear went through her. She tried her best to suppress it. "How can you entertain such a terrible thought? You'd never have—"

"My hand was around your throat, Philly!"

She winced. What he said was nothing more than the truth, but he imbued it with such sinister implication that she knew then there was nothing she could say to sway him. Arthur was far too disturbed by what he'd done to be rational about it. "You need say no more. I'll go back to my own room if that's what you wish."

Her calm acquiescence appeared to unsettle Arthur just as much as her objections to leaving him had. As she began to rise from his bed, he caught her by the wrist.

"It's not what I wish," he said quietly. "But I've promised to protect you, Philly. And I will. Even if that means I must protect you from myself."

TWENTY-ONE

At daybreak, Violet entered Philly's bedroom carrying a breakfast tray. While she drew the curtains and lit the fire, she made her excuses for having failed to come the night before, explaining that she'd put her head down on the kitchen table for "just a tick" and ended up falling asleep. She went on to tell Philly that her dogs were eating their morning meal down in the kitchens under William's supervision, and that Arthur had risen well before sunrise and was now closeted in the library with Mr. Pebmarsh on important estate business, stating, "Mr. Crofton says he's not to be disturbed by anyone."

Philly hid her disappointment. She'd hoped she and Arthur might breakfast together. Indeed, she'd lain awake for the remaining hours before dawn thinking about what would happen when next she saw him. She'd imagined many different scenarios, but she hadn't once considered that he wouldn't even wish to see her. Did he really have pressing business with his steward? Or was he simply avoiding her?

Whatever his reasons, the end result was the same. She was to be left alone in a strange house surrounded by strange servants. It was enough to blue-devil a person.

But Philly had no intention of feeling sorry for herself. No matter what else had happened between her and Arthur, she was still the new mistress of Heywood House. She had much to learn and even more to do—more than enough to keep her busy for weeks.

The first thing she must address was the cook. The cold collation presented to them last night was unremarkable, but the morning meal Violet had brought on a tray was absolutely awful. The tea was foully pungent, the food was either undercooked, burned, or congealed, and not a single item was hot.

"Violet, how long has the cook been with us?" she asked.

"Going on a year, ma'am. But Mrs. Davies don't fancy herself a cook."

Philly moved her fork through a suspicious gray lump on her plate. "No?"

"She were a housekeeper at her last place." Violet busied herself with shaking out Philly's traveling clothes and putting them away. "But there's not much choice for cooks round these parts, and Mrs. Lamb says Mrs. Davies does right enough for a bachelor's house."

Philly set aside her breakfast, unable to stomach it. "Violet, from now on, you needn't bring me a tray. I'll be eating my morning meal in the breakfast room."

"Yes, ma'am, but...the breakfast room?" Violet's voice trailed off as she lifted Philly's stays, eying the cut laces with undisguised curiosity.

Philly suppressed a surge of embarrassment. "You may leave those out, Violet. I'll mend them myself." She waited until the maid complied before asking, "Does Heywood House not have a breakfast room?"

"I reckon so, ma'am, but I think it's one of them rooms that's shut up."

"Where is breakfast served to Captain Heywood? The dining room?"

"No, ma'am. The master has a tray in the library. Spends most of the day in the library, he does."

Philly frowned. She didn't want to disrupt Arthur's life, but she'd definitely have to make some changes.

She sent Violet off to fetch a can of hot water, and once she was alone, went into her dressing room. She pulled her hair back from her neck and examined herself carefully in the mirror.

Though it was still sensitive to the touch, her throat bore no visible marks.

She sighed with relief. There were no high-necked gowns packed in her valise, nor any scarves or wraps that would have covered her throat, and such an injury would have been impossible to explain to the servants. She was thankful she no longer had to worry about such things.

Indeed, she wished the entire incident with Arthur could be resolved with as much convenient expedition.

She wasn't angry with him. How could she be? He hadn't meant to hurt her, and though he'd scared her enough to make her cry, she was physically no worse for it. But she wondered *why* he'd done it. It was clearly connected to the nightmare he'd been having—a nightmare she assumed was about something that had happened to him in Spain. She wished she knew what it was. Unfortunately, her only piece of information about Arthur's experiences in the war had come from her two unreliable cousins.

Had he truly been left for dead on the battlefield?

And what was the nature of the injuries he'd suffered?

Even after their night together, Philly was no closer to understanding. Arthur had doused the candles well before he removed his clothes. But in the dark, when she'd touched his bare chest and his shoulders, she'd felt his scars. It seemed to her that they were very like the scars she'd seen on his left hand. What had caused them? *Who* had caused them?

Until now, she'd dealt with Arthur's past by pretending it didn't exist. It had seemed kinder not to remind him about the war and all that he'd endured while fighting it. But after last night, she knew she'd been wrong to remain silent. Arthur wasn't going to forget the past simply because he didn't talk about it. His nightmare was enough proof of that.

When Violet returned, Philly washed with the rose-scented soap she'd brought with her from her uncle's and dressed in a printed muslin gown. After Violet arranged her hair in a rather haphazard style—not unlike something Philly could have achieved on her own—Philly sent her off to summon Mrs. Lamb.

Her grandmother had always said that in order to successfully run a great house, the mistress and the housekeeper must work together in harmony. Philly planned to start out as she intended to go on.

A short time later, Mrs. Lamb knocked at the bedroom door. She was a tall, thin woman with black hair, hooded eyes, and a harshly slanting mouth—a medieval oil painting come to life. At first glance, it was impossible to tell whether she was cruel or kind, intelligent or calculating.

Philly invited her in and bade her sit down in one of the chairs near the fireplace.

They began to talk.

Within ten minutes, Philly had come to the conclusion that the sinister-looking Mrs. Lamb was neither cruel, nor calculating. She was merely a very unhappy, very dissatisfied housekeeper—and one intent on maintaining her meager authority.

"Captain Heywood's a good master," Mrs. Lamb said. "And he pays a fair wage, but there's naught to do in Heycombe, and precious little to do in the house with so much of it not in use. I always said keeping house for a single gentleman who don't entertain, and rarely leaves his library from dawn until dusk, was a difficult business. I've managed it as well as can be, though I daresay, now you're in residence, you'll have complaints aplenty about how I run things."

Philly ignored Mrs. Lamb's defensive tone. She wasn't unsympathetic to the housekeeper's plight. A new mistress in an established household always disturbed the order of things, and sometimes not for the better. "A difficult business? How do you mean?"

"It's not easy to keep on good servants when there's so little for them to do, and no chances for them to display their particular skills. Our former cook is a fine example. In her last place, she was accustomed to making fine cakes and puddings. She wasn't content to cook simple fare for a single gentleman. She gave notice within two months. And then there are those younger maids and footmen who fancy a more exciting life in Bath or at Melton Abbey, in service to some fine lady or gentleman."

"Of course. I understand." Philly paused. "Where is Melton Abbey?"

"Lord and Lady Markham's estate. It's not far from here. They're always having house parties with all manner of London society folk in attendance."

Philly's brows knit in a pensive frown. She hadn't considered that Arthur would have society neighbors. Certainly not the sort who regularly entertained ladies and gentlemen from London.

Did her uncle ever visit Melton Abbey?

Did the Duke of Moreland?

The very thought set Philly's stomach in knots.

"A rather adventurous lot, if you ask me," Mrs. Lamb went on. "Young bloods racing their carriages up and down, and even a duel fought right out in Mr. Tuttle's north pasture last summer."

"Good heavens."

"Indeed, ma'am. It was a right scandal. And just the sort of thrilling event to tempt away two of our young footmen. They're working in the abbey stable now, or so I hear—and good riddance to them."

"Surely the servants know the many benefits of working in a quiet, respectable household? They need never worry about their wages being lost in a card game, for instance, or some visiting rake taking undue liberties during a raucous party."

"Oh, Heywood House is respectable, to be sure. And Captain Heywood is an honorable gentleman. No one would ever say otherwise. But he keeps himself to himself. Perhaps a little too much, if I may say so. He don't tolerate company, if you know what I mean, and he has his black moods to contend with. You could have knocked me over with a feather when the express came saying he was bringing home a wife. 'This house ain't fit for a lady,' Crofton said to me when he read the letter, 'and nor is the master.'" Mrs. Lamb met Philly's eyes, her mouth set in a grim line. "But now you're here, ma'am, and we must make the best of things, mustn't we."

Philly looked steadily back at her. "So we must."

Arthur couldn't sleep after Philly left his room. Instead, he dressed and went downstairs to the library. He tried to keep himself busy—so busy that he wouldn't have a single spare moment to reflect on what he'd done to her. But even after hours spent with his land steward dealing with the tedious minutiae of estate business, he couldn't stop going over it in his mind.

Nightmares had been a common occurrence when he first returned from Spain. As the years passed, they came with less frequency, but they'd never completely ceased. Every few weeks he would dream the same nightmare anew, waking in a cold sweat as memories of the aftermath of his last battle returned to plague him.

The nightmare was vivid, but Arthur had never thought himself capable of hurting anyone because of it, least of all Philly. If he'd known there was even the smallest chance he might do so, he wouldn't have allowed himself to fall asleep beside her. Indeed, he wouldn't have made love to her. He'd have kept as far away from her as he could. Anything to keep her out of danger.

What might have happened if he hadn't awakened when he did? If he'd remained lost in his nightmare for one moment longer? She was so small and fragile. He was sure he'd have killed her. That he hadn't done so was the merest chance.

Philly didn't yet appreciate the full implications of what he'd done. Not yet. But how long would it be before she began to regret having married him? How long before she grew to hate him?

The whole predicament was the result of his own selfishness. And it *was* selfishness. He could call it nothing else. Marriage had surely not been the only way to keep Philly safe from Moreland, yet he'd rushed her into marrying him, promising her that it would be a marriage in name only.

A promise he'd broken rather spectacularly last night.

He propped his head in his hands, reflecting on the experience with a dull ache in his heart.

By the time Pebmarsh left, it was midafternoon. Arthur's guilt over what he'd done to Philly on their wedding night was now compounded by guilt over having left her alone for the better part of the day. It seemed he could do nothing right where his new bride was concerned.

He reached for his cane. His leg was more painful than it had been in London. After the fifteen-hour carriage drive yesterday, it was no wonder. He hadn't helped matters by sitting half the day away at his desk.

With an effort, he rose and went out into the main hall. Two maids hurried by with mops and buckets. Their aprons were dirty and their hair disheveled. When they saw him, they stopped and bobbed awkward curtsies. He didn't know either of them by name.

"Is Mrs. Heywood about?" he asked.

"She went down to the kitchens with Mrs. Lamb, about an hour ago, sir," the taller maid answered.

"And then she were going outside, sir. For a walk with her dogs," the smaller maid added.

Arthur turned and walked down the hall, leaning heavily on his cane. It was going to be difficult to keep track of Philly in a house this size. And with his leg giving him more trouble than it normally did, he was in no fit state to traipse all over the grounds looking for her.

Yet another reason he should have made some effort to see her at breakfast. He might have learned how she planned to spend her day, and then he wouldn't have had to ask the servants where she was and what she'd been doing.

He made his way outside, conscious of how uneven his gait was as he walked across the grounds. It did nothing to improve his mood.

Fortunately, he didn't have to go any farther than the stable yard. Basil, Jasper, and Dash were lazing in the sunshine outside the entrance to the north stable block. When they spotted him, their tails thumped slowly, but none of them made even the smallest attempt to get up. Their commitment to remaining by the plank doors that led into the stables was all the confirmation Arthur needed that Philly was inside.

He entered to find her leaning against one of the loose boxes, petting the muzzle of Hyperion, his giant blood bay stallion.

Arthur's heart contracted in his chest at the sight of her.

She was standing up on the toes of her scuffed brown half boots, one arm resting on the edge of the box, and the other stretched out to Hyperion as she murmured something to him that Arthur couldn't make out.

The thin material of her gown hung softly on the curves of her body. It was surely no more revealing a dress than any of the other modest muslins he'd seen Philly wear, but after their night together it might as well have been transparent. He knew the feel of her now. And as his eyes drifted over her, warmth infiltrated his veins for the first time all day.

Until his gaze came to the slender column of her throat.

There were no bruises, and the red impressions left by his fingers had gone. It did nothing to assuage his guilt. His gut still wrenched with self-recrimination.

Where could their marriage possibly go after such an event? They could never share a bed again, he was sure of that much. What then? Would they revert to their original arrangement? Would theirs be a marriage in name only after all?

His thoughts were thus occupied when Philly glanced in his direction. Her cheeks flooded with color. "Arthur! I thought you were still in the library."

"I've finished with Pebmarsh for the day." He came to stand beside her, absently reaching up to stroke Hyperion on the neck. He debated reaching out to Philly instead, but after how their night together had ended, it didn't feel right to take such a liberty with her. He wondered if it ever would again. "I regret I was engaged with him for so long."

"Estate business must be very tiring."

"No, I—" He turned his full attention on Philly, only to discover that she was more focused on his horse than she was on him. "What I meant to say was that I regret I was so long away from *you*."

"You need have no regrets on my account." She held out the flat of her palm to Hyperion and let him nuzzle it. "I've managed to keep myself occupied all morning. As a matter of fact, this is the first time I've been at my leisure. I was going to take the dogs for a run in the woods, but I've been waylaid admiring your beautiful horse."

"His name is Hyperion."

"Hyperion," she repeated to herself. "Is he the blood bay Lord Edgeworth mentioned at my uncle's dinner?"

"He is."

"How did Lord Edgeworth know of him? I didn't get the impression that the two of you were particularly good friends."

"Indeed not. Hyperion is by Titan, a rather famous stallion that once belonged to my father. Titan sired only three foals before he died. No doubt Edgeworth considers himself an expert on the bloodline, along with everything else on which he's an authority."

Philly smiled faintly as she scratched Hyperion's heavily whiskered chin. "He certainly gave his opinions very freely. And very loudly."

"He and his wife are well suited in that regard."

After a few more cursory pets to Hyperion's velvety nose, Philly stepped back from the loose box and looked up at him. "Would you like to come for a walk with me?"

Arthur was taken aback by the invitation. She'd scarcely been able to meet his eyes. The last thing he'd expected was that she'd want to spend any more time in his company.

"I understand if you don't wish to—"

"I'm completely at your disposal." His leg was throbbing with pain, but he wouldn't have refused Philly for the world. "How far did you have a mind to go?"

"Not far." She retrieved Fox from an empty loose box, where the disheveled little terrier had been resting comfortably on a pile of fresh straw. "Mrs. Lamb told me of a path through the woods that leads to a pond. She said it was a lovely prospect."

"I know it well."

Philly came to stand at his side, and before he could offer it, she took his arm, pressing herself to him as determinedly as she had that first afternoon in the park. "Well then, sir, I shall let you be my guide."

TWENTY-TWO

Philly hadn't anticipated feeling so shy in Arthur's presence. She was a sensible creature, and had fully expected that, when they met again, she'd talk to him as normally as she had on any other occasion. Instead, when he approached her in the stable, all rational thought had fled. Her stomach had fluttered with rampaging butterflies, and her mind had filled with memories of his kisses, his caresses, and all the sweet words he'd spoken to her the night before.

Was Arthur feeling the same way? She didn't think so. He'd said precious little to her since they set out, and as they walked together, he remained solemn and quiet. Philly suspected that, rather than reflecting on the intimacy of their wedding night, he was still excoriating himself over what had happened when he woke from his nightmare.

She didn't try to draw him out of his melancholy. Not yet. But she held tight to his arm, intermittently moving her hand along the sleeve of his coat in unspoken reassurance.

The path they took into the woods led them through a vast,

overgrown wilderness, dense with wildflowers, shrubs, and trees that bowed overhead. Shafts of sunlight shone through the branches, and the intermingled songs of warblers, wagtails, and tree pipits filled the air.

At the next bend in the path, the woods opened up quite unexpectedly into a clearing, at the edge of which was a large tranquil pond. It curved gently against grassy banks, flanked with crumbling benches of old stone, and strewn with fallen leaves and flower petals.

Mrs. Lamb was right. It was a very lovely prospect indeed.

Philly removed her arm from Arthur's. "Shall we sit awhile?"

"If you like."

As they made their way to one of the stone benches, a squirrel burst out of the underbrush and ran ahead of them. Basil, Jasper, and Dash happily gave chase. Fox wriggled in Philly's arms. She carefully lowered him to the ground. Without hesitation, he tore off after the three larger dogs, putting tentative weight on his injured front paw with every stride.

Philly watched him go. "I've been waiting for such a moment."

"For him to walk on his own?"

"Fox could have walked months ago had he wanted to." She made her way along the edge of the pond. The water was dark green, and the depths were murky, appearing limitless beneath the surface. Had the sunlight not sparkled so invitingly across the water, it might have been rather ominous. "All he lacked was the will." She sat down on one of the stone benches. "I was hoping that one day something would reignite it."

Arthur took a seat beside her, resting his cane against the edge of the bench. He massaged his leg. "He must have seen many squirrels before today."

"It wasn't the squirrel that brought him back to himself. Not precisely. It was simply the right time, and the squirrel acted as a spark to the tinder." She turned slightly so she could face him, intending to say something more about Fox, but when she met his eyes, she couldn't summon a single word. A deep blush worked its way up her neck and into her face. Flustered, she turned her attention back to the pond.

"Philly."

A tremor of awareness coursed through her at the sound of Arthur's voice. It was low and grave, different from the tone he'd used with her before.

"Since I came upon you in the stables this afternoon, we've talked of my horse and your dogs, but you have yet to say a single word about how you yourself are feeling...after last night."

She willed herself not to blush again. For all the good it did her. If the blazing heat in her cheeks was any indication, she must already be as red as a ripe tomato. "I'm perfectly well."

"Are you? I don't see how you possibly can be. You can hardly bear to look at me."

Is that what he thought? That she couldn't bear the sight of him? Foolish man. She turned to face him. His expression was no less grave than his voice. "You're speaking of what happened between us after your nightmare, I suppose, and not of what came before."

Along the edges of Arthur's elegantly tied cravat, his neck turned a dull shade of red.

"I only ask because...well, it seems to me that you may have forgotten that part of our night together."

"Forgotten it?" he repeated. "I'll remember it for as long as I live."

Her pulse skipped. "Will you really?"

"Never doubt it." He searched her face. "And you...I hope that you, as well...?"

"Yes. Though I must confess—"

"What is it?" he asked at once.

"Only that..." Philly smoothed the skirts of her gown quite unnecessarily. "If I'm having difficulty looking at you, it's only because I'm feeling so unaccountably shy about the whole thing. I expect it's a normal reaction for a newly married lady, but I must say I'm beginning to find it trying. I've been looking forward to seeing you all day, and now—"

"Have you?"

"Of course." She abandoned her preoccupation with her gown. "You sound rather surprised."

"After how our night together ended, I didn't think you'd have any interest in seeing me again."

"Why not? I hope you don't imagine I blame you for what happened."

"Who else should you blame?"

"Not you, or anyone. It was an unfortunate accident. As you can see, I'm no worse for it."

Arthur was incredulous. "An accident."

"Yes, I call it an accident. It wasn't done purposefully."

"Purposefully or no, it was unforgivable. What manner of person would treat you thus? Not a man with honor. Not a gentleman. It was the action of an animal. A damnable brute."

"No," she objected softly. "It was the action of someone having a terrible dream. Nothing more."

Arthur stilled at her words. Very briefly, a spasm of the deepest anguish crossed his handsome face. It was gone as soon as it came. "It doesn't matter why it happened. There's no excuse for it. It was a reprehensible act. And it shall never happen again. Of that I promise you."

"Did you think it might have?"

His anger and frustration were palpable. "Yes. I know now that it would. If we ever shared a bed together again."

"If we ever...?" Philly was stunned. "Is this what you had in mind when you said you were going to protect me from yourself? That we should live separately?"

"However we live, we can't ever be as we were last night. These dreams—these nightmares—they come too frequently. I should have realized... But I didn't think about the consequences when I proposed marriage to you. I was blinded by my own selfishness."

She frowned. "I don't remember your proposal that way at all."

"Of course not. I convinced you I was being noble, that I was rescuing you, but in truth I was thinking only of myself. I was no better than Moreland."

At this dire pronouncement, Philly fell silent. She turned away from him, staring out across the surface of the pond.

No better than the Duke of Moreland? She didn't believe that for a moment.

Yet, Arthur was utterly convinced of it. He was determined to condemn himself on every count, and it all stemmed from those few seconds when he'd woken from his nightmare and seized her by the throat.

She cast about for something she could say that might help to alleviate his anguish over what he'd done, but couldn't think of a single thing that would make any difference. How was she to handle such a situation? Her experience in helping and healing was in the realm of animals, not men. She could hardly treat Arthur as she would an injured dog.

And yet, in essentials, it couldn't be so very different, could it?

"I've upset you," he said quietly, when, after a time, she still hadn't turned back to him.

She looked up. "I'm not upset. I've just been thinking about some of the things you've said to me." Slowly, and a bit distractedly, she began to pull off her York tan gloves. "Arthur, I want to show you something, but I fear I might shock you."

"I doubt you could."

Philly took this as tacit permission, and before she could lose her nerve, hoisted up her skirts to just above her knees, revealing her stocking-clad legs.

"What the devil!" Arthur moved quickly toward her, positioning himself to shield her from view.

"No one will see me," she assured him. "The clearing is very secluded." She untied her right garter and set it down on the bench beside her gloves. The cool afternoon breeze instantly blew it into the grass at Arthur's booted feet.

He swept up the delicate bit of satin up, staring at it intently for a moment before thrusting it into the pocket of his waistcoat.

Philly expected he might raise an objection, but he said nothing more, only looked at her and her exposed legs as if his emotions were warring within him. She felt the heaviness of his gaze as she rolled her stocking partway down her leg, baring her knee and calf. "You'll have to come closer in order to see it."

"What is it exactly I'm supposed to be looking at?"

"Just here. On the back of my leg. Right above my knee." She attempted to angle herself so he could get a better view. She knew the very second Arthur saw her scar for she heard him mutter an oath.

And then his large hand closed gently around her calf, holding her leg still so he might examine the faded marks more closely.

"What did this to you?"

Philly's breath caught as the pad of his thumb brushed just over the surface of the scar. "It was a dog."

"*A dog?*"

"Yes, I know. It looks as if it had been something more serious." She began to roll her stocking back up and he removed his hand. "May I have my garter, please?"

He retrieved the dainty little ribbon from his pocket, holding it out to her on the palm of his hand.

She secured it back around her stocking. "Sometimes in Fox Cross the fog would come in early in the morning and blanket the village." She lowered her skirts. "Once, five years ago, it came in so heavily that you could hardly see in front of you. When it lifted, there was a dog lying injured in our kitchen garden. We didn't know where he'd come from or how it was he'd found his way to Satterthwaite Court."

"He must have been a very large dog by the look of that scar on your leg."

"He was. He was also near death. He was starved, and bleeding from a terrible gash on his side. I knelt down next to him so I could see to his wound, and quite unexpectedly, he lunged at me and caught me by the leg. Had he not been so weak, I think he might have done me a greater injury. As it was, the apothecary insisted on bleeding me, applying horrible poultices, and subjecting me to a month-long course of cold baths."

"They thought him a mad dog."

"Some of the servants did, yes. But my grandfather and I knew that he wasn't. He was only insensible with pain. He thought he was defending himself."

Arthur looked at her for a long time before he spoke again. "Philly, you can't compare what I did to you to what you suffered because of that dog."

"Indeed not. What the dog did to me was far worse."

"It's not the same. Some things are—"

"Unforgivable. Yes, I know. As you've told me. I can't imagine what terrible condemnation you would've had for that poor dog. By your measure, he'd have been a thoroughly irredeemable creature. It wouldn't have mattered under what circumstance he hurt me, only that he'd done so." She looked out across the clearing to where her dogs had come to rest in the tall grass after their fruitless pursuit of the squirrel. "Had I judged that dog as harshly as you're judging yourself now, I'd have been deprived of my most loyal and fearsome protector."

Arthur followed her gaze. "It was *Basil*?"

"Of course it was Basil."

Basil lifted his wiry gray head at the sound of his name. His attention fixed on Philly for a moment, as if to ascertain that all was well. Once satisfied, he heaved a sigh and lay his head back down on his oversized paws.

"He's been my trusted companion these five years, and never once let anyone harm me. Indeed, my grandfather always said that if I were ever in any real danger, Basil would gladly give his life to save mine. It's never come to that, thank heaven, but just yesterday he protected me from Evans. If he hadn't been there with me, who knows what might have happened?"

Arthur turned back to her. "And he never attempted to bite you again?"

"No. He growled at me a bit in those early days as if to scare me away, but I don't think his heart was in it. He always seemed rather relieved when I ignored his threats and remained beside him." She hesitated before adding, "I should have ignored you in a similar manner last night."

"Ignored me? When?"

"When you told me that I must leave your room."

"Philly..."

"I can't think why I allowed you to send me away, except that... well...perhaps I thought it was kinder to do what you asked of me. But it wasn't kind. Nor has it been kind to show so little curiosity about what happened to you in the war."

He visibly tensed at her mention of the war, but he didn't withdraw from her. Indeed, he maintained the same protective posture he'd assumed when she removed her garter, his large frame slightly inclined over her own. "Is that what you've been doing? Showing a lack of curiosity?"

"Not by design, no, but it amounts to the same, for I know absolutely nothing about the nature of your injuries or what you experienced while in Spain. Wouldn't it help to talk about these things more openly? I'm certain that, if I'd stayed with you last night and you'd told me about your nightmare—"

"It would have changed nothing."

"Perhaps not. But I think you'd have felt better for sharing it with me, and you wouldn't have ended up in so much anguish over it today." She touched his arm. "It's not too late. You can talk to me about it now, if you like. You can tell me what it was about your nightmare that upset you so much. You can tell me about what happened to you in Spain."

"I understand your need to make sense of all this, Philly, and God knows you have every right to ask me after what I did to you last night, but you must know I'm not accustomed to discussing these subjects with anyone."

"But, Arthur...surely, I'm not just anyone?"

He contemplated her with an unreadable gaze. "No," he said after a time. "You most certainly are not. Nor have you ever been."

Her heart swelled at his words. She closed the small distance between them in one quick movement, and before Arthur could anticipate her action or express any surprise at her boldness, her arms were tight around his neck and her face was buried in the folds of his cravat.

He responded at once, enfolding her in an embrace so powerful she could scarcely breathe.

For several long minutes they didn't speak, only held fast to one another. When Philly finally managed to find her voice it was to discover that all reasoned argument had gone. She could no longer formulate the gentle assurances she'd given to Arthur as they sat beside each other. Instead, she spoke to him fiercely, urgently, whispering against his neck that which had troubled her deeply from the moment he said it, "Don't ever tell me again that you're like the Duke of Moreland."

"I won't," he promised gruffly.

"And never say that it was wrong to marry me. I cannot bear to hear it."

"No. Never."

Philly melted at the rough tenderness in his voice. Somehow, on a deeply feminine level, she now understood that he'd needed this physical reassurance from her far more than he'd needed her words. The mere act of holding him in her arms did more to ease his tortured spirit than anything else she could have said or done. "I won't let you send me away ever again, Arthur," she vowed to him in the same half whisper. "It doesn't matter if you growl at me and attempt to frighten me. You're my dearest friend. I will never leave you."

In answer, Arthur's arms tightened around her. She felt him press his face into her hair. Some of the tension seemed to go out of him then, but the strength with which he held her didn't falter. "The nightmares are all the same," he said. "All about the same man."

Philly made no reply, only clung to him and waited for him to continue on his own. She sensed that he no longer needed her prompting and was reluctant to say anything that might discourage his confidence.

"When you leaned over me last night and touched me, I reacted as if you were that man. And now I can't stop thinking about what I might have done to you had I not awakened. It's driving me mad. If you knew... If you understood..."

"I do understand."

Very slowly, he loosened his hold on her and drew back just enough to look her in the eye. His expression was stark. "How can you?"

Philly slid her hands down to the front of his waistcoat, resting them there as she looked up at him. "Is the man in your nightmare an enemy soldier? It's all right, Arthur. I'd already guessed as much on my own. It was the only explanation for why you were so certain you might have done me greater harm. If the man you mistook me for was an enemy soldier that you killed in battle—"

"He wasn't an enemy soldier, Philly."

"Wasn't he?"

"No," Arthur said. "He wasn't a soldier at all. But you're right. I did kill him. I caught hold of him just as I caught hold of you last night. I crushed his throat."

TWENTY-THREE

Philly went very still in his arms. "That's why you were so certain that you might have killed me? Because of what you did to this other man?"

Arthur felt a sinking sensation in his stomach as he looked down at her. "I've frightened you."

"Yes. Perhaps a little. I didn't believe you when you said you could have harmed me. I thought you were merely distraught. But now..." She was trembling. "If you woke from a nightmare and thought I was this man..."

"I shouldn't have told you. It's served no purpose except to upset you."

"It's too late for that now. You must continue." She tightened her fingers on the front of his waistcoat. "Who was he, Arthur? Why did you have to kill him in such a brutal manner?"

If he hadn't told her so much already, Arthur would have said nothing more. But Philly was right. He must continue. "The last battle I fought in Spain...It was at Albuera."

Her brows drew together in an elegant line. "It didn't have a favorable outcome, I fear."

"We won the battle," Arthur informed her dryly. "We were annihilated by cavalry, cut to ribbons by musket fire, and by every measure smashed beyond all recognition, but we won the battle. Unfortunately, there were precious few of us left to enjoy the victory."

"Oh, Arthur."

"My regiment fought until we weren't a regiment anymore. It was chaos, Philly. Cannon fire, smoke, and driving rain. The French pouring over the hills from every direction like a flood, and our own men outflanked and outnumbered. My horse, a chestnut named Lucius, took a musket ball through his shoulder, and I took one in my leg. I managed to continue fighting until a shot from a cannon cut Lucius out from under me. At the same time a piece of artillery shell struck me in the back of the head. I was unconscious before I hit the ground."

She clutched his waistcoat even tighter, crushing the fabric in her fingers.

"There were too many wounded to treat, and those of us who couldn't walk off the battlefield were left to lie there. It rained all night, even worse than it had during the battle, and there were sounds—all sorts of sounds like the howling of the wolves and the carrion birds that came to scavenge amongst the bodies, the sounds of men crying out for help, the sounds of men dying. I stayed on that battlefield, bleeding and insensible, for more than a day, halfway sunk into the mud and the mire beneath the dead bodies of my men. When the search parties finally came through, they didn't see me."

The sound of the wind rustling through the trees and the water lapping in the pond faded away. Arthur had a sense that he was somewhere else entirely.

"At nightfall, the human scavengers came. They stripped the

bodies. Stole whatever was of value. If the soldier they robbed happened to have a little life left in him, they snuffed it out with a knife or a hammer. On the second night, a man found me there in the mud. He leaned over me to remove the buttons from my coat. It was enough to bring me round. I opened my eyes and I saw him there. His hand was on my chest, his fingers closed over one of the buttons. I took hold of his hand—to plea for help, I imagine. But he wasn't there to help me. And when he felt the touch of my hand, he drew out the knife he'd brought with him."

Philly's already pale face drained of the little color it had left.

"I don't know how I had any strength left to defend myself, but as he drew the knife, I took hold of him by the throat." Arthur flexed his scarred left hand. "He slashed out at me. He cut at whatever he could reach, but most of all he cut at my hand, trying to get me to release him. It made no difference. I was a man possessed. The more he slashed the knife, the tighter I held him until, finally, I crushed his throat in my hand. It felt as if it lasted for hours. In truth, it was the work of minutes. Seconds. Fortunately, one of the search parties saw the struggle and came to investigate. That was how they found me."

"But you had to kill him, Arthur! You were fighting for your life."

"I know that. I've no regrets about killing that man. God knows why he's haunted my dreams these three years. I assume it has something to do with the state I was in when he found me. Weak and vulnerable, unable to properly defend myself."

Her lips compressed. "I think you defended yourself remarkably well."

A shadow of a smile crossed Arthur's face at the hint of pride in her voice. "I suppose I did."

"I know I shouldn't wish such a fate on any fellow creature, but he sounds an absolute scoundrel. A man without any honor at all. To steal the buttons from the coat of an injured soldier? What need had he of your buttons? And then to cut your hand with a knife in such a cruel and heartless fashion?" She took his left hand in both of hers and held it in her lap. "Still, I expect I must be grateful to this villain. After all, if you hadn't struggled with him so violently, the search party would never have seen you and come to your rescue."

"That's certainly one way of looking at it."

She traced her fingertips over his scars. Her touch was warm and soft and heart-wrenchingly tender. He wondered if she had even the slightest notion of the effect it had on him.

"Did they take you straight to hospital?" she asked.

"There was no hospital. They took me to an aid station. There was a harried surgeon there doing one amputation after another. He would have taken off my leg and removed part of my skull, except that I was so ill with fever by then it didn't seem likely I'd survive."

Philly's eyes jerked to his. "They wanted to remove part of your *skull*? But why?"

"It had been fractured by the artillery shell that struck me during the battle. The surgeon thought to relieve the pressure on my brain. And so he might have, but I was already half-dead, and there were an endless number of soldiers for him to tend to. Soldiers who had a much better chance of recovering from their wounds than I did. I wouldn't have the surgeon wasting his efforts on me when he could be saving one of them. I told him he'd better leave me to die. So, they dressed my wounds with lint, and propped me out in the rain with some of the poor souls who had just undergone amputation. There was no room in the tent for all the wounded.

"Later in the day, when I still hadn't succumbed, they loaded me along with hundreds of other wounded soldiers in the backs of wooden bullock carts and we were evacuated to Lisbon. Many men died along the way, and those of us who lived arrived in Lisbon somewhat worse off than when we left Albuera. It was in Lisbon that I spent the next several months in hospital making my recovery."

She pressed his hand. "And then you came home."

"What was left of me." He couldn't keep the bitterness out of his voice. "I should have been thankful that I returned alive with no greater injuries, but I confess it gave me little solace to know that many men fared worse. For a time, I was cursed with blinding headaches, my leg was in a state of perpetual agony, and my hand… That scavenger cut my hand so deeply that I can no longer hold or fire a pistol with anything even approaching accuracy. The pain I can bear, but to lose all my abilities. To be left helpless—" He broke off, unable to finish.

"Could you not learn to shoot with your right hand?" Philly asked.

"I've always been able to shoot with my right hand, though never as competently as with my left. Under different circumstances I might have made an attempt to practice—to improve myself—but I must use my right hand to hold my cane. I couldn't shoot with it if I wanted to."

She continued to caress his hand as she held it in her lap. In time, Arthur returned her caresses, their hands slowly moving along each other, fingers twining together for a moment before once again resting quietly in each other's grasp. "Maybe one day you'll no longer have need of your cane."

"I doubt that day will ever come. The musket ball did a great deal of damage. It took three separate surgeries to remove it. It was only by chance that I didn't lose my leg entirely. No. I expect I'll always need my cane. Although, for a time—"

"Yes?" Her blue and amber gaze lit with expectation.

He instantly regretted having spoken. The last thing he wanted to do was give her false hope. "It doesn't signify, but by the end of my stay in London I had the impression that all the walking might be effecting some small improvement."

"It didn't increase your pain?"

"Initially it did, but on the last day it was a little better. I'm sure it was nothing, for it's just as painful today as it was before I left Somersetshire. Indeed, I believe that all of my injuries are as well now as they'll ever be."

"And your nightmares? Do you think they'll ever cease?"

He frowned. "They used to come much more often. Now, several weeks can go by without my having one. I still have some hope that one day I'll be free of them. I only wish I knew when that day might be."

Philly appeared to consider this for a moment. Her fingers threaded through his. "Arthur?"

"What is it, my dear?"

"Did you never wake up from a nightmare with anyone else the way you did with me last night?"

Heat rose beneath his cravat. A gentleman didn't discuss such things with a lady. Not even his wife. But Arthur could be nothing but honest with her. "Philly, I haven't shared a bed with anyone since I returned from the war. Believe me, if anything like this had ever happened before, if I'd had any warning at all, I would have never—"

"I do believe you." She leaned against his chest, resting her cheek on the slightly rumpled fabric of his waistcoat.

Arthur wrapped her close. He was sure he'd overwhelmed her. Not only with his confessions about the war and his injuries, but with everything that had happened between them since he'd proposed to her so unexpectedly in the park.

"Three years ago, I was in Fox Cross with my grandfather. I didn't even know you then. And yet..." Her voice thickened with emotion. "To think that I was safe and happy in Devonshire while you were suffering and in pain so far away from home. It's almost more than I can bear."

Arthur felt something deep within him give way. "Are these tears for me?"

"I'm not crying."

"Of course not." His hand moved soothingly on her back. "But if you were, I'd tell you that you mustn't waste your tears. It's all in the past. I'm no longer in pain. I'm home now."

There had been no lady to weep for him when he was away fighting on the Peninsula. Not a mother, a mistress, or even his fiancée. It had made little matter. He hadn't pined for the sympathy of a woman in his time of trouble. In truth, he'd never believed such feminine comfort could make any difference. But now, even these three years later, to know that the tears Philly shed were for him and for what he'd suffered moved him more deeply than he could have imagined.

"No wonder you've preferred to remain alone in the country all these years. How hollow and foolish everything else must seem after what you've been through."

"Here, sweetheart." Arthur held out his linen handkerchief to her.

She took it, drawing back from his chest only the distance necessary to blot her tears. "And then to come back to London at last only to be subjected to the ignorant speeches of a man like Lord Edgeworth. How could you endure all of those awful things he said at my uncle's dinner?"

"I didn't have to endure them. A very lovely young lady intervened on my behalf each time Edgeworth attempted to engage me."

She sniffled into his handkerchief. "Were my efforts so terribly obvious?"

"You could hardly be subtle with a man like Edgeworth." Arthur tucked a lock of her hair back into an escaping hairpin. It was a small gesture, but one that sent a surge of possessiveness through him. Philly was his now. Completely and irrevocably his. He felt it with every fiber of his being. "Do you feel better?"

She looked up at him, her eyes still shining. "Oh, Arthur, I meant to comfort you, and instead, you've been obliged to console me."

"I can't say it feels like much of an obligation to hold you in my arms."

"You needn't be so gallant about it. I know you must think me one of those ladies who burst into tears at the slightest provocation."

"I assure you I don't."

"The truth is, I've cried more in the last several days than I have in my whole life."

"A great deal has happened that was worth crying about."

"I suppose you're right."

Arthur searched her face, that calm, sweetly serious face that had tilted up to his throughout the entirety of his tale. She'd listened to him with the whole of her being, drawing more out of him with her silence than anyone else had ever done with their probing questions. And she was right. He felt better for having shared it with her.

But Philly clearly didn't feel better. The knowledge of what he'd suffered was painful to her. And she was tired. How had he not noticed it before? She was pale as marble and there were shadows under her eyes.

"Did you sleep last night when you returned to your room?" he asked abruptly.

"No," she admitted.

He scowled. It was in his every instinct to read her a lecture on the dangers of making herself ill. But such concern seemed hypocritical after how he himself had treated her.

"You needn't worry over me," she said. "I'm not fragile. A night or two without sleep isn't likely to kill me."

"Don't even jest about such things."

A chill breeze stirred the leaves of the trees, rippling over the surface of the pond. Dash raised his head from the grass and growled low in his throat as the bushes beside him quivered in the wind.

Philly turned to watch her dogs for a while, making sure all was well.

"Perhaps it would be best if we return home now before the weather takes a turn for the worse?" he suggested.

"If you like."

Arthur retrieved his cane and rose from the stone bench. "You can have a lie-down before dinner." He helped her to her feet.

"I'm not that tired, Arthur. And I won't allow you to become one of those husbands who are constantly sending their wives to their room."

"I shall try my utmost not to succumb to the temptation." Arthur offered her his arm. She took it as unreservedly as she always did.

The dogs sprang to their feet to escort them back along the

path. Fox peered up at Philly, but gave no indication that he wished to be carried. He trotted along with the other dogs, soon leading the way ahead with Jasper as if they intuitively knew the way their mistress was headed.

The way toward home.

TWENTY-FOUR

*T*he next two weeks went by rapidly, and very soon their days began to fall into a sort of pattern. Every morning when Philly came downstairs to the breakfast room, Arthur was there waiting for her. He didn't talk much while they ate, but before the end of their meal, he never failed to query her about her plans for the day. She soon learned that, for whatever reason, it was important to him that he know exactly where she was at all times. She indulged him in this for it seemed a harmless fancy, not unlike something a new, rather possessive husband might do.

They had their meals together, they went for walks, and in the evenings, she played to him on the old, out-of-tune pianoforte in the drawing room. There wasn't a great deal of current sheet music at Heywood House, and after a few antiquated, off-key songs which Arthur didn't criticize but Philly knew were deplorable, she'd give up the pianoforte and end the evening listening to him read aloud from one of her favorite Greek classics.

Arthur never showed the slightest regret about relinquishing his solitude in order to be with her. In fact, Philly began to suspect he rather preferred her company. There were still many hours of the day that he spent in his library, but more and more, he sought her out. Once he'd even come upon her in the small parlor while she was engaged with her needlework, and instead of withdrawing, he'd joined her there, alternately reading his newspaper and watching her sew until it was time to escort her into luncheon.

As much as he desired to be near her during the day, Arthur never visited her room at night. Philly had come to the conclusion that he'd meant what he said that day in the clearing. They could never again be together as they were on their wedding night. She was sure he feared hurting her and was still punishing himself for what he'd done to her after his nightmare, but she made no effort to broach the subject. In many ways, she didn't know how she could.

It didn't seem right to complain when everything else was so wonderful. He'd given her his name, and he'd given her and her dogs a home of their very own. Sometimes she still yearned for her old life in Fox Cross, but her new life didn't feel so very isolated or confining. Arthur provided more than enough companionship, and when she wasn't spending time with him, she was well occupied arranging things in the house for their comfort.

She hadn't managed to win over the servants yet. Not entirely. Though Mrs. Lamb showed signs of gradually warming to her, she still eyed Philly with suspicion on occasion. And Philly had more than once come across the housemaids giggling and gossiping at her expense.

To make matters worse, within a few days of her arrival, the staff had somehow got wind of her previous association with the duke. It was a source of great speculation among them. Only yesterday she'd heard Violet and a young parlor maid whispering about it in the hall outside her bedroom.

"To think she could've been a duchess!" Violet had proclaimed. "And she gave it up to run away with Captain Heywood? Don't sound right, if you ask me."

"It must've been a love match," the young maid had replied.

To that, Violet had made a disparaging noise. "She can't love him. I'll wager he ravished her and she were forced to marry him."

Such an exchange bothered Philly enough that she mentioned it to Mrs. Lamb during their next morning meeting.

The housekeeper's face set into deep lines of disapproval. "Those two girls have no more sense than a pair of newborn chickens. I shall deal with them, Mrs. Heywood, make no mistake."

Philly refilled Mrs. Lamb's teacup, the long, full sleeves of her French cambric morning gown billowing gracefully around her arms as she moved. When the baggage coach had finally arrived, her London-made wardrobe had been scrupulously included amongst her things. She'd thought it a terrible mistake. Surely the servants were only meant to pack the old dresses and underthings she'd brought with her from Satterthwaite Court? She had no claim to the elegant clothing Uncle Edgar had purchased for her.

But when she'd confronted Arthur with the error, he'd quite calmly admitted to arranging it all. He'd repaid her uncle for every fashionable gown, shawl, and stocking. There was little Philly could do to thank him for such generosity except to wear the clothes he'd purchased for her.

"You needn't reprimand the maids too harshly," she said.

"What they need is more work," Mrs. Lamb declared. "If they had enough to do, there'd be no time to stand about gossiping. No. I shan't be harsh with them, Mrs. Heywood, but I'll increase their daily duties, you can be sure of that."

"I don't begrudge them their gossip," Philly said. "Heaven knows it must all seem dreadfully exciting. But the simple fact is, I refused an offer of marriage from one gentleman and accepted an offer from another. There's really nothing more to it, and I hope they won't waste any more time in idle speculation."

"Indeed, ma'am, but if you'll forgive me…" Mrs. Lamb shifted in her chair. "I suspect it's the identity of the gentleman you refused that has them all atwitter."

Philly set down her teacup on a small carved table. The morning room was the most feminine room in Heywood House. It was carpeted, papered, and upholstered in soft shades of cream and blue, and filled with delicately made walnut furniture. She briefly admired how well it looked with the sunlight streaming through the windows and everything cleaned and polished to perfection. It was hard to believe that only a short time ago it had been shrouded in holland covers and blanketed with a layer of dust.

"I don't care for myself, Mrs. Lamb," she said. "It's my husband that concerns me. I don't want him to ever hear the sorts of comments I've overheard."

Mrs. Lamb nodded gravely. "No, ma'am. The master wouldn't be as forgiving as you are."

No sooner had Mrs. Lamb spoken than a slight noise alerted them they were no longer alone. Philly looked up to find Arthur leaning against the doorframe. Her heart leapt.

He was clad in his customary country attire of buckskins and top boots, with a well-cut coat and a simply tied cravat. He looked stern and imposing, carrying himself with the same austere, soldierly reserve she'd noticed the first day she saw him in the park.

Mrs. Lamb rose at once. "Captain Heywood, sir, I beg your pardon."

Arthur gave the housekeeper a dismissive nod. His eyes were only for his wife. "Can you spare a moment to come outside with me?"

Philly smiled. "As many moments as you require."

Arthur moved out of the doorway so the housekeeper could pass him, his gaze never leaving Philly. He hadn't failed to notice how she brightened at first sight of him. It was a reaction he'd seen often since their marriage, and one he didn't think he'd ever become used to. "Have I interrupted something of importance?"

"No indeed." Philly came toward him, straightening the pale blue ribbon sash that was tied around her waist. "Though I'd better change my gown before we go outside. It wasn't meant for walking in."

"We aren't going for a walk. Not yet." He offered his arm to her and she took it. "What were you discussing with Mrs. Lamb?"

She glanced up at him. "Nothing important. Why? What did you hear?"

"Enough."

The dogs had been lying outside the morning room. As Philly and Arthur passed through the hall, they sprang up to follow.

"It's only silly servants' gossip," Philly said. "I've asked Mrs. Lamb to see to it."

"And how do the servants know about Moreland? From William, I suppose."

"Not necessarily. All of the servants who returned with us from London must know something of the circumstances under which we married. And the footmen who retrieved my things from my uncle's house must certainly have got an earful about it from the servants there. Any one of them could have relayed the tale."

"I don't care to have my servants gossiping at all, but when they gossip about you—"

"All servants gossip. Some more discreetly than others." Philly squeezed his arm. "I'll see to these sorts of domestic worries. You needn't trouble yourself."

Arthur said nothing else on the subject as he led her outside, steering her in the direction of the stable yard.

He'd been walking with Philly at least once a day, and though they weren't long walks, he couldn't deny that the outings had been beneficial. The fresh air and sunshine had helped his mood, and the exercise had been working a gradual improvement on his uneven gait and the pain in his leg. But it wasn't the fresh air and exercise alone that was affecting an improvement.

It was proximity to Philly.

Many times in the past two weeks, he'd been reminded of the hairpin he'd removed from her hair the night of Townsend's dinner party. He'd thought then that she had the ability to make everything around her better than it was, and he hadn't been mistaken.

It was a strange phenomenon and one he didn't fully understand, but he was experiencing it for himself now.

Since Philly had come to live with him, things had begun to change. It was nothing drastic, indeed much of the effect she had was very probably unintentional, yet he felt it as surely as he felt the improvement in his leg.

She managed Heywood House skillfully, and by her mere presence made it feel like a home. But it was more than that. It was the way she looked across the table from him during their meals. It was the way she sat so gracefully in their drawing room as she engaged in her needlework. And it was the knowledge each night as he went to sleep that she was in the bedroom beside him doing the same—even if he wouldn't allow himself the privilege of joining her there.

One day, as he was coming out from meeting with Pebmarsh, he'd seen several footmen hauling a metal tub up the stairs so Philly could have her bath. Another day, he'd come upon her as she practiced the pianoforte and heard her softly singing to herself. And during a quiet evening, when he'd enquired after her sewing, she'd held up a scrap of fabric so Arthur might examine her handiwork, and he'd realized, with a painful tightening in his chest, that she was mending one of his cravats.

Her feminine presence was quiet and subtle, but it was there, and Arthur felt it profoundly.

He'd been raised in a house without women. His mother had succumbed to childbed fever shortly after he was born, and the earl had never remarried. There were female servants, of course, and occasionally an old aunt would come to stay, but it was nothing like the consistent presence of an elegant lady in the house. He hadn't realized how much he desired such a thing until Philly had come.

"The weather is very fine," she remarked as they entered the stable yard. "I thought we might walk to the old apple orchard later this afternoon."

"You may yet change your mind about how you wish to spend the rest of your day," he said.

"I don't think so, but if you'd like to do something else..." Her words trailed off.

The head groom, Mr. Greene, stood in the stable yard holding the halter of a large, dark bay mare. She was heavily boned, with a broad back, and a decidedly stubborn glint in her liquid brown eyes. At their approach, she let forth an earsplitting whinny of recognition.

Philly stared at the mare for several seconds, uncomprehending, before she dropped Arthur's arm and flew to her side. She cradled the mare's giant head in her arms. Even from a distance, Arthur could hear her soft voice saying, "Oh, Persy!"

A deep sense of satisfaction coursed through him. It mattered little that Philly had temporarily forgotten his existence. He'd been anticipating her reaction to her horse's arrival for the past week, and had hoped for just such a joyful response.

He wasn't the only one watching Philly. Several of the grooms and a few of the house servants stopped to stare, as well. Was there no work for them to do? Or were they hanging about in hopes of gathering more gossip to pass around the servants' hall? He was just on the verge of losing his temper when Philly left her mare's side and made her way back across the stable yard.

She came to a halt in front of him, so close that she had to tilt her head back in order to meet his gaze. "How?"

Arthur looked down at her. Her eyes were shining and her cheeks were flushed. The entire front of her pretty French frock was now streaked with dirt. "I arranged for her purchase through my solicitor the day before we were married."

"Just like you did with all of my clothes?"

"Yes."

"But my uncle—"

"You need have no worry about Townsend. Everything was handled with the utmost discretion."

She stepped even closer to him. Her voice dropped. "Why didn't you tell me?"

"There was no way of knowing if the purchase would be successful. I didn't want to disappoint you. Not about something you hold so dear."

Without warning, she stood up on the toes of her delicate kid slippers, and with a little leap, threw her arms around his neck. "You've never disappointed me, Arthur. And I know you never shall."

Arthur's left arm closed around her waist. And suddenly, it no longer mattered that the servants were staring. He turned his face into her hair, inhaling the sweet, floral scent of her. "After how appealing you made your mare sound at your uncle's dinner party, I worried that Edgeworth might decide to buy her for his own." He felt the corner of her mouth curve into a smile as she pressed her silken cheek to his. "I couldn't allow such a fate to be inflicted on any living creature."

"Was that your motivation, then? To thwart Lord Edgeworth?"

"What else would it be?"

Philly drew back just enough to see his face, and then, right there in the stable yard, in front of Greene and all the other servants, she kissed him full on the mouth.

Arthur was thunderstruck, reflexively tightening his arm around her as she pressed her soft lips to his. He bent his head to return her kiss, but had only the briefest of moments to respond before she pulled away from him.

She slid her arms from his neck, bringing her hands to rest flat on his chest. A delicate blush suffused her cheeks.

He could think of no way to quell her embarrassment except to continue their conversation as if nothing untoward had happened. It wasn't an easy task. Not when his heart was galloping madly and his blood was roaring in his veins. "I didn't just arrange to bring back your horse," he said, his arm still firmly around her waist. "I had my solicitor see to the purchase of anything else still remaining at Satterthwaite Court that might have been yours.

The men who delivered your mare this morning also brought with them two trunks. I understand it to be books, clothing, and jewelry."

"My grandmother's jewelry?" she asked in an astonished whisper.

"Did Townsend make you leave it behind?"

"He said it was part of the estate. That it belonged to him now." Her expression betrayed a rare glimpse of the pain and loss she'd suffered since the death of her grandfather. "I never thought I'd see it again, Arthur. Not any of it."

"It's yours, my dear. Had Townsend been a gentleman he'd never have taken it from you." Arthur brushed a kiss against her forehead, and then, reluctantly, released her from his embrace. "I must go back to the house. The men who delivered your horse are waiting. I need to speak with them before they return to Devonshire. It won't take long and then we can go for our walk—if you still have any interest in my company now your horse is here."

A smile tugged at the corner of her mouth. "Don't be absurd."

"Captain Heywood, shall I put the new mare in the stable?" Greene shouted.

"I'll do it, Greene!" Philly hurried across the stable yard to her mare. "Persephone is very particular about how she's tied. I'll show you how I've always done it, and then you can instruct the other grooms..."

Arthur watched her awhile longer before heading back to the house.

Crofton was waiting for him in the main hall. "The post came at half past, sir. I've put it on your desk."

Arthur acknowledged him with a nod.

"The two gentlemen asked for refreshment," Crofton continued, following Arthur to the library. "When you've done with them, they can come down to the kitchens." He opened the library door for Arthur.

The men waiting inside were shabbily dressed, their faces burnt by the sun.

Arthur greeted them perfunctorily, and sitting down at his desk, looked over the papers they gave him. There was a letter from a Mr. Renquist, the intermediary Mr. Ombersley had used in Devonshire to negotiate the transaction. There was also a listed inventory of all he'd purchased. It had been written out by the estate agent at Satterthwaite Court and countersigned by Mr. Renquist.

After reviewing the documents and spending a good half hour listening to the two men talk about the weather (*Right cloudy and then uncommonly warm, sir!*), the quality of the roads (*Right uneven and then smooth as glass, sir!*), and the poor temperament of Philly's mare (*Right dangerous, sir! Bites, kicks, and tried to run me down!*), Arthur bid them both good day and sent them down to the kitchens.

It was too early for his walk with Philly. She was likely still down at the stable. Arthur would have liked to join her there but didn't wish to disturb her any more than necessary. He never knew at what point she might begin to find his constant presence more of an annoyance than a pleasure. As for himself, he was well aware that, unless he exercised some restraint, he was in danger of behaving even more like a besotted fool than he already did.

Determined to keep himself occupied, he began to go through the various items that had arrived with the morning post.

He was quickly disposing of the letters, most of which had to do with estate business and could be handled by Pebmarsh, when a small, rather odd-looking missive caught his eye. It was wedged between a copy of *The Times* and *The Gentleman's Magazine.*

It was sealed with black wax, as if it bore the news of a death, or had been sent by someone in mourning. Arthur's name and address were written on it in a barely legible scrawl. It had no other direction.

Arthur couldn't imagine who would have sent it. He didn't know of anyone suffering a recent loss.

On closer inspection, he saw that the letter bore no postal marks. It hadn't come through the post at all. Someone had delivered it by hand.

With a growing sense of unease, he broke the seal and spread the rumpled foolscap out in front of him on his desk.

It was no letter. It was a single sentence, written in large, commanding script:

You have taken what is mine.

TWENTY-FIVE

*T*he contents of the note read more as an accusation than a threat, and the black wax seal was so much window dressing, but the method of delivery left Arthur in no doubt as to the writer's true message. Someone had brought the letter personally into Heywood House. They were telling him in no uncertain terms that his home wasn't safe. That his *wife* wasn't safe.

Cold rage surged through him, the likes of which he'd never felt before. He wasn't a man ruled by his passions. He wasn't reactive, nor was he reckless. In battle, he'd been known for his ordered and methodical mind, his ability to make sound decisions despite the chaos all around him. But when it came to Philly, he was fast becoming irrational.

And yet, even now, when his instinct to protect his wife was clouding judgment, he could see quite plainly that something wasn't right about the letter.

If Moreland truly wanted revenge, would he bother with sending anonymous notes? He was a man of avarice and obsession. Some would say a madman. But he wasn't a man for wasting time. When his vengeance came, it came swiftly. There were no warnings. There were no games of cat and mouse. And there were no half measures. The stories about Moreland all ended the same, with the complete and total destruction of the object that had been denied him.

If Moreland was seeking revenge, he wouldn't bother communicating with Arthur.

He would hurt Philly.

Arthur stood from behind his desk without pausing to reach for his cane. Awash with anger, he walked several steps unaided before a jolt of pain in his leg brought him to his senses. He retrieved his cane with a muttered oath, and after jerking once on the bell pull, exited the library.

William came across the main hall at a trot in response to the summons. "Yes, sir?"

"Where is my wife?"

William blanched. "She was out in the yard, sir. With her new horse. She may have come in since, but I—"

"Mrs. Heywood is in her room, sir." Mrs. Lamb's authoritative voice rang out from the staircase. "Would you like me to fetch her for you?"

Arthur looked up to see the housekeeper descending the final few steps to join them in the main hall. He detected both wariness and alarm in Mrs. Lamb's hooded gaze. He'd never shown the servants the edge of his temper. As far as they knew, Philly was the cause of his anger. They no doubt feared she was about to receive the full force of it. "That won't be necessary," he said. "Are the two men from Devonshire still down in the kitchens?"

"They were but ten minutes ago," Mrs. Lamb said.

"Send them back to the library. They're not to leave until I see them again." Arthur started up the staircase. "And tell Crofton I have need of him, as well."

Mrs. Lamb stared after him. "Yes, Captain Heywood."

The carpeted hall that led to Philly's bedroom was empty. Not a servant in sight, nor the sound of one, either. It was not uncommon. The staff at Heywood House wasn't a large one. Servants were rarely underfoot. Yet now, in light of the anonymous note, the yawning emptiness seemed almost sinister. As if danger lurked in every shadow—in every quiet corner.

As he approached Philly's door, Arthur heard the soft undertone of her voice. She was speaking to her maid—everything just as it should be.

He exhaled an uneven breath.

What had he thought? That Moreland had spirited her away? That she was already lying dead somewhere? Arthur gritted his teeth against such images, and cursed Moreland, Townsend, and whoever sent that blasted note for conjuring them.

He needed to go back downstairs and talk to the men from Devonshire. He needed to speak to Crofton, to see to it that the servants were all questioned as discreetly as possible. Yet all he could think about was seeing Philly. It should have been enough to hear her voice, to know she was safe in her room, but it wasn't.

The men from Devonshire, Crofton, and the rest of the servants would have to wait.

Arthur entered the bedroom to find Philly kneeling next to one of the trunks that had come from Satterthwaite Court, her unpinned hair flowing around her shoulders and down her back. On every side of her were the neatly arranged piles of items she'd so far unpacked. In her lap, she held a large, flat velvet jewel case.

He hadn't seen her with her hair down since their wedding night. To see it now, so unexpectedly, temporarily immobilized him.

"'Tis very fine," Violet was saying from her place on the floor across from Philly. "Almost as fine as one of the necklaces my last mistress had."

Philly lifted a strand of garnets from the jewel case. The delicate stones threaded through her fingers. "Yes, it's very fine."

"Don't know where you'll ever wear such jewels here in Heycombe. Seems a waste to have 'em if you can't wear 'em—" Violet abruptly broke off, scrambling to her feet. "Captain Heywood!"

He gave her the barest glance. "Leave us."

Violet offered a nervous curtsy and scurried from the room, shutting the door firmly behind her.

Philly looked up from the jewel case. "This was my grandmother's necklace. It belonged to her mother before her, the Countess of Merrivale."

He dutifully admired the elegant foiled garnets before extending his hand to her. "Come, sit with me a moment."

After putting away the necklace, she allowed him to help her up and lead her to the settee near the fireplace. They sat down together. "What is it, Arthur? Is something wrong?"

"Need there be something wrong for me to want to see you?"

"No, of course not. But..."

"But?"

"You've never come to my room before."

Arthur looked at her steadily. "You're right. I haven't. And I've no wish to intrude upon your privacy now."

"Oh, no. It's not an intrusion. You're always quite welcome. It's only that, if I'd known you wished to see me, I would have made some effort to put myself in order. I've yet to change into a fresh gown, and Violet hasn't arranged my hair."

"You look very beautiful."

"Thank you, but I..."

He took her hand in his, silencing her speech. "Here, love," he said, tugging her gently toward him. "Let me hold you awhile."

Philly's eyes were wide and questioning, but she didn't resist him. She came to him willingly, only to gasp in surprise when, instead of merely embracing her, he took her by the waist and lifted her onto his lap. She clutched at the front of his coat, the skirts of her gown frothing around his breeches and top boots.

"Closer still," he urged. "You seem very far away from me."

Philly needed little encouragement to wrap her arms around his neck and lean into him as he held her close.

Only then did Arthur begin to relax a little. It hadn't been enough to hear her voice, or even to see her. He needed her in his arms. In truth, after such a scare as that note had given him, he needed her in his bed. "Say something to me, Philly," he whispered into her hair. "Anything. Even if it's only to tell me that I must let you go."

Her face was pressed against his cravat, her words so soft it was a miracle he heard them. "You mustn't ever let me go, Arthur."

He closed his eyes in relief. What had he been thinking to keep himself from her these many weeks? What had been the purpose of it? A fortnight of intimacies no greater than chaste kisses on her cheek or her forehead, and every evening, without fail, the monumental struggle over whether or not he should go to her in her room. Why the devil had he put himself through it?

His conscience had been his only barrier. It had seemed to him something worse than ungentlemanly to take liberties with Philly after how he'd hurt her. But when she'd kissed him in the stable yard, his gentlemanly resolve had begun to weaken. And the fear of losing her to some dastardly plot by Moreland had weakened it even further. Now, holding her in his arms, he was rapidly discovering that he had no gentlemanly resolve left at all.

"Would you like me to come to your room more often?" he asked carefully.

Philly didn't respond right away. Instead, she gave it a moment's thought, seeming to choose her words with the same care as he'd chosen his. "Yes. But only if you'd like to."

Arthur didn't know whether to laugh or to groan. Is that what she'd been thinking? That he didn't want to come to her? "I'd like to very much." He moved his hand slowly up and down her slender back. "Indeed, if I go without you even one more day, I believe I shall run mad. I'd stay with you now if I could."

"Can't you?"

"Regrettably no. I've business I must attend to downstairs."

Philly rubbed her cheek against his. "Then I'll not keep you." She began to pull away from him.

He tightened his hold on her. "Stay with me like this a minute more, sweetheart."

He wondered that Philly wasn't shocked by his outrageous behavior, but in response to his entreaty, she only nestled deeper into his embrace, settling herself against him as if it were the most natural thing in the world for him to come into her room unannounced and hold her on his lap.

"Arthur, do you still carry the hairpin I gave you?"

"Always." He threaded his fingers through her thick tresses. "Why do you ask? Are you short of hairpins at the moment? Is that why you've let your hair down in the middle of the day?"

She gave him a faint smile. "Nothing of the sort. It was in such a tangle when I came back from settling Persy that I had to unpin it. Violet was going to dress it again after we finished unpacking."

"I'd rather you left it down."

"Would you? I confess I wouldn't mind it, but the servants would be bound to think me the veriest hoyden."

"If we lived somewhere all alone, just the two of us without a single servant..." He pulled the bulk of her hair out of the way so he could place a gentle kiss upon her neck. "I'd have you wear your hair like this every day."

Her eyes closed briefly as he kissed her again. "Do you know what I would have you do? If we were all alone?"

"What's that, my dear?"

"I'd have you in your shirtsleeves the way you were on our wedding night."

He nuzzled her cheek. "You liked that, did you?"

"Yes. I thought you looked excessively handsome..." Philly's words dissolved as Arthur's mouth closed over hers in a slow, lingering kiss.

He was gently insistent, expecting to be met with the same maidenish timidity as when they had kissed in the stable yard. Instead, Philly was warm and soft, returning his kiss with a whole-hearted urgency that set his blood aflame.

"My darling," he murmured to her. "My sweet, beautiful darling."

She blushed rosily at his caressing words, and when, after enfolding her in a crushing embrace and kissing her deeply once more, he might have relented in his attentions, she threaded her fingers through his hair and coaxed him back to her lips, compelling him to kiss her again.

Arthur was sorely tempted to consign Crofton and the men from Devonshire to the devil. Indeed, he came very close to doing so. But after a few more heated kisses, and several whispered endearments, he recovered his senses enough to recall the circumstances that had brought him to Philly's room in the first place.

He slid his mouth from hers, pressing a final kiss to her cheek before at last pulling away from her. "Philly, I must ask something of you."

Her gaze slowly sharpened. "What is it?"

"I want you to promise me that you won't take your mare out unless a groom is with you."

She stroked his cheek, looking at him with an expression of affectionate indulgence. "If that's what you wish."

"And I don't want you to go on any more walks alone."

Her hand stilled on his face. "No more walks?" Her brows drew together. "But why? Surely it's not unsafe if I stay on the grounds?"

Arthur thought of the woods surrounding Heywood House. He could well imagine some henchman of the duke's hiding himself amongst the trees, lying in wait for Philly on her afternoon ramble. And what about the pond in the clearing? Philly could drown there just as easily as Molly Cartwright had drowned in Moreland's fountain. There were dangers everywhere. "Not unsafe, no," he said, not wishing to alarm her. "Merely ill-advised. You're my wife now. It would be better if you had a proper escort."

"My dogs are always with me."

He counseled himself not to overreact. Philly was right. She had her dogs with her every time she left the house. Surely she'd be safe if Basil accompanied her. He was as good a guard dog as any Arthur had ever come across, and the scar on Philly's leg was evidence of his power. If he'd done that when near death, what might he do when at full strength? Such a dog could easily fell any man who attempted to harm her.

Unless that man had a pistol.

"A human escort," Arthur said firmly.

Philly gave him a searching look. "I thought I wouldn't have to worry about such things after leaving London. I was so looking forward to my freedom." She frowned. "Of course, I wouldn't like to do anything that reflected poorly on you. If you think it advisable to have someone with me... Well, I suppose I shall have to have Violet accompany me until I hire a lady's maid."

"I'd rather you take one of the footmen with you."

"A footman? I don't understand, Arthur. Even in London, a maid was sufficient. And London is surely more dangerous than Heycombe."

"In many respects, yes, but..." Arthur was loathe to exert his will over her without giving her a reason for it. "There may be poachers or others who might disturb you," he said at last. "The grounds of the estate are vast, and even my gamekeeper can't guarantee there are no trespassers. It would put my mind at ease if I knew you had someone with you in case of trouble."

Her frown deepened. "I hadn't thought of trespassers and poachers. And I certainly don't wish you to become anxious every time I go for a walk."

"Then you'll do as I ask? Every time you go out?"

"If you think it best." She touched his cheek again. "Naturally, I'd much rather walk with you than one of the footmen, but I suppose you'll be too busy."

"I won't be that busy," he said gruffly. "I daresay if you can bear my slow pace—"

"Slow pace? What nonsense. We're perfectly suited." She drew his face close to hers, and after kissing him lightly on the edge of the jaw, settled into his embrace once more.

Arthur held her for just a few moments more before taking his leave. "There are one or two additional matters I must address with the men who delivered your horse. It shouldn't take long.

Will you wait for me here in your room? You can finish unpacking, and when I've done with my business, I'll come and fetch you myself."

Philly gave him another long, searching look, but acceded to his request just as she had all the others. It was only as he shut the door to her room that he caught a glimpse of the same sad and grave expression he'd seen on her face so many times in London.

He was locking her away just as Edgar Townsend had, and Arthur had no doubt that she knew it.

TWENTY-SIX

*A*rthur questioned the two men from Devonshire himself, and wasn't at all surprised when they forswore knowledge of the anonymous letter. He tended to believe them. They were unassuming country farmers with open, rather simple expressions. If they'd been lying, he'd have read it on their faces.

Crofton's face had been more difficult to read. The elderly butler had spent decades concealing his emotions behind a mask of slightly disdainful deference. After a brief inquisition, however, Arthur was convinced that Crofton knew just as little as the men from Devonshire did.

Arthur didn't personally question the rest of the servants. He was well aware that he made them nervous, and he had no interest in dealing with weeping housemaids or stammering footmen. Instead he set Crofton to the task. But when, sometime later, Crofton returned to the library, he reported not only that none of the servants had admitted to knowing anything about the letter, but also that he tended to believe them.

"I've been in service my whole life, Captain Heywood," he said, "and I know when a servant is lying and when they're telling the truth. You can be sure that nobody here knows a thing about any letter."

"I trust you were discreet."

"Indeed, sir. Everyone knows Mrs. Heywood isn't to be troubled."

"Let's hope for everyone's sake that she won't be." Arthur folded his arms. "Mrs. Heywood takes a tolerant view of gossip amongst the servants, but I'm not inclined to be so forgiving. If I discover anyone on the staff discussing this matter, I'll dismiss them without a reference."

"Yes, Captain Heywood." Crofton gave a somber nod. "I'll see they understand."

Arthur watched him leave the library. Crofton seemed to genuinely believe that the servants knew nothing about the letter. Who had brought it, then? Not Moreland himself. Not Townsend. They weren't the type of men who would dirty their own hands. They'd have enlisted someone to do their bidding.

The two men from Devonshire had been the obvious culprits. They were strangers, and could very well have been made willing emissaries for the right sum. But if not them, then who? A former servant? A faceless trespasser?

It occurred to Arthur that one of the bored, dissipated houseguests of Lord and Lady Markham might be behind it. His marriage to Philly was surely the talk of the town at the moment, and the Markhams' raucous house parties at Melton Abbey attracted all sorts of London gadflies. Arthur wouldn't put it past one of them to have written the letter and arranged for its delivery. It was just the sort of malicious prank that certain members of the *ton* might find amusing.

But even this theory had to be ruled out for, as he soon discovered, Lord and Lady Markham were currently in Bath, and wouldn't return to the neighborhood for another week at least.

After much deliberation, Arthur came to the inevitable conclusion that anyone might have written the letter, and for a few coins, anyone might have been persuaded to walk it into his house. He couldn't very well question all of Heycombe, no matter how much he might wish to. The most he could do now was focus on keeping Philly safe.

That night, dinner with Philly was more than a little strained. She was pensive and quiet, focusing a great deal on her food, yet hardly eating a morsel. Under normal circumstances, Arthur would have made some attempt to engage her; however, on this occasion, he was contending with a melancholy mood of his own.

Philly had been distant toward him ever since they'd gone for a walk together in the apple orchard. Initially he'd thought her upset over the limitations placed on her outings, but it hadn't taken long for him to come to the conclusion that she was far more preoccupied with the passionate embrace they'd shared earlier than she was with the fact that she must have an escort on all of her walks.

Now, sitting across from her at the dining table, Arthur was convinced she regretted the answer she'd given when he asked if he might come to her room more often. He was certain that, upon reflection, his request had done nothing but remind her of how he'd hurt her the last time they were together. That she was, in fact, afraid he might hurt her again.

After dinner, they repaired to the drawing room. Some of Philly's sheet music had come from Satterthwaite Court along with the rest of her things. Arthur expected she'd spend quite a bit of time at the pianoforte. Instead, after playing only three short songs, she rose from the instrument and informed him she was going to retire.

He stood, feeling rather dispirited. "Yes, of course. It's been an eventful day."

Philly didn't come to him for the usual kiss on the cheek or the forehead he'd grown accustomed to bestowing upon her each night. In fact, it became quickly apparent that she didn't intend to bid him goodnight at all. She walked straight past him toward the door of the drawing room. Only then did she stop and turn back, saying softly, "I shall be ready for bed in half an hour."

Arthur stared at her, at first uncomprehending, and then completely incapable of speech. He barely managed to give her one solemn nod before she left the room.

Within minutes he was in his own bedroom. He shrugged out of his coat and waistcoat, tossing them onto the bed. His cravat followed. He undressed no further. After pouring himself a glass of brandy, he settled himself in a chair by the fire. It felt as if more than half an hour had passed since he'd come upstairs to his bedroom, but when Arthur looked at the clock on the mantle, the hands were in the same place they'd been the last time he'd checked.

He possessed himself in patience for the next ten minutes, sipping his brandy and reflecting on how badly he'd missed the mark interpreting Philly's mood. She'd been behaving no differently than any other very timid new bride might, and instead of putting her at her ease, he'd attributed to her his own fears and doubts about their marriage.

He was the one who couldn't forget what had happened the last time they shared a bed. *He* was the one who was terrified of hurting her again. If his thoughts hadn't already been so fragmented by concerns over the letter, he'd have recognized this and acted accordingly.

After a long while spent in contemplation of his own idiocy, he heard the unmistakable murmur of Philly's voice dismissing her maid. It wasn't precisely half an hour yet, but he waited no longer.

She answered his knock on the connecting door almost immediately, and he entered her room to find her sitting up in bed. She had on a beribboned lawn nightgown and her hair was spilling loose all around her. His father's copy of *The Odyssey* lay on the bed at her side.

"Were you intending to read?" His cane was soundless on the thick carpet as he walked toward her.

"I wasn't certain you would come."

He sat down on the edge of her bed. "I wasn't certain you wanted me to."

"Why ever would you think that?"

"Because I'm a blind fool."

Philly smiled at that, and at her smile, Arthur leaned toward her and gathered her into his arms. She came to him willingly, almost impatiently, embracing him fiercely around his neck and burying her face in the collar of his linen shirt. "I'm sorry I'm so dreadfully shy about everything," she whispered against him.

"Are you? I hadn't noticed." He kissed her cheek at the same time he ran his fingers through her hair. The sheer weight of it in his hand was evidence as to why she was always losing her hairpins. "Were you shy of me this evening?"

"Yes."

Arthur kissed her once more, this time letting his lips linger against her warm, silken skin. "You needn't be afraid of me. I promise I'll never hurt you again."

"I'm not afraid of you. I'm just a little nervous."

"Nervous of me?"

"No. Indeed not. Well, that is to say, I suppose...yes. Perhaps a little."

Arthur pulled back from her to search her face. A line of worry marred her forehead. "Might I enquire what it is I've done to make you nervous?"

"It's nothing you've done."

"I'm very glad to hear it."

Her hands rested on his chest, her fingers lightly clutching the voluminous fabric of his shirt. "It's only that, this is all still so terribly new to me. If you'd be patient awhile longer, I'm sure that—"

"You think me impatient?"

"No, of course not." Her mouth tugged into a frown. "I only meant that, in time, I hope that... That is, I'm determined to become more sophisticated about this side of things."

Arthur regarded her with solemn attention. "I don't require you to be anything other than what you are," he said quietly. "And you're perfect, Philly."

She lowered her gaze, a blush rising in her cheeks.

With infinite care, he caught her chin in his hand, tilting her face up so she had no choice but to meet his eyes. "You're so perfect that, when I look at you, I can scarcely believe you're mine." His voice roughened with tenderness. "But you *are* mine. By whatever miracle. And though I'm unworthy now, if it takes the rest of my life, I will endeavor to deserve you."

"Arthur..."

"In the meanwhile, it's *you* who must be patient with me. I've never before had a treasure so precious in my keeping. I'm bound to say or do the wrong thing on occasion." He caressed the delicate line of her jaw. "If that happens, if I ever upset you or do something to make you unhappy, you must tell me at once. I can't stand not knowing what you feel. And when you fall silent, when you won't look at me or smile at me, by my very nature, I'm disposed to think the worst."

"If ever you're in doubt of my feelings, you need only ask me, but..." She hesitated. "Well, I must say the next thirty or more years will go very hard on you if you think me unhappy every time I fall silent."

Arthur's hand stilled on her face. "What did you say?"

"Only that I've been shy and quiet all my life, and I don't think it likely I'll change much during the course of our marriage."

He stared at her. "The course of our marriage being thirty or more years."

"Yes. At least, that's how long my grandparents were married. Five and thirty years, to be precise. It would have been longer if my grandmother hadn't succumbed to an inflammation of the lungs. Still, five and thirty years is a good long time to be married, I think."

"It's a lifetime." Hadn't he just promised her as much? And yet he'd never fully comprehended the reality of such a span of time until Philly said the words aloud.

Thirty or more years.

"Exactly. So you see, you mustn't worry over every prolonged silence, else you'll drive yourself to distraction." She paused, adding brusquely, "It doesn't matter in any case."

Arthur raised his brows. "Doesn't it?"

"No, for I don't believe you capable of upsetting me or making me unhappy. In truth, even if you were only half as amiable as you are now, I think I'd still find you as perfect as you find me."

Arthur drew her back into his arms, a faint smile curling the corner of his mouth. "I wasn't aware I was so very amiable to begin with."

She managed a fleeting smile of her own. "You scowl a good deal, but I've never considered it any reflection on your character."

"I can well believe it. You have a particular fondness for disagreeable brutes." He held her gaze for a moment, the wry humor in his tone a stark contrast to the extraordinarily tender manner in which he stroked her cheek. "You imagine Basil to be gentle as a lamb. And only today I find out that the very mare which you told me was well-suited for a young child is, in fact, a dangerous fiend."

Philly's mouth fell open. "Who told you that about Persy? Those two men who brought her from Fox Cross? I'll have you know that she's perfectly agreeable if you handle her in the right way."

Arthur kissed her forehead.

"She may sometimes bite or strike out…but that's only because… because…" Her voice trailed off, the impassioned defense she gave on behalf of her mare fading as he bent his head and kissed the right corner of her mouth. He heard her catch her breath.

"Do you really mean to stay with me the rest of your life?"

"Yes." She closed her eyes as he deliberately kissed the left corner of her mouth. "I vowed it to you the day we married." Her arms moved to circle his neck. "You vowed it to me, as well."

Arthur captured her mouth in his for a long, languorous kiss. Philly was warm, sweet, and responsive, melting into his embrace in the same maddening way she had on their wedding night. He eased her back onto the bed, feeling her fingers tighten in his hair as he came down with her and kissed her once more. "We vowed a lot of things to each other that day. Quite a bit about children, if I recall."

Her cheeks were flushed from his kisses and her blue and amber eyes were as soft as velvet. "I meant everything that I promised you."

Their marriage ceremony had been hastily planned and hurriedly performed, but Arthur remembered every look, every touch, every recited word. The course of his life had been irrevocably altered that day, and now, as he looked down at Philly, there was no response he could give that was equal to the magnitude of his feelings except to admit to her the simple truth.

"So did I, Philly. So did I."

TWENTY-SEVEN

*P*hilly leaned down across Persephone's withers, holding the reins deftly in her gloved hands as the mare stretched into a full, thundering gallop. The wind bit her face, tearing at the veil of her high-crowned riding hat, and caused the thick skirts of her habit to blow back against Persy's flanks. Unbidden, a smile of pure happiness spread across her face.

"Faster, Persy!"

Persephone responded by extending her neck and surging forward in a burst of speed, her giant hooves hardly touching the ground as she moved across the field in what, to any casual observer, would appear to be a bolt.

"Mrs. Heywood!" Mr. Greene shouted from behind her, his chestnut gelding struggling to catch the much bigger, much stronger mare. "Mrs. Heywood!"

She didn't listen, and she didn't stop until she crested the final hill. Only then did she shorten Persephone's stride, bringing her down to a trot, and then to a walk. The head groom wasn't far behind. While she waited for him, Philly patted Persephone's damp neck, walking her on a loose rein around the large Hawthorn tree that graced the hill.

Arthur had thought it best she confine her morning rides to a path that ran near to Heywood House. It was a beautiful ride with an avenue of elm trees, a stone bridge over a small waterway, and a few steep hills, but after riding it for so many days in a row, Philly was anxious to venture farther.

If she were accompanied by one of the younger grooms, she might have been able to convince them to go into Heycombe with her, or in the opposite direction toward Melton Abbey. Greene, however, was the head groom, and one of the few servants who had been at Heywood House as long as Arthur had. He was fiercely dedicated to his post—and equally dedicated to his master. Philly doubted she had the ability to talk him into anything.

"I say, ma'am. 'Tis not safe!" Greene trotted up to join her, his words coming out in gasps as if it were he, and not his horse, who had just ascended the hill. "Uneven ground hereabouts... poachers...sheep!"

"Sheep?"

"Aye. Sleep under this Hawthorn, they do, to shelter from the sun. Galloping horse might scare 'em."

Philly frowned. She'd never seen any sheep sleeping under the tree. If she had, she wouldn't have dared to come up the hill at such a frightening pace.

"No harm done," Greene said. "Not that it mightn't be best to carry on a mite slower."

"Yes, of course." The joy she'd felt during her mad race to the top of the hill was dissipating quickly. "I should never have been so reckless. I wasn't thinking."

"Nothing wrong with a gallop now and then, ma'am. But if

you must do, 'tis much better on the flat by the elms. Much closer to the house, too. Safer, that." Greene brought his horse up to walk alongside her, his saddle shifting dangerously to one side.

"My goodness, Greene. Have a care."

"It's only a loose girth, ma'am." Greene leapt off of his horse to tighten it. His oversize coat caught on the saddle as he landed. "Blast it," he muttered under his breath as he attempted to release himself.

The sun was shining brightly, and as Greene lowered the flap of his coat, it flashed with uncommon brilliance upon a metal object.

Philly blinked. Heaven's sake, it was a pistol!

Was it so dangerous here in Somersetshire? Or was it merely a matter of course for the local men to carry pistols?

"Greene?"

"Yes, ma'am?" He cast a glance in her direction as he vaulted back into the saddle and gathered up his reins.

"Is the poaching so very bad here on the estate?"

Greene was a man of middle age with a muscular build, a shock of sandy hair, and a grim, weather-beaten face. Philly sensed he'd be the last man on earth to share any estate gossip with her, and wasn't at all surprised when he gave her a typically ambiguous answer.

"Not as bad as some places, I'd wager, but best to take care, Mrs. Heywood."

Philly walked on with Persephone, and Greene stayed near her side. Persephone flattened her ears and showed her teeth to the chestnut gelding, warning him not to get too close. "And... are poachers hereabouts particularly villainous?"

"Villainous, ma'am?" Greene furrowed his brow. "Can't ever tell, can you? But, best to take—"

"Yes, I know. Best to take care." She sighed to herself as she guided Persephone down the hill.

Arthur had told her she was his treasure, and it was becoming apparent he meant to guard her like one. She'd known he was overprotective from the day they married, but in the past week it had become markedly worse. She now took a groom with her on all of her rides, and Arthur himself escorted her on most of her walks.

Philly knew she had no cause to be unhappy. She had far more freedom here with Arthur than she'd ever had in London. Besides that, she had the pleasure of Arthur's company, and the growing intimacy they shared together during his now nightly visits to her room. Of course, he still wouldn't allow himself to spend the night in her bed. And he hadn't yet told her that he loved her. But many women were far less privileged than she was. Indeed, Philly considered herself extraordinarily fortunate.

"...right on the arm. Might have bled if he weren't wearing his heavy coat."

She glanced up, uncertain what Greene had been telling her. "Oh?"

"Told him to tie her up short next time, so she couldn't reach back to him."

Philly flushed with embarrassment as she realized, quite suddenly, that Greene was explaining to her that Persephone had bitten one of the grooms.

"Don't you fret, Mrs. Heywood. Can't say your mare will be the only animal in the Heywood stable that's hard to manage. Just you look at that stallion of the master's."

"Hyperion?"

Greene nodded. "A right devil."

"Is he? I thought him rather gentle. At least, he has been whenever I've come to see him."

"No, ma'am. He'd kick down the whole stable if it weren't made of stone." Greene chuckled. "Captain Heywood can tell you as much himself, if he has a mind to."

Philly smiled. "I shall ask him." She drew up Persephone, allowing Greene to take the lead as they descended the steepest part of the hill. "He's had Hyperion a very long time, I believe."

"Aye. He come here from Stratfield Hall as a three-year-old, just under saddle. Was a devil then as much as now. Couldn't no one ride him but Captain Heywood."

"My husband must have been a very accomplished rider."

"I've not seen better." Greene's chest swelled with uncharacteristic pride. "Could handle the most vicious brute in the stable. Not a bit of fear about him. Ready to do or dare anything was Captain Heywood." He fell quiet for a moment before adding rather gruffly, "The path we ride in the morning was his favorite."

"Was it?" Philly looked at Greene. "Did he used to ride this path on Hyperion?"

"Aye, ma'am. See just there, beyond that rise? The master practiced his shooting there."

Philly turned her head to peer out across the grounds, her eyes squinting against the morning sun. Arthur had only ever mentioned his prowess with a pistol to her once, and then only in the vaguest of terms. He was bitter that he could no longer shoot, that much she knew. And from that bitterness, she'd deduced all on her own that his skill must have been something truly extraordinary. "I imagine he was an excellent shot."

"Better at shooting than he was at riding," Greene said. "He should've joined the Rifles, and so I told him. But he was that set on the cavalry."

He said nothing else the entire way back to the stable, and Philly didn't press him. She contented herself with the little scraps of information he'd given her. Along with other things she'd heard about Arthur, it served to create a picture of the man he'd been before he left to fight in the Peninsula.

When they arrived back at the stable, her dogs ran to meet her. Persephone knew them well, and though she flattened her ears, she refrained from kicking out as they leapt about her legs.

Philly dismounted and handed her reins off to a waiting groom. She thanked Greene, and having assured him that she would indeed be riding at the same time next morning, left the stable yard and returned to the house, her dogs trotting along at her side.

When she crossed the threshold into the main hall, Mrs. Lamb rushed to meet her. "Mrs. Heywood, thank heaven you've returned."

"What is it, Mrs. Lamb? Is something the matter?"

"I should say so, ma'am. A young woman arrived shortly after you left for your ride. She's in a right state. I tried to send her off, the impertinent little wretch, but she made such a commotion. I didn't like to bother Captain Heywood—"

"Is she looking for work?"

"I expect she is, ma'am. And she says you're honor bound to employ her."

"Honor bound?" Philly laughed as she removed her hat and her gloves. "Who is this person, Mrs. Lamb? Where has she come from?"

"She claims to have come down from London. Arrived in Heycombe just this morning by common stage, if you can imagine. She says her name is Sara."

TWENTY-EIGHT

Philly received Sara in the morning room. Mrs. Lamb led her in, the housekeeper's expression as disapproving as it could possibly be. No sooner had the little maid spotted Philly sitting on the settee than she ran to her, throwing herself at Philly's slippered feet with a terrible sob.

"Oh, Miss Satterthwaite!" she wailed. "Miss Satterthwaite!"

"Heaven's sake, girl. Get up from there. Get up." Mrs. Lamb shook Sara by her narrow shoulders.

Philly held up a staying hand. "It's all right, Mrs. Lamb. You may leave us."

"But Mrs. Heywood, she's crushed your skirts. And here you are freshly changed after your ride—"

"All will be well," Philly said.

Mrs. Lamb clearly wasn't convinced. She glared at the figure of the sobbing servant once more, and then, with a rigid bow, exited the room.

Sara's tiny frame was engulfed by a worn, drab cloak, and her mousy blonde hair, formerly neat and clean, was now dirty and in complete disarray.

Philly placed her hand gently on Sara's back. She was alarmed to feel how much thinner she'd become. "Sara, you mustn't cry so."

"Oh, miss." Sara drew back to wipe her nose on the edge of her cloak. "I didn't mean to crush your skirts, but I've traveled all night, and two villains tried to meddle with me, and if it weren't for the coachman coming to my aid, I would've met with a fate worse than death." She swallowed another loud sob. "I've no money left for anything, miss. I beg you—"

"Hush now." Philly helped her up. "Here, take this." She pressed an embroidered handkerchief into her hand. "Now, sit down beside me, and tell me what's happened."

Sara wept awhile longer into Philly's handkerchief, and then slowly, with sniffs and sobs, she began to speak. "I was dismissed without a reference, miss, on account of Mrs. Vale said it was all my fault you ran off with Captain Heywood." She cried afresh at the memory of such an injustice. "I tried to get work, miss. I went all around the city. Lady Eustace's housekeeper said I could come on as a scullery maid. A scullery maid, miss!" She gave another wrenching sob. "But after two days, she sent me off again."

As she listened to Sara, Philly's conscience grew heavy. She felt a deep sense of having done wrong by the little maid. Whether she'd intended it or not, her actions had resulted in Sara being reduced to her present miserable state. "How long have you been seeking work in London?"

"More than three weeks, miss."

"Three weeks?" Philly was horrified. "Do you mean you were dismissed directly after I left?"

"Yes, miss. I was made to go on Sunday. I begged to stay one more day, but Mrs. Vale wouldn't hear of it." She sniffled. "'Twas very unchristian of them to turn me out on a Sunday."

"How have you been keeping yourself?"

"Not well, miss. I took a day's work when I could find it, but no one would have me for long, and twice I was refused my wages. What can I do, miss? I've spent everything to come to you, and if you won't help me—"

"You needn't distress yourself any further, Sara. I've no intention of turning you out."

Sara began to weep again.

"You're right," Philly said. "I'm honor bound to help you."

The little maid's face turned bright red. "Oh, Miss Satterthwaite, I *had* to say it. That housekeeper of yours said she would run me off."

"It's perfectly all right. I'm not offended." Philly took in the whole of Sara's bedraggled appearance in one comprehensive glance. "Now, it seems to me that before you begin any sort of work you must first have a meal, a bath, and a good night's rest."

Sara exhaled a long, trembling breath. "Thank you, miss. God bless you. I knew you'd help me. I always said you were the best mistress—"

"There's no need for that. As it happens, your arrival is very well timed. You see, I've been here almost a month and have yet to employee a lady's maid."

"*A lady's maid?*" Sara gaped.

"Indeed. Now, you were only a housemaid at my uncle's, and there will be a lot to learn—"

"I'll learn, Miss Satterthwaite. I'll learn."

Philly smiled slightly at Sara's exuberance. "I'm certain you will. And the first thing you must learn is that I'm no longer Miss Satterthwaite."

"Yes, ma'am. I heard you were married from the coachman. I was ever so glad. Mrs. Vale said you'd run away with Captain Heywood and ruined yourself, but I knew—"

"My reputation was never in danger. I was married the very

morning I left my uncle's house, and William provided my escort."

"William is here?" Sara's eyes darted toward the door, as if the handsome footman might burst in at any moment. "Mr. Evans said he'd left with you, but Mrs. Vale said as how he—"

"Yes. He's here. He's a footman, and doing rather well, I think." Philly rose from the settee and moved to ring the bell pull. "Heycombe isn't an exciting village, Sara, and you'll find this part of the country excessively dull, I fear, even if employed in the lofty position of lady's maid. You think on it tonight, and if you decide you'd rather return to London, I'll speak to Captain Heywood and see if there might not be a place that can be found for you there."

Sara's sharp little chin jutted out. "I won't change my mind, ma'am."

Mrs. Lamb entered the room in response to Philly's summons, wearing the same disapproving look she'd worn when she left it. Philly quickly apprised her of the situation, and after another onslaught of tears and a profusion of thanks, Sara was dispatched down to the kitchen to get something to eat.

"It's your decision who to have as your lady's maid, Mrs. Heywood," Mrs. Lamb said, walking alongside Philly out of the morning room, "but I feel obliged to tell you that Violet will be very disappointed. The girl has her faults, I won't deny it, but she's pinned her hopes on gaining the position."

"I've done nothing to encourage her on that score."

"Nor have I. She's been a poor personal maid to you, if you don't mind my saying so, and far too lazy to improve with training." Mrs. Lamb gave a weary sigh. "But she has a new young man—a gentleman, she says!—and has been talking of marriage. I expect she hopes a higher wage might enable them to set up house."

"I see." Philly stopped, not far from the closed doors of the library. "I wasn't aware Violet had a beau. Perhaps...yes, I think a small bonus might be in order. She has, after all, done most of the tasks a lady's maid might these few weeks."

Mrs. Lamb gave an approving nod. "Very good, Mrs. Heywood."

At the sound of the library door opening, Arthur looked up from the ledger he'd been studying. Philly entered the room, shutting the door carefully behind her.

"Am I disturbing you?" she asked.

He retrieved his cane and moved to stand. "Need you ask?"

Before he could walk toward her, she rushed to him and embraced him round the neck in a wholly unladylike fashion, receiving from him in exchange a very ungentlemanly full kiss on the mouth.

"Have you come to fetch me for our walk?" he asked in a low voice, kissing her once more.

"No. That is, we can walk now if you like, but it's not why I've come." She lowered her arms from his neck. "May I talk to you for a moment?"

Arthur smiled at her suddenly formal manner. "I'm at your disposal." He gestured to the chair near his, remaining on his feet until she sat down.

The dogs had come in with Philly. They milled about awhile before lying down on the carpet.

"I wouldn't bother you if it weren't important," she said.

"What's given you the idea that it's a bother?"

"Oh, well, I..." She was sitting near enough to him that one of his booted feet brushed against her delicate kid slipper, momentarily flustering her. "I mean to say that the library is where you go when you prefer to be alone."

"Is it?"

"And I don't like to intrude on your solitude."

"I see."

"But this is rather important, and you've said I'm to tell you if anything occurs that might be upsetting in any way."

Arthur's indulgent smile vanished. "What is it, Philly? What's happened?"

She took a deep breath and related to him the details of Sara's arrival from London.

He listened without comment.

"So you see," she concluded, "it's all my fault, and therefore I must remedy it if I can."

"It's no fault of yours. The blame lies with Townsend. You can't be expected to right all of his wrongs, and I find it singularly presumptuous that this girl expects you to do so."

"No, indeed. She's made no such presumption. She's desperate, and thoroughly wretched. I don't believe she's eaten very much at all since I left London, and I shudder to think where she's been sleeping." Philly's mouth tugged into a worried frown. "She's so thin, Arthur, and so pitiful. I know if you'd seen her as I did that you couldn't help but have compassion."

"Perhaps I'd better see her then."

"Now? Oh no, I don't think it wise. Not at present. She's in such a state and you'd only terrify her."

"She can't be so terrified of me. Unless I'm mistaken, this is the same maid who complained about your meeting me in the park to Mrs. Vale. The same maid who conspired to isolate you from any suitor other than the Duke of Moreland."

"Conspired! That's rather strong. What does a good servant do but protect the interests of their master? Surely you expect the same from your staff. I daresay if I'd twice met a man on one of my walks, you'd have every expectation that the maid or footman accompanying me would inform you of it at once—even if I didn't wish them to."

Arthur's hand tightened reflexively around the handle of his cane. "The difference being that you're my wife, and I, unlike Townsend, am not up to some underhand scheme."

Fox ambled over to Philly and pawed at her leg. In response, she picked him up and settled him on her lap. "Sara's an uneducated housemaid of barely eighteen. She wouldn't have understood such subtleties."

"And you'd treat this uneducated housemaid no differently than one of your injured dogs. But she isn't one of your pets to be cared for and brought back to health, Philly. She's a maid from Townsend's own house. Her loyalty may still lie with him."

"You weren't so suspicious of William."

"On more than one occasion, William risked his position to help you. While this maid showed devotion to no one but your uncle."

"But, Arthur—"

"Have her sent to me. I promise not to terrify her unnecessarily, but I would judge her sad tale for myself. When I've done with her, you may feed her and coddle her to your heart's content, and if I determine all is not as it seems, I'll personally see to her passage on a return coach to London."

Arthur looked across his desk at the sharp-faced little maid who had so plagued him in London. She was indeed as pitiful to behold as Philly had said, and yet...he couldn't fail to notice her upraised chin and the acquisitive glint in her eye. She might be somewhat worse for wear, but she was a long way from being overcome by her miserable circumstances.

"Why on Sunday?" he asked, already suspecting the answer. "Why not on Friday? Or Saturday?"

Sara's mouth pressed into a thin line. "Mrs. Vale paid me no mind until His Grace's visit on Saturday. If they all hadn't ended up so angry, I expect they'd have kept me on, but cook said they must blame someone for Miss Satterthwaite's leaving, and it might as well be me."

Arthur toyed with a newly sharpened quill pen. "You were called before the Duke of Moreland?"

"Yes, sir."

"And?"

She wrung her hands in her lap. "Mr. Townsend and Mrs. Vale asked me all manner of questions, but I can't see why they bothered, for they didn't believe anything I told them."

"What did you tell them?"

"The truth, sir." She looked anguished. "That *you* were the gentleman Miss Satterthwaite met in the park."

He raised a brow. "Hadn't you told them as much already?"

"No, sir. I only told Mrs. Vale that...that Miss Satterthwaite was often importuned by gentlemen on her walks."

"But when Townsend and Mrs. Vale questioned you on Saturday, you confessed all."

She nodded. "I told them we'd met you twice in the park, and that I fancied Miss Satterthwaite was arranging to meet you again."

"I take it they weren't pleased with this information."

Sara's eyes welled up with tears. "That man of the duke's, Mr. Pritchard, said I wasn't fit for service, and if Mr. Townsend was in any way a gentleman, he wouldn't have employed the likes of me and William." She sniffled. "The duke said he'd wasted enough time, and then he and Mr. Townsend had words, but I didn't hear what they said except that Mr. Townsend had made a fool of His Grace, and His Grace wouldn't be made a fool of by Mr. Townsend, Miss Satterthwaite, or anyone. And then, His Grace said Mr. Townsend would learn he wasn't to be trifled with, and that Miss Satterthwaite—"

"What about Miss Satterthwaite?"

"I couldn't rightly hear everything, sir." She managed to look contrite. "'Twas something about leaving her to her fate, I think, but I can't be certain."

The quill pen cracked in Arthur's hand. He looked at it blankly for a moment before tossing it aside. "Leaving her to her fate."

"Yes, sir." She shrank back into her chair. "'Tis what I heard."

Arthur fell silent for a time. "You intend to stay on here, then?" he asked finally. "In service to Mrs. Heywood?"

"Yes, sir."

"Loyal to Mrs. Heywood?"

"With my whole heart, sir."

"You've been dismissed once without a reference. You know now that it's an uncommonly difficult circumstance to be in."

"Yes, Captain Heywood."

"But as difficult as it is, it will be nothing compared to what you'll face if I discover you're here under false pretenses."

"Beg pardon, sir?"

"If you've been sent here by Townsend or the Duke of Moreland in order to make mischief for my wife, I won't only dismiss you without a reference, I'll see to it that you never find work again. Not in London. Not in the country. Not anywhere. Do you understand me?"

Sara's mouth trembled. "Yes, Captain Heywood."

Arthur looked at her a moment longer, waiting for her to disavow any connection to Townsend or the duke.

But Sara said nothing more.

TWENTY-NINE

———— ❧❦ ————

$\mathscr{A}$ week later, Pebmarsh made an unexpected early morning visit. Arthur was obliged to meet with him in the library. It wasn't wholly inconvenient. Philly was out riding and wouldn't be back for an hour, at least. The time when she was away passed at an agonizingly slow pace. Arthur often felt as if he couldn't properly draw breath until one of the footmen ducked into the library to tell him she'd returned safely from her ride. Pebmarsh's arrival was a welcome distraction.

They'd been talking for half an hour when Crofton entered the room. "I beg your pardon, Captain Heywood. The Earl of Gordon's carriage has just come up the drive."

"*What?*" Arthur stood from behind his desk.

"Mrs. Lamb is already seeing to rooms for the earl and his guest."

"His guest? What guest?"

Crofton cleared his throat. "His lordship is accompanied by Mrs. Ogilvy, sir."

Arthur muttered an oath.

Marianne Ogilvy was his father's longtime mistress. The widow of a wealthy tradesman, she'd never been accepted into polite society, and even if she had, she was certainly not the type of female a gentleman should ever bring to meet his new daughter-in-law. The fact that the earl had done so was an insult to Philly. A slap in the face.

What the devil did his father mean by such behavior?

Arthur made short work of dismissing his steward, and walked quickly out through the main hall and down the front steps. A month of twice daily walks with Philly had made his leg stronger. It was a gradual improvement, the effects of which lengthened his stride and allowed him to take the stairs more easily with the aid of his cane.

"Good God, man. What's this?" Edward Albert Heywood, Seventh Earl of Gordon, stood outside his gleaming black coach. He was dressed far warmer than the climate warranted, a figured silver-and-ebony walking stick in his hand. Now in his sixties, his black hair had gone white, and his tall, formerly athletic figure was stooped with age. "I hardly recognize you, my boy."

"Sir." Arthur greeted his father as a second coach lumbered up the drive and came to an unsteady halt behind the earl's elegant travelling coach. It was loaded with trunks of every variety, and appeared to contain, among other servants, his father's formidable valet, Mrs. Ogilvy's personal maid, and a lofty personage that Arthur very much suspected to be the French chef who presided over the kitchens at Stratfield Hall.

The earl placed a hand on Arthur's arm. "Do I have your new wife to thank for this? Is she the one who has brought you back to me?"

Arthur felt himself grow warm under his cravat. "I'm a little improved, but it's hardly miraculous."

"Don't cozen me, sir. You have a look of health about you." The earl dropped his voice. "And your leg? Your hand? Those damnable headaches? Do they still give you much pain?"

"Less," Arthur admitted gruffly.

"Thank God for that." The earl turned back to the coach to assist his mistress out. "Madam, come and look at how improved my son is."

Marianne Ogilvy was a petite woman of fifty, with a mass of brown hair, laughing blue eyes, and dimples in her cheeks and chin. She had a voluptuous figure, the curves of which couldn't be concealed even in her modest slate-colored carriage gown.

"Captain Heywood," she said with a merry laugh. "Heavens, you do look uncommonly well." She gave a perfunctory curtsy, which was returned by a very stern bow. "Do you see, Gordon? You'd no cause to worry at all. This new bride of his has done him a world of good." She craned her neck, looking about amongst the chaos of the servants. "But where is she, Captain? I'm longing to meet her."

"She's out riding."

"Ah, a sporting sort of girl, is she?" The earl nodded his approval as they walked up the steps to the house. "Some fine horses at Tattersall's of late. You might consider it, Arthur. Anything by Gringolet would do her nicely. Not as impressive as Titan was, mind you, but Gringolet's foals are levelheaded."

"Gordon spends far too much time studying bloodlines." Mrs. Ogilvy gave the earl a dimpled smile. "He'll buy Gringolet himself before the month is out, mark my words."

Arthur ignored their talk of fine horses. He'd grown up with such conversation and was inured to it. Besides, he had no desire to tell his father—whose stable of bloodstock was the envy of every sportsman in England—that his new daughter-in-law was perfectly happy with her bad-tempered crossbreed mare. "If we'd known in advance of your arrival, my wife would have been here to receive you."

"Couldn't be helped," the earl said. "Business and whatnot. My health. Mrs. Ogilvy ill. Your damned brother in trouble with a woman up north."

Arthur cast his father a sharp glance.

The earl nodded. "An opera dancer this time. Not ideal, but better than a blasted adventuress, I'm sure you'll agree."

In the house, there was a flurry of activity as servants rushed about unloading the coaches and preparing things for the unexpected guests. Mrs. Lamb came to meet them in the main hall, and after a brief exchange of words, Mrs. Ogilvy was swept off to an upstairs room so she could refresh herself.

"I mean no disrespect to your new bride," the earl said when his mistress was out of earshot. "But at my age it's damned hard to travel without my comforts. Couldn't leave Mrs. Ogilvy behind." He fidgeted a moment with his walking stick. "I suppose your wife will cut her dead."

"I doubt that very much."

"Or refuse the introduction."

"She'd be justified in doing so." Arthur knew that Philly wasn't likely to be offended at all, but he was offended for her.

"Perhaps you can explain it to the girl? Wouldn't like to insult her so early in our acquaintance. She's likely to be my only daughter-in-law if your brother continues as he is."

"It's a little late to worry about insulting her."

"Indeed. What's done is done. Now, if you've grown tired of looking severe, you might see your way to offering me a large glass of claret and a comfortable chair. I have an item or two to discuss with you, and we may as well get all this unpleasantness out of the way before your wife returns from her ride."

Arthur motioned his father into the library. A footman poured out the earl's drink, placed the decanter at the ready, and then quietly departed, shutting the doors behind him.

"Unpleasantness?"

"Quite so. Can't thwart a man like Edgar Townsend without a bit of unpleasantness now, can you?" The earl settled himself into a chair near the fireplace, watching closely as Arthur sat down in the chair across from him. "I must tell you, my boy, your exploits of the last month put your brother in the shade. I should've known when you finally lost your head over a woman, you'd do a thorough job of it."

Arthur fell quiet. The last thing he'd expected from his father was a reprimand. And he'd certainly not anticipated being compared to his rakehell older brother.

"I received a nasty letter from Townsend several weeks ago. An express, no less. Said you destroyed his investment scheme, spirited off his niece and secretly married her, and then, as a final insult, stole one of his servants."

Arthur leaned back in his chair and folded his arms. "It sounds rather fantastical when you list it all out like that, but I'll not deny it."

The earl fixed him with a repressive glare. "He also said that this niece of his you ran off with was betrothed to the Duke of Moreland."

"I'd hardly call it a betrothal. She refused him."

"Did she, by God." His father mulled this over. "Suppose you're aware the details of your courtship and marriage are the talk of London?"

Arthur shrugged a shoulder.

"Been getting daily reports from all and sundry. Ombersley's written. Even Underhill sent round a note. Informed me he was a witness at your wedding, damn his impudence." The earl harrumphed. "I understand she's a rare beauty. The Work of Art, isn't that what she's called? A rather grand appellation. Different colored eyes, has she? And no fortune to speak of? Yet she refused the Duke of Moreland." He drummed his fingers on the arm of his chair. "I must tell you there are some who think you've taken the girl against her will. Tricked her. Trapped her. Abducted her. All that sort of nonsense. Mrs. Ogilvy takes a more romantic view. Tells me it must have been a love match."

Arthur said nothing.

"Either way, a brutal business this, but then you've never been one to do anything by halves." The earl's gravelly voice held a mixture of pride and reproof. "It wasn't enough to simply marry the girl. You had to destroy Townsend in the process."

"It seems to me that you've already taken a particular view of this situation. A view that isn't very much in my favor."

"Nonsense. Do you think Townsend or anyone can turn me against my own son? Mind you, not that he didn't try. Must have written that letter of his while in a fine rage. He's finished in London, you know. Ombersley's acquainted with Moreland's solicitor. He tells me Moreland has fixed the blame on Townsend for this debacle. Apparently, Moreland's pulled out all support for Townsend's business ventures. I give it six months before the man sells up and leaves in disgrace."

Arthur was unmoved by the prospect of Townsend's impending downfall. "Do you have it with you?"

"What's that? The letter?" The earl took a large swallow of claret. "No, my boy. Left it back at Stratfield. No need for you to read it."

"Why the devil not? What else did he say?"

"Not worth repeating."

"I'd be very interested to hear it."

His father took another swallow, draining his glass dry and then busying himself with refilling it. "Foolishness. Said you insinuated yourself into his household, all for the purpose of stealing away his niece. Called you an embezzler of property, or some such nonsense."

"An embezzler of property?" A dry smile edged Arthur's mouth. "Is that all? Come, sir, I would have you speak plainly. If I'm to be denied the chance to read the letter, you must at least relay to me the entirety of the charges Townsend has laid at my door."

"Blast it, Arthur, the rest wasn't about you. It was about your wife."

A taut silence fell over the room. For a time, neither man said a word.

"Blast it," the earl muttered again. "Townsend said his niece has a fondness for broken things. That she left with you, married you, not in spite of your injuries, but because of them."

"Is that all?"

"Is it not enough?"

"And you thought this would offend me?"

"By God, yes!"

Arthur raked a hand through his hair. What Townsend had said was no revelation to him. Arthur had recognized from the first time she took his arm in the park that Philly—who had shunned the much handsomer Lord Darly—had let her guard down with him solely because he was injured. However, within a week, they'd become friends. And within a fortnight, they'd become something more.

"My wife is exceptionally tenderhearted, as you shall no doubt learn, but you may believe me, sir, when I tell you that Phyllida married me because she cares for me. Pity had nothing to do with it."

"Pity!" His father drenched the word in disapproval. "I should think not."

"As for all the rest, it's true enough—to a point. I never had any design to ruin Townsend. I withdrew from his investment scheme as a matter of conscience, and I married his niece because I care for her. A formal offer of marriage and a long engagement were out of the question. Townsend and Moreland threatened her and terrified her. They may still be doing so. There was nothing to be done except to spirit her off, as you say."

"What's this about them threatening her still? Do you mean to say that Townsend or Moreland—?"

"Possibly." Arthur went to his desk and retrieved the anonymous note from within a locked drawer. He handed it to his father, and upon returning to his seat, explained as clearly and concisely as possible the manner in which the note had arrived.

He reminded his father of the tales of Moreland's vengeance. He told him what Forsythe had related about the death of Molly Cartwright. And he told him of the wager he'd found in the betting book at his club.

The earl listened intently, his sharply intelligent eyes coming alive in his lined face. "Rubbish," he pronounced, when Arthur had finished.

"You don't believe it?"

"Moreland's no friend to me, but men of our vintage can hardly avoid knowing each other. He's arrogant. Ruthless. A bit mad about his damned collection. But he's no more or less dangerous than any other very rich, very powerful man. He has plenty of enemies. Always has had. Might say he cultivates them. Any one of them could've put that wager in the book at your club."

"What about the stories of the vengeance he's exacted? Surely they can't all be falsehoods circulated by his enemies."

"May be there's an element of truth to them. I couldn't say. My own opinion's always been that it was Moreland himself who circulated those tales. It makes it easier for him to acquire things if people are in fear of refusing him. But if you do refuse him, as I have done on one occasion myself, I can promise you that nothing very sinister happens."

Arthur looked at his father in surprise. "Moreland attempted to buy something from you for his collection?"

"Quite so. You weren't in England at the time, else you'd know of it. Moreland wanted to buy Titan. I told him flat out that no amount of money would ever induce me to sell. Poor man didn't take it well, but that was all there was to it. No vengeance."

"Titan died."

"Two years later. Of colic. Can't tell me that had anything to do with Moreland." The earl folded the anonymous letter and handed it back to Arthur. "Might be this was sent by an admirer of your wife. One of her hangers-on in London, or some former beau from the countryside."

Arthur stiffened at the suggestion. "My wife has no former beaux. And she's certainly had no hangers-on."

"Don't be a fool, Arthur. She's known as The Work of Art, for God's sake. Do you think she had no admirers?"

Any reply Arthur might have made was cut off by the unmistakable sound of raised voices in the main hall. Within seconds, footfalls pounded toward the library.

The door was thrust open and William entered. His face was pale. "Captain Heywood," he said breathlessly. "Mrs. Heywood has had an accident."

THIRTY

*rthur entered the hall in time to see Greene carrying Philly into the morning room, the dogs leaping and barking all around, trying to get to their mistress. He had a brief glimpse of Philly's hair, fallen loose from its pins, and the heavy skirts of her riding habit, torn and dirty.

Without a thought for his father, or anyone else, Arthur covered the distance across the hall in a few long strides, entering the morning room just as Greene settled Philly down on one of the faded silk sofas. Her dogs gathered round her, and as she sat back against the cushions, she stretched out a hand to reassure them.

"*What happened*?" Arthur bellowed at Greene as he went to Philly's side.

Greene stood at attention, only a few feet from the sofa. "Mrs. Heywood's mare tripped as we were galloping down by the elms, sir. Mare fell to the ground. Flung Mrs. Heywood a good distance."

Arthur sat down next to Philly. He took her face in his hands, scanning her for injuries. "Are you all right?" he asked in a harsh undertone.

Philly's normally rosy cheeks were white as marble. "Perfectly all right."

A small group of servants had gathered at the edge of the morning room. Violet stood—pale and anxious—next to William and another tall footman named Edward.

Crofton was in front of them, wringing his hands in distress. "Shall I summon the surgeon, Captain Heywood?"

"No, please." Philly's objection was faint but insistent. "If you'll fetch Mrs. Lamb to me. I may have turned my ankle a little, and she'll know best what to do."

Crofton waited for the affirming nod from Arthur before hurrying off.

Philly swallowed. "That's why Greene insisted on carrying me. I told him he mustn't trouble himself, but, Arthur—"

"How the devil did this happen?" Arthur demanded of the groom.

The earl came to stand in the doorway. He leaned on his ebony walking stick, watching the scene in silence.

From his place on the floor near Philly, Basil watched the earl with equal attention.

"Arthur, please," Philly said. "It was an accident. Some poacher had set a snare. That's all. It was covered with leaves, and there was no way anyone could have seen it. But more importantly—"

"*A snare?*" Arthur's blood ran cold. He dropped his hands from Philly's face and turned on Greene. "What sort of a snare?"

"A small trench filled with jagged stones," Greene answered. "It caught the mare's hoof."

"On the avenue of the elms," Arthur said flatly. "On a riding path."

Greene exchanged a weighted look with him. "Aye, Captain Heywood."

"William, bring the decanter of brandy. Edward, Violet, see that a hot bath is prepared for your mistress. Greene, wait for me in the library." As Arthur sent off each of the servants, he noticed his father but turned back to Philly without a word of acknowledgment. "Would you like a sip of brandy for your nerves?" He took one of her hands. "A cup of tea? Or should we see about getting you to your room?"

"I'm all right. And so is Persy. And so are my nerves." Her eyes were shining. She squeezed his hand. "Arthur, I've been trying to tell you...I think you mustn't even realize..."

Arthur removed a stray hairpin that clung to a lock of her hair. "Realize what, my dear?"

"You walked into this room without your cane."

Arthur stared at her for several seconds, uncomprehending before looking down and seeing for himself that his cane wasn't with him. In his urgency to go to his hurt wife, he'd failed to pick it up when he left the library. Without even knowing it, he'd walked all the way across the hall and into the morning room completely unaided.

"I saw it all, my boy." The earl made his way into the room. "Every step."

Philly turned her head with a start, registering the earl's presence for the first time.

Jasper and Dash leapt to their feet, and Fox growled a low warning. Basil stayed where he was, anchored by his mistress, his dark eyes sharp as flint.

"Philly," Arthur said, "may I present my father, Edward Heywood, Seventh Earl of Gordon. Sir?" He looked at the earl, an unmistakable ring of pride in his voice. "This is Phyllida Heywood. My wife."

280

Philly's bedroom was dark as pitch. The curtains were drawn, the fire had died down, and the single candle by the bedside had sputtered out some time ago. Her cheek rested on Arthur's bare chest, her arm draped across his midsection as he absently stroked her hair.

Even if she hadn't felt him touching her, Philly would have known he was awake. Arthur never slept in her bed. He held her until she drifted to sleep in his arms.

And then he left.

The knowledge that he would leave soon, returning to his own bed, made her press herself more closely against him, as if she might hold him to her in just such a way that would prevent him from going.

Arthur responded by closing his arms around her more securely. "You and my father were getting along famously this evening. I began to think I'd never have you to myself again."

Philly smiled to herself. Since the moment of their marriage, Arthur had been accustomed to receiving her undivided attention, but tonight, for the first time, he'd been obliged to share it.

No matter whether she'd been listening to his father's dignified musings about a famous stallion named Gringolet (*Every foal guaranteed to have the temperament of a saint!*), or attending Mrs. Ogilvy's bubbly chatter about an equally famous modiste name Madame Moreau (*Gowns of gossamer, held together by nothing but silken thread and a few French prayers!*), Arthur had remained silent, the shadow of a scowl marring his brow.

When she'd retired to bed ahead of the rest of the company, she'd suspected he wouldn't be long in joining her.

She hadn't been wrong.

Arthur had entered her room less than half an hour later, and with complete disregard for the presence of Sara, taken Philly into his arms and kissed her. There had been no time for talking. His need for her had been too great.

"Will they be staying long with us, do you think?" she asked.

"They haven't said, but my father only ever brings that French chef of his on visits lasting more than a fortnight." Arthur fell quiet a moment before asking, "Do you mind it very much?"

"Not at all. I'm a little out of practice playing hostess, but I hope I shall rally enough to be a credit to you."

"I have no doubt of it."

"Besides, I like your father and I'd be happy to know him better."

"Of course you like him. He spent all of dinner talking to you about horses and hounds."

"Do you think he approves of me?" she asked.

"Approves? He's halfway to believing you're an angel."

"If he thinks well of me at all, it's only because he imagines I had something to do with your walking this morning."

Arthur twisted a lock of her hair around his fingers. "My father has been waiting these three years for me to effect a miraculous recovery. He'd rather believe almost anything than accept the truth."

Philly was rather reluctant to accept the truth herself. According to Arthur, his walk from the library to the morning room had been nothing more than a short-lived physical response to a crisis. He'd told them it had nothing at all to do with actual healing, and had cautioned them not to make more out of it than it was.

She suspected that his words had been as much for his own benefit as for theirs.

How many times in the past three years had Arthur seen flashes of improvement only to have his hopes dashed? It was no wonder he was on his guard against disappointment.

"I was sorry to disillusion him. But it's better to be realistic about these things." He kissed the top of her head, signaling an end to the discussion. "Tell me, sweetheart, how did you find Mrs. Ogilvy?"

Philly considered her answer. She knew she should be insulted by Mrs. Ogilvy's visit. Arthur certainly was. He'd told her that Mrs. Ogilvy was the earl's mistress. A shocking relationship, to be sure. And Philly *was* shocked a little, but try as she might, she could find no fault with the woman. "She seems a cheerful sort of person."

"Excessively so."

"With no false airs."

"I should think not."

"Oh, but I do like her," Philly admitted at last. "She isn't at all how I imagined a gentleman's mistress to be."

Arthur's hand stilled on her hair. "And how is that, my dear?"

"Well, I don't know precisely, but my cousin Elizabeth sometimes spoke of women who rouged their cheeks, drank immoderately, and told vulgar stories. Perhaps she was referencing some other class of disreputable ladies? For you must own that Mrs. Ogilvy isn't anything like that."

"Not as far as I can tell." There was a faint quake in Arthur's voice.

She poked him. "You may well laugh. I'm sure I know nothing about mistresses and tradesmen's widows."

"Nor does your cousin, by the sound of it. Her description brings to mind a dame in a pantomime."

"Well, no matter her appearance, I think it abominably unfair that a woman as amiable as Mrs. Ogilvy should be treated poorly on account of her position."

"Marianne Ogilvy can have no complaints about her treatment here. You've made her and my father very welcome. So much so that I fear they'll never want to leave."

"She's invited me to go for a walk with her tomorrow."

"You're to stay indoors and rest tomorrow," said Arthur severely. "It's too soon after your fall to go walking with anyone."

"Nonsense. Mrs. Lamb gave me a thorough going over, and says I'm perfectly fine." She leaned over Arthur to kiss one of the knife scars that marked his chest. His breath caught the instant her lips touched his skin. "Indeed, I feel extraordinarily well."

"I can see that." Arthur pulled her farther up across his chest and captured her mouth in his.

Philly could feel his heart hammering in time with hers as she melted along the length of his body, her lips giving way to his with a contented sigh. "Stay with me tonight."

He gave a low groan of frustration. "You know I cannot."

"But your nightmares have lessened. You told me so yourself. I'm sure that nothing—"

"Philly, I won't take even the smallest chance of hurting you again." His hands moved over her linen-clad back in a warm caress. "But I promise I'll stay until you fall asleep."

"Perhaps I won't fall asleep, then," she said. "I'll make you stay awake with me all night."

"That's hardly a threat, my dear. Besides, after the scare you gave me today, I doubt whether I shall ever sleep again."

She lay her cheek down on his shoulder. "I'm sorry you were scared. Greene shouldn't have carried me in as he did. It made everything appear so much worse. You must speak to him. I told him to put me down and he wouldn't listen to me at all. What was I to do? It's really too much when one's servants pretend they can't hear you."

Arthur ran his fingers through her hair, lifting it off of her shoulder. He bent his head to kiss her neck. "If he's offended you, I'll speak to him, but Greene was right to carry you in. You could have died in that fall."

"Do you think he meant me to?"

Arthur's lips stilled on her neck mid-kiss. Very slowly, he drew back. "Who?"

"The poacher who was digging on the riding path, of course. I didn't like to say so to Greene, but I can't believe that little trench was a snare for an animal. It seems to me the poacher was trying to hurt someone. And Greene and I ride that exact path every day. It wouldn't be difficult for someone to memorize our habits."

Arthur gently eased her off of him. "I'm going to light the fire."

Philly sat up, as well, uncertain of Arthur's change in mood.

He shrugged on his dressing gown and picked up his cane. The tinderbox was on the mantle. He went to it and occupied himself with lighting a fire in the hearth. When he'd done, he returned to sit beside her on the bed.

Philly met his eyes. His expression was troubled.

"You're right," he said. "Whoever constructed that snare may well have meant to do someone harm. Until I know more...I'm sorry, but you must restrict your riding to the paddock by the stable."

She looked at him in disbelief. "You can't mean that. The paddock is nothing but a square of grass and dirt. How could anyone properly ride there?"

"It's large enough for a canter."

"Am I to just canter round and round in a circle for an hour?" She shook her head. "No. You mustn't prevent me from riding out on the estate. I promise I won't gallop anymore, but I won't be confined to a small pen behind the stable. It's my only occupation outside of the house. My only freedom. You can't take it from me."

He raked a hand through his already disheveled hair. "You know as well as I do that it's presently not safe on the estate. Until I'm confident that there's no further danger, you must stay near the house when you ride. Either that, or stop riding altogether."

Philly experienced a wholly unwelcome flicker of resentment at the choice he'd given her. Do as he bid her, or give up the one thing that made her happy? It was no choice at all.

She opened her mouth to argue with him. To tell him he was being unfair to her. That he was becoming a tyrant. The very sort of man she'd sought to escape.

But though she wanted to rail at him, she found she could not.

Arthur was protecting her. He'd been protecting her since the morning they'd met at dawn in the park and she'd put herself into his keeping.

"I've made you angry," he said.

"No. Not angry."

"What then?"

"Unhappy," she said. "Dreadfully unhappy."

Arthur reached out to her. She went into his arms with slightly less enthusiasm than was usual. "I know I have," he said against her hair. "And I'm sorry for it. But it can't be helped. You must let me look after you. You have to trust that I know what's best."

Philly made no reply. She was reminded of how trusting she'd been when first she'd arrived in London with Uncle Edgar. She'd acquiesced to all of his restrictions without question, never understanding how isolated she'd become until it was too late. It was an unfair comparison, she knew, and she felt guilty for making it. Arthur was nothing like her uncle.

He took her chin in his fingers and gently tipped it up from his chest. "Tell me you trust me."

"You know that I do."

At her answer, some of the uneasiness receded from his eyes. "The paddock won't be so terrible, will it?"

She sighed. What could she say? Arthur wasn't going to change his mind. There was little point in arguing. "No."

He stroked her cheek, holding her gaze with his. "What can I do to make it more bearable?"

Philly pictured the paddock in her mind. It was indeed large enough for a canter—though not much else. The ground was even, and the wooden fence surrounding it was aged, but sturdy.

Greene had mentioned that it had once been used when they were breaking young horses to saddle, or teaching children on the estate to ride. She often saw Hyperion wandering there, nibbling grass and whinnying to the mares.

Hyperion.

The idea struck Philly like a thunderclap. "Do you truly mean that? Because I've just had a wonderful thought." She extricated herself from Arthur's embrace and knelt back on the bed. The more she contemplated her idea, the more enthusiastic she became. "Oh, Arthur, do you think that…? Would you ever…?"

An amused smile tugged at the corner of his mouth. "As much as I'd like to, I can't read your mind."

She flushed with excitement. "I know you said that when you walked today it didn't mean anything. But you must admit that your leg has been getting stronger since you first came to London. You've said yourself that it gives you less pain."

The warmth in Arthur's expression faded.

"And you've always been able to put some weight on it, have

you not?" Philly waited for his reluctantly affirming nod. "And now you can bear even more?" He nodded again. "I think you must be strong enough to—" She hesitated before pushing forward in a rush of words. "To try and ride a horse again."

As she'd expected, all traces of the indulgent amusement he'd exhibited only seconds before were now gone.

"Please don't refuse me out of hand," she pleaded. "Please let me finish."

Arthur said nothing to prevent her.

"You're an excellent rider. Everyone tells me so. And even if, after these many years, you've lost some of your skill, I daresay you'll still be more accomplished than most." She swallowed, uncertain as to whether she was encouraging or discouraging him. "If we attempted it in the paddock, and on a calm enough horse, you could get the feel of it again, and you could see how much you're still capable of."

"I'm not capable of anything anymore."

"Arthur—"

"Not on a horse. Not with a pistol. Not with a rapier. It's not only my leg that's weak, it's my hand. And after such a head injury as I had at Albuera—" He broke off abruptly. "No. You mustn't ask this of me. At the very least I'll look like an incompetent fool. And at the worst I'll do myself some greater injury."

Philly leaned against him. "I won't ever let you look like a fool," she vowed softly. She reached for his hand and was heartened when he met her halfway, his fingers threading through hers. "We can go to the paddock in the early dawn hours. Just you and me. And Greene, of course, for we'll need him to help with the horses. But there will be no one else there. I'll make sure of it."

Arthur met her eyes, his stare weighted with something inexplicable. "I don't care what anyone else thinks of me. It's you I don't want to look a fool in front of."

She was stunned by his admission. "You never have!"

A bitter smile ghosted across Arthur's mouth. "I've taken great care not to."

It was inconceivable to her that Arthur should worry about such things. She'd never seen any weakness or insecurity in him, not even in his most melancholy moments. "You're not serious. You can't be. For you know very well that there's nothing in the world that could change the way I feel about you." She released his hand, moving back into his arms. "I love you, Arthur."

For the barest second, she imagined that he froze. That even his breathing stopped. But she knew she must be mistaken. "Do you?" he asked quietly.

"More than anything." She encircled his neck in a fierce embrace.

And she waited for him to say it back to her. To tell her that he loved her, too.

But Arthur said nothing in response. He only held her fast, his arms as strong as bands of iron about her waist and back.

She told herself that it was enough. Knowing that he needed her, and that he cared for her. Knowing that she was his dearest friend. He didn't have to love her. Not in the way of some romantic hero.

Besides, it wasn't the words that were important. It was the actions of a person. Expressions of respect, and tenderness, and all of those fine feelings which she and Arthur shared in abundance.

As for the twinge in her heart...well. It would pass, surely.

Until then, she'd ignore it.

She pressed a brisk kiss to his cheek. "But I won't let you

distract me. Not about something so important. If I must walk aimlessly about the paddock on my horse, I would have you on a horse beside me. It won't be bearable otherwise."

"My sweet, determined little love. I believe you're attempting to blackmail me."

"Nonsense. I'm merely offering my point of view." Philly drew back, her eyes searching his. There was a peculiar warmth in his gaze. "It's not so unreasonable to think you might be able to ride again, is it? It's just sitting on a horse, after all. Far less exertion than walking, I feel."

"Riding is more than just sitting on a horse, and well you know it."

"But you'll try, won't you? Because I ask it of you? Because I need you with me?"

Arthur bowed his head, his forehead coming to rest gently against hers. "Yes," he said. "For you. For all of those reasons. Yes."

THIRTY-ONE

Lord Gordon and Mrs. Ogilvy gave no indication of how long their stay might be, and Philly, for one, had no wish to hurry them away. Over the past two weeks, she'd grown rather accustomed to having an older gentleman round the house. In many ways, living with the earl reminded her of life with her grandfather.

Meanwhile, Mrs. Ogilvy provided some much-needed feminine companionship. She'd already accompanied Philly into Heycombe on two occasions. They'd visited the draper's, the dressmaker's, and the milliner's, and—though the selection of goods was even less varied than in Fox Cross—Philly had managed to find herself two very pretty bonnets and a beautiful amber Georgian cloth, which she planned to use for a new riding habit.

Arthur wasn't as happy with their guests. Nevertheless, he was a good deal more affable than he'd been on the day of their arrival. It was clear that he both admired and respected his father. He was even beginning to soften a little toward Mrs. Ogilvy.

Even so, he took no pleasure in their evenings now being a

party of four instead of two, and he proved especially disagree-able when the earl or Mrs. Ogilvy invited themselves on one of his and Philly's walks. In truth, the only times Arthur was in perfect humor were the nights they lay in each other's arms, and the early morning hours, when they slipped away to the stable to go riding.

Greene had chosen a good-natured gelding named Erasmus for Arthur's return to the saddle. That first morning Arthur had mounted him with seemingly little difficulty. Yet Philly had known by the subtle change in her husband's expression that getting on Erasmus was painful to him. It had likely conjured memories of the last horse he'd ridden, the one killed beneath him at Albuera.

Arthur hadn't said a word. Not about his pain, and not about his memories. He'd simply gathered up the reins as if it had been days and not years since last he rode.

The sight of Captain Arthur Heywood on a horse had quite taken Philly's breath away. He cut an elegant, purely masculine figure that evoked the dashing cavalry officer he'd once been. Even now, more than two weeks later, she still stole glances at him as they walked side by side in the paddock. Arthur had caught her in the act of admiring him more than once.

Between waking early to go riding and staying up late in the evening with their guests, Philly found herself increasingly tired. Mrs. Lamb advised her to take more rest, and by the end of the first week of the earl's visit, Philly was retiring every afternoon to her room for a short nap.

Within two weeks even that was not sufficient.

"You're a married lady now, my dear, and there's no need to keep these abominable early hours," Mrs. Ogilvy said one morning, while she and Philly were sewing together in the drawing room. "It's no wonder you've exhausted yourself. You must follow my example and stay abed until well past ten o'clock. Your maid can bring your breakfast on a tray."

Philly was seated on the settee with her needlework on her lap. She'd been able to do only a few stitches before losing interest. It was unlike her to be so unfocused. She wondered if Mrs. Ogilvy might be right. Perhaps she *had* exhausted herself. "I can't abide staying in my room until late in the morning. It's my favorite time of day to be out of doors."

"Hmm." Mrs. Ogilvy considered for a moment. "I had a spell some time ago. An awful bout of malaise. I took two or three glasses of bitters each day to fortify myself. Might you not try something similar for your relief?"

"I assure you, I'm not ill. Although..." Philly hesitated to share too much. "Mrs. Lamb has been giving me a special decoction. It's meant to help me keep up my strength."

"It doesn't seem to be working, my dear."

"No. Not yet. But Mrs. Lamb is confident I shall soon see a benefit."

Mrs. Ogilvy picked up Philly's abandoned needlework to examine it. "And does Captain Heywood know that Mrs. Lamb is looking after you?"

"Indeed not. It would only worry him."

"I wonder that he can be ignorant of anything that concerns you. He watches you every moment. One would think he was afraid you might run off and leave him." Mrs. Ogilvy laughed.

Philly attempted to smile along, but found she could not. "I'm sure such a thought has never crossed his mind."

"You might be surprised, my dear."

The sun was streaming through the windows of the drawing room. It was a particularly warm day. Arthur had gone out in a carriage with his father to view some of the improvements on the estate. They were due back within the hour, and then she and Arthur were to go for their afternoon walk.

If only she weren't so dreadfully tired. It was inconceivable to her that but two weeks ago she'd argued to continue her daily rides out on the grounds. Now she was so weary that she couldn't even imagine going for a gallop on Persephone.

"Naturally I always knew how it would be. And so I told Gordon. A gentleman as solemn and stern as the captain—"

"Oh, but he isn't," Philly objected, turning toward her guest. "Not really."

"No? It's often the way, you know, when one has an elder sibling who's gone a bit wild. The younger must needs go the complete opposite direction. The rub of it is, Captain Heywood has no less passion than his brother or his father. More, perhaps. Until he met you, I daresay he expended it in killing people."

Philly gave Mrs. Ogilvy a look of gentle reproof. "It was war, ma'am."

"So it was. And everyone always did say what a brutally effective soldier he made. Indeed, I've sometimes felt a bit sorry for that godless wretch who came upon him while he was injured. Anyone who knew the captain could have predicted the result of that encounter. Heywood isn't a man to be trifled with."

Philly didn't need to ask how Mrs. Ogilvy had learned of Arthur's unfortunate experience. Even on such brief acquaintance, it was plain that the earl shared far more with his long-time mistress than mere physical intimacy.

"And now, my dear," Mrs. Ogilvy continued with a dimpled smile, "instead of war and soldiering, all of the captain's energies are directed toward you. It's exactly as I told Gordon it would be. 'Let him marry,' I said. 'That will give him something to think about besides his troubles.' And so it has. Though..." She paused, her brow puckering. "One might wish he would be a bit less intense about it."

"You may blame my accident on the riding trail for that," Philly said. "It's worried him so desperately. I don't think he'll be at ease until he catches the person responsible."

"Better to leave it all to Pebmarsh, I say. Let him sort out the mischief on the estate. What you and Captain Heywood need is a proper honeymoon. Somewhere away from here. The Lake District, perhaps. Or the seaside." Mrs. Ogilvy appeared to warm to the idea. "I have it! When Gordon and I leave Heycombe, you and Captain Heywood must accompany us to Bath."

Philly's brows lifted in surprise. "I'd no notion you intended to travel on to Bath."

"It was our plan, but now that Gordon and Captain Heywood have found matters with which to occupy themselves on the estate, one wonders if we shall ever get there." Mrs. Ogilvy sighed. "Ah, but it's lovely there this time of year. And the waters would do you a world of good, my dear."

Their conversation was interrupted by the arrival of Crofton. He entered the drawing room with uncharacteristic haste, bringing with him a silver salver on which lay a visiting card.

There had been few callers since Philly's arrival in Heycombe. Mr. Fordham, the vicar, had paid a visit just three weeks prior, and following that she'd entertained three of the elderly church-women of Heycombe for tea, but no one who could be termed fashionable had yet come to call.

"Two gentlemen and three ladies have come, Mrs. Heywood," Crofton intoned. "Shall I tell them you're not at home?"

"My word," Mrs. Ogilvy said. "Are you expecting visitors, Phyllida?"

Philly took the card from the salver and read the name engraved upon it.

Miss Elizabeth Townsend.

"It's my cousin from London!" she exclaimed. "Crofton, with whom has she come?"

"Lord Darly, Mr. Forsythe, Abigail Townsend, and Lady Eliot, ma'am."

Philly's excitement evaporated in an instant. The specter of Lady Eliot still persisted in haunting her at her most vulnerable moments. She could think of no person in the world she'd rather see less.

Mrs. Ogilvy laid a hand upon Philly's arm. "Come, now. You can't consider turning them away."

"I'm not at my best at the moment, I fear." Philly looked down at her French cambric gown with its simple blue trimmings. It hadn't a flounce or a frill. Little had she thought when she'd put it on only an hour ago in anticipation of her walk with Arthur that it was soon to be judged by the likes of Lady Eliot.

"You look lovely, my dear. There's not the least need to fret." Mrs. Ogilvy rose from the settee. "Now, if you will excuse me, I intend to follow your example and retire to my room for a little rest."

Philly stood up quickly, her cousin's card still clutched in her hand. "You can't go!"

"I can and I must. If I were to remain, my presence would do nothing but offend the ladies and scandalize the gentlemen."

"But surely—"

"It would reflect poorly on you, Phyllida, and I like you far too well to let your reputation be injured on my account." Mrs. Ogilvy smiled, giving Philly a pat on the cheek. "Crofton," she said as she exited the room, "see that refreshments are made ready for Mrs. Heywood's guests."

"Yes, madam." Crofton turned back to Philly. "Mrs. Heywood?"

Philly watched Mrs. Ogilvy go with a heavy heart. She felt utterly alone. "Captain Heywood hasn't come back yet, has he?"

"No, ma'am."

Her eyes drifted over her dogs. They were in various states of repose all around the drawing room. "You may send my guests up, Crofton," she said at last. "But first, you'd better have William come and collect the dogs. The last time Basil met Lord Darly, he attempted to remove his arm."

"Very good, Mrs. Heywood."

Elizabeth and Abigail Townsend had changed little in the nearly two months since Philly had left London. They were garbed in jonquil muslin with corresponding slippers and parasols, as expensively dressed and excessively quarrelsome as Philly remembered.

The gentlemen of the party were equally well turned out. Indeed, with their fair hair, double-breasted coats of corbeau superfine, and biscuit-colored pantaloons, they all but matched.

Lord Darly greeted Philly with a warm smile. Mr. Forsythe smiled too, but there was a guarded expression in his eyes.

"I'm relieved to find you well, ma'am," he said, bowing over her hand. "And you *are* well, I trust?"

"Of course, she is," Lady Eliot replied, laughing. In her flowing white embroidered muslin gown—complete with two rows of flounces and pleating to showcase her magnificent bosom—she looked every bit the sophisticated society lady. "Mrs. Heywood is a happily married lady now. Isn't that so, Mrs. Heywood?"

Philly pasted on a smile. "Quite happily. But...what are you all doing here? I hadn't expected—"

"We're all come down for the Markhams' house party," Lady Eliot said with another crystalline laugh, "and your cousins couldn't wait to call upon you."

"We've brought a basket of fruit, Phyllida." Abigail clasped Philly's hand in greeting. "One of your maids took it from me else I would show you—"

"She knows what fruit looks like." Elizabeth gave Philly a stiff kiss on the cheek. "The rhododendrons by the front steps are overgrown. Why does your gardener not attend them? It looks horribly untidy."

"It's done on purpose, Lizzy, to make it look like a wilderness garden. Is that not right, Phyllida?"

Ignoring her bickering cousins, Philly ushered the party in and bid them sit down. In due course they were all supplied with tea and everyone proceeded to speak at once, engaging in multiple conversations that Philly could scarcely begin to follow.

"I say, where has Heywood got to?" Mr. Forsythe asked. "Don't tell me he leaves you alone here all day."

She attempted an answer. "No, indeed, sir—"

"I always suspected you had a fondness for Captain Heywood," Abigail said. "From the first day he walked you home. Didn't I say so, Lizzy?"

Lord Darly chuckled. "I wish you'd have shared your suspicions with me, Miss Abigail. It would have saved me a packet on a wager I made."

"None of us suspected any such thing." Elizabeth cast a severe glance at her sister. "When you and William didn't return from your morning walk, Aunt Vale said perhaps you'd met with some villain in the park, but Evans told us you were carrying your valise, and Papa knew straightaway that you'd fled."

Abigail nodded. "He said you'd try to return to Fox Cross by the stage. He sent men out to find you."

"They returned no news of you," Elizabeth went on. "It seemed as if you'd simply disappeared. Which you very well couldn't have done with all of those dreadful dogs of yours."

"I say, Mrs. Heywood." Lord Darly's gaze drifted warily around the room. "About those dogs..."

"They won't trouble you, my lord," Philly assured him. "I've sent them down to the kitchens."

"Are your dogs often confined, Mrs. Heywood?" Mr. Forsythe asked.

Philly gave him a quizzical smile. "Not at all, sir. They spend most of their time in company with me."

"And are all of them as vicious as Darly claims?"

"No, indeed. They're truly quite gentle."

"They bark excessively," Abigail said. "The small one loudest of all. Papa was glad to be rid of them."

"The dogs, perhaps, but not you, Phyllida," Elizabeth said. "You should have seen the look on his face when Captain Heywood's baggage coach came to collect your things later that morning. Aunt Vale fainted straight away into a chair."

"Not straightaway," Abigail corrected. "First, she called for her smelling salts. And then she insisted upon seeing the letter from Captain Heywood's solicitor. It was while reading the letter that she fainted, for the solicitor had written that you and Captain Heywood were to be married."

Elizabeth edged closer to Philly on the sofa. "They're ever

so angry with you. Papa says that because of you we may have to leave London."

Philly's conscience twinged. "I sincerely hope that won't happen."

"Who will handle my investments if Townsend decamps?" Lord Darly asked.

"You shall have to come and visit us often," Abigail whispered to him. "I know Papa would give you advice on your investments if I asked him to. And since we are particular friends—"

"Ha!" Elizabeth gave a crack of laughter. "Papa would do nothing of the sort."

"Tell us, Mrs. Heywood, what makes a lady refuse a duke only to accept a comparatively penniless second son?" Mr. Forsythe asked. "This has been troubling me no end. I have a personal interest in your answer, you see, being a second son myself."

Lord Darly groaned. "Forsythe, you have been bemoaning your plight as a second son from the womb."

"It's a matter of love, Mr. Forsythe," Abigail declared. "If a lady is in love, then it makes no difference whether the gentleman be a duke or a—"

"Love," Mr. Forsythe repeated in a flat voice. His smile was brittle. "In my experience, when it comes to a lady's heart, it isn't love but lucre that carries the day."

"Have you been disappointed in love, sir?" Abigail asked. "You shouldn't let it discourage you from—"

"My sister's knowledge of love comes from Lord Byron," Elizabeth said. "Pay her no heed."

The room once again devolved into several separate conversations. Philly's guests spoke to her, and to each other, laughing, whispering, and talking over one another. Elizabeth murmured into one of Philly's ears something about Mrs. Vale, and Lady Eliot made the occasional remark to Abigail, who was, in turn, straining to listen to a hushed conversation that Lord Darly was having with Mr. Forsythe.

"He was the devil of a shot with a pistol," Lord Darly said. "Do you remember when...?"

"He's nothing to fear now," Mr. Forsythe responded.

"Everyone wants to know the truth of it," Elizabeth said. "We've had ever so many callers since you left."

Philly turned to look at her. "I beg your pardon?"

Abigail leaned forward in her seat. "Constance Penniman said you might have been tricked into a carriage and stolen away, and that after you were compromised, you'd have had no choice but to marry."

"You'll put our minds at ease on that score, won't you, Mrs. Heywood?" Lord Darly flashed a teasing grin at Abigail.

"Yes," Mr. Forsythe agreed. "Tell us once and for all. Has Heywood kidnapped you and forced you to wed him?"

Philly's expression tightened. She'd heard similar nonsense from her own gossiping servants, but she hadn't thought to hear it from her guests. It took an effort to keep her countenance. "What utter absurdity. I'll thank you not to repeat—"

"It's what people are saying," Abigail murmured over the edge of her teacup. "Else why would you marry him instead of the duke?"

"Pray don't listen to them." Lady Eliot covered Philly's hand with her own. "Those of us who *truly* know Captain Heywood can attest that he is, at all times, a gentleman. Is that not a fact, Mrs. Heywood?"

A vague feeling of dizziness caught Philly unaware. She was becoming overwhelmed by all the overlapping talk. And the tea she'd been sipping had made her feel rather nauseous. She wished Lady Eliot would remove her hand. It was too hot, and the weight of it was smothering.

"Why, Mrs. Heywood, you look as if you might be ill. I daresay it's the fault of this drawing room. It's always been too much in the sun at this time of day. You're surely overheated."

Philly looked up at Caroline Eliot, certain she hadn't heard her correctly. "You've been here before?"

"Oh heavens! Many times." Lady Eliot lowered her voice to a soft purr. "I don't like to be indelicate, but I'll wager that on more than one occasion I occupied the very bedroom you sleep in now. Blue brocade hangings and a rather monstrous mahogany bed? Ah well, it was the fashion once, I suppose. As for this room, I always advised that the paper be changed. There's a section that's peeling. Just there. Do you see it? Now, I've found some marvelous hand-painted Oriental paper for my townhouse. It might do for you, if you'd like to copy my style..."

As Lady Eliot ran on, Philly stared, unseeing, at the section of claret-colored flock paper on the wall that had begun to peel away. Her mind was in turmoil.

How long had it been since Lady Eliot was last at Heywood House? Had she really advised Arthur on how to decorate? Had she really slept in Philly's own bedroom?

It must be true, but Philly couldn't credit it.

"...which you should do if you can bear the expense," Lady Eliot continued, "for Heycombe has absolutely nothing to offer in the way of fine paper hangings."

Elizabeth rose to refill her teacup, and having done so, moved to sit nearer to Lord Darly. Abigail came immediately to take the vacant seat next to Philly on the sofa.

"May I see your wedding band, Phyllida? They're rubies, are they not? I could see them sparkling all the way across the room."

Preoccupied with her own thoughts, Philly made no protest when her cousin lifted her hand to admire her ring.

"How delicate it is!" Abigail exclaimed.

"Yes, it is quite flattering," Lady Eliot remarked. "I wasn't persuaded it would be, rubies being far more suitable to someone of my complexion. But Captain Heywood was quite determined on it. I'd even go so far as to say that there was nothing at the jeweler's he liked better."

Lady Eliot's words seem to hang in the air for an eternity. Philly couldn't quite absorb them. She told herself she'd misheard. It couldn't be true. Arthur wouldn't have taken his former fiancée along with him to choose her wedding band. He could never have been so cruel.

Lady Eliot smiled a slow, languorous smile. "Now, I must be naughty and confess something to you."

"Must you?" Lord Darly asked under his breath.

"There was a pair of ruby earrings to match it."

"Matching earrings!" Abigail cried out with delight.

"I tried them on myself to display for Captain Heywood, and I can attest that they were, indeed, superb stones." Caroline Eliot met Philly's eyes. "But you needn't take my word for it, Mrs. Heywood. I shall wear them the next time I come to call, and you may judge for yourself."

THIRTY-TWO

"*S*hooting. Fencing. Boxing with Gentleman Jackson."
The earl climbed out of the carriage. "One doesn't
simply forget a lifetime of excellence in such pursuits."

Arthur watched Greene remove the wooden case of dueling
pistols from the back of the carriage. His father was right. There'd
been a time, whether at Manton's shooting gallery or on a battlefield, when a weapon had been nothing more than an extension
of his own hand. He'd thought that after three years he would
have forgotten what it felt like, but holding a pistol still came as
naturally to him as breathing.

Of course he was far from what he once was. Indeed, Arthur
considered his present level of skill to be little more than a mockery
of his former proficiency. "I'm unsteady, unbalanced, and weak.
I'll be lucky to regain some passing ability with a pistol, and even
then, only in my right hand."

"I daresay your passing ability with one hand is equal to
another man's mastery." His father made no attempt to conceal
his pride. "Don't know why you left it so long. You might have

picked up a pistol any time these last three years. If you had, who knows what you'd be capable of by now?"

"I'd likely be capable of nothing," Arthur said. "For had I picked up a pistol three years ago, I'd have no doubt blown my own brains out."

The earl frowned. "The pain that bad, was it?" He considered a moment. "Well, it makes no matter now. Your health is much improved. And you're shooting again. By God, that's a miracle in itself. Though I can't but regret the circumstances that led you back to it."

The day of Philly's fall, Arthur had gone out with his father and Greene to see the snare on the riding path for himself. It was a narrowly dug hole, just large enough to catch a horse's hoof. Save for the jagged stones placed inside, it might have been made by an animal. That it was meant for Philly, Arthur had no doubt, but it could just as easily have injured or killed Greene. There was a casual sort of malice to the whole thing that had unsettled him deeply.

It had unsettled his father, too.

Later that same afternoon, while Philly and Mrs. Ogilvy were occupied upstairs, Arthur and his father had retired to the library. There, Arthur had opened his box of dueling pistols for the first time in over three years. He'd lifted one of them out, cradling it in his useless left hand for a moment before, resolutely, transferring it to his right. "I'll need to practice," he'd said.

"Quite right," the earl had agreed.

Every day since, they'd travelled out onto the estate under some pretext or another, only to stop instead at Arthur's old shooting range.

"As you stand now," said his father as they walked back toward the house, "if you had to issue a challenge—"

"I've no intention of issuing a challenge to anyone."

"Why the devil not? I would've thought you'd prefer facing the man. Put an end to the business once and for all."

Arthur's jaw hardened. "The man who attempted to harm my wife is a coward. When I discover him, I'll deal with him as a coward deserves."

"And if it's Moreland? What then? How is he to be dealt with?"

Arthur glanced at his father. "Two weeks ago, you dismissed Moreland as a suspect. I believe you said he was no more dangerous than any other very wealthy man."

The earl looked steadily back at him. "Indeed. Thought it all a load of rubbish when first you told it to me. But..."

"But?"

"Moreland's been known to go a little mad over the odd painting or trinket. It does make one wonder. What lengths might he go to over a woman?"

"As far as cold-blooded murder, if you believe the rumors about Molly Cartwright."

"Ah, yes. His last duchess." The earl nodded. "Some of the fellows at my club would have it that she cuckolded him with a younger chap. They say he caught them together one night. Fell into a rage."

"Even if that were true, it would have little bearing on what's happening now." Arthur walked up the front steps of Heywood House with his father. "The anonymous note. The snare. They're malicious games, not crimes of passion."

The earl grunted in acknowledgement. "Perhaps. But as I say, one never knows what lengths a man will go to over a woman. Even a sensible man might act a fool. You need look no further than your brother for evidence of that."

Upon entering the hall, Arthur removed his hat and gloves and handed them to Crofton. His clothes smelled of horses, leather, and gun smoke. He'd have to change before his walk with Philly. He prayed she wouldn't mind waiting a little longer for him. "Is Mrs. Heywood still in the drawing room?" he asked Crofton.

"No, sir. The mistress has retired to her room. She's sent word that she's not to be disturbed until dinner."

"Not even by you, Captain." Mrs. Ogilvy descended the stairs, her skirts held in one hand. "I've just looked in on her and she's sleeping as peacefully as a child. You must let her rest."

The earl took Mrs. Ogilvy's hand to assist her down the last few steps. "What's this? Is the girl ill?"

"I expect she's tired, my dear. She entertained a party of callers not long after the two of you left. By the time they departed, she was quite overdone."

Arthur shot a sharp look at the butler. "What callers?"

"The misses Townsend, Lady Eliot, Lord Darly, and Mr. Forsythe, sir."

"Lady Eliot!" The earl's face reddened with outrage. "The Battersby creature? Bloody unmitigated nerve. Damned adventuress."

"Now, Gordon, you'll have an apoplectic fit if you keep on this way." Mrs. Ogilvy took his arm. "We shan't mention the woman's name again. Isn't that right, Captain?"

Arthur paid no attention to Mrs. Ogilvy's addresses or to his father's ire. He started up the stairs to Philly's bedroom without a backward glance, his hand clenched tight on his cane.

He didn't know which of the callers troubled him more. Townsend's daughters had no doubt brought tales of their father and Moreland. Caroline couldn't speak without levying barbs. And as for the two gentlemen, they were the type who considered married women fair game for romantic liaisons. For all he knew, Darly and Forsythe might have spoken to Philly improperly, attempting to impose themselves on her in some way.

When he reached Philly's bedroom, Arthur opened the door and stepped inside, his boots and cane soundless on the thick carpet. Jasper rose from his place in front of the fireplace to come and greet him. The rest of the dogs remained where they were, lying down at various points of the room as if keeping silent guard over their mistress.

The heavy curtains were drawn across the windows, blocking out the bright afternoon sun. Philly's small figure was just visible in the dim light, lying in the giant mahogany bed, a quilted coverlet draped across her.

Arthur went quietly to her side. As he gazed down at her, he felt a fierce rush of tenderness. She looked much younger than her three and twenty years. The ruffles and ribbons of her nightgown enveloped her frame, and a cascade of dark hair veiled her face. She'd buried her cheek determinedly into her pillow, much as she often did against his bare chest when he held her at night.

He smoothed the hair away from her face. She'd been overtired of late and had been napping in the afternoons, but she'd yet to miss one of their walks in order to do it. He'd have to insist she rest more. No more catering to his father and Mrs. Ogilvy. No more fretting over the running of the household. And under no circumstances would he allow her to exhaust herself entertaining groups of parasites come down from London.

He straightened the coverlet around Philly's shoulders and stroked her cheek once more before leaving her room and going into his own. He'd see her again at dinner. And this evening, after they bid their guests goodnight, he'd at last be at liberty to take her in his arms.

Philly didn't know how she'd managed to get rid of her callers. The last ten minutes of their visit was nothing but an unpleasant blur. She remembered standing and bidding them good afternoon. She remembered Abigail clasping her hands and Lord Darly saying they'd come back again soon in hopes of seeing Arthur.

And then they were gone.

She'd told Crofton quite calmly that she wouldn't be going for a walk with Arthur. That she was retiring to her room for the afternoon and wished not to be disturbed. And then she'd curled up in her bed and promptly burst into tears. She'd wept until she fell asleep, only to wake several hours later just as heartbroken and miserable as she'd been before.

At quarter past six, Sara came to her room to help her dress for dinner. The little maid blinked in surprise at Philly's tearstained face, but she said not a word. Instead, she set right to work fetching water for Philly to wash with, helping her to dress in a beautiful blue muslin gown and arranging her hair into an elegant array of soft curls.

But no sooner had Sara placed the final pearl encrusted pin in her hair than Philly's courage deserted her.

No matter how well she looked, she couldn't go down to dinner. Not tonight.

Sara looked at her with undisguised disappointment. "They'll all be in the drawing room for sherry by now. Couldn't you go down for just a minute or two? You look ever so pretty, ma'am. "Tis a shame for no one to see it."

Philly made an effort to compose herself. "Perhaps I can wear the same for dinner tomorrow. I'm certain I'll feel better by then." She sank down in a chair by the fireplace. Basil came to lay at her feet, and Fox, Jasper, and Dash reclined on the carpet near the hearth.

"Shall I help you to undress? Or fetch Mrs. Lamb with your special tonic?"

"You needn't trouble over me, Sara. Go on ahead to the servants' hall. I wouldn't have you miss your own dinner. I'll ring if I need anything."

Sara made a small curtsy. "I'll send word that you won't be coming down this evening." She opened the door to leave. "And I shall tell them all you're not to be disturbed." On that pronouncement, she left, shutting the door behind her.

Philly lifted Fox onto her lap and wrapped her arms around his wiry little body, her handkerchief still clutched tightly in one hand. She'd been tired long before her callers had arrived, and now, after so much weeping, she was as weak as a kitten. She should eat something. Call for a tray or send for Mrs. Lamb's decoction. But Philly was incapable of motion. All she could do was think of Arthur and Caroline Eliot.

She didn't know how she could have been so blind. So foolish. Arthur had always loved Lady Eliot. Everyone in London said so. And he hadn't been the one to break their engagement. Why, if Lady Eliot had remained true to him, he'd be married to her even now.

It was on this dispiriting subject that Philly was ruminating when Arthur's low-pitched voice sounded from the doorway.

"Philly," he said, as he entered her room.

Jasper and Dash sprang up from their place near the fireplace to welcome him, but Basil and Fox didn't move. Philly didn't move, either. She might have known he would come to ask after her. How long ago had Sara given him her message? Minutes? Seconds?

As he crossed the floor, Philly steadfastly refused to look at him. Even when he came to stand in front of her, her eyes remained downcast, focusing on the embroidered handkerchief she held in her hands.

"Are you unwell?" he enquired.

"I'm a little tired, that's all."

His gaze drifted over her, taking in her gown and the decorative pins in her hair. "You're dressed for dinner. Would you like me to escort you down?"

Her fingers tightened on her handkerchief. "No, thank you."

He sat down in the chair opposite, leaning toward her until only inches remained between them. "Won't you look at me?"

She hesitated before slowly lifting her eyes to his. Her heart gave a traitorous thump. He was unutterably handsome—inherently masculine in that soldierly way of his. His broad shoulders filled out the topline of his black dress coat, and his long legs framed her own.

Concern etched his stern features. "You've been crying." He reached out to take her hands in his.

She stiffened at his touch, instinctively drawing away from him.

Arthur's hurt and alarm at her rejection were palpable. She'd never before recoiled from his touch. "What is it, Philly? What's upset you? Was it your cousins' visit?"

She stared down at her hands, remaining silent for some time before finally raising her eyes back to his. "It wasn't my cousins. It was something else."

His face went cold with anger. "Something else, or someone else?"

"Lady Eliot."

He searched her face. "Not Darly or Forsythe, then?"

"Lord Darly and Mr. Forsythe did nothing to make me cry, if that's what you mean."

Fox struggled from his place on her lap. Before she could help him down, Arthur lifted the little dog from her arms, setting him gently on the carpet.

"What has Lady Eliot done to make you cry?" he asked.

"Nothing," Philly answered truthfully. "I'm crying because of you."

THIRTY-THREE

Arthur stared at Philly, imagining all of the reasons she might be upset with him. He'd restricted her walks and her riding. He'd confined her. Kept things from her. Set the servants to watch her.

"Arthur, do you remember how I answered the first time you asked me to marry you?"

"You refused me."

"Do you remember why I refused you?"

"You believed I was in love with Caroline Eliot." He almost smiled at how ridiculous the idea of it was, but something in Philly's eyes stopped him.

"Please tell me the truth." Her voice quavered. "When you left the park that morning...when you went to the jeweler to buy my wedding band..." She swallowed. "Was Lady Eliot there with you?"

Arthur's expression hardened, the beginnings of a cold rage seeping into his veins. Curse and confound the woman! Is that what she'd told Philly? That he'd taken her with him to choose Philly's wedding band? "Whatever she's said to you—"

"Yes or no. It's a simple enough question."

He clenched one hand. "Yes, she was there, but—"

"I could almost forgive her having come here to Heywood House." Philly blotted away a fresh flood of tears. "Perhaps even for all the times she slept here with you in my bed—"

"*The devil you say!*"

"She described my room to me. She knew everything about Heywood House." Philly dashed away a few more tears with trembling fingers. "I've no right to be upset about that, I know, for it was before we married, but that you went to her the day I accepted your p-proposal. And took her to choose the w-wedding band that you gave to me. And had her try on the m-matching earrings."

Arthur's gut twisted with anguish to see Philly so distressed. "It wasn't like that. If you'd only listen to me—"

"Do you deny that you made a present to her of those earrings?"

"Good God, is that what she told you?"

"You've broken my heart, but perhaps, if I weren't such a naïve little fool—"

"Enough." He reached for her hands. This time he didn't give her a chance to pull away. He took hold of her with an iron grip, his eyes locking interminably with hers. "That woman...that creature...has the morals of a common—"

"She can't be so very despicable. You were engaged to her, were you not? You must have cared for her once." Caught in his grasp, Philly could no longer blot her tears. They slid down her face unchecked. "Perhaps you care for her still? Perhaps that's why you've never said that you love me."

"Damnation, Philly, you're upset beyond reason."

"I assure you, sir, I've been thinking on this quite rationally all day long." She attempted to pull away from him.

Arthur held her fast. "Look at me." He moved his hands to her upper arms, his fingers pressing into her soft flesh. He gave her a little shake. "*Look at me.*"

She reluctantly raised her eyes to his.

"I showed you that you were my love our first night together, and I've affirmed it every day since. It's in everything I do for you. Every look and every touch. I may not have said the words—God knows why. Some ridiculous desire not to render myself vulnerable, I daresay. But it was never because I didn't feel it. I feel it too damned much. There are days when I think I'll run mad from it." His gaze held hers. "I never loved Caroline Eliot. I've never loved any woman in the world but you."

Tears clung to Philly's dark lashes. She blinked them away. "Then why...?"

"It's true Lady Eliot was at the jeweler in Bond Street. But not with me. She came in with Forsythe after I'd already purchased your wedding ring. The jeweler was showing me the matching earrings. Lady Eliot and Forsythe spoke to me at the counter. She picked up one of the earrings and tried it on of her own accord. I left without buying them. I'd never give you something that had been worn by that viper. If she has those earrings now, she's bought them for herself or manipulated some fool into buying them for her."

He loosened his hold on Philly's arms. When she didn't pull away, he removed his hands completely so he could reach into his waistcoat and retrieve a clean handkerchief. He offered it to her and she took it without a word. "After I left the jeweler's, she must have asked the proprietor what I'd purchased. I'm sure she's been waiting to challenge you with that bit of information since first she learned it. No doubt it's the very reason she arranged for your cousins to be invited to the house party at Melton Abbey.

It gave her the perfect excuse to call here and make trouble." He watched as Philly dried her tears. "As for all the rest...my engagement to her and her having stayed here at Heywood House—"

"Please don't. I can't bear to hear it."

"By God, Philly, I've never taken that woman to my bed. We've never shared so much as a lingering look." Arthur ran a hand through his hair in frustration. "This is my own fault. I should have told you the truth the day I proposed. But I wanted you to trust me. I didn't want to scare you away with stories about my older brother."

Her eyes flew to his. "Your *brother*?"

"George Heywood, Viscount Carlisle. I assume you've heard something of him?"

She nodded. "My cousins said he was a rake."

"My brother would make your average rake look like a vicar. He preys upon women for his own amusement, and when he becomes bored, he discards them. Married women, shopkeepers' daughters, governesses, opera dancers. There are no females safe from him." His expression softened. "You needn't look so worried. He doesn't force himself on anyone. They all go to him willingly enough. He's rich, titled, and considered uncommonly handsome. He's thoroughly dissolute now, but for a long time, he did behave as a gentleman in his own way. He made it a rule never to involve himself with young virgins on the marriage mart." A bitter smile edged the corner of Arthur's mouth. "Until the season that Caroline Battersby made her debut."

"You don't mean to say that your brother and Lady Eliot—"

"Oh, yes. They had quite a torrid affair. They met at house parties, and at my brother's townhouse in London, and through the assistance of Lady Eustace—a woman who's just as immoral as Lady Eliot herself—they even managed to meet each other on holiday in Bath. I'm assuming it was during their trip to Somer-setshire that my brother availed himself of Heywood House. I was in Canterbury then, with my regiment, but Pebmarsh would be able to confirm it."

"Lady Eliot wasn't here with you at all?" Philly's face lit with guarded hope. "She was here with your brother?"

The tension within Arthur slowly began to unknot. "It wasn't unusual for my brother or father to make use of Heywood House whenever I was away with my regiment, and George wouldn't have scrupled to bring one of his mistresses here. When I returned from Canterbury, his affair with Caroline Battersby was at an end. She and her chaperone—an old maiden aunt who was deter-mined to put her up to the highest bidder—had expected that if my brother compromised her, he'd be honor bound to make her an offer of marriage. Instead he left for his estate in Ireland with his latest paramour. Caroline wrote him letters to no avail. When she couldn't contact my brother, she came to me. She told me she was with child."

"With child! But surely not?"

"My father and I had no knowledge of her true character then. We believed her when she said she was carrying George's child. Naturally, my brother claimed she was lying, but considering his past behavior, we could hardly take his word." Arthur exhaled. "I was set to leave for the Peninsula. I didn't expect to return alive. It was the most honorable thing to do to offer marriage to her before I left. My father agreed. It would give the child a name, at least." He grimaced at the memory. "By the time I departed for Portugal, it was apparent that she wasn't with child. That it had all been a ruse to trap my brother."

"What about your engagement?"

"I considered it at an end, but I heard in letters from my father that she continued to tell people we were set to marry. I probably would have gone through with it, but thankfully, while I was lying in hospital at Lisbon, Caroline Battersby married Baron Eliot. I didn't see her again until two months ago in Bond Street."

Philly looked down at her handkerchief for a long while. When she raised her face to him again, her brows were drawn together, her mouth tugged down into a pensive frown. "I met her at the Worthings' ball."

He blinked. "Did you?"

"She asked to be introduced to me. She wasn't very kind, but I thought... She was so beautiful and...she was the most sophisticated woman I'd ever seen. I remember looking at her and saying to myself, *This is the woman who has Captain Heywood's heart.*"

"She never had my heart," he said gruffly. "No one has ever had my heart but you."

"Oh, Arthur." She leaned toward him.

The movement was hardly discernable. It might not even have been purposefully done. But Arthur needed no other encouragement to reach for her. In one breathless motion, he closed her in an unyielding embrace, pulling her from her chair and straight into his lap.

Philly put her arms around his neck and buried her face in the crook of his shoulder. "I love you so much. I can't bear to think of you with anyone else."

"There will never be anyone else," he vowed. "Not so long as I live."

"I don't care about the jewelry."

"I know."

"But when Lady Eliot described my bedroom... And when she said..."

"Hush, love. You needn't waste anymore words on her."

Philly tightened her arms around his neck. "I'm so sorry."

He held her fast in his arms, moving his hand soothingly along her back. "My silly little sweetheart, what the devil do you have to be sorry for?"

"I've enacted you a proper domestic tragedy."

"Is that what this was?"

"Yes," she said. "You must wish you'd never come to fetch me for dinner."

"My love, don't deceive yourself. I'm precisely where I want to be." He nuzzled her damp cheek in silent entreaty, and when she answered by turning her lips to his, he kissed her with such painstaking tenderness that she seemed to melt into his arms.

The moments that followed passed without a word between them. Arthur was vaguely conscious of Philly unknotting his cravat, and at some point, he must have divested her of her hair-pins—a fact of which he became achingly aware when her hair tumbled down around her shoulders.

Only then did he pause to catch his breath, resting his forehead gently against hers for several heated seconds. "Come," he said at last, easing her away from him. "It's past time for dinner."

She looked at him in disbelief. "Surely you don't mean us to go back downstairs to the dining room."

"No, I'm going to have our dinner brought up on a tray. We're going to eat together in my bedroom. And then I'm going to take you to my bed and make love to you."

Philly flushed pink. "Oh my," she breathed.

Arthur felt the inexplicable urge to grin. "Oh my, indeed."

THIRTY-FOUR

"It can all be done quite easily," Mrs. Ogilvy assured. "New beds, of course, with the Parisian silk bed-hangings as I described. New window curtains, new carpets, and new paper-hangings, as well."

Philly looked up from her notebook, her pencil poised in her hand. "Perhaps damask would be preferable for the bed-hangings?"

"It's your choice, my dear." Mrs. Ogilvy walked around the bedroom, looking upon the décor with a critical eye. "Shades of amber. Yes. It will be very beautiful for your room. But what of Captain Heywood's bedchamber? Have you consulted him about colors? Or does he not care about such things?"

"He's requested his room be done in shades of blue."

Mrs. Ogilvy raised a winged brow. "Blue and amber? I wonder what's given the Captain that idea."

Philly's mouth curved into a smile. "I can't begin to guess."

"And has he advised you on how much you're allowed to spend?"

"He said I may spend what I like."

"How very obliging of him."

"Oh, but I don't intend to go to any great expense. Indeed, I think that if I'm reasonably careful, I can contrive the whole for a very modest sum. I've been jotting down some estimated figures, and—"

"Don't trouble your head with accounting, my dear one," Mrs. Ogilvy interrupted with a twinkle in her eye. "You may leave it to me. I'm acquainted with all of the best furniture warehouses in London, and you can trust that the widow of a tradesman knows something about driving a bargain."

Philly laughed in spite of herself.

"Beg pardon, Mrs. Heywood." Violet entered the room. "Two ladies have come calling. Miss Abigail Townsend, and Lady Eliot, ma'am."

Philly's laughter faded. It had been only a week since last they'd called. She'd known they would return, but hadn't anticipated it would be so soon. "Show them into the drawing room, Violet. I'll be there directly." When the maid had gone, Philly turned to Mrs. Ogilvy. "Will you join us?"

"It wouldn't be wise."

"What does that signify? You're my guest here. You're Lord Gordon's dear friend, and I hope you've become mine. I'd be honored if you would join me in receiving my callers. Indeed, I fear I must insist upon it."

Mrs. Ogilvy gave Philly a thoughtful look. "If you insist upon it, I suppose I cannot refuse."

"No. Indeed you cannot." Philly removed her apron. Arthur wouldn't approve of her receiving Lady Eliot. Fortunately, he was out on the estate somewhere with Lord Gordon, and wasn't likely to return for another half hour, at least. "Our guests won't be staying long, but if you could endeavor to occupy my cousin…?"

"Ah. You'd like a word with Lady Eliot, I gather."

"I would." Philly smoothed the skirts of her sprigged muslin gown as they made their way down to the drawing room.

They entered to find the two visitors in polite repose.

Abigail leapt up from her chair. "Phyllida! Lady Eliot has driven me here in her new curricle!"

Philly greeted her exuberant young cousin, her gaze moving straight to Lady Eliot as she quickly dispensed with the introductions.

Lady Eliot was resplendent in a white sarsnet spencer robe trimmed with Chinese silk fringe. Her dark, indolent gaze drifted first to Philly, and then to Mrs. Ogilvy. Abigail clearly had no idea who Marianne Ogilvy was, but recognition registered immediately on Lady Eliot's face.

"Madam," she said stiffly.

"Lady Eliot," Mrs. Ogilvy replied with a dimpled smile. "It's been so many years since last we met that I'd almost forgotten your partiality for virginal white."

Lady's Eliot's lips thinned so severely that they all but disappeared.

"The gentlemen have gone hunting all day with Lord Markham, and we're bored out of our wits," Abigail said. "Lady Eliot said we'd best drive into Heycombe and have a look about the shops, but the curricle only seats two, and Lizzy has an awful megrim for she was up until three playing piquet, and Lady Markham told her—"

"We cannot stay," Lady Eliot announced.

Philly felt a surge of indignation on Mrs. Ogilvy's behalf. Mrs. Ogilvy herself only twinkled with amusement.

"What?" Abigail's brow puckered. "But I thought—"

"If you'll walk us out, Mrs. Heywood," Lady Eliot said, "you may see my new curricle."

Philly readily agreed. As they all made their way down the stairs, Mrs. Ogilvy positioned herself by Abigail, engaging her in a discussion about the newest styles in autumn bonnets.

Lady Eliot fell in beside Philly. "Allow me to advise you, Mrs. Heywood. It's one thing to entertain such a woman as Marianne Ogilvy in your home, but to introduce her to your guests—"

"Did you love him very much?" Philly asked.

Caroline Eliot stopped where she stood. She stared at Philly, at first with surprise at her quiet interruption, and then with smug satisfaction as she comprehended Philly's question.

"Did I love him?" she repeated in a languid purr. "But my feelings are hardly important, ma'am. *You* are his wife now. You've no need to be jealous of me—"

"I'm not talking about my husband."

The silence that met Philly was deafening. Lady Eliot's expression grew cold, her eyes hardening to flint. It seemed as if she wouldn't say anything. Then, at last, she answered. "Yes, I did."

Philly's gaze didn't waver. "He treated you very badly."

"You know nothing about it."

"I know that whatever might have happened between you and the Viscount Carlisle has nothing to do with my husband."

"Nothing to do with your husband?" Lady Eliot gave a brittle laugh. "My dear Mrs. Heywood, I suspect you've been getting an earful about the past from your infamous guest." She cast a disapproving glance down the stairs at Mrs. Ogilvy. "Whatever fairy story she might have told you in an attempt to spare your feelings, the fact remains that Captain Heywood and I were engaged to be married. If I hadn't lost my heart to Lord Eliot, we'd be married even now."

"No, indeed you would not, ma'am," Philly said gently. "For my husband severed your engagement before he left for the Peninsula."

Lady Eliot's laughter died away. She stared at Philly in ill-disguised astonishment.

"I'm sure it was a balm to your injured pride to have everyone believe that my husband was devotedly in love with you. That you'd broken his heart and he was pining away for you here in the country. Perhaps having your name forever linked with his even alleviated some of the gossip and ridicule over your scandalous behavior with Lord Carlisle? Whatever the logic behind it, you must know it was dreadfully unkind of you and Lady Eustace to spread such lies. Especially after my husband behaved so honorably toward you."

Lady Eliot's alabaster skin mottled with splotches of red. "Oh, yes, Captain Heywood has a surfeit of honor. He's positively brimming with it." Her voice dropped to a venomous whisper. "But if you think he's a good man, you're mistaken. He's heartless and cold-blooded. Everybody knows it. Do you expect me to be grateful to him that he once condescended to save my reputation with his toplofty proposal? I never cared a snap of my fingers for my reputation. Carlisle could have taken me without benefit of marriage. You wouldn't understand that sort of love, would you? But then, you have married a man with ice in his veins."

Philly ignored her outburst. "You're hurt. No, don't scoff. I can see that you are. But it's no reason to attempt to cause trouble in my marriage. I'm not the one who hurt you, and whether you are pleased to admit it or not, neither is my husband."

Lady Eliot made a disparaging noise. "I have neither the time nor the inclination to cause trouble in anyone's marriage, Mrs. Heywood. If you and your husband are at odds, it has nothing to do—"

"I see you've worn the ruby earrings you mentioned," Philly

interrupted. "They're very lovely, though—if I may point out—not quite suitable for the daytime. Why did you wear them here today? Did you hope to upset me? To make me believe something that isn't true?"

"I've said nothing to you that wasn't the truth."

"You've said many things, and implied a great deal more. I don't require you to issue a retraction. It would hardly be possible at this late date, and I've no wish to humiliate you further. I believe that if you simply cease contributing to the gossip about my husband, it will die down all on its own."

Lady Eliot opened her mouth to speak and then shut it.

"You'll understand that I cannot receive you again." Philly resumed walking down the stairs. "This is probably the last time we shall ever meet."

Lady Eliot followed after Philly in a rush of white sarsnet. "How dare you? To speak to me in this manner? To refuse me admission to your home as if I were no better than a common—"

Philly stopped abruptly only a few steps from the hall. "You're mistaken. I'm not judging you."

"Then it's your husband who forbids my coming here? Or is it the Earl of Gordon himself? He has a bloody nerve. Do you know that Lord Gordon put it about that my chaperone during my come-out was no better than an abbess? That I was a fortune-hunting adventuress who sought to trap his heir? They all behaved as if *I* were the one who had done wrong. Me! A green girl not much older than your cork-brained little cousin. When all the while it was Carlisle who sought *me* out—"

"He treated you very badly," Philly said again.

Lady Eliot's eyes blazed. "I don't want your pity."

"You don't have my pity. You have my understanding."

"Understanding!" She laughed bitterly.

"Yes. For what's past, you have my understanding. But the lies and the gossip can't continue. All of that must end today." Philly took the final steps down to the main hall, sensing Lady Eliot close on her heels.

"—horses are pure white to match the curricle," Abigail was in midsentence, gesturing to the front doors, outside of which was parked Lady Eliot's stylish new carriage.

Lady Eliot visibly collected herself. "Wait until you see my tiger," she said in an artificially light voice as she strode up to join them. "I've had a suit made for him of silver-threaded cloth trimmed with lace. He looks an absolute macaroni. I vow you've never seen the like."

Abigail led the way out the front doors of Heywood House, rushing down the steps to Lady Eliot's curricle, which was attended by her woebegone little tiger. The rest of the ladies followed.

"It's quite fashionable, I'm sure," Mrs. Ogilvy said.

"The very height of fashion," Abigail agreed.

While her cousin was assisted up into the curricle, Philly turned back to Caroline Eliot. She wasn't surprised to see the lady's eyes were still upon her.

Without hesitation, Philly extended her hand.

Lady Eliot started, her cold expression momentarily disrupted by confusion. She recovered herself quickly, her dark eyes appraising Philly's outstretched hand with characteristic coolness.

Taut seconds passed.

And then, quite suddenly, Lady Eliot moved to clasp Philly's hand in hers. "I shan't apologize to you."

"I didn't expect that you would," Philly replied. "But I wish you happy all the same."

"I almost believe you mean it!" Lady Eliot laughed. "Very

well then, Mrs. Heywood. I shall wish you happy in return. But you'll get no more from me."

Their handshake was observed by Mrs. Ogilvy, and as Lady Eliot climbed into the curricle and gathered the reins, she edged close to Philly's side.

"My dear, I accompanied you to meet your guests in anticipation of a terrible row." She linked arms with Philly as they walked back into the house. "Instead, I've seen you shake hands with that horrible woman as if she were your dearest friend. Whatever can you mean by such behavior?"

Philly looked back over her shoulder to see Lady Eliot's curricle disappearing down the drive. "A wounded animal will bite and claw," she said to Mrs. Ogilvy. "And it often cannot tell friend from foe. One mustn't judge such a creature too harshly."

THIRTY-FIVE

Philly bounded down the stairs in her newly made riding habit, her dogs running alongside her. She was to meet Arthur at the stable for their early morning ride, and though she was even more tired than usual, nothing could diminish her spirits. The previous day they'd cantered together in the paddock. It had been utterly thrilling, and she had every hope they would repeat the experience today. Arthur was getting ever so much stronger. She was sure it wouldn't be too long before they could ride out on the estate together.

The sun was just creeping up over the horizon, burning away the edges of an unusually heavy morning fog that had settled over Heywood House. Visibility was poor. Indeed, it wasn't until she reached the stable yard that she saw Arthur.

And then she saw Hyperion.

The giant bay stallion was saddled and bridled. He tossed his head and stamped his hooves, barely under the control of Thomas, the young stable boy who held him.

Her breath caught in her throat. "Where's Greene?"

"A mare foaled in the north pasture, ma'am. Mr. Greene told me to—"

"It seems he instructed Thomas to saddle our riding horses," Arthur said.

Philly looked at Hyperion, understanding at once the mistake the young groom had made. She was on the verge of telling him that he must put Hyperion away and saddle Erasmus, when she glanced at Arthur.

His eyes were fixed on Hyperion, a strange expression on his face.

She wondered what was going through his mind. Images of all he'd been capable of before the war? Memories of how he'd galloped Hyperion across the grounds? Bitterness? Regret? She saw it all manifesting its melancholy weight across his brow.

"He's a bit fresh today," Thomas said breathlessly, struggling to quiet the giant stallion.

Philly turned her attention back to Hyperion just in time to see the boy narrowly avoid being stamped on. "Oh, do be careful!"

Suddenly, Hyperion reared up, striking out with his powerful forelegs. Thomas strained to pull him back down by the bridle. For a few seconds, the boy's feet were lifted straight off the ground.

Arthur stepped forward to assist him. "Here." He reached out to catch Hyperion's reins. "Give him to me."

It happened so quickly that Philly couldn't say a word. Arthur had reflexively extended his left hand. His fingers closed around the reins. The great horse shook and leapt. Arthur hadn't the strength to hold him. The reins were torn from his injured hand as Hyperion bolted, nearly knocking Arthur down in the process.

"Arthur!" She rushed to his side to support him.

Thomas ran after Hyperion, who cantered out of the yard and through the gate, disappearing into the morning fog.

"*Leave him!*" Arthur shouted at the boy.

Philly flinched at the anger in Arthur's voice, even as she took his arm securely in her own. "But he must fetch him back, surely."

"He'll find his way back to the stable in time for his supper. There's no point chasing him." Arthur was tense underneath Philly's touch. "You needn't cosset me," he said under his breath. "I'm not a cripple."

Philly blinked in surprise. Arthur had never spoken to her thus. "Of course you aren't. I only meant to—"

"Forgive me. I'm returning to the house."

"Arthur, wait." She tugged on his arm, willing him to look at her. "You mustn't let this experience sour you on riding altogether. Greene told me that Hyperion was the most ill-mannered beast in the stable. He said he was impossible to handle—"

"Yet I once handled him with ease." Arthur's expression was closed off. Unreadable. "Thomas, stay with Mrs. Heywood while she rides in the paddock and then escort her back to the house."

Philly allowed Arthur to disengage from her arm. "Are you angry with me?"

"I'm angry with myself. And in my present mood, I'll be poor company for your ride this morning."

"Then I'll come back to the house with you."

"No. Don't suspend your pleasure on my account. Stay. Have your ride on Persephone. I'll see you at luncheon."

She watched him walk away, her heart heavy. He was terribly upset. The sight of Hyperion under saddle had wrenched him into the past, and his inability to control the great beast had been a brutal reminder of his own limitations.

"Do ye want your mare, ma'am?" Thomas asked.

"What? Oh, yes. Well…" Philly looked out into the distance. The fog was still very thick. She couldn't see how far Hyperion had gone.

Arthur had pretended it didn't matter, but she knew better.

It wasn't safe for Hyperion to run loose with his reins hanging down about his legs. He might trip on them, or catch them in a branch and injure himself trying to break free. Had Arthur not been so angry, he'd have realized this. Indeed, he'd have ordered Thomas, or one of the other grooms, to chase after the disobedient equine.

Philly had no doubt that, when Arthur was a bit calmer, he'd come to regret his neglect. What if, by then, it was too late? What if Hyperion had torn his mouth or lamed himself—or worse? She couldn't allow it to happen. Not only because of her fondness for the horse, but because of her love for her husband. She wouldn't permit anything else to upset Arthur today.

"Thomas," she said, "if you'll wait with Persephone, I shall be right back."

Thomas gave an awkward bow and ducked into the stables.

Philly had expected an argument from the boy and was pleasantly surprised by his ready compliance. She whistled to her dogs. In all likelihood, Hyperion had stopped as soon as he reached the first tempting clump of grass outside the gates. If he'd gone a little farther, her dogs would help to discover him. If she knew anything about horses, he'd be calmer after his outburst, and she'd have no difficulty in taking him firmly by the reins, and leading him back to the stable. It was the least she could do to set Arthur's mind at ease.

Of course, he wouldn't be pleased that she'd ventured out onto the grounds alone. And she did hate to disobey him. Someone was up to mischief on the estate. Someone dangerous, if the snare on the riding path was any indication. Arthur wouldn't thank her for putting herself at risk.

But it was only just a step outside of the gate. And her dogs were with her, after all.

She started out at a brisk pace, Basil close at her side. Fox, Jasper, and Dash ran ahead. The stable yard was quiet. Thomas remained inside the stable with Persephone. None of the other grooms were about. There was no one at all to witness Philly leaving the grounds of Heywood House. No one at all to watch as she stepped into the fog with her four dogs.

And disappeared.

THIRTY-SIX

*rthur's temper had been building for days. It was a culmination of frustration over his lack of progress with shooting, walking, and riding. He'd foolishly begun to allow himself a modicum of hope, daring to believe that if he worked hard enough at it, he'd regain some approximation of his former proficiency. But he'd recently come to the bitter realization that whatever improvements he'd made since marrying Philly had reached their limit.

He was getting no better.

That was no excuse to have behaved like a sullen child in front of his wife. He should have stayed with her. Gone riding with her. It was one of the things she loved most, and he'd been too consumed with his own bitterness to give it to her.

She'd been right about Hyperion. Most riders couldn't handle such a foul-tempered beast. That he'd been skilled enough to do so once was a miracle all on its own. That he could do so no longer shouldn't have upset him.

He resolved to apologize to Philly the moment she returned from her ride.

The papers across his desk required little of his attention, but Arthur immersed himself in them nonetheless. The bracket clock on the mantle said it was half eight. Philly's ride should have been completed an hour ago, yet none of the servants had come to inform him that she'd returned to the house.

Perhaps she'd slipped past them and gone straight to her room to have her bath? Or perhaps she was still at the stable? She often lingered there after their rides, fussing over the horses and handing out treats.

He made an effort to quell the first stirrings of unease. She was safe in the stable yard. No harm would come to her there. Besides, she was probably enjoying her time away from him. And who could blame her? His dark moods would try the patience of a saint.

No. He wasn't going to allow himself to hover over Philly night and day, no matter how much he might want to. And he certainly wasn't going to go outside and fetch her back into the house like some overbearing, tyrannical husband.

Not yet, anyway.

A brisk knock at the library door interrupted his thoughts. He looked up from his desk to see Crofton entering with Greene close behind him. Fox, Jasper, and Dash ran ahead into the room. They came to Arthur directly, leaping and barking for his attention.

Crofton cleared his throat. "I beg your pardon, Captain Heywood. The head groom has informed me—"

Greene shouldered past the long-winded butler. "Did Mrs. Heywood not come back with you, sir?"

Arthur rose from behind his desk. The dogs continued to bark, but he didn't heed them. His every attention was trained on Greene. "No. She stayed at the stable to ride."

"Thomas tells me Mrs. Heywood didn't ride. Said she told

him she'd be back shortly. But she didn't come back, sir." Greene leaned toward the open door. "Thomas!"

The stable boy came in, cap in hand.

"Tell him," Greene commanded.

"You see, sir..." Thomas clutched his cap. "She said she were coming back directly. So, I saddled her mare. When she didn't come back...I thought..."

"It's not your job to think, is it now?" Greene growled. "The lad thought Mrs. Heywood had come back to the house with you," he said to Arthur. "Didn't think to tell anyone until I returned from the north pasture."

Arthur's blood went cold. The dogs' barking was more insistent. He registered for the first time that Basil was not amongst them. "Crofton, send for my wife's maid. Find out if she's in her room. Greene, why are only three of the dogs here?"

"They was out in pasture, sir," Thomas offered, shamefaced. "They come back half an hour ago."

"Only three of them?"

"Yes, sir."

Arthur fixed Thomas with an icy stare. "Did my wife go out into the pasture?"

The boy visibly swallowed. "I don't rightly know, Captain Heywood. I was in the stables—"

"I've a few men at the ready to go out searching for her," Greene said. "And a gig for you, if you like. She can't have got far."

Arthur moved from behind his desk, striding past the servants out into the hall, his cane clacking against the floor as he went. The dogs scrambled after him, along with Greene and Thomas.

Mrs. Lamb was just coming down the stairs with Sara in tow. Violet trailed behind them.

"Mrs. Heywood hasn't come back from riding, sir," Sara said.

Arthur could no longer keep his temper in check. "And it didn't occur to you to *tell* anyone?"

Sara cringed back against Mrs. Lamb.

The housekeeper did a creditable job of keeping her composure. "Sara thought Mrs. Heywood was with you, sir. We all did."

Mrs. Ogilvy appeared on the landing in a beribboned wrapper with a lace nightcap perched on her head. "What's all this commotion? Has something happened to Phyllida?"

Arthur's father soon joined her, emerging from the drawing room with a book in his hand. "What's going on?"

"Mrs. Heywood went out for her ride and hasn't come back, my lord," Mrs. Lamb informed him. "No one can find her."

Questions and answers were shouted out across the main hall. Mrs. Ogilvy withdrew to her room to dress, and the earl came downstairs to join Arthur. Mrs. Lamb organized the female servants to search the house. Crofton directed the male house servants to search the gardens. Arthur removed to the stable yard with Greene, Thomas, and William, the dogs following in their wake.

"He's a good boy is Thomas," Greene said as they walked. "I told him to saddle your horses, but naught else. Never for a minute thought he'd—"

"Not now." Arthur's voice was rigid with controlled fury. The last thing he wanted to hear were excuses. Not that any were needed. The fault was his and his alone, and well he knew it.

The shrill whinny of Hyperion reverberated through the stable yard. He trotted loose in the paddock, tossing his head to the men as they went by.

"When did Hyperion return?" Arthur asked.

"An hour ago, sir," Thomas said. "He come back just like ye said he would."

Arthur's stomach was leaden as he divided the men to go out

onto the grounds and search. Greene and several of the grooms mounted horses. Most were on foot. Arthur himself got into a gig with William at the reins and the three dogs in the back. He'd be damned if he was going to stay behind simply because he couldn't walk out with the same vigor as the rest of the men.

"The pond, the apple orchard, the riding path through the elms!" Greene shouted to the men as he wheeled his horse around toward the gate. "She can't have walked far. If she's met with any mischief—"

"She won't have met with mischief, Mr. Greene," William proclaimed. "She has Basil with her."

Arthur's hand tightened on his cane until the wood creaked beneath his fingers. He could hear Philly's voice as clear as anything: *My grandfather always said that if I were ever in any real danger, Basil would gladly give his life to save mine.*

The other dogs had returned.

Basil had not.

Arthur and William traveled straight out of the gate from the stable yard and onto the grounds, heading toward the fields that lay over the rise ahead. The voices of the other searchers echoed in the distance, their intermittent calls of "Mrs. Heywood!" carrying along on the crisp morning air.

All of the shouting excited the dogs. They barked and whined in the back of the gig, craning their heads to see.

"Stop," Arthur commanded.

William pulled up the horse. "Do you see her, sir?"

"No." Arthur alighted from the gig, his cane tottering on the uneven path. He went to the dogs, and one by one, assisted them onto the ground. Jasper raced off over the hill. Dash was quick to go after him, with Fox close behind. "Follow them," Arthur said, as he climbed back aboard.

William's face lit with understanding. He snapped the reins, and the horse sprang forward in its traces. "You think they'll lead us to her, Captain Heywood?"

Arthur hid his growing panic by sheer force of will. "To her, or to Basil."

The dogs were not trackers by any means. They had neither the instinct nor inclination to follow a trail or a scent. Instead, they ran ahead in a pattern of undisciplined chaos, stopping to sniff the grass several times, or to mark their territory. They barked, yipped, and scuffled with each other as they went, but they progressed, leading Arthur and William along a stone-covered path that led up and over a small rise.

"Wait," Arthur said. "Do you hear that?"

Amidst the barking of Jasper, Dash, and Fox, a fourth dog's voice rent the air in a deep, mournful howl.

"It sounds like Basil!" William urged the horse forward in its traces, following after the dogs at a brisk pace. "I never heard him make a noise like that before. Do you suppose he's hurt, sir? Or do you think... Wait, I see him. There he is, Captain Heywood. He's sitting by those hawthorn trees at the top of the rise." He craned his neck. "What's that beside him?"

Arthur's heart contracted. "It's Philly."

She was crumpled on the ground in a heap of amber fabric. Her eyes were closed, her skin as white as marble. Basil stood guard over her, refusing to move, even as Jasper and Dash leapt around him. Fox ran to Philly, bending his bedraggled little head to lick her cheek. When she didn't respond, he let out a pitiful whine.

Arthur was out of the gig before William had fully stopped

it. He rushed to his wife, and knelt beside her, heedless of the pain it caused his injured leg. "Philly," he said sharply. He pressed a hand to her face. She was cold to the touch. "Philly, wake up."

William came to stand behind Arthur. "Is she dead, sir?"

Arthur slid his hand beneath her head. His fingers came away wet. He didn't need to look to know what it was. He'd felt it countless times during the war. "You're bleeding, love," he muttered, feeling the unfamiliar sting of tears in his eyes.

"Someone's struck her on the head." William's voice was thick. "They've killed her."

Arthur realized that he was shaking. Whether with rage or fear, he didn't know. As carefully as he could manage it, he felt the back of her head, his fingers probing through her matted hair until he found the source of the blood. He withdrew his handkerchief and pressed it to the wound.

With his free hand, he reached inside the neckcloth of her riding habit, trying to determine if she had a pulse. There was nothing. Not a single, solitary heartbeat.

She was gone.

Dead.

A thunderous roar of anguish tore through him, seeming to emanate from the very depths of his soul. The smaller dogs cringed back. William blanched. And Basil growled low in his throat. Arthur wasn't aware he'd cried out at all until he heard the sound of his own voice. It was the sound of a soldier in the heat of battle.

Philly's pulse leapt in response to it.

His breath stopped in his chest. He didn't dare believe what he'd just felt beneath his hand.

"Who could have done this to her, sir?" William moaned. "Who would want to kill Mrs. Heywood? She's the kindest—"

"Quiet!" Arthur moved his fingers along Philly's throat, certain he'd imagined it.

Then he felt it again. The unmistakable pulsation of her heart.

It was alarmingly faint, but it was there.

A shudder of relief racked his body. "She's not dead."

"Isn't she?" William's brow creased. "Oh, but she looks very poorly, sir."

Arthur ignored him. With a single-mindedness born of half a lifetime spent on the battlefield, he untied Philly's neckcloth and opened up the fitted jacket of her riding habit so that she might breathe more freely. He then gathered her up into his arms, and very slowly got to his feet. His leg gave a deep throb of protest, but it didn't give way beneath him. As William looked on with wide, disbelieving eyes, Arthur carried Philly to the gig.

"It's going to be all right, love," he said to her. "I'm taking you home."

THIRTY-SEVEN

Arthur was fighting a herculean battle to keep calm. He sat in a chair beside Philly's bed while Mr. Graves examined her. The stout elderly man looked more like the village butcher than the village surgeon. As he moved his brawny hands across Philly's head, Arthur tensed with every touch.

"I've seen worse," Graves pronounced, as he completed his inspection. "Over at Mr. Tuttle's last year, the gardener's lad took a fall that near broke his head open. Never regained his senses, poor chap, and only two days later—" A speaking glance from Mrs. Lamb caused the old surgeon to break off from his grim reminiscence. He looked warily at Arthur, cleared his throat, and continued in a more sober tone. "Yes, yes, as I mean to say, there's no need to worry just yet, Captain Heywood. There was a great deal of blood, to be sure. 'Tis the nature of a head wound. But as for the rest—the swelling and loss of consciousness—well, that's only to be expected with a concussion."

"When will she wake?" Arthur's gaze rested on Philly's face. She was pale and drawn, lying so still upon the bed that the rise and fall of her chest was scarcely discernable.

"Ah, well that's the question. Could be as soon as an hour. Then again, she mightn't wake for a day or more. I counsel patience in these situations."

"What about her pain? She looks as if she's...suffering."

"Oh no, Captain Heywood," Mrs. Lamb said. "She's sleeping peacefully, I'm sure of it."

"Quite right," Mr. Graves agreed. "Now if she wakes with a headache, you can give her a dose of laudanum. Otherwise I don't think she'll suffer too much. There are no broken bones that I can find, and the cut on her head is a small one. I'd as soon not bind it now it's stopped bleeding. The best course is to let her sleep. If she worsens, send for me quick as you can, but I daresay you won't need to. A young lady in good health won't have any trouble recovering."

"She wasn't in good health." Arthur's voice sounded cold and flat to his ears. As if all emotion had been wrung out of him. He rather felt as if it had been.

"What's this?" Graves was suddenly alert.

"She was tired. She couldn't seem to get enough sleep. For the last three weeks, she—"

"It's all right, Captain Heywood." Mrs. Lamb ushered the surgeon away. "I can explain, Mr. Graves. You see..."

Arthur couldn't hear the whispered exchange. His attention was entirely on Philly. When he'd brought her home, Mrs. Lamb and Sara had carefully removed her riding habit and dressed her in one of her ruffled white nightgowns. Now, with her hair loose and the coverlet pulled up across her chest, she looked so unbearably vulnerable that he didn't know what to do.

Sara approached with a basin of water, some strips of cloth, and a small bottle of lavender-water. She busied herself preparing a cold compress, and when she'd done, she pressed it to Philly's forehead. The maid's birdlike little face screwed up in concentration as she leaned over her mistress, bathing her face with the utmost care.

Arthur waited for Philly to stir, to show in some small way that the ministrations of her maid were giving her comfort, but she remained as still and lifeless as she'd been since first he found her. He took one of her hands in his, hardly registering the sound of the bedroom door closing behind the surgeon or the presence of Mrs. Lamb as she came to stand beside him.

"Captain Heywood, I expect you'll be very angry to hear this now. Indeed, it's not my place to tell you. But—"

Arthur finally lifted his eyes from his wife, fixing them on Mrs. Lamb with an intensity that stopped her speech. "What is it?"

Mrs. Lamb took a deep breath. "I've taken the liberty of summoning Mrs. Ingram from the village."

"Mrs. Ingram."

"Yes, sir."

"The village midwife."

Sara rapidly gathered the basin and cloths and beat a hasty retreat to Philly's dressing room.

"Yes, sir," Mrs. Lamb said. "As I said, it's not my place, but I've suspected that Mrs. Heywood may be...that is to say, in my experience...a lady in Mrs. Heywood's condition—"

"What the devil are you telling me? Are you saying that my wife is with child?"

Mrs. Lamb drew back from him. "I've reason to think so, yes. There have been various...symptoms." She turned a dull red. "I've been giving her a special decoction to ease her, but I couldn't be sure. These are early days yet—"

"She said nothing of this." Arthur's heart pounded painfully in his chest. He looked down at Philly again, squeezing her hand in his. "Why wouldn't she tell me?"

"She mightn't have realized it herself, sir. For some ladies it can be quite common to...occasionally..." Mrs. Lamb gave a discreet cough. "I beg your pardon, Captain Heywood, but these matters are best left with women."

He was silent for several moments before asking, abruptly, "What can the midwife do?"

"Very likely nothing at all, but I have a hope she might be able to tell us if..." Mrs. Lamb withdrew another few steps. "If this... accident...has caused Mrs. Heywood to lose the babe."

"I'll kill him."

The earl looked at Arthur in alarm. "What do you intend to do? Shoot him down with a pistol? Come man, don't be absurd."

"I have no need of a pistol. I'll use my bare hands."

"You'll calm yourself before you do something foolish," his father commanded. "You don't even know Moreland's at fault. Anything could have happened out there."

Arthur raked a hand through his hair. He and his father had been consigned to the drawing room while Mrs. Ingram examined Philly. He'd wanted to stay with her, but the wizened old midwife, along with Mrs. Ogilvy and Mrs. Lamb, had driven him out.

"It's all my fault. If I'd acted as soon as I received that note—" Arthur muttered an oath. "If I'd told Philly she was in danger—"

"No point in what you're doing now. It's a damned waste of energy." The earl downed the entire contents of his brandy glass. "Nothing to be done except to leave Heycombe for a spell until this is all sorted out. Mrs. Ogilvy and I depart for Bath end of the week. You and Phyllida had better join us. From there we can contact Bow Street. Past time we got the runners involved."

"My wife could have been killed today," Arthur ground out.

"You don't think I know that?" the earl barked. "Heaven and earth, man, she might very well be carrying my only grandchild!"

"And you want us to go to Bath and take the bloody waters?"

"The danger's in Heycombe! Not in Bath!"

"My dear, we can hear your raised voices all the way in Phyllida's room." Mrs. Ogilvy entered the drawing room with Mrs. Ingram close behind. "I insist you cease this quarrelling at once."

"We're not quarrelling!" the earl bellowed.

Arthur crossed the room in a few large strides. "Well?" he demanded of the elderly midwife.

Mrs. Ingram bristled at Arthur's peremptory tone. "I don't claim to be an educated woman, Captain Heywood, not like those fancy doctors you have up in London, but I've been looking after women for nigh on fifty years here in Heycombe, and though others might disagree with how I do things—"

"They won't hold you accountable if you happen to be wrong," Mrs. Ogilvy assured the old woman.

"I'm never wrong," Mrs. Ingram replied with some asperity. "Mind you, I couldn't look at Mrs. Heywood proper as I'd like, but I know all the signs, and I don't reckon she lost the babe today. She may yet, and so I warn you. Keep her quiet. None of this gadding about on horseback, or walking for miles on end as these young ladies are wont to do when they come to the country."

Arthur was frozen where he stood, the slight tremor of his hand upon his cane the only outward indication of the torrent of emotions that had been unleashed by her words. "Then you're certain that my wife is...? That she...?"

"Aye, Captain Heywood. Your wife is with child."

THIRTY-EIGHT

Philly woke confused, not sure where she was or what had happened to her. Some hazy impressions had permeated her restless sleep—the sound of murmured voices, the scent of lavender water, and the feeling of someone holding her hand. For a moment, she imagined she was back in her bedroom at Satterthwaite Court recovering from a terrible illness, but the hand that was holding her own was too large and far too strong to belong to her grandfather.

"Philly," Arthur said. "Wake up, sweetheart. Open your eyes."

Her lashes fluttered. "My head."

"Are you in pain? Shall I summon Mrs. Lamb for the laudanum?"

She squeezed his hand with a faint pressure. "No. Please stay."

"I'm here."

She swallowed. The details of what had happened came back to her slowly. She wanted—needed—to tell Arthur, but couldn't seem to formulate the words. Her throat was unbearably dry. "Hyperion..."

"It's all right, love. Here. Have a sip of tea." He slid his arm under her shoulders, carefully supporting her head as he held a teacup to her lips. She took a small drink, but when he pressed her to take more, she weakly pushed the cup away. "You needn't worry about Hyperion," he said, easing her back down upon the pillows and once again taking her hand. "He came home not an hour after he ran off. He's safe in the stable now."

She thought she might drift off again. "I'm glad of it."

"Philly, stay awake just a little longer. Open your eyes. Look at me." Arthur was insistent. "Do you remember who did this to you?"

Her last clear memory was of Hyperion standing near the Hawthorn trees. He'd been munching on the grass, his tail swishing idly, and one ear cocked forward in an attitude of lazy attention. He'd watched her approach with seeming disinterest, but as soon as she'd touched him, he had exploded with energy.

The rest was all rather dim. She knew she'd fallen backward, and she could recall the shocking sensation of her head striking against something hard and brutally unforgiving as she hit the ground. After that, her world had gone mercifully black.

She nodded. The small movement sent a jolt through her already throbbing skull, causing her to give a small sob of pain.

"My love, my love, you mustn't try to move. You must lie still. It will be all right soon, I promise you, but you cannot, you must not, move."

Philly closed her eyes until the sharp pain had subsided. When she opened them again, Arthur was a shade paler. It suddenly seemed very important to tell him something. "Hyperion..."

"He's perfectly fine." Arthur lifted her hand to his lips and pressed a kiss to it. "Who did this to you, Philly? Did you recognize him?"

"No." She struggled to say what she meant. "It was Hyperion. I followed him. I thought to...to catch him for you. To bring him back."

"Of course, you did. Why else would you have wandered off into the pasture?"

She gave him a wan smile. "Yes." Her lashes fluttered again. "He was over the hill. By the hawthorn trees."

"Where you were hurt?" Arthur visibly tensed. "Was someone in those trees, Philly?"

"What? No. Arthur. Please, listen." She squeezed his hand again with the same weak insistence. "Hyperion knocked me down. I think...my head must have hit a stone when I fell."

"*Hyperion did this to you?*"

"Please..." She looked at him imploringly. "Don't be angry with him. It was my fault. I tried to take his reins. He reared up and tossed his head. He's so strong."

"Hyperion knocked you down and your head hit a stone." Arthur leaned closer to her. "Is that what happened?"

"Yes." Philly sighed with relief, and having assured herself that Arthur understood what she had told him, she at last closed her eyes.

This time he made no attempt to stop her.

When Philly next woke, it was the early hours of the morning and she was in Arthur's arms. She had no real idea of how much time had passed or how badly she'd been hurt.

"You're awake."

Philly started at the sound of Arthur's deep voice. She looked up from where she lay to find him watching her intently. There was a worried frown across his brow and an expression in his eyes that she couldn't interpret. He was still in his shirtsleeves, his hair disheveled and a shadow of stubble across his jaw. She had the vague impression he'd been keeping vigil over her. "Arthur."

"I'm here."

"You're here," she agreed softly. "I thought it must be a dream, but I..."

"It's not a dream." He touched the edge of her jaw with the back of his fingers. "How do you feel?"

"My head aches."

He levered himself up on one elbow, his gaze drifting over her face. "Very badly?"

"No, just a little. Here, where I fell." She reached to feel the back of her head, only to wince when her fingers brushed the site of her injury.

Arthur caught hold of her hand, gently restraining her from further exploration. "You've had a concussion. There's a good-sized lump on your head, and a wound from where you hit the edge of a stone when you fell. It might be better not to touch it for now."

Her brows drew together. "I know I hit my head, but—after that—I can't seem to remember."

"I'd be astonished if you could. You were unconscious when I found you and didn't begin to wake until several hours after I brought you home. Even then you were a bit confused."

"I imagined I was at Satterthwaite Court."

"That you did. And when you first opened your eyes, I believe you mistook me for your grandfather." A strained smile edged the corner of Arthur's mouth. "Naturally, it was a great blow to my conceit."

Philly managed a weak smile of her own. "What a lot of nonsense you talk."

"Do you think so?" He smoothed her hair from her brow, his expression once again reverting to lines of the deepest concern. "Tell me, sweetheart, what can I do to ease your aching head?

Would you like a few drops of laudanum? Or one of Mrs. Lamb's decoctions?"

"Neither, if you please."

"Shall I be a very unpleasant husband and force you?"

"No. Truly, I'm not in any great pain. Indeed, I feel very much myself again, except...I fear I must look absolutely dreadful."

"You look charmingly. A trifle pale, perhaps, but that's easily remedied."

"Is it? How? Not some awful cordial, I hope."

Arthur gave her chin an affectionate pinch. "I have an idea that you might be wanting your breakfast. What do you think of that, my love? Would food suit you a little better than your medicine?"

Philly brightened. "I *am* excessively hungry."

"I don't doubt it. You've had nothing since yesterday morning."

"And then only a cup of chocolate."

He frowned his disapproval. "What sort of a meal did you consider that?"

"No meal at all. We were meant to breakfast together properly when we returned from our ride. I didn't want to spoil my appetite."

Her words, though innocently spoken, had a quelling effect on Arthur. He fell silent a moment, as if reflecting on a particularly troubling thought.

"What is it?" she asked.

His jaw tightened. "I behaved abominably toward you outside of the stable."

Her eyes searched his. She noticed, for the first time, the decided tension in the set of his shoulders and the ragged harshness to his features. It was more than strain and fatigue. He might almost have been angry. "But that was nothing but a misunderstanding. Hyperion...and Thomas...and I shouldn't have clung to you as I did."

"You did nothing wrong. It was my fault. I was angry with myself. Angry. Frustrated. Unable to keep my temper." A flicker of anguish passed over his face. "To think those sharp words might have been the last I ever said to you."

"Oh, my dear. Has this been preying upon your mind all this while?"

"Amongst other things."

Philly touched a caressing hand to his cheek. "What a lot of trouble I've caused you. I thought only to help by going after Hyperion, and instead I've worried you ragged and no doubt inconvenienced the entire household."

Arthur stared down at her, his brooding gaze heavy with unspoken emotion. "Trouble and inconvenience? Do you think I give a damn about those things? My God, Philly, I thought I'd lost you. From the moment I found you lying in the pasture, I've been in hell."

Her hand stilled on his cheek. "Arthur..."

"In hell," he repeated. His voice deepened to a fierce undertone. "And so I should remain if you were ever taken from me. There would be nothing else worth living for."

Philly had no words to offer in reply to such a desperate statement. She did the only thing she could think of. She coaxed his face down to hers and she kissed him.

It was a sweet kiss, slow and gentle and uncompromisingly tender. Arthur responded with unexpected caution, his hand reaching up to cup her face as his lips softened under hers, returning her kiss with as much tenderness as she'd given it, and then, reluctantly, pulling away from her.

"Have a care, love," he said huskily. "I don't want to hurt you."

THE WORK OF ART

"You never could."

"I could and I will, if you kiss me like that again."

She was tempted to smile, but something in his expression stopped her from making light of his words. "What is it? What's wrong?"

"Nothing's wrong, but...we must talk a moment."

"Must we?" She stroked his cheek, kissing him softly once more. "What about?"

"I summoned the surgeon yesterday."

"Oh?"

"And then Mrs. Lamb summoned old Mrs. Ingram from the village."

Philly looked up at him, uncomprehending. "Mrs. Ingram?" And then, in a flash, understanding came.

The warmth she'd experienced after their kiss drained away. She drew back from him. "Did I...? When I fell...?"

"Good lord, no. I didn't mean to imply that anything was amiss. Mrs. Lamb feared it might be, but all is well, I promise you."

"But then, did Mrs. Ingram say that I'm increasing? She's sure of it?"

"I don't know how much her opinion is worth. She seems an odd, eccentric sort of creature, and owns to not having properly examined you, but since she's all but staked her fifty-year reputation on your being with child, I suppose we must have no doubt."

Philly had heard enough. She pressed her face back into her pillow. It was all too much. The accident with Hyperion, the throbbing in her head, and now this. A baby.

The news should have been joyous. And it was. Truly, it was. It was also completely overwhelming.

Arthur moved his hand soothingly on her back. "You might have told me."

"I didn't know."

"But you suspected?"

Philly hadn't suspected. Not at first. Her courses had always been irregular. It was only when she'd missed them a second time that she'd begun to wonder. "A little," she admitted.

"Will you not look at me?"

She grudgingly turned to face him. He didn't look angry. Nor did he look unhappy. He looked anxious. Anxious for her and her health? Anxious about becoming a father? She couldn't tell. "If it's true...If I am in a promising way..." she faltered. "Do you wish us to have a child?"

Arthur lowered himself down next to her. "I confess, I didn't expect it to happen so soon, but—"

"It's *too* soon."

"That could hardly be avoided, my love."

Heat rose in her cheeks. "But this can't be what you wanted."

"You think not?"

"It's all come about so quickly. And it's all so much chance. If Basil had never run into my uncle's library that day, or if we'd never happened upon each other that afternoon in the park when I was out walking with Sara—"

Arthur gave a wholly unexpected, and completely uncharacteristic, shout of laughter. "Happened upon each other? I waited over an hour for you to walk by that day."

Philly gaped. "You did not!"

"And the next time, as well."

"I don't believe it. You were far too somber and dignified to—"

"To behave like a besotted fool?"

Hope swelled in her breast, warm and bright. "Is that what you were?"

"Yes." Arthur gathered her up in his arms. "It's what I still am." And he lowered his mouth to hers and kissed her.

THIRTY-NINE

———— ❧ ❧ ————

*A*rthur had stretched those blissful moments in Philly's bed out for as long as he could, all the while knowing that the sweet and tender affection she'd lavished upon him was shortly going to come to an abrupt, and possibly very unhappy, end.

At breakfast, he was going to tell her everything about the Duke of Moreland.

He'd made the decision during the seemingly endless hours of her unconsciousness, realizing then that if only she'd known the truth, she would never have wandered off onto the estate alone. It didn't matter in the end that it was Hyperion who had harmed her and not some evil henchman of the duke. The fact remained that his silence had put Philly in danger. He'd vowed that if, by some miracle, she came back to him, he would confess all to her—the consequences be damned.

After taking his leave of Philly so that she could perform her morning toilette, he'd retreated to his own room to put himself in order. He'd washed, shaved and changed into a fresh suit of clothes.

When he returned, Philly met him at the connecting door,

dressed in a long-sleeved India muslin morning gown with an amber ribbon sash. She'd insisted on having a bath before breakfast so she could wash the dried blood out of her hair. Her long tresses were still damp, tumbling over her shoulders in a mass of wild curls.

"You must be dreadfully tired after staying up all night with me," she said as he helped her to her seat at the small table the servants had laid in her room.

He sat down opposite her, watching as she began to preside over their intimate breakfast with the same elegance of manner in which she presided over the dinner table and the tea tray. She seemed all that was feminine and beautiful, and he wondered, not for the first time, how the devil a man like him had ever won her.

"I didn't stay up all night, my love," he answered. "In fact, I slept very soundly for quite a few hours. In your bed."

Her hand froze in the act of pouring out his coffee. She caught herself just before it spilled over, returning the coffeepot to its place on the table and fixing him with a wide, hopeful gaze. "Oh, did you really?"

He nodded. It was hard to tease her when she looked at him that way. In truth it was hard to say or do much of anything at all.

"It must have been quite accidental," she said.

"So it was."

"And…is it an accident you intend to repeat?"

Arthur seriously doubted whether he'd ever have the fortitude to sleep away from her again. "You have an exceedingly comfortable bed, my dear. Perhaps I'll sleep awhile there again tonight." He paused, adding, "If I'm invited."

Her mouth quirked. "How absurd you are. You're always welcome in my bed, and well you know it."

For the briefest moment, Arthur wondered how wrong it

would be to postpone telling her about Moreland, but no sooner had he begun to consider it than it struck him, rather forcibly, that to prolong the inevitable would only compound his crime.

He could put it off no longer. "I hope you'll still feel that way after what I have to tell you."

Philly was buttering a piece of bread while her dogs looked on with expressions of shameless longing. A hint of a smile played on her lips. "Ah. I suppose you're about to restrict my movements to the house or some other such act of domestic tyranny."

"No, indeed."

She lowered her knife, raising her eyes to his in enquiry. "Good gracious, Arthur, you haven't got it into your head to sell Hyperion, have you? I told you it wasn't his fault, and that if—"

"Don't distress yourself. I've no intention of selling Hyperion, temperamental brute that he is. What I must say to you is in the way of being a confession."

And then, before he could lose his nerve, Arthur proceeded to do just that.

He confessed.

It all came out in a succession of clear, concise sentences— rather as if he were making a report to a superior officer. He told her of the sinister reputation Moreland had earned as a collector of rare and valuable objects, his infamous obsession with those items that were one of a kind, and of the legendary stories of his vengeance. He told her all he knew about the death of Molly Cartwright. He told her about the wager in the betting book, the anonymous note that had come to Heywood House, and Sara's report that the duke had spoken of leaving Philly to her fate. Last of all, he talked of the snare that had been dug on the riding path through the elms. A snare that had undoubtedly been placed there to injure or even kill her.

Philly listened to him, never once interrupting as he recounted all the things he'd been keeping from her, and when he'd finished, she responded to him with silence. Ominous, wretched silence.

Arthur looked at her from across the small table, searching her face with growing anxiety. Her hair had been damp when they first sat down near the fire. Now it was dry. How much time had passed? Minutes? An hour? It felt like an age.

He'd promised himself he would tell her everything about the threat from Moreland—and tell her he had, but Arthur was beginning to suspect that he'd made a profound error in judgment. "Say something," he urged. "Please."

Philly was staring down at her plate, but when Arthur spoke, she lifted her gaze back to his. Her face was pale. "Why did you keep all of this from me?"

"I wouldn't have had you frightened, Philly. Not over something that originally seemed so utterly ridiculous."

"But you don't think it ridiculous now."

"Not after you fell from Persephone, no. The arrival of the note made me uneasy, I won't pretend it didn't, but it seemed… off, somehow. It struck me as the overly dramatic sort of thing a child would do. But the snare on the avenue of the elms was something entirely different. Whoever was responsible for it meant to do you actual harm. That's why I restricted your rides to the paddock. Why I didn't want you out alone outside of the house anymore. And when you wandered off after Hyperion—"

"You thought the Duke of Moreland had taken me."

"Yes. Not the duke himself, but someone in his employ. Some villain. I don't know." Arthur raked his fingers through his hair. "I wasn't thinking clearly at that particular moment."

"You thought he'd taken me so that he could…what? Kill me? Like he killed Molly Cartwright? Or that he meant to destroy me like some work of art he's been unable to procure for himself?" Philly shook her head. "Arthur, you can't believe the duke is truly so dangerous. Not really. For if you did—if you thought for even one moment that he might do me harm—you'd never have considered leaving London."

Arthur stilled. "What?"

"After my uncle's dinner party. You knew the duke had an interest in me, and yet you would have returned to Somersetshire that Friday. You would have left me to him." She leaned forward. "Don't you see? If he'd really been dangerous, you'd never have gone. Or if you had, at the very least, you'd have warned me of the danger. We were friends then. More than friends, though we hadn't yet acknowledged it. You wouldn't have simply abandoned me to a monster."

Arthur stared at her, momentarily speechless. By God, she was right. If he'd believed the rumors about Moreland…

But he hadn't believed them. Not then.

"You must understand," he said at last. "When we were in London, all those stories about the duke…I didn't credit them. I've been hearing such things about Moreland my entire life. I never once thought any of it more than fantastical tales. Fictions. It's true, I didn't like him. And I didn't want you to marry him. But for all that, he *is* a duke. If you'd wanted to become his duchess, there was no legitimate objection I could have given then except that I loved you myself."

"Are you saying that you no longer think the stories about Moreland are fictions? That, after the note and Persy's fall, you've changed your mind?"

"Yes." Arthur thought of the morning of their marriage, their hurried trip from London to Somersetshire, and the fears that had plagued him along the way. "No," he amended, surprising himself. "It wasn't the note, nor even your fall that changed my mind. The truth is... I began to take the rumors about Moreland seriously as soon as we married."

Philly raised her brows. "Before any threats had been made?"

Arthur struggled to explain what he didn't quite understand himself. "Once we married, once you became mine, I was consumed with the urge to protect you. Perhaps it's like that for all husbands? I don't know. But by the time we were in the coach and on our way here to Somersetshire, I found I could no longer dismiss the potential threat from Moreland. When the note came, it was the confirmation of all my fears."

"'You have taken what is mine,'" Philly recited with a thoughtful frown. "Can the duke really feel that I belong to him? Even though I refused his offer, and am now married to you?"

"It's possible, I suppose."

"But he didn't even seem to like me. Indeed, the day he took me driving in the park, he scolded me and accused me of being as stupid as his dogs."

Philly's own dogs had long since given up begging at the table and were now lying asleep by the hearth. At her words, Basil raised his head enquiringly.

"And then..." She frowned. "He told me that no one had ever seen my equal and compared me to a Botticelli or a Titian. Yet, he didn't seem to be complimenting me as a woman. He spoke of me as a...as a *thing*."

"The Work of Art," Arthur mused. "Something for his collection."

"Oh, how foolish!" Philly's cheeks flushed with rare anger. Her eyes dropped once more to her plate.

Arthur followed her gaze. Her buttered bread was uneaten, and the rest of the dishes on the table had no doubt gone cold. He felt a stab of guilt for confessing to her over breakfast. She wasn't only recovering from an injury, she was expecting their child. She shouldn't be missing her meals.

In one quick motion, he rose from the table and jerked the bell pull. "The cook can send you something hot," he said as he sank back down in his chair. "You must eat."

"Yes."

He waited for her to say something more. When she didn't speak, he found himself unable to endure the silence. "I should have told you."

"Yes," she agreed. "You should have done. If I'd known, perhaps I might have been frightened, but at least I would have understood why you watched over me so closely. As it was, I thought you simply a very possessive husband."

Arthur had the grace to redden. "I *am* a very possessive husband."

"But not one who arms his wife's servants and sets them to guard her, surely."

"I'd like to say no, but...." He gave a wry smile. "Now you're with child, I can't promise anything."

A tap at the door announced the arrival of Violet. She entered the room with a nervous curtsy. "You rang, ma'am? Sir?"

"Take all of this away," Arthur said. "And bring Mrs. Heywood the same again. Hot."

"A fresh pot of coffee, as well, Violet," Philly said in a gentler tone.

Violet cleared away the dishes on the table, her hands trembling. Philly watched her. "Is everything all right?"

A cup skittered out of Violet's hand. She scrambled to retrieve it. "Yes, ma'am."

Arthur waited impatiently for the maid to leave.

Violet balanced the breakfast things on a tray and turned to go. She got as far as the door, and then stopped to look back at them. Her face was stark white. "Beg pardon, Mrs. Heywood. Is it true what happened to you yesterday...that it were the *horse's* fault?"

Philly smiled. "Yes. It was an accident. Nothing more."

Arthur glowered at the nosy servant. He'd have said something to hurry her along, but one look at his expression and she shot out the door all on her own.

"You scare the servants on purpose," Philly observed.

"Do I?" Arthur's ill temper faded quickly now he was alone with his wife again. "Then they shall be glad to be rid of me when we leave for Bath at the end of the week."

"Bath!"

"There's no need to sound so astonished. It's an easy journey from Heycombe, and I daresay you'll find it as fine a city as when you were last there with your grandfather."

"I saw nothing of the city then. I was all of fifteen and hardly left our lodgings except to go with my grandfather for sweets at Molland's."

"In Milsom Street." Arthur's spirits lifted at the chance to please her. "I'll take you there if you like."

Philly's face shone with pleasure. "I'd like that very much." And in a rustle of muslin skirts, she was out of her chair and in his arms. "Will we stay with your father?"

Arthur settled her on his lap. "If you don't mind it."

"Naturally I don't. But will *you* enjoy it?"

He gave her a wry smile. "*Enjoy* is a rather strong word."

"It's an unexceptionable word. And you needn't pretend to hate it. It's perfectly all right for you to enjoy the company of other people again."

"Again?"

She stroked her fingers through his hair. "Your father says—"

"If my father has been telling you that I was sociable before the war, I must inform you that he's been embellishing the truth beyond all recognition. I fenced, I boxed, I shot at Manton's, and on occasion, if forced, I attended a ball. That was the sum total of my life in town before I left for the Peninsula—and even then, I was as moody and cross as I am now."

Philly's blue and amber eyes glimmered with laughter. "Moody and cross. What nonsense."

Arthur returned her smiling gaze with one of sudden solemnity. By heaven, but she was beautiful. More than beautiful. She was radiant. Glowing. From the sparkle in her eyes to the luminosity of her creamy skin. If he hadn't known for a fact that she'd been injured the previous day, he'd never have believed it. "When we're in Bath, I shall engage a miniaturist to paint you just as you are now."

"Will you indeed? And what need have you of my likeness when I'm always with you?"

"Not always."

"As near as can be."

"Nowhere near enough." Arthur drew her closer. His voice deepened. "I'm jealous of every second you spend away from me."

Philly tightened her arms around his neck. "Perhaps," she whispered into his ear, "I shall have this Bath miniaturist paint a picture of you, as well."

"Good God."

She nuzzled his cheek. "And then, if you haven't become too bored, you can accompany me to the modiste, the milliner, and the—"

"I shall squire you to the ends of the earth, my love."

She laughed softly. "You shall thank me some day for not taking you at your word. Besides, how would your father feel if we were to spend every moment together? Surely he expects us to make a family party of it. Unless... Oh, I hope he wasn't looking forward to time alone with Mrs. Ogilvy. She did mention once that we might join them in Bath, but if I thought we were intruding—"

"We're not. My father suggested the trip himself after your accident." Arthur hesitated, before adding, "He advised we leave Heycombe for Bath at once, and from there, contact the Bow Street Runners."

Some of the happiness faded from Philly's face. "And that's what you intend to do? Even though you know it was Hyperion who hurt me and not the duke?"

Arthur gave her a solemn nod.

"Because you think he may still hurt me?"

"I don't know, love, but yesterday, when I thought I'd lost you, I felt..." Arthur couldn't describe it to her. Fear, panic, rage, unbearable grief. He knew now that he couldn't withstand such a loss. That if something were ever to happen to Philly, it would be the end of him. "I'm not going to wait for tragedy to strike. I'll contact Bow Street. And then..."

She looked down at him, a line of worry across her brow. "And then?"

Arthur met her eyes, realizing in a flash that Philly knew his answer—indeed, that she expected his answer—even before he gave it her. "If they're unable to do anything," he said with grim determination, "then I'll confront the Duke of Moreland myself."

FORTY

❧❦

The morning of their departure for Bath dawned crisp and clear. Philly had spent the past three days overseeing their travel preparations. They wouldn't leave until midday, and the morning hours were taken up with last-minute odds and ends. Mrs. Ogilvy and the earl were still in their rooms. Arthur was in his library for a brief meeting with Pebmarsh. And Philly was in the morning room going over her list of completed tasks.

She ticked off the final two items, racking her brain for anything else she might have missed. It wouldn't be disastrous to forget something. Indeed, she needn't have done as much as she already had. But keeping herself busy helped to distract her from her worries.

"Mrs. Heywood!" Sara called from the doorway. "I've found these two wraps in your wardrobe. Mightn't you need them for Bath?"

Philly turned, her eyes drifting over the folded fabric in Sara's hands. One of the wraps was Sardinian blue silk, the other a deep amber gauze. She could still remember the day the modiste in

London had recommended them to Mrs. Vale. It seemed a lifetime ago. "You'd better pack them."

"Edward and William have already taken your trunks down with the others, ma'am."

Philly rose from her writing desk, glad to have some diversion. "Here. I'll take them out to the coach myself. I could do with the fresh air." She collected the wraps from Sara. "Would you check my bedroom again for anything else we might have overlooked?"

"Yes, ma'am."

Philly left the morning room, her dogs at her heels. In the hall, she crossed paths with William. He was rushing toward the servants' stairs that led down to the kitchens. It looked as though he'd spilled something over the front of his livery. "William, is my trunk already at the coach?"

"Yes, ma'am. Right out front. Shall I—?"

"No. That's quite all right. Carry on." Philly went out the front doors of Heywood House and down the steps only to find utter chaos. There were trunks everywhere, and the earl's servants, Mrs. Ogilvy's servants, and the staff of Heywood House were shouting instructions back and forth to each other as they attempted to put everything in order.

Philly stepped out of the way. As yet, only Violet had noticed her. The slender housemaid was struggling with what looked like a stack of hatboxes. When she caught sight of Philly, she dropped them all to the ground. Edward trotted to her side to help her.

Was Edward Violet's sweetheart? The young man Violet hoped to marry?

If Philly were at Satterthwaite Court, she'd have known the answer. But here at Heywood House she still had much to learn about the servants and their lives.

She took a step farther out of the way, moving back toward

one of the oversized rhododendrons that flanked the front stairs.

"Mrs. Heywood! *Mrs. Heywood!*"

Philly turned sharply, startled by the sound of a familiar voice calling to her in low, frantic tones from just behind the shrubbery. She followed the sound of it.

"Thank God, it *is* you. You're just the person I was looking for."

Philly stopped short, her dogs close behind her. "Mr. Forsythe! My goodness. What are you doing here?"

Mr. Forsythe stood, hidden by the rhododendrons. His hair was disheveled, his chest rising and falling as if he'd run a great distance. "I've come to fetch you. I could think of no one else to turn to."

"Whatever is the matter?"

"A great deal, ma'am. There's a dog that's been hurt. A small fellow, not too different from your little one there. I found him while out walking in your woods. He's in a terrible way."

Philly's heart leapt. "An injured dog?"

"Quite. I couldn't tell what's befallen him. He wouldn't let me near. I've no skill with animals. But surely you—?"

"Yes. Yes, of course. I'll come directly." Philly hesitated, glancing back toward the servants. She'd better send someone for Arthur, or perhaps the gamekeeper. A small dog wasn't dangerous, but if it were hurt, it may snap and bite.

"I fear he was on the verge of expiring. We shouldn't tarry. But then...perhaps it's best? An injured creature like that. Crying piteously. Frightened and alone. Perhaps death is better?"

"Indeed not!" Philly was appalled.

"You know more about these things than I. Come. I'll you show you the way."

She glanced back toward the house once more, torn between

the urgency of the situation and her inherent desire to summon Arthur.

"Are you coming, Mrs. Heywood?"

"Forgive me, I... Yes. I'm right behind you." Her mind made up, Philly followed at a quick pace, her dogs racing along with her.

"Wait!" Mr. Forsythe stopped short. "I beg your pardon, ma'am, but will your dogs not scare the little wretch? He's already terrified. If he were to see a pack of—"

"To be sure, they would only frighten the poor beast further." Philly felt a fool for not having thought of it herself. Turning back, she gave her dogs the command to stay. Basil edged forward, the hackles on his neck raised. She held up her hand again. "Stay," she repeated firmly.

"Will they obey you?"

"What? Oh...yes. Yes, they're quite obedient."

His lips curled into a smile. "Excellent."

Philly wasted no time in contemplating the questionable obedience of Basil, Fox, Jasper, and Dash. She strode ahead, consumed by urgency. Indeed, she had to quell her urge to run.

The poor little dog! Where had he come from? And who—or what—had harmed him? Why, he might have been caught in a metal trap. Or attacked by a wild animal. A very small dog could have easily bled to death by now.

What if she were too late?

"Is he very far?" she asked breathlessly as the woods that ran along Heywood House rose up to envelop them.

"No, Mrs. Heywood. Not far at all," Mr. Forsythe said. "He's in the clearing. Just by the pond."

Philly would never have thought Mr. Forsythe the sort of gentleman to care about the fate of an injured dog. He'd always seemed to be more focused on superficial matters—with particular attention given to the manner of his dress.

But perhaps she'd misjudged him? Perhaps there was more to him than met the eye?

"I must commend you, sir." She hurried after him along the path through the woods. "Most gentlemen wouldn't have cared enough to bother with a hurt animal."

Mr. Forsythe made no response.

She glanced at his face. Beads of perspiration covered his brow. "You needn't distress yourself, Mr. Forsythe. If we're too late, it's not for lack of effort on your part. No one could have done more."

Just around the bend, the woods opened to the clearing. The surface of the pond glistened in the sunlight, and the surrounding trees cast shadows on the crumbling stone benches.

Philly ran ahead, looking all around. "Where was he, sir?" There was no sign of any dog, nor any tracks or marks of blood that she could discern. "Perhaps he's crawled back into the woods? A badly hurt animal will often attempt to hide."

Mr. Forsythe's stride shortened. All signs of urgency left him. "Yes. Perhaps he's crawled away."

Philly walked the edge of the clearing, her wraps still clutched in her arms. She could use one as a makeshift bandage. If the dog were small enough, she might even fashion a sling with which to carry him.

A sudden crunch of leaves and branches in the woods brought her to an abrupt halt. She stepped closer to the edge of the clearing just as a shadow of movement caught her eye. "I think I see him!"

She peered through the dense growth of trees and shrubs that made so much outside of the perimeter invisible. There was a flash of chestnut. A long, bent neck and swishing tale. Reins lightly tethered to a tree.

It was someone's horse.

A twig snapped.

Philly whirled around to find that Mr. Forsythe had come to stand directly behind her. "You startled me, sir." She took an unconscious step backward. She was suddenly, quite unaccountably, afraid.

"I see you've noticed my horse."

"No. I mean... *Is* that your horse? Did you ride here? I thought you'd been walking in the woods when you found the dog. Perhaps I misunderstood?" She swallowed. Every instinct within her told her to take another step back, but she didn't. "In any case, it seems the poor creature has run away. Or maybe someone else has found him? So many people come to this clearing."

"Do they?" Mr. Forsythe didn't appear impressed by this revelation.

"Oh, yes. Frequently. Now, if you'll excuse me, I'd better return to the house. My absence will be remarked."

"I'm counting on it." His hand lifted to the front of his bottle-green double-breasted coat, and with a lazy, casually indifferent flick of his fingers, he opened one of the buttons.

Philly's eyes widened, her gaze jerking to his hands as he opened another button, and then another. Was he disrobing in front of her? She shot a glance to the path that led out of the clearing. She wanted to go. To run. But she hesitated to do anything that would destroy the illusion of normalcy that existed between them.

"Mr. Forsythe, I—"

"Pray, disregard my bad manners, Mrs. Heywood." He continued to work at his buttons. "I have my coats cut by Weston and they fit me like a second skin. They're an absolute devil to remove without a valet."

"Oh?" Philly thought she heard the sound of another twig snapping in half. It seemed to come from somewhere near the path, but she couldn't tell. Then the horse moved again. Another twig cracked, this time under its hoof. "Is it necessary to remove your coat, sir?"

"It's essential."

She looked at him, completely nonplussed. With his artfully tousled flaxen curls, fashionable clothing, and bored, disdainful mien, he appeared every bit the dandy. She couldn't imagine him engaging in anything more strenuous than a hand of cards. Surely, he wasn't intending to ravish her?

Mr. Forsythe finally managed to work loose the final button. He removed something from an inner pocket, and then, after struggling out of the tight-fitting sleeves, he folded his coat with reverent care and laid it on one of the stone benches. When he next looked up, there was a burning glint in his eyes that hadn't been there before.

"I'm glad you didn't attempt to run away," he said.

Philly took a few steps backward along the edge of the clearing. Except for her grandfather and Arthur, she'd never seen a gentleman in his shirtsleeves. It struck her as being thoroughly indecent. "Why should I run away? We may yet find the injured dog you spoke of."

Mr. Forsythe stalked her. "We both know very well that there was never any injured dog."

"No?" She affected a tone of relief as she took another few steps. "I'm glad of it. I don't like to see any creature suffering."

"Please be still, Mrs. Heywood. I don't want to hurt you any more than I must." Mr. Forsythe raised his hand, revealing what it was he'd taken from his coat.

A small ivory-handled pistol.

She froze. It was impossible to continue pretending that nothing was wrong. "Mr. Forsythe," she said as calmly and as reasonably as she could. "Why must you hurt me at all?"

He shrugged a shoulder. "I don't care for your husband, but other than that it's nothing very personal, I assure you."

"Then why?" She scanned the clearing, looking for anything that might be of help to her, anything she might use against him. "Are you *mad*?"

"Indeed, I'm not, madam," he replied, showing a hint of temper for the first time.

"Yet you mean to shoot me with that pistol?"

"Not at all. I mean to strangle you and throw you in that pond." He took a decisive step toward her.

"*Stop!*" she cried. "Don't move another inch."

Mr. Forsythe hesitated at her tone, but only for a moment.

"No, please," she begged when he advanced once more. "My dog has followed us. He's even now in the woods. If you attempt to touch me, I won't be able to stop him."

Mr. Forsythe looked at her in blatant disbelief only to have his disbelief arrested by something inexplicable that he saw in her face. He jerked his head around the clearing, scanning the trees for some sign that a dog did, indeed, lurk within them. He kept the small pistol trained on Philly, his hand unwavering. "Stop him from doing what?"

Philly's eyes were on the pistol, her mouth dry with fear. "From ripping your throat out."

He gave a bark of laughter. "Ripping my throat out? You jest, Mrs. Heywood. I know full well there's no vicious dog lurking hereabouts. Indeed, I see nothing of any danger to me in these woods."

"I suggest you look again, Forsythe."

"*Arthur!*" A wave of unimaginable relief tore through Philly

371

at the sound of Arthur Heywood's deep voice.

She turned, expecting to find her husband standing at the entrance to the clearing. Instead, her eyes fell upon someone else entirely. A man she'd often heard about but never seen.

It was undeniably Arthur. But it wasn't *her* Arthur. It wasn't the husband who kissed her and called her his sweetheart. No. This was a different man. A dangerous man. This was Captain Arthur Heywood. This was the soldier who had crushed a man's throat with one bare hand.

FORTY-ONE

Arthur surveyed the scene before him with seemingly dispassionate coldness.

"It didn't look right, Captain Heywood," Sara had said to him. "Mr. Forsythe taking the mistress off like that. And making her leave her dogs! 'Tis not something she'd have done on her own, sir. He must've made her do it. I wonder what he can be up to?"

Arthur had needed to hear no more. Indeed, from the first moment Sara had stopped him in the hall and informed him of what she'd seen from Philly's bedroom window, everything had become clear. He could only wonder how he'd ever been so blind as to not see it to begin with.

There had been no time to reflect.

Arthur had fetched his pistol from the library with a single-minded purpose, and as his fingers closed around the polished wooden handle, he'd felt an all too familiar sensation. It was a sensation he'd experienced countless times during the war. All of his senses sharpened. All of his muscles tensed for combat. His emotions went numb.

THE WORK OF ART

In this state, he'd taken the field with his regiment dozens of times. He'd strategized and given orders.

He'd killed more men than he could number.

But never before, not even on the battlefield at Albuera, had his heart pounded so erratically. And never, not in his entire history as a soldier, had he tasted the bite of what was, undoubtedly, fear.

Forsythe was holding a pistol straight at Philly's heart.

"Heywood," he said. "What an unexpected surprise."

Arthur briefly met Philly's eyes. She was pale and frightened, her bosom rising and falling rapidly beneath the bodice of her muslin gown. "Are you all right? Has he hurt you?"

"He hasn't touched me," she said.

Forsythe took in the whole of Arthur's appearance with one disdainful glance. "I see you've come armed."

Philly's breath caught as she, too, lowered her gaze to the pistol in Arthur's hand. When she lifted her eyes back to his face, her expression was one of disbelief.

"What did you intend to do with that pistol, Heywood?" Forsythe's mouth twisted into a sneer. "Frighten me?"

"I intend to kill you," Arthur said.

A flash of anxiety briefly shadowed Forsythe's face. And then his eyes dropped to Arthur's cane. The sight of it seemed to hearten him. "With a *pistol*? Don't make me laugh! Everyone knows you can't shoot any longer."

Arthur took a decisive step into the clearing. "Let's find out, shall we?"

Forsythe responded by immediately moving closer to Philly. "You always were the most insufferably arrogant boor, Heywood. Perhaps you once had reason, but not anymore." He gave a contemptuous snort. "My God, how I used to despise you. You and all your rot about duty and honor. Where has it got you, I ask?

You came back from the Peninsula a cripple. Nothing honorable about that, as far as I can tell."

"What do you know of honor, Forsythe? You've been a coward all your life."

Forsythe's face went red with anger. "Damn you. Why could you not have stayed in the country? If you'd never come to London, this would all be over by now."

"To what end?" Arthur asked in the same controlled voice. "Did you think to see Moreland tried and executed?"

"Why the devil not? Even a duke can't get away with murder twice."

"You were ever a fool, Forsythe. A member of the House of Lords hasn't been hanged in over fifty years. Besides, Moreland hasn't murdered anyone. It was you who drowned Molly Cartwright in that fountain."

Philly stifled a gasp.

Forsythe's hand trembled on his gun. "No. I loved Molly. I'd never have done her harm."

"She refused your hand in marriage so she could marry Moreland. She wanted money and a title. You had neither." Arthur took another step into the clearing. A searing pain shot through his right leg. He ignored it. "Did you follow her to Moreland Park? Argue with her? Murder her in a fit of rage?"

"No!" Forsythe shouted.

"Or perhaps she allowed your affair to continue for a while after she married? Perhaps she strung you along with promises, until one night, when you came to meet her—"

"Moreland influenced her. He turned her against me. She'd never have cast me off of her own accord."

"Is that what she was doing the night you killed her? Breaking off your affair?"

Forsythe edged closer to Philly. He was almost touching her now. "Men like Moreland believe they can do whatever they want. Take whatever they want. He never cared about Molly. She was a possession to him. No different than one of his horses." He skimmed Philly's face and figure with fevered eyes. "He'd have taken possession of you, too. He'd have showered you with clothes, and jewels, and all manner of fine things. What would you have thought of Heywood then, I wonder? If old Moreland had said you had to choose, would you have thrown him over? Told him he was nothing but a worthless second son? Told him that no woman in her right mind would ever be his wife?"

"It sounds as though she spoke to you in a very cruel manner," Philly said.

"She was raving! I held her head under the water to bring her back to her senses!"

Philly blanched.

"It was seconds, merely. Just long enough to settle her. To make her see reason. I promised her I'd let her up as soon as she'd calmed herself, but she wouldn't stop struggling." Forsythe's face contorted in a strange mixture of fury and anguish. "When she grew still, I thought she'd come to her senses. I released her then. I was going to warm her with my coat. I didn't want her to catch a chill." He gave Philly a desperate look. "It was too late, don't you see? There was nothing I could do to save her."

"No, I..." Philly broke off with an anxious swallow, her attention briefly arrested by Forsythe's hand quavering on his pistol. "I don't suppose there was."

"I had to put her body into the water. I didn't want to do it. Molly was deathly afraid of the water. But it was the only way." Forsythe glanced at Arthur. "Moreland believed she fell into the fountain and drowned, the damned old fool. He barely mourned her. He couldn't wait to find his next wife. His next possession."

A glimmer of rage broke through Arthur's cold veneer. "So, you thought to murder her, as well."

"It was Darly who gave me the idea. He told a group of us at the club that he'd met Townsend's niece. That she was a rare beauty. A Work of Art, he called her. Said he hoped she wouldn't go the way of Molly Cartwright. That's when I knew what must be done."

Philly looked at Forsythe in bewilderment. "But I didn't marry the Duke of Moreland, sir. Surely your scheme had no more reason to include me?"

"You're all politeness, Mrs. Heywood," Forsythe mocked. "But even you must realize that by refusing Moreland's money and title to run off with Heywood, you've done more to humiliate him than Molly ever did by cuckolding him. You've made him the laughingstock of London. He has every reason to wish you harm. If you'd been killed, I knew that society would blame Moreland. Even better, Heywood and the earl would have blamed Moreland. Justice would have been done at last, don't you see?"

Arthur had had enough. "What did you promise my servant in exchange for helping you?"

Forsythe's brows shot up in surprise. "Violet told you? Directed you here to the clearing in a sudden burst of conscience?"

Philly tightened her fingers into the fabric of the silk wraps she carried in her hands. "Are you Violet's gentleman?"

"Nothing so refined as that, my dear. I tumbled her a time or two, and now the stupid little fool expects I'll marry her. It's all been a rather tedious affair, I must say. Hardly worth the few services she rendered in exchange."

"She delivered the note for you," Arthur said.

"Obviously."

"And the snare?"

Forsythe shrugged. "There was already a shallow hole on your riding path. I simply made it deeper and added a few stones. It was an easy enough task to accomplish during one of my daily rides from Melton Abbey."

Arthur nodded solemnly, and then he raised his hand, leveling his pistol at Forsythe. "That's all I needed to know."

Alarmed by the action, Forsythe took a step backward, angling himself partway behind Philly. "You reckless fool. Do you think to shoot me? I have my pistol inches from your wife's heart. She'd be dead by the time you pull the trigger."

Arthur's blood ran cold. But he didn't lose focus. He couldn't afford to.

Philly stared at him from across the clearing. She was clearly petrified. Too scared to speak or to move. But when Arthur had raised his pistol to point at Forsythe, her eyes had followed it. They widened briefly, and then suddenly, lit with guarded hope.

He knew then that she'd registered, for the first time, a fact which she'd been too frightened to notice before. A fact which Forsythe had, as yet, failed to appreciate.

Arthur's pistol was in his right hand.

Philly dropped her eyes from Arthur's raised right hand to his injured left. It was presently resting on the handle of his cane—resting there far too lightly to be doing anything more than preventing the cane from toppling to the ground. Dear heaven, he was standing with virtually no support at all! It must be causing him the most dreadful pain.

"Lower your pistol, Heywood," Mr. Forsythe said. "Lower it and toss it away from you. Into the pond, there. Do it, and I may yet let your wife live."

"No, Arthur!" Philly protested.

In response to her outburst, Forsythe grabbed Philly roughly.

No sooner had his fingers closed around her arm than a low rumbling erupted from the underbrush.

"*What the…?*" Forsythe spun around.

Basil's giant gray body hurtled from out of the woods. Fangs bared, he leapt at Forsythe, colliding with him in a snarling fury. His teeth clamped down on Forsythe's thigh, tearing straight through his expensively tailored pantaloons and sinking into his flesh.

Reggie Forsythe's scream rent the air. His fingers squeezed convulsively on the trigger of his pistol.

A shot rang out.

Philly was knocked backward. The crumbling stone of one of the benches abraded the backs of her legs. She reached out, seeking purchase as she fell down upon it, a wave of nausea nearly sending her into a faint.

And then Arthur's arms were around her, gathering her up and crushing her against his chest in a fearsome embrace. She couldn't move. She couldn't even breathe. Never had he held her so tightly.

"You killed him," she whispered.

"Yes."

"Just like you told him you would."

"Yes."

She had only a fraction of a second to look before Arthur blocked her view. It was enough time to see Mr. Forsythe's body lying in a crumpled heap beside the pond. Basil stood over it, teeth still bared and flecks of blood on his muzzle. He bore a look of savage triumph, as if he were responsible for the gunshot wound to Forsythe's head, as well as for the vicious bite to his leg.

Philly lifted her eyes to Arthur's face, expecting to find the same savagery in his expression. But whatever deadly ferocity lurked within Arthur Heywood was once again under ruthless control. "He said there was an injured dog that needed my help."

"Damn him to hell."

"I went right along with him. And all the while he meant to...he intended to..." She trembled. "If you hadn't come when you did..."

"Don't say it." Arthur's gaze was stark. "Don't even think it."

She felt the first sting of tears. "However did you find me? Did Violet truly confess?"

"No. Violet said nothing. It was Sara who told me. She saw you following Forsythe into the woods from your bedroom window."

"And she came to you? So quickly? Oh, what she must have thought!" Philly's brows drew together in distress. "What *you* must have thought."

Arthur's expression softened. "Never, my love. I understood straightaway what had happened."

"You did?"

"I did. In fact, all at once everything made perfect sense. Forsythe. Molly Cartwright. The Duke of Moreland. If I hadn't been so out of my head with worry over you these last months, perhaps I might have seen it sooner." He stroked her cheek. "As for your maid, I don't believe the thought of an amorous assignation ever crossed her mind. Oddly enough, the servants seem to be quite convinced that you're madly in love with me."

"I am," she vowed. "Most desperately."

Arthur lowered his head to kiss her.

Philly clung to him, melting for a moment into the tender caress of his lips and the strong, unyielding strength of his arms before an abrupt and startling reality brought her back to her senses. She stared up at him in vague alarm. "Arthur, your arms are around me."

"That they are. And happily so."

"Both of your arms." Philly looked frantically about them on the ground. "Where is your cane?"

"I believe I dropped it when I ran to catch you."

"Ran to catch me!"

"Before you fainted."

"Oh, but you can't have. Your leg isn't strong enough to run. And I've never fainted before in my life."

"It's been a day of firsts." He steered her away from the pond. "Pray don't make yourself uneasy. My cane and my pistol are at the entrance to the clearing. We'll fetch them as we leave. Here. Give me your arm, sweetheart. Let me take you home."

Philly did as he bade her. "But what of Mr. Forsythe?"

"I shall summon the local magistrate. He'll take care of both Forsythe and Violet. You needn't concern yourself with either of them anymore."

Basil reluctantly abandoned his position over the body, bounding after Philly and Arthur.

As they left the clearing, Philly stole one final look back at Reggie Forsythe. His bottle-green coat was still perfectly folded on the stone bench by the pond. She shivered.

Their journey to Bath was delayed by a week. It took as long to settle things with the local magistrate, as well as to contact the authorities at Moreland Park, where Molly Cartwright had been murdered.

Philly was happy to let Arthur take charge. Along with the earl, he saw to everything. As a result, she spent most of her time in company with Mrs. Ogilvy, engaged in needlework or benign conversation. The shock of Mr. Forsythe's death had been great, but not so great that Philly didn't chafe at her confinement. When Arthur finally sought her out for a walk, she fairly jumped at the chance to get out of the house.

They strolled together on a tree-lined path near the apple orchard, far from the pond and the memory of what had happened there. The dogs trotted along with them, tongues lolling in the midday sun.

"My father insists on calling on Sir Clement personally," Arthur said. "They're friends of old."

"I don't envy him."

"Nor do I. But Sir Clement is no fool. He can't be entirely surprised that his son came to a bad end."

"I suppose not." Philly slowed her pace. Though Arthur had managed to walk unassisted on the day of Mr. Forsythe's death, it was by no means a regular occurrence. Since rescuing her in the clearing, his leg had been paining him greatly. He'd been obliged to rely on his cane more than ever. "Even so, he's sure to be grieved by the news."

Arthur didn't look very sympathetic. "Reggie Forsythe had every opportunity to make a success of his life. More opportunity than most."

"It wasn't lack of opportunity that drove him to do what he did to me. And it wasn't the Duke of Moreland, either. Much as I'd like to blame him, the duke had no part in this—except for that of unwitting victim."

"You don't bear a grudge?"

"Against Moreland? I can't say that I do. He bullied me and insulted me, it's true, but once I married you, he was content to leave me to my fate."

"Do you know, Moreland said that very thing."

She cast him a curious glance. "Did he?"

"Before Sara was turned out of your uncle's house, she heard Moreland consigning you to your fate."

Philly smiled. "He meant you, didn't he? You're my fate."

Arthur responded with an eloquent grimace. "Heaven help you."

A soft breeze ruffled the ribbons of her chip bonnet. It was a bright and beautiful day. The apple trees were in full bloom, the air sweet with the scent of them. "You're not still concerned about the duke, are you?"

"No. My father had the right of it. The man's a collector. A dashed devoted one, at that. But the rumors about his acts of vengeance are just that: rumors. You have nothing to fear from him."

"I wouldn't have thought I had anything to fear from Mr. Forsythe, either. He was always so polite to me in London. And so particular about his clothes—right up until the end." A frown worked its way across her brow. "He must have been mad."

"Quite possibly."

"Driven mad. Over what he'd done to Molly Cartwright."

Arthur gave her a narrow look. "Perhaps."

"He loved her so. And he couldn't accept that he'd done such a terrible thing. It was too much for his heart to bear, I feel. No wonder he blamed the Duke of Moreland."

Arthur stopped walking. "Now this I won't allow."

She looked up at him in vague alarm. "What?"

"There will be no compassion for Forsythe."

"But, if he—"

"No. Not a word in his defense." Arthur cradled her face in his hand. "He nearly took you from me."

"I'm safe now."

"Yes, you are, confound him."

"You saved my life. If you hadn't come when you did... If you hadn't shot Mr. Forsythe..." Philly covered his hand with her own. "How long have you been practicing?"

"Since the day you fell on the avenue of the elms."

"In the afternoons, I suppose. When you and your father went out to inspect the repairs on the estate." She sighed. "I wish I might have been there."

His brows lifted. "To watch me shoot a pistol?"

"Why not?"

"I'd think that after last week's events you'd never want to be around a loaded weapon again."

Philly considered. "Well, I shouldn't like to have one pointed at me. And I certainly hope that in future there's no occasion for you to look quite so fearsome as you did then. Other than that..."

Arthur's gray eyes darkened with concern. "Did I frighten you, Philly?"

She squeezed his hand. "My dearest love, you never could."

"Couldn't I? You've just said that I looked fearsome—"

"Oh, yes. You did. Just like Basil."

Arthur stared down at her. "Like Basil," he repeated. There was a quiver in his voice. "The way he looked when he attacked Forsythe? Like a demon sent straight from hell? Good God."

"Poor Basil. He *was* very overwrought. I did warn Mr. Forsythe, but I daresay he didn't believe me. I gave all of the dogs a command to stay behind, you see. He must have trusted that they'd obey. Indeed, I *hoped* that they would. But...I'm afraid none of my pets are as well trained as I like to pretend they are."

Arthur bent his head and kissed her. "And yet you love them all regardless."

"So I do."

"Horses. Dogs." His voice deepened. "Husbands."

"Especially husbands."

"Every moody, unpredictable last one of them."

Philly's mouth lifted in a rueful smile. "Yes, well…you did say once that I had a particular fondness for disagreeable brutes."

Arthur returned her smile with a rare smile of his own. "A lamentable situation, to be sure," he said as he captured her lips once more, "but one that I wouldn't change for the entire world."

The End

AUTHOR'S NOTE

I wrote *The Work of Art* long before I wrote any of my other historical romance novels. It was originally meant to be a two-book series with *The Viscount and the Vicar's Daughter*. At the time, both books were set during the Regency era. In the end, *The Viscount and the Vicar's Daughter* was rewritten and released as a standalone Victorian romance, leaving *The Work of Art* to languish on the shelf.

This wasn't because it wasn't good enough, or because I didn't love the characters, but simply because I decided to move away from Regency romance, and *The Work of Art* didn't lend itself to being rewritten as a Victorian.

All that to say, if you're curious to discover what Arthur's rakehell older brother is like, you need look no farther than Tristan in *The Viscount and the Vicar's Daughter*. The names and the setting have changed, but the characters are pretty much the same.

And if you're at all interested in learning more about the Battle of Albuera, I highly recommend Guy Dempsey's excellent book *Albuera 1811: The Bloodiest Battle of the Peninsular War*. It was a tremendous help when researching my story.

ACKNOWLEDGMENTS

*R*evising a book that you wrote many years ago isn't easy. There were moments during the process when I didn't think this manuscript would be salvageable. More than ever, I relied on feedback from my wonderful editor, Deb Nemeth, and my amazing beta readers and critique partners, Flora, Sarah, Lauren, Lena, and Alissa. I don't know what I would do without them.

Special thanks also go to my cover designer, James Egan, who always succeeds in capturing the mood of my stories; to Richard Jenkins, who very kindly permitted me to use one of his beautiful photographs; to Colleen Sheehan for her gorgeous formatting; to Tara Mandarano for proofreading; and to my parents who act as pet babysitters, assistants, and purveyors of sweets whenever I'm writing.

Lastly, I'd like to thank you, my readers, not only for your readership, but for your emails, comments, tweets, and reviews. You don't know how many times, during a low point, a message from one of you has kept me writing. I appreciate all of you so very much.

ABOUT THE AUTHOR

USA Today bestselling author Mimi Matthews writes both historical non-fiction and proper historical romances set in Victorian England. Her articles on nineteenth century history have been published on various academic and history sites, including the *Victorian Web* and the *Journal of Victorian Culture,* and are also syndicated weekly at *BUST Magazine*. In her other life, Mimi is an attorney. She resides in California with her family, which includes an Andalusian dressage horse, two Shelties, and a Siamese cat.

To learn more, please visit
www.MimiMatthews.com

OTHER TITLES BY
Mimi Matthews

NON-FICTION

The Pug Who Bit Napoleon
Animal Tales of the 18th and 19th Centuries

A Victorian Lady's Guide to Fashion and Beauty

FICTION

The Lost Letter
A Victorian Romance

The Viscount and the Vicar's Daughter
A Victorian Romance

A Holiday By Gaslight
A Victorian Christmas Novella

The Matrimonial Advertisement
Parish Orphans of Devon, Book 1

A Modest Independence
Parish Orphans of Devon, Book 2

A Convenient Fiction
Parish Orphans of Devon, Book 3

Made in the USA
Middletown, DE
20 April 2020